Alien Abduction

Irving Belateche

Laurel Canyon Press

Los Angeles

Library of Congress Control Number: 2015919147

ISBN: 978-0-9840265-9-3 (ebook)
ISBN: 978-0-9840265-8-6 (print)

Edited by David Gatewood
www.lonetrout.com

Cover design by Kerry Ellis
www.coveredbykerry.com

Formatting by Polgarus Studio
www.polgarusstudio.com

Author Website
www.irvingbelateche.com

Printed in the United States of America

Laurel Canyon Press
Los Angeles, California
www.LaurelCanyonPress.com

Also by Irving Belateche

Einstein's Secret
Science Fiction Thriller

The Origin of Dracula
Supernatural Thriller

H$_2$O
Science Fiction Thriller

The Disappeared
(A short story)
Supernatural Thriller

Under An Orange Sun
Autobiographical Novel

BEN

CHAPTER ONE

I wasn't worried in the least about kidnapping Tess Payton, the target. This assignment was going to be a piece of cake.

My job had become second nature to me. The fear of getting caught had disappeared. This was a bad thing, and I knew it. But it was also the truth. So I actively wished for fear to make an appearance. Fear kept me alert. Fear kept me from taking too many risks. And most of all, fear kept me from getting caught.

I turned onto Orange Grove Avenue, a sad, narrow Hollywood street. It was one of hundreds of such streets in Hollywood, all crowded with rundown apartment buildings. Though these buildings didn't have much variety, regardless of which street you found yourself on, the tenants did: young, wannabe actors, struggling writers, students, Russian immigrants, Latino families, and the elderly living on nothing but their social security checks.

It was exactly this variety of tenants that made this an easy assignment. Plucking Tess here, even in plain sight, wouldn't cause much of a stir, if any. This wasn't the type of neighborhood where people looked out for each other. There was no "neighborhood watch" here. This was the type of neighborhood where, for the most part, people avoided each other.

I wasn't always given a target as easy to abduct as Tess Payton. But after four years of working for Abel—my employer—I knew this was part of his calculation. Abel wanted to keep a low profile, so whenever possible, he'd select a target I could scoop up without leaving much of a ripple in my wake.

Halfway down the block, I swung into a parking lot that sat under a boxy, three-story apartment building known as a "dingbat," probably so named because it stood on stilts, though I had never been able to confirm that. Dingbats had flourished in Southern California during the fifties and sixties. They provided cheap housing to transplants flooding into LA looking to make their dreams come true. And dingbats still provided the cheapest housing in LA, though now the vast majority of the buildings had turned into visual blights, littering great swaths of the city.

I knew the history of dingbats because I had plenty of time on my hands. Running surveillance on my targets gave me hours of free time, which I spent surfing the net on my smartphone, digging ridiculously deep into whatever subject caught my fancy. And the days between assignments, waiting for Abel to give me my marching orders, provided me with even more free time to dig into random subjects. At home, I spent hours on research, while my wife, Diane, and my son, Mason, thought I was hard at work.

I parked in the open parking space, the one I had scouted out in advance. The space would remain vacant until nine p.m. because the tenant who parked here worked long hours. I also knew that none of the other tenants would chase me away from this space. My scouting had revealed that each tenant had to defend his or her own turf. Besides, my wait under the dingbat wasn't going to be long.

Within the next ten minutes, Tess would pull into her parking space, two spots away from mine. She worked half days, then rushed home to grab a quick bite to eat, before heading across town to

UCLA, where she was taking computer programing classes. Through my investigation—not an in-depth investigation, as this assignment didn't call for one—I'd learned that Tess was expanding her skill set so she could rise above her lowly work as a production assistant. She'd been working as a PA since moving to LA three years ago.

I thought her smart. She was improving her marketability while she was still young—twenty-eight—rather than waiting until it was too late. She was hoping to avoid the fate of so many other young people who moved to LA hoping to break into the film or TV industry, but who, years later, in their mid-thirties, found themselves stuck in low-paying, low-skill jobs that were at best peripheral to the film industry, or at worst, not in the film industry at all.

I wondered if kidnapping her would alter her career plans. But I never checked on a target after I completed my assignment. It wasn't worth the risk. And I had never asked Abel what happened to the targets. Not that he'd tell me. He rarely spoke about his operation. If I had to sum up what I knew about the operation for sure, it would come down to one sentence—

Alien abductions are real.

Absurd, but true. And more absurd was the fact that I, Ben Kingsley, a once successful executive with DirecTV, was part of the operation.

Yeah, alien abductions were real all right, but they were nothing like how the kooks and conspiracy theorists described them. They weren't high-falutin', high-adventure exploits, chock-full of advanced alien technology.

Instead, the abductions were low-tech, more akin to common, street-level crime. Though my employer was an alien, the abductions I pulled off were no different than they would have been if he'd been a human. They were no different because a human—meaning me—was the one actually doing the abducting.

The *alien* part of the operation—the part I wasn't privy to—happened after I delivered the target to Abel. But what exactly that alien part was, I didn't know. I saw no evidence that Abel was "examining" the targets, as was alleged by those who believed in alien abductions. And I knew for a fact that not one target had any idea that she'd been abducted. So those kooks who told the world that they'd been victims of alien abductions also got that part of their conspiracy stories wrong. Abel wouldn't have been able to keep a low profile if his targets even suspected they'd been abducted.

I glanced at the dashboard clock. Tess would be here any minute.

I prepared the tranquilizer.

Sedating the target was a part of the operation that *did* involve alien technology, though the technology was remarkably simple. My bet was that Abel could have given me more alien tools. But more alien tools meant more risk, and the key to the whole operation was minimizing risk—the risk to him.

As I waited, the tranquilizer ready and my eyes glued to the spot where Tess's car would soon appear, my thoughts went back to the mystery of what Abel did to the targets.

I had long ago concluded that the targets provided the alien with something of value. It had been obvious almost from the start that he wasn't some sort of alien biologist assigned to Earth to "examine" the human species in order to learn as much about this form of life as possible. He wasn't curious about the human species in the least.

I also had long ago concluded that Abel selected specific targets because only *those* targets could provide him with this thing of value. Otherwise, he would have chosen any human from anywhere—humans whose disappearances would never register—reducing the risk of getting caught to almost zero.

But even after four years on the job, I had no clue as to what this thing of value was. It didn't show up when I researched the targets' lives. Nothing in their backgrounds pointed to it. And I didn't see it when I was doing surveillance on them. Nothing about their current lives—not their behavior, not their physical characteristics—revealed anything about it.

Though the targets shared very similar demographic characteristics—they were single women between twenty-five and thirty-five, and from what I could tell when I researched them, all of them were smart—this wasn't nearly enough for me to deduce what Abel wanted with them.

Tess's blue Honda Civic rounded the corner at the end of the block.

Without hesitating, I leaned down across the front seat of my car so she wouldn't see me when she pulled in. From scouting her, I knew exactly what she'd do next. In my prone position, clutching the thin copper straw in my hand—the copper straw loaded with the tranquilizer pellet—I counted off the seconds.

Forty-five seconds later, I heard the Honda's engine echoing under the dingbat as Tess pulled into her parking space. Then the roar of the engine died as she turned off the car. Five seconds later, I heard her car door open, then slam shut.

As I counted off twelve seconds, I pictured her moving around the front of her car, then walking briskly, as was her style, in my direction. She'd pass in front of my car when my countdown was over.

At eleven seconds, I lifted the thin copper straw to my lips, sat back up straight, and saw Tess just clearing the front of my car to my right. I aimed the straw at her back and let out a gentle breath.

The pellet—moving at lightning speed—traveled through the windshield, and Tess's brisk pace took a hit. She slowed down—way down—then stopped. She grabbed one of the dingbat's stilts and started to sway.

I got out of the car and hurried around the front toward Tess, timing it perfectly so that I caught her—just as I'd caught dozens of women over the past four years—as she collapsed. I'd had to let some targets tumble all the way to the ground only because those abductions were more complicated and had required elaborate ruses.

But Tess was an easy target, and I had become good at timing a target's descent into unconsciousness.

I scooped her up into my arms and carried her the few feet to my car. Then I opened the passenger door and buckled her into the seat. The seat was already reclined, so that during my drive to Abel's, anyone who glanced into the car would think Tess was sleeping.

I pulled out from under the dingbat and turned onto Orange Grove Avenue.

Once again the abduction had gone well—not that this one had been much of a challenge. I turned onto Santa Monica Boulevard, then onto Fairfax, and headed toward the hills, toward Abel's house. I was relaxed and complacent, and didn't feel even the slightest inkling of fear over getting caught. My heart wasn't pounding, my stomach wasn't in knots, and my breathing wasn't quick and shallow. Again, I couldn't help but think that my lack of fear was a bad omen.

I'd soon find out it was.

EDDIE

CHAPTER TWO

I looked up from my computer, took in the nearly empty newsroom, and thought myself lucky.

But it wasn't really luck, was it?

Of course it wasn't.

And I knew damn well it wasn't.

What had saved my job—a reporter for the *Los Angeles Times*—was my willingness to take one pay cut after another. I much preferred this slow death, a death by a thousand cuts, to undertaking the grueling search for a new job, or worse, a new career. I just didn't want to start over.

Who does?

I supposed a younger person would. But I was too old.

So, by hanging on to my job, by accepting one pay cut after another, I now had a paycheck that was just as pitiful as the *LA Times*'s bottom line. For the paper—a venerable LA institution—was doing its own kind of hanging on. It was hanging on to a business model that was no longer profitable, just as I was hanging on to a job that barely made ends meet. And "barely made ends meet" was just an expression, because if you actually crunched the numbers, the job *didn't* make ends meet.

Bob's voice boomed through the newsroom—and there was plenty of space through which it could boom, because there were very few reporters left to absorb the sound. I was a member of an endangered species.

I watched Bob, the paper's editor in chief, lead two men, both in their early thirties, across the vacant expanse of the newsroom. Bob was in full sales mode, his voice loud, cheery, and annoying. And while he was dressed old school, in a suit, the other two men wore jeans and pressed button-down shirts.

My bet was that the two younger men—whose confidence reached across the empty newsroom all the way to my desk—were representatives of the *LA Times*'s new owner, a venture capital firm in Silicon Valley. According to the firm's press release, our new owner was planning to "leverage" the *LA Times*'s "brand"—meaning the paper's name—to support a "wide variety of news aggregators across multiple platforms."

In other words, the firm was planning to use the only asset the paper had left, its name recognition, to market whatever they deemed legitimate news sites. These sites, mostly Internet startups with very little in the way of news-gathering resources, and which dealt mostly with trumped-up news stories, would suddenly become the *LA Times*.

I laughed. Man, was I feeling bitter today. And watching the two entrepreneurs step into Bob's office did nothing to curb my bitterness. I knew that part of the discussion in that office would center on more job cuts.

I shook my head, then looked back down at my computer and focused on the task at hand: coming up with an Internet-worthy headline for the story I was polishing. My story was good; that I was sure about. But the headline was the critical missing piece. Headlines were now called "clickbait" and were more important than the story itself. Clickbait was what made the Huffington Post, Buzzfeed, and a slew of other sites the go-to sites for online news. Those sites were killing the *LA Times* and dozens of other traditional papers across the country.

In the online edition of the paper, the number of times a reader clicked on your story was tracked. In general, my numbers were low. And once again, I was coming up blank when it came to a clickbait headline.

"Hey," Rick said, coming up behind me, which he often did, and which I hated. Bob had hired Rick, twenty-nine, as an editor. Rick's strength was creating clickbait headlines. "We're ready for the LA River piece," he said.

That was another thing I hated: there were no longer set times for posting stories. The online edition had to be kept fresh. So we posted a new story not when it was ready, but when the online edition became stale—when the readers stopped clicking.

I turned to Rick. "Yeah, it's done, more or less. But I don't like the headline."

"I got a couple," he said, even though he hadn't yet read the story. "Go ahead and submit it."

I typed a few commands into my keyboard, then said, "Done."

"Are you going to do the illegal road racing story next?" he asked.

"Nah. I thought I'd work on the school board story."

Rick smiled, though the smirk hidden in his smile was obvious and was sending a clear message—the same message Bob told me to my face: If you want to keep your job, you need to pick better stories. Because of my seniority, I had some say in the stories I wrote, but apparently I was exercising that privilege unwisely.

"Are you sure?" Rick said. "We're talking about teens racing down Figueroa. It's bound to get eyeballs."

"It didn't look like there was much meat on the bone there," I said, though rejecting the story wasn't going to help my shaky tenure at the paper.

"Okay, suit yourself," he responded, then turned and started back toward his desk. "I'll put up the LA River story. Make sure you respond to comments. If there are any."

And that was another thing I hated. I was expected to track the comments on my stories and respond to them if warranted.

I sat up straight in my chair, ready to defend my decision to go with the school board story, ready to explain how the board's new ruling would impact more than a hundred thousand teens in LAUSD, but instead I swallowed my pride.

"I'll do the racing story first," I said.

He turned back to me. "Twisted your arm, huh?"

"Yeah." I needed to play ball.

"Great. Check your inbox. You'll have the police info in one minute."

With that settled, Rick went merrily on his way, and I took another look at the practically empty newsroom. When I'd started working here twenty years ago, the place had been packed with reporters. Now, less than twenty percent of the space was occupied. A few of the remaining reporters, like me, were old school, but unlike me, the other survivors had successfully transitioned to the new model of journalism: low-quality, quickly written stories, without depth or facts, and full of opinions, many actually written in the first person. And most of the reporters now on staff were younger and had started their careers working within this new model—so they churned out these kinds of stories by the dozens.

Of course, there were exceptions to these low-quality stories. Some of the old school reporters still managed to squeeze in a proper story here and there, a thoroughly vetted and researched story, with plenty of reliable sources. The problem was that the LA Times's new owner didn't value those stories. Those stories didn't bring in readers, and without readers, the advertising dollars that kept the paper afloat went elsewhere.

Bob's office door swung open, and the two entrepreneurs stepped out. That had been a short meeting. So short, I concluded the two must have come to LA to give Bob bad news. Regardless of whether it was coming from an established company or an upstart, bad news was always delivered in person.

The two men confidently strode toward the elevator, their mission accomplished. They didn't so much as glance at any of the reporters along the way. I looked back toward Bob's office and saw the editor in chief standing in the doorway.

He motioned for me to come on over.

A minute later, I entered his office, wondering if another pay cut or reduction in benefits was headed my way.

Bob was glued to his computer screen, undoubtedly watching the real-time analytics that sealed the paper's fate. The analytics tracked every story the paper ran, dictating the shelf life for each. Bob, as well as the paper's Silicon Valley overlords, could track the popularity of each story, click by click, in real time. I wondered if my LA River story was already up on the paper's website, living and dying by the click.

Probably dying.

I closed the door behind me and took a seat across from Bob. His desk was tidy. He'd probably cleaned it for the entrepreneurs.

"So, more changes are afoot," he said.

"Let me guess. They don't want to publish a print copy of the paper at all anymore."

"Print isn't dead. It's just a niche product." He grinned. "That's the term they use."

"I guess that's putting a positive spin on the low subscription numbers."

"Yeah—and it comes with more good news. This 'niche product' gives the brand we're leveraging some prestige."

"So the print edition lives."

"So far. But they want to cut the number of pages—again." He leaned back in his chair and his grin disappeared. "Listen, Eddie, I don't want to beat around the bush here."

"I don't expect you to."

He took in a deep breath and the corners of his mouth turned down, as if what he was going to say next pained him. "I'm going to have let you go, Ed. I'm sorry."

My body went numb, and then I heard myself laugh—a quick cackle. "Let me go?" I blurted out. "Go where, Bob? There's no place for me to go."

"I know you saw this coming." Bob was calm. "Hell, we both did. Whatever your plan B is, it's time to put it into action."

My numbness was turning to anger. I felt a heat in my gut. "I played ball," I said. "I took the cuts in pay, the cuts in health insurance, the cuts in pension contributions. You name it, I took it."

"I know."

"So what's the problem?"

"The problem is, these guys are bottom line guys, and they want to implement changes at a faster rate."

"Can you tell them that *I'll* change at a faster rate?"

"I already went to the mat for you. More than once." He shook his head. "I hate to say this, but you should've taken the severance package while it was on the table."

"Well, too late now, huh?"

Bob didn't respond.

"What about Sam and Greg?" I said. "Are they being let go, too?" They were two of the reporters from my generation.

"I can't talk about their employment status. You know that. It's private."

"I'm doing the street-racing story. I'll turn those teens into folk heroes."

"There's nothing you can do, Ed. We're retooling. Like I said, it's all about the bottom line." A despondent look flashed across his face. "I really am sorry. You know that. I mean, we had a good run."

"What about you? Are the overlords letting you go, too?" That was uncalled for, but I couldn't help myself.

"Would it make you feel better if they were?"

"I'm just wondering how much retooling they want to do."

"The print edition is going to get pretty thin," he said, "and the plan is to go with younger, more versatile personnel in the newsroom. You know, writer/podcasters and writer/videographers and more freelancers."

"I can learn those skills."

"I know you can, but it's too late. The decision's been made."

"I can change."

"Ed—you don't want to change."

That was the truth. No beating around the bush there. I didn't have a comeback.

"I'm sorry I couldn't save your job," Bob said.

"Me too."

CHAPTER THREE

I started looking for a new job immediately. I called all my contacts, but times were tough. Not just for me, but for everyone. None of my contacts had any good leads, and I discovered that many of my former colleagues had long ago opted for new careers. Apparently, I was the only one who hadn't gotten the memo.

Though honestly, the truth was that I *had* gotten the memo, I just hadn't accepted its conclusion: that it was time to move on. Bob was right when he said I didn't want to change.

It had been four weeks since I was fired, and I still hadn't told Jenny, my wife, nor my teenage kids. Bob had agreed to let me work those four extra weeks so I could add a little extra pay to the terrible severance package I'd received. But more importantly, he had let me search for a new job while I was wrapping up my old job. That had been a big help when it came to hiding the truth from Jenny.

But now I found myself at the dinner table, having just left the newsroom for the last time after twenty years on the job, and unable to share this milestone with my family. I had to keep the swirl of mixed emotions inside me bottled up.

If I had been realistic, I would've told my family about getting fired weeks ago, but instead my ill-conceived plan had been to land another job first, so I could deliver the good news with the bad. That had truly been wishful thinking. The odds of a man in his late forties landing a decent paying job in under four weeks had always been grim. It was going to take a hell of lot longer than that.

"How was work today?" Jenny asked, out of the blue. She had long ago stopped asking me about work because she knew it would only lead to my complaining about the state of journalism. So her question caught me off guard.

"Good," I said.

"That's a change, isn't it?"

I amended my lie by turning it into a bigger lie. "*Today* was good."

"I thought there might have been a truce with the new overlords since you haven't complained about them for a few weeks."

"They're still overlording," I said, weighing whether to just come clean and tell her the overlords had tossed me out on my butt. Meanwhile, I stalled. "Have you made that doctor's appointment yet?"

"No. But I'm feeling better."

"What's wrong?" Jake said with genuine concern. Though he was seventeen, and was supposed to be well into his teenage rebellious years, he was still very close to his mom.

"Nothing really," Jenny said. "I've just been feeling tired lately." She shot me a look: *Why'd you have to say anything?* She didn't want to worry the kids.

Hannah, our defiant sixteen-year-old, who more closely matched the profile of a rebellious teen, looked up from her plate and joined the conversation for the first time tonight.

"Maybe forcing us to eat dinner together is wearing you out," she said.

"It's just twice a week," Jenny shot back.

"Torture's bad even if it's just once a week." Unlike her brother, Hannah didn't get along with her mom.

"If you'd make an effort at conversation," Jenny said, "it might not be so bad."

"I don't hear dad chatting it up much."

Jenny looked over at me, acknowledging Hannah's point. "Why don't you tell us what you're working on, honey?"

For the sake of preventing another dinner table battle between mother and daughter, I obliged. "I'm working on a story about unemployment."

"And…?" Jenny said.

"And… well… Rick doesn't want me to do the story."

"What story does he want you to do?" Jenny asked, doing her best to keep the conversation going.

"Teens drag racing downtown."

"That's a better story," Jake said. "Kind of retro. Like from the fifties."

"The YouTube video got a million hits," Hannah said.

"How do you know?" I asked, amazed that she'd even heard about the underground craze.

"Everyone's seen those videos," she said. She could barely contain her disdain toward my ignorance. "It's old news, Dad."

So Rick had had it right. If the story was clickbait on YouTube, it would've been clickbait on the *LA Times*'s website. *And* it would've appealed to a younger demographic. But after Bob fired me that day, I didn't go back to my desk to write the drag racing story. I wrote the school board story instead, as an act of defiance. Another bad move, career-wise.

I smiled at Hannah. "You should be my editor and assign my stories."

"You'd quit if I assigned you stories."

I laughed, then Jenny and Jake and Hannah all joined in. This was the upside of Hannah's rebelliousness. She had a great sense of humor, and I loved her for it.

With the mood better, I decided to ask Jake about a touchy matter. "How are the last of the college applications going? Do you want me to look at any more of your essays?"

"I got it under control."

"Good."

Before getting fired, I hadn't worried too much about Jake's college applications. He'd been meticulous about filling out the necessary forms for his top choices. But not so much when it came to his safety schools. And now, some of those safety schools—the schools where he had the best shots at receiving scholarships—were more important. Without a job on the horizon, who knew how much tuition I'd be able to afford next year?

"Can I take a look at them?" I said. "Just to make sure."

"I said I got it under control."

"I just want to make sure the last of the applications are as good as the ones you did months ago."

"You don't trust me."

"Of course I trust you."

"You're not acting like you trust me."

"Okay—don't worry about it."

"I'm not."

I decided to drop it for now. I'd have to ask Jenny to talk to him about the essays. Of course, I couldn't tell her why the safety schools were now a priority. *Or I could tell her.* For how long was I planning to wait?

And there was a more pressing reason to tell her. She needed to go to the doctor for that checkup, to find out why she'd been feeling fatigued, before our insurance lapsed. My lousy severance package didn't include health insurance, and though I was ready to move us onto COBRA—the program where you could extend your company's insurance for a short time by paying the premiums yourself—it had restrictions. I thought it wiser for her to go to the doctor before our official insurance lapsed, which was in ten days.

Also, from here on in, it was going to be much harder for me to hide my unemployment. Since today was my last day of work, what was I supposed to do when I got up tomorrow morning? *Pretend* I was heading off to work? That was ridiculous. We had a strong marriage, and I had never lied to her. Of course, we had our arguments and disagreements, but lying wasn't an issue between us.

After dinner, as we both cleared the table, I was on the verge of telling her.

But I didn't.

It was my night to do the dishes, but she volunteered, so I went into the den, opened my laptop, and wrote an email to another former reporter, a friend of a friend, who now worked for a large public relations firm. He'd gotten the memo about the seismic shift in journalism and he'd taken action. He had long ago parlayed his reporting and writing skills into a public relations job.

I was reading over the email, verifying that I didn't sound too desperate, when Jenny walked in. I quickly closed my laptop.

She flashed me a sympathetic smile, the kind that says *I'm sorry for your woes*, and I thought that she somehow knew I'd been fired.

"Do the overlords want you to take another cut, honey?" she said.

"Do I look that down?"

"You're quiet. I mean, much more so than usual."

"Have you heard anything more about the job at CBS-Radford?"

"Why? I thought that discussion was over."

It was, but I wanted to open it up again. Not only because I wanted to change the topic of conversation from me to her, but also because I'd had a change of heart—a forced one—about her taking the job. Of course, I couldn't tell her about my change of heart without telling her what had prompted it.

Jenny worked as a prop master and liked her job. She'd been working in the art departments of TV shows for twenty years—but she wasn't going to take a job this year.

That had been my doing.

Sure, it was a joint decision, but I had pushed hard, arguing that it would be best if one of us was around while Jake was applying to colleges and while Hannah, a junior, was prepping for the SAT and the ACT, as well as taking a heavy class load and swimming for the varsity team.

Now that decision had turned out to be a colossal mistake. We could have had a paycheck coming in during my job search, a search that was looking like it might last quite a while.

A dull ache was growing in my stomach, an ache fed by my rapidly increasing anxiety. Anxiety about not having a job to go to in the morning. Anxiety that my sorry severance package wouldn't come close to paying our monthly bills. Anxiety that I hadn't told my wife the truth.

"I was fired," I blurted out, thinking this would ease the ache in my stomach. It made it worse. My stomach tightened into an agonizing knot and pulled the rest of my body toward it as if I was contracting into a tight ball of panic—I was too old to start again.

"Wow…" Jenny said, her brow furrowing into an expression I recognized. It wasn't sympathy. It was incipient anger, and I knew why: ever since my first pay cut, seven years ago, she'd been pushing me to consider a career makeover. *She'd* read the memo, and she had been trying to explain it to me.

"That's why you've been quiet," she said. "How long have you known?"

"Four weeks."

"You're kidding, right?"

I shook my head. "I had this stupid idea that I'd find a new job and then tell you about getting fired *and* getting hired at the same time. To ease the blow."

"That *was* a stupid idea. You want to know how stupid? They called me about the CBS-Radford job two days ago to check in before giving it to someone else. If you'd told me you'd been fired, I could've taken the job."

"No sympathy, huh?" I smiled wanly.

Her face softened, and she came over and sat down by me. "I'm sorry," she said, then gave me a peck on my cheek. "You know I'm sorry."

"Adapt or die," I said. It was what she'd been telling me for seven years. "Looks like you were right."

"I'm not killing you off yet."

"Thanks."

"But I did tell you to start adapting sooner."

"I tried."

"Really?" She looked me in the eye.

"No. Not really."

"The writing was on the wall," she said. "I remember the first time we talked about it. Jake was just starting middle school."

"I wasn't ready to give up and start a new career back then."

"Eddie—it's not giving up. You can't look at it like that."

"But you don't just switch careers."

"Actually—you do. Look at everyone we know who did just that."

She was right. Off the top of my head, I could list quite a few of our friends and acquaintances who'd made career changes over the last seven or eight years.

But I was out of gas. And I'd been out of gas for a hell of a long

24

time. I was too old to start at the bottom. Too tired.

Adapt or die.

I was destined for the second option, unless a miracle came my way.

CHAPTER FOUR

I pulled up to Larry's house and parked. Another couple of weeks had passed, and there were still no job prospects on the horizon. I hadn't totally given up on landing another staff reporter position, but I was throwing my name in the hat for a wide variety of openings, everything from marketing positions to paralegal work.

But so far, no luck. My age was working against me. I was almost fifty, and I could tell you that fifty wasn't the new thirty, as had been wildly reported in those clickbait headlines. Fifty was over the hill, just as it had always been.

So I was turning to Larry for advice. He was my closest friend, and that right there said a lot about me, because he was also my only real friend. I'd long ago stopped nurturing friendships, and that had now come back to haunt me. If most jobs were gained by networking with friends and acquaintances—as statistics suggested—I was doomed. I had damn few of either.

Larry had done exactly what Jenny had wanted me to do, which was why I was turning to him for advice. And he'd done it seven years ago, exactly *when* Jenny had wanted me to do it. While he was still one of my fellow reporters at the *LA Times*, he'd felt the winds of change blowing across the economic landscape, and he'd started laying the groundwork for a new career.

It had paid off.

He hadn't just read the memo, he'd taken decisive action. He dove head first into the new form of journalism. He created clickbait headlines and started writing stories in the first person, adding entertaining asides and opinions, and opting for spin rather than facts.

Within two years, he had his own online blog/column for the *LA Times*, focused on California politics. The blog/column didn't get into nitty-gritty policy questions, but instead focused on political infighting and his own opinions about those clashes. It all made for an entertaining read.

Bob not only approved of Larry's column, but gave him more resources. The result was that Larry was able to grow his own "brand" on the *LA Times*'s dime. Then, once he had a substantial following, he quit and started his own news site.

In other words, Larry had adapted and thrived.

Since he'd left the *Times,* he'd grown his news site to include investigative stories. And not just any investigative stories. His brand focused on unsolved Southern California murders, especially those that could generate sensational headlines. And, of course, each story contained commentary and opinions about every aspect of the crimes.

"I'm sorry they let you go," Larry said at the door.

"Me too. But thanks for not saying anything to Jenny."

"I'm still on the record as thinking that was a bad idea."

"Yeah—well, congrats. You were right. She turned down a job."

"Ow. That hurts."

"That's why I'm here. I've got to turn this around."

But my outlook was gloomy. So gloomy that, as Larry led me through his house and into his office, I found myself resenting the bounce I saw in his step. I supposed I never noticed it before because the contrast between us had never been so great. He'd always been outgoing, while I'd been more introverted, but right now, in addition to that, he was blossoming while I was in retreat.

I'd retreated so much that a few weeks ago I had declined Larry's invitation to go to the Oregon/USC football game, something I would never have done if I'd still been employed. He was a Duck—a graduate of the University of Oregon—and I'd taken a liking to USC football during my first year in LA. It was a tradition for us to watch that matchup, either in person or on TV. We'd seen the last fourteen games between the rivals together.

But not this year.

Larry sat down at his desk. Behind him, through the window, stood a lush tree, heavy with bright yellow lemons. *Time to make lemonade,* I thought, which was trite, but at least it was my first positive thought all week. Maybe Larry would come through with some good advice.

He swiveled his chair away from the three computer monitors that graced his desk, and motioned for me to take a seat.

I did, and jumped right in. "I need a job. And I need it yesterday."

"How did you leave it with Bob?"

"He fired me. That's how I left it."

"Did you make a counteroffer?"

"It wasn't a negotiation."

"I mean, did you offer to work as a freelancer?"

"I can't afford to work as a freelancer."

"You can't afford *not* to work as a freelancer."

"I'm not following you."

"It's time to build your own brand. And if you can use the *Times's* resources to do it, then you should."

"I don't want to build my own goddamn brand. I just want a job that pays a decent wage—enough to keep Jenny and me afloat, and enough to pay Jake and Hannah's college tuition."

"Listen, I get it." Larry was unruffled by my frustration. "You know I love my job. But it's not because I made myself into a brand." He used dismissive air quotes around "brand," which made me feel a little better. "It's because I get paid to do what I love. That's what I'm getting at. You have to go back to basics and figure out a way to get paid to do what you love."

"I was hoping for concrete leads, not a Tony Robbins pep talk."

He laughed. "I'm getting there. But you need to take stock. Otherwise you're floundering."

I let out a deep breath. He'd hit a chord.

"When it comes right down to it," he said, "that's what I did when I realized the shit was going to hit the fan. I took stock. I lived and breathed Southern California politics—that was me regardless of my job at the *LA Times*. So that's what I based my transition on. And when I started my own site, I looked to other things I loved. Murder mysteries—sounds ridiculous, right? But I'd loved them since I was a kid, so I added that to my site, and it's been a boon. So what do you love, Eddie? Do you still love reporting on the LA City Council? Do you still love digging up what's going on behind closed doors at the DWP? What about the school board?"

I looked away from him as I considered his questions. I stared at the lemon tree, hoping for an insight, hoping for a glass of lemonade packed with insights. After ten seconds or so, I looked back at my friend and told him the truth.

"No, I don't love any of that anymore."

His eyes widened. "Wow. Really?"

"Yeah. Really."

"That's a shocker."

"To me, too. I still like the investigating part, but not the stuff

I'm actually investigating."

"So you really do need to take stock."

"I don't have time to take stock. And even if I did, landing a job is hard as hell. I've applied for all kinds of jobs, but I can't get any traction. Not even an interview. And most of the time, not even a return email." I frowned and told him something I hadn't planned on telling him. "I'm resorting to tutoring. I registered with agencies yesterday." I was ashamed of that, but I wanted to tell someone, other than Jenny, how bad things were.

"That's how fucked up our society is," Larry said. "We consider tutoring—teaching—as 'resorting' to something awful."

"Yeah, and if you go by the pay, we consider substitute teaching worse than tutoring. I looked into that first—the pay was pathetic."

"You might have to accept pathetic pay for a while if you move into a new career."

"I can't. I just don't have the savings to do it. Not with college tuition coming up."

"That makes it tough."

"Yeah. Tutoring is just to have some cash coming in. I was really hoping you might have some ideas up your sleeve."

"I'll reach out and see if I can dig something up. But it's going to be freelance. A lot of online news sites use freelancers."

"That's fine. It's not like I have a choice."

Larry glanced over his shoulder and checked his computer monitors. "I wish you were a techie, Eddie. I'm hiring one to boost my web traffic so I can get more advertising dollars."

"You're doing well enough to hire an employee?"

"Yeah—I turned another corner in the last couple months. And it looks like I'm going to hire a USC Trojan. The Annenberg School has a major that fits right in with what I need." He grinned, trying to lighten the mood. "I wanted to hire a Duck, but USC grads have the goods."

"Fight on," I said, quoting the USC fight song, with false enthusiasm.

*

I drove along Mulholland to my next tutoring session. I loved the view from up here at night. It truly inspired a leave-all-your-troubles-behind outlook on life. The Valley's wide boulevards were laid out in long ribbons, and decorated in red taillights and yellow streetlights stretching all the way to the Santa Susana Mountains up north. And between those long glittering ribbons, thousands of neighborhoods sparkled and glowed, built solidly and forever out of ephemeral California dreams.

I hoped that I, too, could build a solid foundation again for my life. I'd done it once, but it was increasingly looking like doing it again was going to be impossible. On the bright side, I had already increased the income I was getting from tutoring, even though I knew the job was just a temporary fix.

At first, I hadn't liked the job because of the pay. The teaching was rewarding, but the money was so piss poor that it soured the whole experience.

Then I saw the light.

By not going through a tutoring agency, I earned five times more per hour. It still wasn't anywhere near what I needed for my family—the bills were piling up—but it was enough that we were falling behind at a slower rate. And tutoring also broke up the drudgery of looking for a full-time, professional job.

Tonight, I was adding a new tutoring client to my roster, which meant a little more money would be coming in. The clients I'd gotten on my own had all come from an ad I'd put up in a coffee shop in Sherman Oaks. A coffee shop frequented by an upscale clientele. The ad had netted five good clients—wealthy parents willing to pay top dollar to give their kids an edge. And those five clients had turned out to be enough, because they had passed on my name to other parents, and two months later, my plate was full.

Tonight's client was the last of the new ones. I couldn't take on any more or it would cut into my job search. Not that the job search was going well. I'd had three interviews, all for marketing jobs, and not one offer. But every time I was tempted to give up, to quit looking for a professional job, I'd think back to something I'd overheard during one of my tutoring sessions.

Brad Vogel, a smart kid who didn't need tutoring, but whose parents insisted on it, had taken a bathroom break. A couple of minutes later, I heard his mom yelling at him.

"Get back in there!" she said. "I'm not paying for you to check your iPhone."

"If he's so smart," Brad snapped back at her, "why is he like fifty years old and tutoring, huh?"

What dignity I still had left crumbled. My body closed in on itself, as if it was involuntarily retreating. I felt small and insignificant, and I was once again forced to face the reality of my situation. Brad Vogel was right. He'd spoken the unvarnished truth.

I didn't hear what his mom said back to him, but I didn't need to. I knew it was something along the lines of: "He's here to help you with your paper, and if you listen to him, maybe you won't end up like him."

*

I turned off Mulholland onto Beverly Glen. Then, just a few blocks down, I turned into a new housing development. It consisted of McMansions, one after another. And not of the kind that was almost acceptable. These were of the sprawling, gaudy variety, which I hated.

I cruised through the development, keeping my eyes peeled for the correct address and waiting for my Waze app to tell me I'd arrived at my destination. As I approached the house, unease crept over me, as it had been doing more and more lately. I felt queasy and unsure of myself.

How the hell am I going to make it? How the hell am I going to make sure my family can make it?

"You have arrived at your destination," the Waze app informed me.

"Not really," I said. I wasn't even close to arriving at my destination: a stable life built on a new career. But what I didn't know, as I pulled up to the house, was that I *had* arrived at my destination. I was on the doorstep of an opportunity that would change everything.

I parked the car and sat there for a few seconds, putting on my game face, which consisted of a jovial smile, a smile that covered up my desperate state.

Then I headed to the oversized, double front doors, engraved with the silhouettes of lions, as if this were the entrance to a French castle. How much more gaudy could you get?

I rang the doorbell and heard the sound of overly eager chimes. Within a few seconds, the door swung open, revealing a broad-shouldered man in his mid-forties. It was almost always the mom who greeted me, so having the dad open the door was unexpected.

"I'm Ben Kingsley," he said, and reached out to shake.

"Eddie Hart," I replied, and shook his hand. My smile was still plastered across my face.

"Come on in."

I stepped inside, and he led me through a cavernous living room populated with expensive furniture and modern artwork. I wondered what he did for a living. All my clients were well off, but he seemed more well off than the others, which didn't fit in with him being at home at seven p.m. If he had a high-paying, high-powered job—the kind needed to maintain the upkeep of a faux French castle—then he should have still been at work.

"So, you got the scoop from my wife about Mason?" he said.

"Sure did." That sounded jovial enough, didn't it? "We're going to be working on his writing. Focusing on clarity and conciseness."

He laughed, a nice hearty laugh, as if he didn't have a financial care in the world. "Yeah—and if that great summary is any indication of your work, then Mason should be in good hands."

"Before you know it, he'll be writing like Hemingway."

"If that's true, you're a bargain."

We both laughed. Ben Kingsley was so relaxed and quick with the joke that I wondered if he was independently wealthy. I imagined that if you didn't have to work for a living, you'd be as easygoing as he was.

We entered a sleekly furnished den, and he motioned toward a desk along the far wall. Two chairs had been pulled up to it.

"Is this a good work space for you?" he asked.

"Perfect."

"Great. I'll round Mason up."

"Have him bring his last couple of English papers."

"Will do."

Ben exited the room, and I sat down at the desk and pulled out my MacBook Pro. I'd bought a new, opaque, hard-shell case for it, hoping my clients wouldn't notice how beat-up it was. Of course, who was I trying to fool? As Brad Vogel had made so painfully clear, anyone could see that I was a middle-aged man who had resorted to tutoring. At the *LA Times*, I'd never felt self-conscious about my ancient laptop. It was a point of pride that I was banging away on my old workhorse.

I opened the computer, turned it on, and looked around the den.

Like the living room, it was adorned with expensive furniture. So what did Ben do for a living? Maybe Mason would drop a hint during the tutoring session.

The boy stepped into the room, and I introduced myself, then made small talk before we started working. He was a straightforward kid, and I liked him immediately.

"Even though I want my writing to improve," he said, "it's not like I plan to get a job writing."

Wise choice, I thought. *Stay away from writing—especially journalism.* "So you're already thinking about what kind of careers you're interested in," I said.

"Yeah. Why not get an early start? It's something I'm going to be doing for a long time."

I smiled. "Any ideas so far?"

"Something where you actually make a product."

"What kind of product?"

"I don't know yet."

"Maybe apps?"

"No—that market is flooded. Apps are commodities now."

Commodities. That put a grin on my face. The kid was smart.

"Does your dad make an actual product at his job?" I said.

"Nope—he's an investor."

I was so desperate for a new career that, in that moment, I actually thought I could become a successful investor too. As if anyone could just wake up one morning and make a good living investing, without training or previous experience.

That crazy scenario passed just as quickly as it had come, and I pulled out a writing prompt, the one I used to assess a student's writing skills. I gave it to Mason and went through the instructions with him. As he worked on the prompt, I read through his English papers.

Then we got to work. We went over the prompt, focusing on sentences that were egregiously out of control. He pushed back a little—most bright kids were defensive, so this was to be expected—but I persisted. I'd discovered that it was hard for bright kids to admit they weren't the best at something. But when they finally conceded the point, they were also the most dedicated to improving.

About an hour into our two-hour session, Mason was getting restless, so I suggested a ten-minute break.

"Sounds great," he said, and pulled out his cell phone. He hadn't checked it even once during our session, another sign that he was good kid.

I checked my cell phone, too, then asked him where the bathroom was.

"Out the door, to the right, at the end of the hallway," he said, while texting.

I exited the room and made my way down the hallway, past what appeared to be a dedicated screening room. A ridiculously large TV screen took up an entire wall, and a sectional leather couch stretched forever across the room.

Then I passed a door that was shut—except for a slight opening. If that door had been shut all the way, everything that followed would've never happened. My life would probably still have changed in some way, but not in the drastic way it did. It's still hard for me to believe that everything that followed started with a door that was left slightly ajar.

I glanced at the tiny sliver of an opening and saw Ben Kingsley placing a brick of cash into a wall safe, where other bricks of cash were already resting peacefully.

My curiosity was piqued.

I hesitated in the hallway, watching Ben pull out more bricks of cash from an expensive leather satchel and place them into the safe.

But I didn't linger, for I understood I was watching something I shouldn't be privy to. I quickly continued down the hallway and stepped into the bathroom.

For the rest of the tutoring session, it was hard for me to concentrate on anything but the source of those bricks of cash. It was clear that if Ben was an investor, he wasn't an investor in any typical definition of the word. It was more likely that the "investor" label was a cover story. The only thing I knew for certain was that Ben made a lot of money, and it came in droves.

And it was probably illegal. Why else would he have all that money in cash?

Of course, there were different degrees of illegality. Ben could have been skimming money off the top of a legal business that dealt in cash, like a restaurant or grocery store or liquor store. But that would be a lot of skimming. So much so that I had to believe the cash came from another source.

And whatever source that was, I wanted to know if it was a line of work I could get into.

Sure, this was a ridiculous notion, fueled by desperation. But I needed a way to cover my family's expenses. And I needed to cover Jake's college tuition next year, and Hannah's the year after that. And what if we were hit with a huge, unexpected expense—like a medical emergency?

I had let COBRA lapse this month because it was just too damn expensive, so we no longer had health insurance. There was the possibility of getting onto a Covered California plan, but so far, I hadn't been able find a plan with an affordable premium. Going without health insurance was the biggest risk I'd ever taken, but I couldn't keep going into more debt.

Maybe it took that risk to lay the groundwork for the next risk, a much bolder gamble, one I didn't see coming that night. Or maybe it was the drive home that planted the seed for that gamble—for the lights of the Valley, the dazzle of the ephemeral California dream, were particularly bright on my ride home.

Or maybe it was just the down and dirty, but very tangible, image of those bricks of cash taking root.

JENNY

CHAPTER FIVE

Eddie would be happy that I had finally taken the time to see a doctor, but he wouldn't be happy that I had waited until we were uninsured. As I stood in line behind two patients, I glanced around the waiting room, wondering how many other patients were paying for their visit out-of-pocket. My guess was not too many. I'd be the only one paying with a credit card.

But I had no choice.

The fatigue had gotten worse over the last month. Much worse. And it had been getting worse before that, but I'd been in denial, blaming it on my freelance gigs. I'd started working again, because we needed the money. Unfortunately, I hadn't been able to land a full-time gig on a TV show, so I was cobbling together day jobs here and there.

On a day job, you were the low man on the totem pole—far from a department head—and you therefore had to do a lot of heavy lifting, both literally and figuratively. I told myself that the overwhelming fatigue that hit me at the ends of those days was due to my age. I no longer had the strength and stamina of my thirties. But this month I hadn't had any freelance gigs, and yet the fatigue was worse than ever—bad enough to finally drive me to the doctor's office.

The receptionist called me up to the counter and asked for my insurance card.

"I'm not covered by Blue Cross anymore," I said. "And my new insurance won't kick in for another three months." I lied because I was ashamed of being uninsured.

"So you're paying for the appointment yourself?"

"Yes."

"Let me check on the fee." The receptionist typed something, studied her computer monitor, then typed some more.

Again I glanced at the waiting patients. How many had picked up that I was uninsured? *What do I care?* I thought. But I cared. I cared so much that I had a plan to fix the problem, a plan to get Eddie and me out of our financial tailspin.

The receptionist looked up from her monitor. "It's going to be a hundred eighty-three," she said.

I took my MasterCard from my purse—the only card that wasn't maxed out for the month—and handed it to her. She ran it through the reader, and as we both waited for the charge to be approved, I had a pang of doubt. Had Eddie used the MasterCard and maxed it out?

Twenty seconds later, to my relief, the card reader clicked and began printing out the receipt. The receptionist grabbed it and put it on the counter. "Please sign here. The nurse will call your name."

I signed the receipt, adding a little more debt to our growing pile, then took a seat and began to regret my decision to visit the doctor. I was feeling guilty about throwing away almost two hundred dollars. Once you hit your late forties, your stamina decreases, and there's nothing you can do about it. Going to a doctor wasn't going to help.

The best solution was to follow the advice that I'd been giving Eddie for the last seven years. *I* needed to retrench and find a new career, and that was exactly my plan. But unlike Eddie, I didn't need to retrench because there was no longer work in my chosen profession. I needed to retrench because I'd gotten too old for the physical demands of my job. It was a young man's—or woman's—game. And now there was an even greater incentive to find a new career: going forward, one of us needed a stable job if we were going to get out of our financial tailspin.

Lila, my closest friend and former cohort in production, had long ago retrenched. She'd smoothly transitioned into a new career, one more suited to her age—*my* age. Six years ago, she'd started taking accounting classes at Pierce College. After finishing up her course work, she'd immediately taken on any production accounting jobs that came her way, regardless of the company, or the pay, or the work hours. Now, six years later, she was working in Disney's accounting department. She had a new career at forty-four, with benefits, holidays off, and security. A *great* career. She liked working at Disney.

That's what Eddie should've done seven years ago. Not the accounting part, but the retrenching part. He could have easily transitioned into a new career. But now he seemed lost. He wasn't sure how to retrench, and he worried that it was too late.

Maybe some people had to hit rock bottom in their careers to make a change. But I certainly didn't want that for Eddie—or for myself. And that was why I was going to take the initiative. By preparing myself now, I'd have a new career in a few years.

But I had yet to tell Eddie about my plan, because I didn't want him to think I didn't believe in him. He was already feeling bad about his prospects, and if I told him I was making my own move, he'd feel even worse.

Still, I was going to move forward. I was going to follow in Lila's footsteps. And not just in general, but specifically. I was going to move into production accounting. But unlike Lila, who'd taken only one or two classes at a time, I'd enroll in as many classes as I could to expedite the transition. I'd also use my TV production contacts to see if I could land work as an accounting trainee or assistant. I'd already called Lila, and she was more than happy to help me get started.

The door to the inner chamber of the medical office swung open, and a nurse stepped out. She looked up from a manila folder. "Jenny," she said. "Jenny Hart."

I got up and headed toward her—toward a destiny completely different than the one I'd just laid out. The best-laid plans of mice and men often go awry.

*

The doctor examined me, then read me questions from a form. This was the new protocol: doctors no longer chatted with you, working in their questions as they saw fit; instead, they stepped methodically through a prepared form. I'd read this approach led to far better diagnoses, but I didn't like it.

After he finished with his questions, I asked him mine. His answers were vague, as if he didn't want to commit to a diagnosis. But I could hear the concern in his voice. He said there could be a number of causes for my fatigue, and we'd find out more after a blood test and a urine test.

At least he didn't send me to some specialist, I thought. That would've surely meant something was wrong.

Three days later, he sent me to a specialist.

A nurse from his office called and told me that my blood tests showed unusual levels of a certain kind of protein. The doctor wanted me to schedule an appointment with an internist. He'd already sent over the referral authorization.

When I asked the nurse what the unusual levels of this protein meant, she said the doctor could answer my questions and that she'd leave a message for him.

"When can he call me back?" I asked, trying not to sound too anxious.

"He usually tries to make his calls around lunchtime."

That was two hours away. So after I scheduled the appointment with the internist—for next week, which was the earliest available appointment, even though I wanted to get in there this afternoon—I scoured the Internet looking for answers.

That turned out to be a big mistake.

I kept finding the same two words associated with unusual levels of the protein: "tumor marker." This didn't mean I definitely had cancer, but I couldn't deny that bad news—terrible news—might be just around the corner.

It was hard to breathe while I waited for the doctor to call. I felt lightheaded, as if I'd stepped into another world—a world that revolved around a dreadful fate, one I hoped could somehow be avoided, but feared couldn't. My body trembled.

I needed to tell Eddie, didn't I? Normally, in times of crisis, that would have been my first call. But I didn't want to worry him until the bad news was confirmed.

Or was it that I didn't want to call him because it would make the bad news even more real?

Two hours passed, and the doctor didn't call. He didn't call after four hours passed either. So as five o'clock approached—seven hours after the nurse had called—I called his office and demanded to speak to him. The receptionist said she'd see what she could do, then put me on hold.

Three minutes later, the doctor came on the line. That alone—the fact that he'd acceded to my demand—was already proof the news was awful.

I pressed him with questions, asking him directly, twice, "Do I have cancer?"

Each time I asked, he gave me the same answer. "The blood test isn't definitive." Then he patiently explained that I'd be undergoing tests specifically designed to make that call. His patience was just more proof that my situation was grave.

*

An hour later, when Eddie came home, I was absentmindedly making a sandwich, purposely trying to keep my mind blank. I didn't want to think about what lay ahead.

Eddie stepped into the kitchen, and I asked him, "How was it?" He'd been attending a networking function for professionals looking to make career changes.

"It was basically a bunch of people like me," he said. "Over-the-hill ninety-nine percenters, telling war stories about their dead-end job searches."

"Can you make it sound any more depressing?"

He chuckled. "I bet I could if I tried."

"Did you grab a bite to eat?" I asked.

"Nah."

"I didn't make dinner because Hannah went to In-N-Out with Camilla after practice, and Jake is eating at Sam's." *And because I've been in a panic all day.* "Do you want me to make you a sandwich?"

"Thanks. That would be great." He sat down at the kitchen table and pulled his laptop from his shoulder bag.

"What time are your sessions tonight?" I asked.

"Eight and ten. I probably won't be home until midnight."

That meant I should tell him now. Tell him about the proteins running wild in my bloodstream. Tell him before he came home exhausted. But I hadn't even told him I'd finally gone to a doctor. How long had he been bugging me to go?

I should've gone while we were still insured.

Now, nothing would be covered. Not the specialist. Not the next round of tests. Not the treatments. And not the surgery, should that become part of this nightmare, too.

"Are you okay, honey?" he asked. He was staring at me from the table. I had finished making my sandwich and was just standing there, hovering over it.

"I'm just anxious for Jake," I said. "He should be hearing from quite a few colleges this week."

"Batten down the hatches, huh? We're going to have some major battles."

"I know—I'm not looking forward to it," I said, and I wasn't. The battles were going to be over costs. Jake was no longer going to be able to pick a college based just on his preferences.

I wasn't hungry, so I brought my sandwich over to Eddie.

"Isn't this your sandwich?" he said.

"I'll make another one. You're going to have to hit the road in a few minutes, so why don't you go ahead and eat first?"

"Thanks."

I began to make another sandwich while Eddie ate his. We talked about how we were going to get Jake to accept our new financial reality. I wanted to talk about the proteins running wild in my bloodstream, but I couldn't do it.

And I didn't tell Eddie about the proteins when he came home later that night either. Or the next day. Or the day after that. I somehow managed to talk myself into believing that it'd be better to wait until I was sure of my fate. Why make life prematurely miserable for him, and for Jake and Hannah?

Things turned miserable anyway.

At the end of that week, I went to the mailbox and found an envelope from Northwestern. The envelope wasn't thin, but it wasn't thick either. Northwestern was one of Jake's top choices, if not his first choice. When Jake had first applied to colleges, before Eddie had lost his job, I would have hoped with all my heart that the letter I now held in my hand was an acceptance letter. Jake would be ecstatic. But oh, how things had changed. Was I actually hoping for a rejection letter? Though Jake would be crushed by it, it would mean Eddie and I wouldn't have to tell him we couldn't afford Northwestern.

With the envelope on the kitchen table next to my laptop, I finished laying out a schedule of accounting courses I could take at Pasadena City College. Over the last few days, I'd forced myself to focus on my career pivot rather than my upcoming appointment with the internist. The career pivot was another subject I hadn't yet talked to Eddie about.

I kept glancing at the envelope. I was tempted to open it, so I could prepare for Jake's reaction. But Jake had long ago demanded that I not touch his mail.

Fifteen minutes later, I heard a car door slam outside and knew it was Jake. Sam always gave him a ride home after the Economics Club meeting.

When Jake walked into the kitchen, his eyes immediately went to the envelope. He knew I always left the mail on the kitchen table, so every day for the last two weeks, his first stop after getting home from school was the table. The stop had already yielded some results. He'd heard from a few schools—but none that he really cared about.

"Another one," he said.

"Yep. Northwestern."

His body tensed for a second, then he grabbed the envelope. His eyes were wide and his lips were pursed with apprehension. He turned the envelope over in his hands.

"What do you think?" he said. "Thick or thin."

"Hard to tell, sweetheart." I suddenly realized that I *did* hope, with all my heart, that he'd gotten in.

He slowly tore open the envelope, then pulled out the letter and unfolded it—a fraction of a second later, he yelled, "I'm in!"

I leapt up and hugged him.

"Hell, yes!" he said. "I'm going to Northwestern!"

"Congratulations—and don't curse."

He pulled out his iPhone and began to text, spreading the news. He must've fired off at least five texts before I spoke up.

"Jake—remember. We need to see what kind of financial aid package they're going to offer."

"I'm going to Northwestern," he said, as he texted away. "Unless I get into Columbia or Berkeley. And even if I get into those, I'm pretty sure I'm going to Northwestern."

"Honey, we need to talk about it as a family after we hear from all the schools."

"You can talk about it all you want, but count me out. This changes everything. I'm going to Northwestern."

"You're not listening. You still have half a dozen schools to hear from, and you can't just reject UCSD—it's a good school." He'd been accepted to UCSD a few weeks ago.

"Yes, I can. You're the one who's not listening. I'm rejecting UCSD—got it?"

"Don't raise your voice. We're having a discussion. We have to take cost into account."

"You already told me that—a million times. But that was before I got into Northwestern. And Northwestern is where I'm going."

"We're all going to talk about it."

"You know what? You're a damn liar. What happened to 'We'll figure out a way to pay for any school I want to go to'? Remember that?"

"I remember—but that was before your dad lost his job."

"That's not my problem!" He stormed out of the kitchen, and a few seconds later, the sound of his bedroom door slamming shut rocked the house.

I felt awful. Why couldn't I have let him enjoy a few days of validation? Why couldn't I have let him enjoy the fruits of four years of hard work? Normally, I would have. *Wouldn't I?* But things weren't normal. Proteins were running wild in my blood.

When Eddie came home and learned about Jake's acceptance letter, he congratulated him.

Jake responded with: "You don't need to pretend. I know you don't want me to go there. So just leave me the hell alone."

*

My argument with Jake turned out to be mild compared to the one I had with Eddie two days later. I still hadn't said anything about my blood test, nor about my upcoming internist appointment. Hiding that from Eddie, plus the fact that Jake hadn't talked to us since getting accepted to Northwestern, made for a tense household.

"You think Jake is ever going to talk to us again?" Eddie asked me when I walked into the kitchen. He was eating an early dinner of scrambled eggs before heading out to tutoring sessions.

"Eventually," I said. "But when he does, it's not like he's going to tell us he changed his mind about Northwestern."

"I know, but we have to talk to him. He needs to be realistic, whether he likes it or not."

"Don't you think we should wait until he hears from all the schools?"

"If we cut it too close to the deadline, we'll have less time to talk it out. And he might not get as much financial aid."

"Then why don't you talk to him?" I wasn't ready to battle Jake. I had my own problems to deal with. And I was feeling bad for Jake.

After all, he was right: we *had* promised him he could go to the school of his choice.

"It might go better if you laid the groundwork first," Eddie said.

"That's not going to go well," I replied, while thinking: *It's your fault we have to renege on our promise.* If he'd done a career pivot when I'd told him to, we wouldn't be in this position.

"You haven't given up on finding a real job, have you?" I said.

"Of course not."

"Because if you found one, we might not have to argue with him. He might be able to go to Northwestern."

"You know I've looked high and low. By the way, it's not as if UCSD is a bad school. It's a great school. Look at all the kids who didn't get in there."

Hearing him say that made my anger boil over. "You know Jake worked hard as hell to get into Northwestern."

"Of course I know."

"But you want him to settle, just like you've settled."

"I don't have time to fight about this now," he said, then stood up and looked at his watch. "I'm going to be late if I don't scoot. We'll talk about it later."

"When? At eleven, when you get back? That's a little late for a serious discussion."

"Okay, then we'll talk about it tomorrow." He started toward the kitchen door. "And I haven't *settled.*"

"Give me a break. You've settled on tutoring."

"Come on—you know I'm not doing it permanently."

"No, *you* come on, Eddie. Be serious. That's exactly what you're doing."

"I can't find a goddamn job, so I'm doing what I can."

"Really? Tutoring is the best you can do? That's how you plan to pay the bills—to pay for Hannah and Jake's college—to pay for medical expenses? Really?"

"Give me a break—I'm working my butt off!"

"I don't think so. I don't think you're working your butt off!"

He stared at me, ready to escalate the argument. But then he turned and walked out. I wanted to yell at him to come back and have this out. Now. But I was disgusted with him. He was a loser. That's right.

I suddenly felt tears well up in my eyes and then spill down my cheeks.

Why was I thinking my husband was a loser? Was it because the proteins were running wild in my blood?

EDDIE

CHAPTER SIX

I told Jenny I had lined up an interview for a sales job. One that I had a very good shot at landing. It was with a high-tech company in Playa del Rey that sold software to international business clients. I told her the company was willing to give me a shot because they were looking for older salesmen who engendered a feeling of trust with clients.

It was ironic that I was talking about trust, because I was lying about the job. Not only was there no interview, there was no such company.

I lied to buy myself some time. Lying to her was totally out of character for me, and I didn't feel good about it, so I promised myself I wouldn't lie to her again.

Then I did something else out of character. I did something at Ben Kingsley's house that I wouldn't have done in a million years if I hadn't been so desperate to find a job. And if Jenny hadn't basically told me she thought I was a failure.

I was ensconced in Ben Kingsley's McMansion, going through the first draft of a history paper with Mason, when I started to feel the tug of those bricks of cash. This wasn't a new feeling. Every time I was in the McMansion, that feeling would come over me.

Weeks had passed since I'd last seen Ben at the house, and tonight was no different. During some of those past weeks, on a few occasions, I had walked down the back hallway to use the bathroom, even though I hadn't needed to. It was the lure of those bricks of cash that had drawn me.

While down the hallway, I had discovered that the room with the wall safe was a sparsely furnished office. If this was Ben's office, it offered no hint of what he did for a living. As for the wall safe, it was hidden behind a beautiful tapestry, a weave of the galaxy, with swirling solar systems, red-orange planets, and golden suns.

Tonight I once again heard the call of the siren's song, the one coming from the wall safe. So after I pointed out the three areas in the history paper that I wanted Mason to focus on, I once more succumbed to its lure.

I excused myself to go to the bathroom.

But this time, instead of perusing the office from the hallway, as had been my custom, I stood on the threshold of the room for only two or three seconds before I—and I don't know if I'd planned this all along or not—rushed into the office and over to the tapestry.

I knew this was a crazy move—that Mason might catch me, or Ben, if he was home, or Mason's mom, Diane, for she was definitely home. She had answered the door when I arrived, and sometimes she'd peek into our tutoring sessions and ask if we wanted a drink or a snack. She could easily check in on the tutoring session, then decide to head a little farther down the hall and find me snooping.

I considered shutting the office door, but decided that might look suspicious. And it would take a few precious seconds; whatever I was going to do, I had to do it quickly.

I lifted the tapestry and saw the wall safe right where I remembered it.

Now what?

I wasn't sure. I stared at the safe. Judging by its sleek design, I could see that, like everything else in the house, it was top of the line. But I wasn't trying to figure out how I could crack it. No. That wasn't it at all.

I was standing there because it was my way of accepting the truth: my only goal in life right now was to find the source of the cash inside this safe. I would do everything within my power to find it, no matter what it took. My family's life, their happiness and security, depended on this—

I heard something and quickly lowered the tapestry. Then I realized it was my heart thumping madly in my chest.

I hurried out of the bedroom, down the hallway, and into the bathroom. My body was shaking. I was fearful. But after closing the bathroom door behind me, and taking a few deep breaths, I realized that I felt more than fear. I felt energized.

I now had a mission.

I had hope.

JENNY

CHAPTER SEVEN

Without telling Eddie, I went to the internist for my appointment. I put the charge on the Discover card, but I didn't feel as guilty about it this time. Eddie was on the verge of landing a job in Playa del Rey, and from what he'd said about it, though we wouldn't be rolling in the money, it would put us back on the road to financial stability.

The internist turned out to be compassionate and direct. He didn't deal in vague answers like my general practitioner had.

"I wish I could say that the odds are with you," he said, after carefully explaining the battery of tests I'd be undergoing. "But the truth is we might be in for some bad news. I want you to be prepared."

"I think I am." I gave him a feeble smile.

"Good—because there's a high likelihood that we'll find something. But I also want you to understand that just because we find something, it doesn't mean it'll be life-threatening. Patients tend to think that a tumor means a serious illness—incurable."

"You can count me in that column."

"There are a lot of patients in that column. But we've come a long way with treatments. Let's get the diagnosis and we'll go from there. I can assure you, there will be plenty of options, all with great outcomes."

I still couldn't help but think of cancer as a death sentence.

*

I spent the next few days gritting my teeth, unable to focus while I waited for the test results. I also decided that, at this point, I would just wait until I got those test results before I said anything to Eddie and the kids.

And when the day came to take the MRI, I told Eddie that I had an interview for a job as a prop master on a Netflix TV pilot.

He wished me luck.

Two days later, the internist's office called to schedule an appointment. The doctor wanted to go through the results with me in person.

It was time to tell Eddie.

I wanted him with me when the doctor ran through my treatment options. And I was sure that this was what the doctor was going to do—right after he told me the bad news.

That evening, after I'd gotten the call to schedule the appointment, Eddie was at a tutoring session nearby. After that session, he was planning to come home to grab a bite to eat before heading out for two more sessions. Hannah was at swim practice, and Jake was at Sam's house, so this was a good opportunity to tell Eddie.

The only downside was that he'd just come off a terrible argument with Jake about college. Jake had gotten into both Berkeley and Columbia, and though no college was looking affordable right now, we'd been pressuring him to choose Berkeley. It was in no way inexpensive, but at least it was less expensive than Columbia and Northwestern.

The most logical choice was Lehigh, a small school in Pennsylvania, one of Jake's safety schools. Lehigh had awarded him a substantial financial aid package.

Jake refused to even consider the school. And Eddie not only wanted him to consider it, he wanted him to go there. Period.

They'd had another argument about it this afternoon. It had been so loud and so full of "fuck you"s from Jake that I'd gone into the bedroom and put a pillow over my ears. In the end, Jake had stood his ground, and Eddie had marched into our bedroom, fuming.

"The belligerent bastard wants to major in economics," he said, "but he doesn't understand a fucking thing about the reality of paying for college."

"He'll come around," I said, though I knew Jake well enough to know he wouldn't.

"Deposits are due in two weeks," Eddie shot back.

"We'll put down a deposit for Northwestern and Berkeley, *and* for Lehigh, and we won't tell him."

"More money flushed down the toilet." Eddie sat down on the bed, the fight suddenly gone out of him. "And then what? How do we get him to go to Lehigh?"

"We bully him until he understands that it's the only school we can afford."

"I could use your help."

"I'll talk to him again," I said, though it would be a futile conversation. Then, hoping that there might be some good news on the horizon, I asked, "Have you heard anything about the job in Playa del Rey?"

"No—not yet. They're dragging their feet." He slumped, and didn't say anything more.

"You think they might have hired someone else?"

"I don't know. I hope not." He shook his head, exasperated.

That had pretty much been the end of the conversation. Eddie had then taken off to go to the early tutoring session. But it was the image of him sitting on the edge of our bed, slumped over, desperate, that had stuck with me. It had stayed in my mind for the rest of the afternoon, and it was still there when he came home for a bite to eat.

So I couldn't bring myself to tell him about the doctor's appointment, even though I wanted him there with me. Instead, I made him a burger, with cheese and avocado and onions, just the way he liked it.

"Thanks, honey," he said, when I brought it over to the table.

"No problem," I responded—though there were a ton of problems.

*

The internist told me I had pancreatic cancer. And that was the good news. The bad news was that it was at an advanced stage, and my options were limited. But what exactly those options were, I couldn't say, because once I'd heard the diagnosis, I couldn't focus on much of what the doctor said afterward.

I found myself wondering why the world around me suddenly looked fake. When I'd walked into the doctor's office, the doctor had looked like a real human being, made of flesh and bone. Now he appeared to be an android, spouting off words he was programmed to say, and most of those words sounded like gibberish. Sure, I heard emotion in his voice, reflecting the gravity of my situation, but I wasn't fooled.

I was the only human in the room.

The office had also changed. When I'd walked in, it had looked inviting and comfortable, decorated in warm beige tones. Now it looked like a cheap set from a low-budget infomercial, like the one I'd worked on in Ventura four years ago. I was sitting in a God-awful replica of a medical office.

"Do you have any questions?" the android asked.

"No." I just wanted to get out of the robot's line of sight.

But I couldn't. I was trapped in this fake world.

A few of the things the android said did make it through to me, even though I was focused on escaping this facade of an office: surgery was too risky, unless they could shrink the tumor; aggressive treatment might prolong my life, but it was risky and expensive, and the outcome was uncertain; my life expectancy was two years.

I stared at the android's eyes—steely blue, beautifully lifelike, but not made well enough to fool me. I could tell they were cut glass.

"I know this is a lot to take in right now," the android said. "But this isn't the last consultation. We should talk again next week, after you've had some time to digest this." His computer-generated voice was a million times better than Siri—better than any I'd ever heard—but I could still tell it was synthesized.

"Are you going to be okay, Mrs. Hart?" the android asked, feigning concern.

I nodded. I had to get out of here.

"It's okay to tell me if you're not feeling okay," he continued. "I can give you something for that."

I stared at his skin. Like his voice, it was synthetic.

The android shifted in his seat, then said, "Why don't we schedule another appointment? After you've had some time to process."

"Okay."

*

On the way home, I tried to force myself to stop my irrational thinking. It was tough. Everything I drove past looked fake. Painted, wooden facades of buildings, plastic life-size cars, and badly made props of all types.

I tried to ignore the phony world around me because I wanted to recall exactly what the doctor had said. I had to get that straight before talking to Eddie.

By the time I pulled up to the house, I had managed to remember the basics. Pancreatic cancer, advanced, not many options, but with aggressive treatment—expensive treatment—I might live for... *How long had the doctor said?*

Two years. *Was that right?*

I entered the house and stood there, motionless. I knew where to find Eddie: in the den, feet up on the coffee table, computer on his lap. He was probably reading newspapers online. He was still a news junkie, though he was no longer part of the profession. Why did he harbor hopes of getting back in the game? Couldn't he see that the herd had been thinned?

Of course he sees that, and it's killing him.

And what I have to tell him now will kill him even more.

I stepped into the den, and he looked up from his laptop.

I felt bad. For him.

"It's tough, isn't it?" I said.

"What's tough?"

"Changing careers. Getting kicked to the curb. After so many years."

"It is..." He smiled, and I could see he appreciated my words. He was a good man whose career had imploded through no fault of his own.

"When is your first tutoring session today?" I asked.

"I've got an early one today. Two-thirty."

"You want me to make you some lunch?"

"Sure—thanks."

But I didn't turn to head out of the room. Again, I found myself standing there, motionless. A morbid picture had formed in my head. It was my funeral, and Jake was staring at my casket. He was devastated and lost. I was heartbroken. How could I abandon my son?

"What's wrong, honey?" Eddie said.

I tried to rally—that's what I was going to have to do from here on in. Wasn't it? I'd have to find a way to give my family strength. The strength they'd need to carry on without me. That would be my goal before I died.

But how?

I felt warmth around the edges of my eyes, and then the tears began to flow. Down my cheeks they fell. I quickly wiped them away.

Eddie leapt off the couch and headed toward me. "What's wrong, honey?" he asked again.

I shook my head and continued to wipe away the tears. But they kept coming. Why the hell was I crying? How the hell was that going to help?

Eddie hugged me. "I'm sorry it's been so rough," he said.

"That's okay." My voice was shaky.

"It's not okay—I lied to you," he said. "There isn't a sales job in Playa del Rey. I guess I can't get it through my thick skull that I have to come up with a new game plan. Applying for jobs isn't enough. It's not working."

"I—" That was all I managed to say before my throat constricted.

"I'm so sorry I lied to you," he said.

"Th-that's okay. Y-you had to. I cornered you."

"You'd think the way some of those kids I tutor look at me, like I'm the world's biggest loser, would be plenty of motivation for me to find a way out of this. I have to regroup and—"

"I—I have cancer," I blurted out. "Pancreatic cancer."

Eddie's face went pale, and his upper lip quivered. He hugged me again and didn't say anything for a minute or so.

Then he whispered in my ear. "Honey... I'm so sorry."

"It's bad," I said.

He kissed my cheek gently. "We'll survive. I promise."

I buried my head in his shoulder. "I was in a d-daze when the doctor went through my diagnosis." My voice was muffled by the soft cotton of his shirt. "I think I have two years to—" My words caught in my throat.

He hugged me more tightly, and neither of us said anything for a while. Finally, with my head still buried in his shoulder, I managed to go on.

"It's my fault. I made it worse," I said. "If I'd gone to the doctor when you asked me to, they would've caught it sooner."

"It's not your fault. How could you have known?"

"It's my fault that we won't have the money to pay for this. If I'd gone while we were insured, at least that would be taken care of."

"We'll find a way to pay for this. Don't worry."

I suddenly pulled away from him. What was wrong with him? *He* was the one living in a fantasy world. Not me.

"It's going to cost us hundreds of thousands of dollars without insurance!" I said. "Don't you get that? You know about those families who lose everything because of a 'catastrophic medical issue'?" I used air quotes. "We're going to be joining them. That's the most horrible part of all this. You and Hannah and Jake will get over my death—I know you will—but you won't have anything left. And that'll be my fault. Can't you see that?"

He was about to respond, but I ran out of the room first. I didn't want to talk to him anymore. I was mad at myself and at him. He should've landed a job already. We should've had health insurance by now. Why wasn't he being realistic? Couldn't he see we weren't going to make it?

I ran into the bedroom and closed the door behind me. Why hadn't *I* gotten a full-time job? I had my own career—a good one. I could take care of myself, and Eddie, and my family. Was that the real source of my anger? That I hadn't done my part?

Or was I angry because life had dealt me a cruel blow?

EDDIE

CHAPTER EIGHT

Over the next couple of days, whenever Jenny and I spoke about our new crisis, we kept our voices down. Neither of us was ready to break the news to Jake and Hannah, and I couldn't help but think that we were all starting to keep secrets from each other.

Of course, I had been the one to start this trend. I was the one who'd waited more than a month to tell my wife I'd been fired. It was only after that transgression that she had followed suit and hidden her doctor's appointments and subsequent bad news from me. But I thought I understood why she had chosen to do so. She didn't want to acknowledge that more terrible news was just around the corner.

Now, with everything out on the table, I wanted to be by her side during every minute of her ordeal. Because it was *our* ordeal. And that meant I wanted her to go back to the internist, this time with me. But she didn't want to spend the money on another appointment, not for just a consultation. She wanted to move on to the oncologist, the surgeon, and the other specialists. They were next on the agenda, regardless of what the internist had to say.

But after a little cajoling, she conceded. She trusted the internist, and she agreed that hearing him lay out the options again would help us make better decisions down the line. Both of us understood that reading about pancreatic cancer on the Internet, without being able to ask the internist questions, would only make this crisis worse.

*

The internist laid out the options. He was patient and easy to talk to. And when it came to the cost of the treatments, Jenny had been right. It was going to cost hundreds of thousands of dollars, and could easily pass the million-dollar mark, especially if we got "lucky"—meaning the tumor shrank enough to allow for surgery.

The doctor knew we weren't insured, so he suggested some clinics that could help out with consultations and some of the treatments. But he was cautious with this advice, and it was easy to read between the lines. He was saying that we might not yet be poor enough to go to these clinics. We were caught in the middle. Even though we were broke, we would have to lose our assets, too, before qualifying for help from the clinics.

In the car, on the way home, Jenny threw out an idea. "I'm going to call Lila and beg her to find me a job at Disney. I won't tell her what's going on, and we'll hide that I'm sick until I get insurance."

I glanced at her. That was crazy talk. Which wasn't like her at all. She was never irrational. She had to know that hiding her diagnosis was an implausible plan, and we *both* knew there were very few staff jobs in the art departments of the major studios. Ninety-five percent of prop masters were freelancers.

I gave her a minute to realize her plan was absurd, then spoke up. "I'm the one who needs to get a job right now. With insurance and no waiting period." That was the only solution.

But I had no idea if we could actually get insurance now that she'd already been diagnosed. Obamacare was supposed to have outlawed the practice of denying insurance coverage due to a pre-existing condition, but I'd read that insurance companies had found loopholes in the law that allowed them to continue this practice.

Neither of us said anything as I drove past the familiar sites on Riverside Drive: Bob's Big Boy, Trader Joe's, the quaint little post office. I loved walking this stretch of Riverside in the evening—perfect for pedestrians out on a casual stroll—but my heart sank when I thought about walking it alone, without Jenny.

She turned to me, and I could feel her eyes on me before she spoke. "What if I don't do anything?" she said.

"You mean no treatments?" Of course that's what she meant, but I asked out of surprise.

"Yes."

"Is that what you want?"

She didn't answer. I looked over at her and met her eyes. They were gloomy eyes, swimming in confusion. She turned away.

"I don't know," she said. "What do you think?"

"I don't know either—but I promise I'll get a job. One that doesn't have a waiting period for insurance. I don't want money to be part of the decision."

She smiled, but it was a sad, downturned smile.

*

I drove up Beverly Glen toward Ben Kingsley's house. It had been a long time since I'd used Mulholland to get to my tutoring sessions up this way. I'd been avoiding taking the celebrated road because I no longer enjoyed sneaking peeks at the glittering lights of the Valley below. The view was no longer a leave-all-your-troubles-behind kind of view. The long dazzling boulevards now looked like dead ends.

On the Bel Air side of Beverly Glen, I turned into the familiar development of McMansions. When I pulled up to the Kingsley house, I noticed a new car in the driveway—a Tesla. Need I say more?

Ben clearly had way more money than he knew what to do with. The guy already had a Mercedes SUV and a BMW.

Mason greeted me at the door and led me into the den. Over the last few weeks, his writing had turned the corner. All his hard work had paid off, and I was impressed. Not only because of his improvement, but also because the kid was incredibly motivated, even though he came from a privileged background. He was hard on himself and would never take the easy way out.

In the den, Mason pulled out his iPhone and shut it off. I noticed that, like the Telsa, it was brand new.

"New toy?" I said.

"Yeah—my dad got it for me for getting an 'A' on that Cold War history paper." He put the phone back in his pocket. "I guess you deserve part of it, huh?"

"It was all you, Mason." In this case, with this kid, it really was. But I did wonder if I should ask his dad for a bonus. Obviously his dad could afford it. But a bonus wasn't even a drop in the bucket when it came to what I needed. What I needed was the job his dad had.

But exactly what is that job? I thought. And right then, I decided that I'd find out. Tonight.

"Your dad hasn't been around much lately," I said.

"He works a lot," Mason responded.

"He likes to burn the midnight oil, huh?"

"I guess. But he's home tonight."

"Oh."

We both sat down at the desk.

"So, what's your dad invest in?" I said, trying to sound casual.

"Something to do with agriculture."

I pulled out my workhorse laptop, and Mason pulled out an English essay from his folder.

"Does he work for himself or for some kind of hedge fund?" I hoped this wasn't beginning to sound like an interrogation.

"Why don't you ask him yourself?"

I glanced at Mason. His eyes had narrowed—it was clear that I'd entered the interrogation zone.

"No big deal," I said, shrugging.

"You sure? Because it sounds like you're fishing for information."

"Don't worry about it. Really. I was just rambling."

"Okay." He relaxed. "It's just that my dad is secretive about his job. That's the thing. He doesn't tell me or my mom much about it."

So that's why the kid had quickly become defensive. Still, even though he hadn't wanted to answer questions about his dad's job, he'd used the word "secretive" to describe it. That, for me, was a further call to action. Tonight, I'd talk to Ben himself, and find out what he did for a living.

Of course, my call to action was really fueled by Jenny's diagnosis, but I didn't want to think about that. It was too painful.

When the tutoring session ended, Mason led me through the house toward the front door as he usually did. But tonight, I was on the lookout for Ben the entire time. I didn't see him in the hallway, or in the living room, or in the dining room.

So at the front door, before heading out, I stopped and turned to Mason. "Can you get your dad for me?" I said. "I want to ask him about adjusting our schedule." But as soon as those words were out of my mouth, I realized I'd been stupid. First of all, wasn't Mason the one to talk to about his schedule? And second, wouldn't he figure out that the reason I wanted to talk to his dad was to continue my interrogation?

But Mason simply responded with: "Hang on. I'll get him."

I waited in the foyer, and thirty seconds later Ben ambled in. "Good to see you again," he said. "You're doing a terrific job with Mason."

"Thanks. But Mason's the one doing the terrific job."

"You gave him the confidence. He didn't think he was a good writer before you started tutoring him. I hope this change in schedule doesn't mean we're losing you."

"I don't know exactly. Not yet anyway." I hadn't come up with a way to work in the only question I wanted to ask him. So I decided to play along with my change-in-schedule lie, hoping it'd take me where I wanted to go. "I'm taking on a freelance editing job, and that means I have to cut back on the tutoring."

"Well, I hope you can still squeeze Mason in."

"That depends on his schedule. Can you email me all the times he's free and what works with Diane's schedule and yours?"

"Sure. I'll get that together and get it over to you ASAP." He moved toward the front door, ready to open it for me.

"Great," I said, and turned to the door. I was scrambling to come up with something to keep the conversation going and to get me closer to uncovering the source of those bricks of cash. "I wish I didn't have to take on this second job," I said, "but my son is starting college next year and that's going to put a big hurt on the old wallet."

"College tuition is out of hand," Ben said, and opened the front door.

You'll be able to pay for college a hundred times over, I thought. But that's not what I said. Instead, I went with, "You're not kidding, and I'm not even sure this new job is going to help."

"I hope it does," he responded. He was waiting for me to mosey on out.

I took a step toward the open door, and then let a Hail Mary fly. "By the way, what do you do for a living?" I asked. Then, to soften the brusqueness of the question, I quickly added, "I'm definitely in the market for suggestions."

"I'm an investor," he answered.

That wasn't going to cut it. I turned back from the open door. "That's right—I forgot," I said. "Mason told me. What do you invest in?"

"It depends. Mostly agricultural products."

"You mean you're a commodities trader?" Maybe this was why Mason knew the term "commodity."

"Something like that," he responded.

I was going to have to press him if I wanted answers. And pressing him would probably cost me the tutoring job. But what did that matter? Tutoring Mason wasn't going to pay the staggering medical bills headed my way.

"Something like what?" I said.

Ben's face went taut. He moved closer to the door, as if ushering me out. "Something like commodities trading, but it's more specialized," he said.

I didn't make a move to exit. "How is it specialized?"

"It involves all sorts of esoteric analysis."

"Like derivatives trading?"

"It's more complicated than that. Sometimes I barely understand it myself." He chuckled, but there was no humor in it. It was forced.

"You're saying I wouldn't understand it?" I said.

"You seem awfully curious about it. But I really don't have the time to explain it all right now. Maybe we can talk about it some other time."

But it was more than obvious that he didn't want to talk about it some other time. The man didn't want to talk about it at all. Ever.

"I'm sure you can sum it up for me," I said. "Just so I have a general idea."

"Listen—I know what you're getting at. You're looking for a potential job." He shook his head, then flashed a grin. "But believe me, what I do isn't the type of job you can just jump into."

"Maybe if you fill me in, I can decide for myself."

Ben's grin disappeared and his eyes turned hard. "You think if you had my job you'd be better off—financially. Well, maybe you would, or maybe you wouldn't, but the grass isn't always greener. And take my word for it, that's the bottom line here." He started to close the door, even though I was still in the doorway. "Now if you'll excuse me," he said, "I've got some phone calls to make."

If I didn't want to get hit by the door, I had no choice but to step out onto the stoop. So that's what I did. And that's when he delivered the grand finale.

"You know what?" he said. "I think Mason is doing pretty well. Why don't we take a break from the tutoring?"

And with that, he shut the door in my face.

I walked to my car, slid in, then stared at Ben's house before pulling away. The McMansion held a secret. The secret of what Ben did for a living. And I was determined to uncover that secret. I was determined to uncover the source of those bricks of cash.

For the sake of my family, that was my mission.

CHAPTER NINE

Because of my career as a reporter, I had strong investigative skills. But using them for what I had to do next ran counter to my character. I had never used those skills to move into morally shady territory.

That was about to change.

My plan was to learn everything I could about Ben. Or, in crasser terms, to snoop on him, to tail him, and to leave no stone unturned.

I was motivated to get started right away. Jenny had decided to begin chemo treatments, and the result of her first treatment made it perfectly clear that getting on with my mission was the only thing I could do to help her.

We'd both made the decision to go with chemo. The expense worried us, but we wanted to see if the chemo could stop the cancer from spreading. When we dug in and looked at the numbers behind the studies, we both knew we were hoping for a miracle. But a miracle was our only option.

The first chemo infusion left Jenny weak and sick. I couldn't remember ever feeling so bad for another human being. And what made that feeling worse, what moved my soul to tears, was that this was the woman I loved with all my heart. Watching her suffer, without being able to help her, was heart-wrenching.

And it was this crushing sorrow that reinforced what I had to do. For there was only one thing I *could* do for her: give her peace of mind.

Give her security.

So as soon as she'd recovered from her first chemo infusion, I began to implement my plan. Unfortunately, this had to start with a lie.

After what had been a good day for her, we were both in bed reading, before hitting the hay. She was perusing a book about cancer treatments. She'd discovered that books about treatments were far better than scouring the Internet for information. With books, you didn't suddenly find yourself down a rabbit hole, where fact and conjecture were mixed together, offering either unsubstantiated hope or unsubstantiated doom.

I put down my book and picked up my cell phone from the night table. Then I scrolled through my emails and served up my lie. "It looks like I have an early appointment in the morning," I said, as if I'd just learned this from one of my emails.

"A new job interview?" she asked.

It would have been easier to say "yes," but I guess I was trying to soften the lie, so instead I said, "Not exactly a job interview. I'm going to see someone who's in a line of work that I might be able to get into."

"Sounds mysterious—what kind of line of work?"

"I don't mean to sound mysterious." I had meant to sound vague. "Let me see how it goes before I say anything more about it." I set the alarm on my cell phone for five a.m.

Jenny looked over at me. "You don't want to jinx it, right?"

"Yeah."

"I don't blame you. We've been jinxed enough."

"I'm sorry." I kissed her on the forehead. "We'll fight our way back."

"I know," she said. But I could hear the lack of faith in her voice.

"I promise we will," I said.

She kissed me. "I love you."

"I love you, too."

*

I was out of the house and driving up Beverly Glen, travel mug in hand, sipping coffee, by 5:40. My binoculars were in the glove compartment. I hadn't used them in a while. It had been over a decade since my investigative reporting had required a stakeout.

My plan was to start staking Ben out at six, and as it looked now, I'd be starting a little early. Of course, it was possible that Ben left for work—for his "specialized" commodities trading—much earlier than six. His workday might coincide with the hours of the New York Stock Exchange, or of the Chicago Mercantile Exchange, or of a foreign stock exchange.

The point was that I might not get his schedule down for a few days, but during this first stakeout, I'd begin to get a handle on it. If I didn't see Ben leaving for work, I'd stick it out until I had to leave for my first tutoring session at three. That way, I could at least begin to lay out Ben's schedule. I could infer that he didn't travel back and forth from his house to an office between the hours of six a.m. and three p.m.—unless his schedule differed depending on the day of the week. But eventually I'd find that out, too.

I didn't stake out Ben's house directly—that would have been too obvious. Luckily, there was a great alternative. There was only one street—Tiffany Circle—that connected Ben's neighborhood to Beverly Glen, and Beverly Glen was the only way out of the neighborhood. So I parked my car on Beverly Glen, a half block up from Tiffany Circle. I had an unobstructed view of that intersection and its traffic light. My car was one of a handful of cars parked on the road, but it would be less conspicuous as the morning wore on. Beverly Glen was a busy thoroughfare connecting the Valley to the Westside, and soon the blur of traffic would obscure my presence.

Still, I didn't fool myself. Parking here for nine hours straight could raise suspicion. A neighbor might call the cops. But I'd cross that bridge when, and if, I got to it, for it was possible that I'd get what I needed soon and be on my merry way. Ben might head to work in the next couple of hours.

I began my vigil, sipping coffee and waiting for Ben's Tesla, or his Mercedes SUV, or his BMW. Over the next hour, cars pulled up to the traffic light, waited for it change, then turned either south to the Westside or north to the Valley. Most headed south to the Westside.

At 7:15, I perked up. Ben's Mercedes pulled up to the traffic light. Its blinker indicated that Ben was going to turn left—north toward the Valley—which meant I'd already miscalculated. I had guessed that Ben worked on the Westside, so I'd parked my car facing south. I needed to pull a U-turn if I had any chance of following him, and pulling a U-turn was going to be near impossible. Traffic on Beverly Glen was now thick in both directions.

I started the car, hoping to force myself into traffic. I inched forward along the curb, blinker on, but no one was slowing down to let me cut in. I was also moving closer to the intersection, and I didn't want to look toward the Mercedes for fear that Ben would spot me.

But I couldn't help myself. Just before passing right in front of the Mercedes, I glanced over at it—

—and realized I had a long way to go before I learned how to play the stakeout game. Diane, Ben's wife, was behind the wheel, and Mason was in the passenger seat, looking down at his spanking new iPhone.

Of course, I thought. How could I be so stupid?

Mason went to Harvard-Westlake. I should've expected to see

him heading to school this morning. Not only did I have a lot to learn about preparing for a stakeout, but my investigative skills were rusty. I should've parked closer to Tiffany Circle. That way I could've seen who was behind the wheel. Or I should've used the binoculars.

A couple hundred yards past the intersection, I finally managed to merge into traffic. A quarter of a mile farther down, I turned into another housing development, then swung back onto Beverly Glen, and back up to Tiffany Circle.

I parked in the same place, facing south again, still betting that Ben would head to the Westside, and hoping that I hadn't missed him.

By ten a.m., I worried that I had. Maybe he'd left minutes after Diane and Mason had. But I stuck with my plan to stay until three o'clock. My only break came just after one p.m., when I drove up to the strip mall just below Mulholland. I went to the bathroom, grabbed a sandwich at Starbucks, and noted that on my stakeout tomorrow, I needed to cover the twenty-minute gap I'd just missed.

At three o'clock, I left. I hadn't seen Ben.

After my tutoring sessions that afternoon and evening, I told Jenny, over dinner, that I'd be leaving early again the next morning.

"I want explore that new job possibility some more," I said. "But I have a lot to learn and a lot of questions."

"Can you tell me a little about it?" she asked. "Or are you still worried about jinxing it? I'm really curious."

I felt so bad about lying that I lied some more, just so I could give her answers. "It's investing," I said. And maybe it was. Maybe Ben had been telling the truth.

"Are you thinking of becoming a stockbroker?" she said. Her frown gave away her reaction. She was doubtful about that choice. So I pivoted a little.

"No—nothing like that. It's a specialized kind of investing."

"Is it commission-based?" *That* was her concern.

"Don't worry," I said. "I know it's stupid to take on something where the salary is commission."

"If you're making a career change, you should go for stability."

I was about to say that the only way to have any stability these days was to already be wealthy. But I didn't say that. It was absurd to pick a fight over a make-believe job.

"It's working for an investment group," I said. "It would be as stable as any other job. Whatever that's worth these days."

"That's an interesting change."

"Yeah... But I still feel nervous talking about it while it's a long shot."

She didn't ask me any more questions, and I didn't tell her any more lies. Not then, anyway.

The next morning, I was back on my stakeout, trying to uncover exactly what this investment job was. But Ben didn't show up at the intersection of Beverly Glen and Tiffany Circle that day either.

So, on the way to my five-o'clock tutoring session, I decided I'd cancel tomorrow's tutoring sessions in favor of doing a nighttime stakeout. My reasoning was that if Ben had left his house over the last two days, it must have been during the late afternoon, evening, or night.

But I didn't wait until the next night for the stakeout.

I went to my five o'clock tutoring session, then canceled the others.

By seven-thirty, I was staking out my favorite intersection again.

Forty minutes later, a jolt of adrenaline shot through my body: a Tesla was pulling up to the traffic light. But when I took a closer look at the silhouette of the driver inside, I realized it wasn't Ben, nor was it Diane. It was the silhouette of some other person who had money to burn on a new Tesla.

But as the adrenaline receded, I suddenly realized that I felt good. I felt energized by this hunt, by this investigation, by this mission. I felt more alive—invigorated even—than I had in a long time.

I kept my eyes glued to the intersection, and I considered the research I'd done on Ben one more time. This had been another phase of the hunt that had energized me. When it came to putting together a person's profile, years of investigative reporting had trained me well. I was good at online sleuthing.

But Ben had a very low profile on the Internet. It was as if he'd hired a cyber-security firm to scrub his presence from the web, especially when it came to information about the last four years or so of his life. Except for some public records, like the one listing the purchase of his current home, I hadn't found much.

Still, that was a clue in itself.

He'd taken quite a big step up the socioeconomic ladder from his previous address. *Movin' on up to the east side,* he finally got a piece of the pie. In this case, his piece of the pie was Bel Air. And my hunch was that his sudden change in fortune coincided with the first few deliveries of those bricks of cash.

Before he'd moved to Bel Air, Ben's digital footprint on the web was bigger, though still not as big as it should have been—it appeared that some details, even from the earlier periods of his life, had been scrubbed from the web. What I did know was that he had worked as a manager for DirecTV in El Secondo, and he had lived in a middle-class neighborhood in Torrance. I couldn't tell if this had been his first job, but it looked like he'd worked there for more than fifteen years. He had climbed the ladder into management during DirecTV's period of explosive growth.

I also found that he'd graduated from UC Irvine with a business degree, and that his parents lived in San Diego. He appeared to have no other living relatives, which struck me as odd, especially because that was true on both his mother's side *and* his father's side. He was an only child, as were his parents, so he had no aunts and uncles.

But even stranger was the fact that there was no record of what Ben did for a living now. No record about his segueing from DirecTV to investing.

Zilch.

*

An hour and a half passed without much activity on Tiffany Circle, so I decided I'd cruise up to the Starbucks and grab a cup of coffee. It could be a late night.

But just before I started my car, I saw Ben's gray BMW pull up to the intersection.

My first thought was that he was driving the most inconspicuous of his cars. When you owned a Mercedes SUV, a Tesla, and a BMW, the BMW was the most inconspicuous.

Its blinker indicated that Ben was heading to the Valley.

That meant I'd have to make a U-turn, for again I'd counted on Ben heading south. But there wasn't much traffic, so that wasn't going to be a problem. I just had to wait long enough after Ben drove by so he wouldn't see my U-turn in his rearview mirror and become suspicious. He might notice that the car making the U-turn was the same model as the tutor's car—the tutor who was too nosy for his own good. On the bright side, I drove a Camry, which was such a common car, it probably wouldn't raise a red flag.

I wasn't worried about actually trailing Ben. I'd trailed people as a reporter before, and I knew how to hang back and not be spotted.

The light turned green, and Ben swung out from Tiffany Circle onto Beverly Glen. When he drove past me, I started my car. Then I craned my head around and watched his taillights. As soon as they disappeared around the bend, just past the strip mall, I checked to make sure the road was clear in both directions, and pulled a U-turn. I sped up until I saw his car up ahead, but I didn't get too close.

I followed him through the Mulholland intersection and down into the Valley. His BMW snaked down Beverly Glen toward Ventura Boulevard. I caught a glimpse of the Valley lights glittering below, and I realized that the view had changed again. The lights now shone with hope. The Valley's long dazzling boulevards led to the Promised Land.

At Ventura, Ben took a right, heading east. I was about a hundred yards behind him, but I sped up. If he made a quick exit from the boulevard into one of the adjoining neighborhoods, I didn't want to miss it.

He didn't make a quick exit. I ended up trailing him down Ventura for a few miles, theorizing about what he'd do next. He wasn't planning on going far, or he would've turned west on Ventura and gotten on either the 101 or the 405. And he probably wasn't headed out for a quick bite to eat, because he'd already passed dozens of eateries, which dotted this stretch of the boulevard.

When Ben hit Studio City, a pang of fear shot through me. What if the guy took a left turn onto Colfax and headed toward Valley Village—toward my house? Had my prying into his business set off some kind of alarm? Was *I* the reason he was on the move tonight?

Ben didn't turn off onto Colfax; he took a left onto Tujunga. That still left open the possibility that he was headed to Valley Village—to my place—but it also added another possibility to the mix. I knew that on Tujunga, among the boutiques, coffee houses, eateries, and yoga studios, was a low-slung office building. Maybe Ben kept an office there. It would definitely be a great location if he wanted to keep a low profile.

On Tujunga, he slowed down as if he was looking for a parking spot. If so, he wasn't headed to that office building—it had its own parking lot. I scanned the shops that lined the block, wondering which of them he was planning to visit.

He pulled into a parking spot, which meant I needed to find one too. I continued forward, past his car, making sure not to look over at him. Instead, I checked my rearview mirror so I wouldn't miss him climbing out of his car.

That was when I noticed that he had some kind of paper stuck on the far right corner of his windshield. I didn't think much of it then—I wrote it off as some kind of parking sticker—but that would soon change.

I found a parking spot far enough in front of him that he probably wouldn't take note of me as I parked. He still hadn't gotten out of his car. I weighed whether to get out of my car and find a place where I could monitor him, or just wait in the car until he got out of his BMW.

Seconds turned into minutes, and he still hadn't gotten out of his car. What the hell was the guy doing just sitting there? Maybe he had arrived early for a meeting and preferred to wait in his car, rather than in the eatery or coffee shop where the meeting was to take place.

I couldn't see what he was doing, only that he hadn't gotten out of his car. But after another fifteen minutes passed, I had the wild thought that somehow I *had* missed him getting out of his car. Again I considered whether to get out. People were strolling up and down the block; I could easily blend in.

But then Ben did something strange. He pulled out of his parking spot, drove farther down the block, past me, and just as I was ready to pull out and follow him, he parked again, in a space four spots up from mine.

What was he up to? Why had he switched spots? The parking wasn't metered right now; it was past eight o'clock. Besides, it wasn't like the guy needed to save a buck or two.

Once more, he didn't get out of his car, and this time I came up with a possible answer to the vexing question "Why?" But my answer was absurd.

He was on a stakeout, just as I was.

After another five minutes passed, that answer didn't seem so absurd. Did his job entail surveillance of some sort?

My attention drifted from his car to farther up the block, where a string of women were trickling out of a yoga studio, their mats in hand. Some of them were strolling in our direction, and I unexpectedly found myself enjoying the sight of a couple slim and attractive women in yoga pants.

I hadn't felt any kind of sexual desire since I'd been fired. Up to that point, my sex life with Jenny had been great—for both of us. But after losing my job, I lost my desire in that department. When Jenny realized that my interest in sex was waning, and that it was a side effect of getting fired and nothing more, she tried to revive it.

Until the cancer diagnosis came down. Then she lost interest too.

Now, I suddenly wanted to have sex with her. My desire had come roaring back, and it wasn't the slim women in yoga pants that had rekindled it. It was the stakeout itself—the hunt—and the entire investigation. And the bricks of cash at the end of the yellow brick road. I was feeling the same kind of transformative energy in the sexual desire department that I was feeling in other departments.

I looked back toward Ben's car, and just then, one of the approaching yoga women starting tottering and swaying. And before she completely lost consciousness and collapsed, one of the other women caught her. Then, while holding on to her, this woman frantically shouted out for someone to call 911.

Ben leapt from his car and ran up to the two women. He put his hand on the unconscious woman's neck as if he was feeling her carotid artery for a pulse. As people gathered around, Ben helped lay the woman down on the sidewalk. Then he pulled a penlight from his pocket, opened the woman's eyes, and checked them, as if he were a doctor. He followed this up by gently putting his hand on the woman's chest plate, and at that point, I actually wondered if the guy *was* a doctor.

But I knew he wasn't. That would've definitely come up in my search. Ben Kingsley had graduated from UC Irvine with a business degree.

I supposed it was possible that he was a certified EMT. But that seemed even more ludicrous. From what I'd found, the guy had worked for DirecTV his entire career—until he'd segued into whatever he did now. And I was sure that whatever he did now wasn't EMT work.

The only other possibility was that he had taken a CPR course.

But even if that was the case—which it probably was, since it was the most plausible explanation—that didn't matter right now, did it? For all intents and purposes, my stakeout was over, interrupted by this emergency. And that was bad luck, because I was sure that if there had been no emergency, I would've been one step closer to discovering what Ben did for a living.

The crowd of bystanders around the unconscious woman now obscured my view of Ben. But I still wanted to track what he was doing, because the entire incident didn't sit right with me, even with the CPR explanation. Maybe it didn't sit right because Ben had had that penlight with him. And that's probably what drove me to get out of my car.

Before I knew it, I was on the sidewalk, walking toward the crowd. I figured I could hang behind the gawkers and go unnoticed by Ben.

When I stepped up to the bystanders, I saw him scoop the woman up.

"Please make way, guys," he said. His voice boasted absolute confidence. He was the man in charge.

The crowd opened up, and Ben headed toward his car with the woman in his arms.

"I'm taking her to St. Joseph's," he said.

He got to his BMW and barked an order at the crowd: "Please open the door."

A bystander did as he requested, swinging open the passenger door.

But another bystander—a brunette in her forties, dressed in yoga pants, piped up. "We should wait for the ambulance." The woman's tone betrayed doubt about her own suggestion.

"We don't have time to wait," Ben said. He buckled the unconscious woman into the passenger seat and shut the door.

"You can't just drive her away," the brunette said. But there was still too much uncertainty in her voice to sway anyone—and Ben was already rounding the front his car.

He looked back at the crowd. "If any of you know her, please call her home and tell her family to meet us at St. Joseph's."

The brunette protested again. "The ambulance will be here any minute."

Ben pulled a card from his pocket and reached across the top of his car with it. "Please," he said. "Don't worry. I'm Dr. Straub. You can follow me to St. Joseph's. But we can't waste any more time or she's going to suffer some serious damage."

The brunette took the card, glanced at it, then looked back up at Ben.

He was already in the BMW.

The engine roared to life.

I wondered if I should intervene. I knew the brunette's instincts were right—something terrible was unfolding here on Tujunga.

Ben pulled away from the curb.

I hurried back to my car, but kept my eyes on the BMW. It headed down the block and turned right onto Moorpark.

At least he's headed toward St. Joseph's, I thought, *because one thing's for sure: he isn't Dr. Straub.*

What the hell was Ben Kingsley up to?

I jumped into my car, pulled out, and raced down the block. When I rounded the corner onto Moorpark, I saw the BMW in the distance.

It took a right onto Vineland—which meant Ben wasn't going to St. Joseph's.

I sped up, and so did the questions running through my mind. If Ben wasn't taking this woman to St. Joseph's, where *was* he taking her? To another place where she'd receive medical attention—like an urgent care center?

Or was his plan not to help her at all? Was his plan just the opposite—to hurt her? Was it possible that he'd parked on Tujunga precisely to wait for the opportunity to swoop in and kidnap this woman?

No, that couldn't be it. How would he know she was going to pass out? It was more likely that he'd seen an opportunity and seized it. But an opportunity for what?

I turned onto Vineland and saw that the BMW was stopped at a light a couple blocks up ahead. I slowed down, hoping the light would turn green before I got too close. It did, and the BMW moved forward. I followed, keeping my distance.

When Ben hit Ventura, he took a right, heading west. Was he headed back to his house? That couldn't be right. Not with this woman passed out in the passenger seat.

We hit the heart of Studio City, where the boulevard was very well lit, and I noticed something about Ben's car—something that had registered before, but which I hadn't given any thought to. There'd been no reason to.

The BMW didn't have a rear license plate. Instead, it just had a plate advertising "Center BMW," as if Ben had just purchased the car and hadn't gotten the plates for it yet. But I knew Ben hadn't just purchased the car. He'd had it since I'd started tutoring Mason.

It was right then that I realized what I'd seen stuck to the BMW's windshield: temporary registration papers. The kind you got while you were waiting for your new plates; the kind that exempted you from having plates while you waited. I had no doubt the BMW was also missing its front license plate.

And more importantly, I had no doubt that the temporary registration stuck to the windshield was fake. If a concerned citizen back there on Tujunga, like that brunette, had wanted to take down Dr. Straub's license plate number, they couldn't have.

With that revelation, what I had just witnessed started to make more sense. Ben had been prepared for the opportunity to kidnap that woman. He was not only prepared with a car that had no plates, but he'd also been prepared with his spiel, with his performance, with his penlight, and with his card—Dr. Straub's card.

So how had he known the woman was going to pass out?

Ben took a left onto Coldwater and began to drive up into the hills that overlooked the Valley. As I followed him, the gravity of his crime started to hit me. I had to wonder if Dr. Straub was headed up to Mulholland with the intention of pulling into one of the many secluded wooded areas nestled in the canyons.

What the hell had I stumbled onto? Should I intervene right now and call the police?

Whatever Ben was up to had nothing to do with the original purpose of my stakeout. This wasn't about Ben's job at all. Was I watching a sociopath? A serial rapist in action?

I made a decision. Not a tough one. I'd intervene if Ben pulled off into the woods. I'd help that poor woman. I didn't see myself as a hero. Anyone—even someone with a barely working moral compass—would do the same. But shouldn't I have called the police as soon as I saw Ben buckle the unconscious woman into his car?

When Ben reached the top of Coldwater, he turned west on Mulholland. Then, less than a mile later, he took a left. He was headed down the Beverly Hills side of the canyons. The houses down this way were intermingled with swatches of woods, which meant he could still be headed to a secluded patch of land.

I followed, but it was much tougher to keep his car in sight here because the hillside roads were winding, narrow affairs, snaking up and down in convoluted paths, and I didn't want to get too close, or he'd see that someone was following him. So every time he disappeared from view, I risked losing him for good.

Finally, Ben turned onto yet another narrow road, and when I got to it, I saw a "No Outlet" sign. Maybe this road dead-ended in a wooded area, and I had arrived at the end game. I fished my cell phone out, ready to call the police.

I drove past old Beverly Hills homes. These weren't the modern hillside homes and McMansions that had sprung up much later in Beverly Hills's history; these were grand, surrounded by generous patches of forested land. Even under the pale moonlight, they shone brightly with the glory of Hollywood's golden age.

Up ahead, Ben was driving fast, and considering that this was a narrow, unlit road, that told me he was familiar with this street, that he'd driven this way many times before.

I hung back. There was no outlet, so there was no risk of losing him.

He slowed down near a stretch of woods to his right, and I thought this was where he'd pull over.

He didn't. He continued another hundred feet or so before his headlights swooped to the left, illuminating a large wrought-iron gate. He stopped in front of that gate.

I immediately pulled over and cut my lights and engine. Then I grabbed my binoculars from the glove compartment—finally, they'd get some use—and I lifted them to my eyes just in time to see the iron gate swing open.

The BMW drove through, and I slid over to get a better view of the property behind the gate. A grand Neoclassical home rose from the forested grounds.

What was Ben doing? Making a delivery? Was the woman he'd kidnapped going to be used as a party favor? Was she going to be turned into a sex slave for a bunch of sick perverts waiting in that grand home? Was *this* how Ben earned a living?

Through the binoculars, I watched the BMW pull up to a three-car garage attached to the west side of the house. The garage door slid open, and Ben drove inside.

While some things made sense, others just didn't add up. If Ben was collecting sex slaves, wouldn't he kidnap at-risk women? Women whose disappearances wouldn't cause any sort of outcry? As a reporter, I knew that some lives were unjustly deemed more "worthy" than others, and that the news media was complicit in this. The kidnapping of a woman from a well-to-do neighborhood in Studio City rose to the level of "worthiness" that would result in news coverage. The kind of coverage rich men seeking sex slaves would avoid like the plague.

The garage door slid shut, and I admitted to myself that I had believed all along that the bricks of cash lay at the end of this tainted yellow brick road. That was why I hadn't called the police. That was why I'd told myself I'd "intervene" at the last minute. It had been a cowardly choice, born from the possibility that there was money to be had. Big money.

But if I wanted to redeem myself, now was my last chance. *This* was the last minute.

So why wasn't I punching numbers into my cell phone and calling the police?

Because that big money was going to save my family. It was going to give Jenny hope and peace of mind, and it was going to give my kids the college experience they'd earned.

But I wasn't going to start kidnapping women, regardless of the money.

So why hadn't I called the police? What was I still doing here?

Blackmail. That's what I was doing here. I wasn't going to kidnap women, but I *was* going to blackmail Ben Kingsley.

Fifteen minutes or so went by before the garage door slid open. I'd like to believe that I was mired in a moral quagmire during those fifteen minutes, with desperation barely trumping doing the right thing, but I can't say for sure that this was true. All I know is that I waited without calling the police. Instead, I thought about the one question above all others that I couldn't find an answer to: If Ben's job was kidnapping women and delivering them to wealthy clients, how did he know in advance that tonight's unlucky victim was going to pass out on that sidewalk in Tujunga?

The BMW pulled out of the garage.

Through the binoculars, I saw that the woman was back in the passenger seat, her eyes closed, as if she was still unconscious. But what about those fifteen minutes when she wasn't in the passenger seat? What had happened in that house? Rape? All of sudden this didn't seem likely. The fact that Ben's visit to this grand old home had been so brief didn't fit in with my sex slave theory. But I damn well knew that it didn't rule out some sort of deviant behavior on the homeowner's part.

It was time for me to take off, but as I jammed my binoculars into the glove compartment, I realized I'd waited too long to turn my car around. I hadn't planned an exit strategy. Ben's headlights were already on the iron gate, waiting for it to open.

For the second time tonight, a U-turn was a risk. On this narrow street, the maneuver would be slow—a three-point turn—and Ben's car would be on me while I was still executing it.

So as soon as the BMW's headlights swung onto the road, and right before they headed toward me, I ducked. That's what it had come down to. Amateur hour. Now the risk was whether or not Ben would recognize my car as he drove by. Again, Camrys were as ubiquitous as air, so I had that working for me. Also, Ben was probably more focused on the unconscious woman in his passenger seat than on parked cars.

I heard his car drive by—and it didn't slow down, which was a good sign. Twenty seconds later, I sat back up, glanced back, and saw his taillights winding toward the mouth of the dead-end street. I realized that I'd already lost him. By the time I pulled the U-turn, he'd be long gone, and I'd never find him in the maze of hillside streets.

So I made my time-consuming three-point U-turn, and I went with the only plan available to me: I'd head up toward Mulholland and hope that Ben was doing the same. If I could catch him before he got there, and see whether he turned east or west on Mulholland, I'd be able to continue trailing him. But if he headed down toward Beverly Hills, or to visit another nearby wealthy client, then for me the night was over.

I drove fast and recklessly up the winding roads, and I got lucky. I caught glimpses of the BMW up above me in the hills. Ben's car swept into curves, then disappeared into the dark again, winding its way up to Mulholland.

But my luck ran out at the crucial intersection. When the BMW reached Mulholland, I was in a spot far below, where I didn't have a clear line of sight. So I didn't see whether Ben went east or west.

I had to make a calculated guess. My bet was that he wouldn't go back to the scene of the crime. That he wouldn't head east toward Coldwater.

So when I reached Mulholland, I turned west and floored it.

There were a couple of cars up ahead of me, but the BMW wasn't one of them. Then, less than a half mile later, I caught one of those broad views of Mulholland Drive, and I knew I'd blown it. There were no cars along the stretch ahead of me.

Ben had turned east.

I pulled onto a turnout, and ignoring the view of the Valley below, I swung around and raced east to Coldwater.

But the distance was too great. I didn't catch up to him. And by the time I got to Coldwater and headed down into the Valley, I knew I was done for the night.

I'd lost him.

My first instinct was to head home. I was close by, anyway. But when I reached Ventura, I had a change of heart. Who knew how many times Ben ventured out into the night and kidnapped women? If I was going to follow through with any kind of blackmail, I should strike while the iron was hot. I had to strike while that transformative energy, inspiring and action producing, was coursing through my body.

Though I didn't know what Ben would do with the woman next, I knew he'd eventually return home. I decided to head to Beverly Glen and stake out Tiffany Circle Road.

When Ben returned home, I'd be waiting there for him.

*

I parked down the block from the Tiffany Circle intersection and waited. As it turned out, I didn't have to wait long.

Ben showed up thirty minutes later, and I followed him to his McMansion.

He pulled into his driveway and parked.

I pulled up to the curb as he stepped out of his BMW. He was carrying the expensive leather satchel, the one I'd seen that very first night at his house. The one from which he had pulled out the money. And I had no doubt that that's what was in there now. The money he'd just earned by kidnapping that woman.

Before I stepped out of my car, Ben spotted me and picked up his pace. He moved quickly toward his front door.

I slid out of my car and hurried toward him. "Ben," I said.

He didn't stop, and he didn't slow down. He was closing in on the front door.

"Ben—we need to talk," I said, loudly and firmly, enough so that he felt he had to respond.

"I told you: we're taking a break from the tutoring," he said. He selected a key from his key fob and reached for the front door.

"This isn't about tutoring."

He glanced back at me. His face didn't betray fear. Instead, his eyes were narrowed in anger. "Listen—we don't have anything to talk about," he said.

"Yes, we do."

He unlocked the front door. "You have a good night," he said, curtly.

"Let's talk about your job."

"We talked about it," he said, as he opened the door.

"You said we could talk about it again—some other time."

"Not now."

"My guess is not ever. Right?"

"Go home," he said.

"Not until you tell me why you kidnapped that woman."

That got his attention. He shook his head and closed the door without entering the house. Then he turned to face me. "You followed me."

"That's right."

"Forget what you saw," he said.

"I can't."

"You do not want to get involved."

"I don't want to, but I have to."

Ben's lips were pursed and his eyes were no longer narrowed. He looked far more worried than angry. "Go home," he said again.

"Tell me what I saw tonight."

He didn't respond. He just shook his head again.

I pressed him. "I saw you on the job. I know why you don't want to talk about the job."

He took in a deep breath and let it out. "Forget what you saw. I'll pay you to forget. Enough to make it worth your while."

So just like that, my blackmail plan had worked. It seemed ridiculously easy. I hadn't even had to bring it up myself. Operating under the influence of the transformative energy—which was still coursing through me—had paid off.

And maybe it was that same energy that dictated my next move. I suddenly wanted more. Much more.

"I don't want you to pay me off," I said. "I want to know what you do and how it works. And I want to be added to the roster of employees."

"You're kidding."

I wasn't. I wanted the same job he had, and access to the same amount of money.

"Forget about it," he said. "Take what I give you and run."

"No," I responded, without so much as a second thought. Whatever money he was going to give me would never cover all of Jenny's treatments or the kids' college tuition. And I no longer cared about the blackmail—I wanted the job.

He stared at me, but I couldn't tell if I saw confusion in his eyes, or resignation, or regret. I held his stare without backing down.

"I can talk to my employer," he said. "I suppose this has happened before."

"What has happened before?"

"A snoop like you rears his ugly head and we have a problem." He grimaced, and I was suddenly able to read him: he was disgusted. He turned away from me and opened the front door.

As he walked inside, he said, "This isn't going to turn out the way you want it to."

The confidence with which he issued that declaration made me uneasy. Was it a normal warning—that I was getting myself into something I'd later regret—or was it a veiled death threat?

"I'll give you a week to get back to me," I said. But he had definitely put a chink in the armor of my confidence. Maybe I should've taken the money and run.

JENNY

CHAPTER TEN

It couldn't wait any longer; Eddie and I had to talk to Jake about his choice of colleges today. Otherwise he'd lose the scholarship that Lehigh had offered him and the spots at Berkeley and UCSD. We could have delayed the decision by putting down deposits at all three schools, but we didn't want to flush the little money we had down the toilet.

I had tried to talk to Jake on my own, but even our close relationship wasn't enough to get him to understand that we didn't have the money to send him to Northwestern, or to Columbia. Of course, it had been tough to come down hard on him, because of how he'd reacted to my first chemo treatment.

He was the son every mother wished for.

On the days that followed the chemo infusion—miserable days, filled with vomiting, fever, ill temper, fatigue, and other side effects—he did everything he could to help me out. He cleaned around the house, he ran errands for me, he helped me cook dinner. And of all the sweet things he did for me, the one I treasured most was the time he spent sitting at my bedside, cheering me up.

It seemed cruel to reward his compassion by taking away his dream. But we had no choice.

At least Eddie was in a good mood today, and that meant he'd be patient with Jake. It was critical for both of us to be patient, because the discussion was bound to escalate quickly into an argument.

Up until the last couple of days or so, Eddie had been sullen and gloomy. And my chemo treatment seemed to have made his spirit sink even lower. He wasn't used to seeing me weak. I'd always been a pillar of strength, and he was shaken to the bone to see me in such a fragile state.

But why his mood had suddenly brightened, I didn't know. I suspected it was because he'd found out he had a good shot at landing that investment job. And I also suspected that because my initial reaction to that job had been negative, he didn't want to talk about it. He was keeping the potential good news to himself, but still, it had lifted his spirit.

This morning he'd settled onto the couch in the den, and he was now absorbed in his laptop. He was so absorbed that I could almost believe he was working on a story for the *LA Times* again.

I interrupted him, reminding him that we had to talk to Jake today.

"I know," he said. "I'll talk to him myself if you want."

I knew he was offering to go it alone because he felt bad about what I'd just gone through with the chemo. "That's okay," I said. "We can do it together."

"Are you sure you're up to it?" he asked, and closed his laptop. "It could get pretty ugly."

"Yeah. But he might be less angry if I'm there, too."

"Because he feels sorry for you?"

"That sounds horrible, doesn't it?" I said. "Using my cancer to crush my son's dream. What kind of mom am I?"

"We're not crushing his dream. Lehigh is a great school."

"I know, but don't say that to him. It makes him really mad when you put it that way." I'd already put it that way several times and had been verbally punished because of it.

"Maybe we should play it like Berkeley is the compromise school," he said. "We can't afford Northwestern or Columbia, and he doesn't want to go to Lehigh, so it's a fair compromise."

"We can't afford Berkeley either. You know that. Unless something has changed."

"You're right," he conceded.

But I couldn't understand why he'd brought Berkeley up. Was it the possibility of the investment job coming through—meaning a salary would soon be rolling in? Or was it that he didn't want to face Jake's wrath?

*

That afternoon, Jake came home from school and headed directly to his room.

Eddie and I waited in the kitchen before descending on him, to give him time to unwind. I plucked the envelope from Lehigh from the bulletin board, pulled out the letter from inside—the one offering Jake the generous scholarship—and read it again. Jake had read it once, the day it had arrived, and had never looked at it again. The only reason he'd even applied to Lehigh was because his high school counselor had insisted he apply to at least one school that was a sure thing. What the counselor had called a "sleep at night" school. A school where there was almost no doubt Jake would get in. So he'd grudgingly applied, and now the substantial scholarship he'd been awarded was a godsend.

If only Jake could see that.

After we decided he'd had enough time to unwind, I tucked the letter back in the envelope, pinned the envelope back on the bulletin board, and braced myself for the confrontation. I felt the insides of my stomach roll. It was nausea, which hadn't crept up on me for a couple of weeks—not since the side effects from the infusion had subsided.

But this nausea didn't feel like a precursor to vomiting. It felt like a precursor to something worse: crushing my son's dream.

"Are you ready to go in there?" Eddie asked.

"No—but that doesn't really matter, does it?"

*

Eddie knocked on Jake's door.

There was no answer.

I was sure that Jake had his headset on and was glued to his iPad, watching a YouTube channel.

I did the knocking this time—hard and sharp.

"Yeah," Jake said, distracted.

I opened the door, and Eddie and I stepped into the room.

Jake was lying on his bed, headphones on, iPad in hand, just as I'd expected. He slid the headphones off.

"What's going on?" he said, already defensive. "Why is the entire cavalry here?"

I expected that reaction—it was rare for both Eddie and I to appear in his room together.

"Your dad and I wanted to talk to you," I said.

"I figured out that part."

"Can you please sit up?"

"Okay…" He reluctantly swung around. "So what's up?"

I pulled out the chair from his desk and sat down. I didn't want both Eddie and I towering over him. That would make him even more defensive.

"We want to talk to you about college," I said.

He looked from me to Eddie and back again. "Haven't we talked

108

about it enough?"

"Jake," Eddie said, "we know how badly you want to go to Northwestern."

"And I know how badly you want me to go to Lehigh."

"Well, I guess that's a start," Eddie said, with good humor and patience.

But the good humor didn't take. "Guess what, guys?" Jake said. "I'm going to Northwestern." His voice was hard. "That's my decision, and it's final." He grabbed his iPad, then started to slip his headset back over his ears.

"Jake, we're part of that decision," Eddie said, still patient.

"It's my life." The headset was now over Jake's ears.

"It's a family decision," Eddie said.

Jake lay back down on his bed, then put the iPad in front of his face, blocking us from his line of sight.

"Jake—" I said, trying not to raise my voice. "If you don't talk to us about this, we're going to have to make the decision for you."

"I made the decision, Mom. I told Northwestern yes."

"What?" I was shocked.

"You're kidding, right?" Eddie said.

"Nope." Jake was still shielding us with his iPad.

"Well, it doesn't matter," Eddie said. "Without the deposit, they won't hold the spot."

"You're right, Dad." Jake lowered the iPad and looked up at him. "That's why I sent in the deposit."

My stomach rolled, again, and the nausea bloomed through my body. I looked at Eddie, but I didn't see anger on his face—he must've been containing it. As for me, it was a different matter. Maybe it was a way to fight back the nausea, but I couldn't contain my anger.

"Where did you get two thousand dollars?" I said, though I knew where, which made me even angrier.

"The credit card," he said. The one we'd given him for emergencies.

"We're canceling that charge," I said, and stood up from the chair.

"I thought this was a family decision," Jake shot back.

"It was—until you pulled this stunt." I looked at Eddie, expecting him to join me, to lash out at his son's defiance.

He didn't.

So I continued to lead the charge. "I can't believe you sent in a deposit without telling us," I said.

"You're saying if we had talked about it, we would all have agreed on the same school?" Jake smirked.

"That's right—because you would've understood our financial situation."

"You mean you would've forced me to go to Lehigh."

"You'll do well wherever you go, Jake," I said, and looked over at Eddie for reinforcement.

"Lehigh is a great school," he said, finally adding his two cents, exactly the two cents that I'd warned him not to add.

Jake bolted up from the bed. "That's a fucking lie and you know it."

"Jake—watch your mouth," Eddie said.

"This is all your fault! *You* can't find a job! So you want *my* future to take a hit!" Jake's eyes were ablaze. "I'm not going to let that happen! I'll find my own way to pay for college!"

"Jake, come on," Eddie said. "We have to be realistic. All of us. Lehigh is offering you practically a full ride—"

"You be realistic! You said I could go to any school I wanted to! So I'm going to Northwestern, and if you can't make that happen, I will!"

"We can't make that happen, honey," I said.

"Why not? Because Dad's a loser?"

"Your dad's not a loser!" The nausea welled up again, and I shivered. "Please, Jake, don't be like this."

He stared at me, his face rigid with hate.

"I'm sorry," I said. "I'm sorry that it's not working out the way you thought it would."

"It's going to work out exactly like I planned."

"But Jake. It ca—"

"He's right," Eddie interrupted. "It's my fault. I'm the reason we can't afford Northwestern."

"It's no one's fault," I said.

"We both know that's not true." Eddie looked at Jake for a long beat before he added, "You worked hard. You set a goal. And you achieved your goal—"

"But now I have to be realistic," Jake said. "Please save your little speech."

"Okay—how about I just skip the speech part and get to the good part? You're going to Northwestern."

Before Jake could even react, I blurted out, "What?"

"He's going to Northwestern," Eddie said. He didn't bat an eye, and a confident smile crossed his face.

I looked over at Jake. He appeared stunned, his mouth agape in disbelief. "Wow," he said. "Talk about a reversal of fortune."

Eddie stepped forward and patted Jake on the shoulder. "You worked hard to get into a top school, and that's where you're going." He then gave me a peck on the cheek, and walked out of the bedroom.

I didn't budge.

What did he just do? Had he just set Jake up for an even harsher disappointment? Wouldn't we now have to tell him at the very last minute that he couldn't go to Northwestern after all?

But Eddie had sounded confident, not desperate, and again I went back to his mood—how it had brightened over the last few days. Right then, I concluded that he'd probably landed the investment job and was just waiting for the final confirmation.

BEN

CHAPTER ELEVEN

I sat at a table outside M Street Coffee on Moorpark, staring at my latte, weighing my options. The tutor had thrown a monkey wrench in the works. An asteroid-sized monkey wrench.

Usually, I came to M Street Coffee to look over the material I'd gathered on a new target and develop a tentative course of action. The coffee shop was out of the way, served good coffee, and during the day was primarily frequented by customers who kept to themselves—mostly screenwriters who wanted to get out of the house and producers who wanted a low-key place to meet with directors, writers, or actors.

But today, I was here to make a final decision on how to handle Eddie Hart. It was a decision I wasn't prepared to make. I had known that my lack of fear was a bad omen, but I had never guessed it would put me in this bad a position. I should've been more vigilant. And more cautious. I should've taken seriously my suspicion that I was being followed down those dark hillside roads to Abel's place. Those headlights behind me had been a little too persistent.

Too late now.

For four years I'd worked for Abel, getting better and better at abducting targets. But with each passing year, the fear of getting caught had lessened. And it wasn't cockiness that had replaced it. Not by a long shot. It was that I'd become so good at the job that the chances of getting caught were small.

Not small enough, I thought. But it wasn't like the tutor had caught me on the job. Every single abduction I'd done for Abel— even the more challenging ones—had gone off practically without a hitch. And so had this last one. My mistake didn't happen on the job; it happened *between* jobs. The critical mistake was inviting a desperate man into my house.

That was stupid.

Especially because I'd been very careful not to get too close to anyone since I'd started working for Abel. I didn't want to answer any questions about my line of work, and friends were the most likely to ask questions. So the job had required that tradeoff. I would become wealthy, but I wouldn't have any friends.

Making that transition to loner status actually hadn't been too hard. After the move from Torrance to Bel Air, I slowly lost touch with my friends in the South Bay anyway. And the same thing happened with my friends and colleagues at DirecTV. Once I left the job, it was out of sight, out of mind. So, as it turned out, my growing isolation had all looked kosher. My old friends in my old life assumed I'd made new friends in my new life.

I sipped my coffee and looked down Moorpark. The quiet suburban street, lined with mostly two and three-story apartment buildings, looked pleasant and languid in the California sunshine. That was a big contrast to how I was feeling. My chest was as tight as a drum and my muscles were tense with dread.

Did Abel expect me to take care of the tutor on my own? Did he expect me to *kill* him? Murder wasn't part of the job description. Or was it implied?

I had no idea. And the only way to get an idea was to talk to Abel.

Which I was dreading.

But I needed him in the loop, didn't I? And that was the decision that I was really here to make: Should I tell Abel what had happened?

On the one hand, I wanted him in the loop. How else would I know what the proper protocol was? My response to this problem should be based on what Abel had to say. Shouldn't it?

On the other hand, I didn't want to tell Abel that I'd been caught red-handed. Just the thought of telling him made my chest tighten even more, which in turn sent a sharp pain shooting down my back. I clenched my teeth.

So what the hell were you supposed to do when you'd been caught? Certainly this had happened to one of Abel's employees in the past.

Of course, the truth was that this *wasn't* certain. Nothing was certain when it came to my job. There was just too much I didn't know. Abel kept me in the dark about practically everything. I could be one of a long list of employees dating back decades or even centuries; or Abel could have started his operation four years ago, and I was his first hire.

The pain in my back passed.

I took a deep breath and tried to will myself to make a final decision—and the one I was leaning toward was to go ahead and drive up to Abel's house and tell him what had happened.

But before I was able to convince myself that this was the best course of action, I went back to thinking about the tutor. Why hadn't the guy accepted hush money? That would have been an acceptable outcome. There was plenty of money to go around. But no, I had to be stuck with a man who was going for all the marbles. He didn't just want hush money. He wanted much more.

All week long, I'd thought about offering him the hush money again. But the look in the tutor's eyes—desperation mixed with determination—had stuck with me. Not only did the tutor want a lot of money, he also wanted to put his life back together. And the way you put your life back together is by putting a job at the center of it. That was as American as apple pie, even if that job was as far from a mainstream job as you could get.

One way or another, my time for considering the situation was over. In the next few hours, I had to tell the tutor whether Abel was going to hire him. I had to tell the tutor whether his dream of getting back on his feet would come true.

I took another sip of my coffee and looked down Moorpark again. I was just delaying the inevitable. The bottom line was that I had to tell Abel. He had to be in the loop. I didn't want to tell him about my screw-up, but I had no choice. My chest tightened again and another pain shot through my back.

*

I pulled up to the gates of Abel's house, and they opened as they always did. But this time, I didn't feel like a triumphant soldier returning from a successful mission. I felt like a screw-up, and my pounding heart was proof that I was. Fear had returned, big time. The fear of confessing my blunder to Abel.

The only other time I'd come to Abel's serene, hillside home alone, without a target in the passenger seat, had been the first time. I'd received an email from an executive headhunting firm; it touted a potential managerial position for me, one which paid better than my position at DirecTV.

I hadn't signed up with a headhunting firm, but I knew that headhunting firms also worked for employers, not just employees. And that was the case here: the email said the firm had been hired by a telecommunications company looking to expand, and that the company was impressed with my DirecTV resume and wanted to meet me.

I'd been at DirecTV for my entire professional career, and though I wasn't a top executive, I'd moved up the food chain to vice president. But I didn't kid myself; I was one of dozens of vice presidents, and I wasn't going to move up the food chain any further. I had strong analytical and organizational skills, but I wasn't tops when it came to managing personnel.

So the email interested me, and I responded. That led to three more email exchanges before the headhunting firm arranged an interview. In retrospect, it was clear that Abel had been reeling me in, testing me to see if he'd made the right choice. If I had stopped responding to the emails, or failed in some other way, he would've moved on to recruiting someone else.

So I had driven up to Abel's home for the interview. I thought it a bit strange that the meeting was taking place in a private home, but I chalked it up to the company's management style. I had looked up the company, and this fit right in with their freewheeling approach to business. What I didn't know was that, though the company was indeed real, I wasn't interviewing with them.

I was interviewing with Abel.

And that interview had turned out to be very brief—as were all my dealings with Abel. In fact, when he presented me with the job offer, I hesitated, because he hadn't really given me many specifics. But all my hesitation went out the window when Abel told me the pay. It was more than triple my current salary.

*

Today, as I drove through the gates and toward the front of the house, I wondered if the garage door was going to open. Normally that was the routine, but this was no normal visit. And there was no doubt that Abel already knew that. I was sure he had a couple of ways of tracking my movements, so he would already be aware that I was showing up without a target. And that could only mean one thing: something was wrong.

The garage door didn't open, so I parked in front of the house. My assumption that Abel was expecting me was confirmed when I saw that the front door was open and ready for my arrival.

As I got out of the car and walked up to the door, my heart was pounding even harder than it had been at the gate. I wanted to turn and run, for here on the threshold of Abel's doorstep, I finally admitted to myself that there was another possible way for him to deal with my screw-up. An option even more chilling than Abel ordering me to murder the tutor.

What if Abel decided that I, too, had to be taken out? What if Abel decided to murder *me*?

But running wasn't an option. There was no getting away from Abel.

So I stepped inside.

The house was quiet. It was always quiet. I walked across the foyer and into the living room.

Abel appeared from the back hallway. I knew he wasn't going to speak first. It was up to me to start the conversation. Before I did, I took in the living room. I couldn't help but wonder if this was the last time I'd see it. I noticed once again how the fireplace appeared to have never been used. Its cast-iron grate, and matching poker, tong, and shovel set, were pristine, free from the ravages of flames and ash. The patio doors were open—Abel always left them open— and I admired the unique fountain beyond the patio. I'd never seen water spout from the odd-shaped fountain.

After another few seconds spent staring at the thick woods that ran up the hillside behind Abel's house, I made my move. I crossed the living room and stopped a few yards from Abel. He always stayed on the far side of the living room, the side that wasn't visible from outside those patio doors. Why he didn't just get curtains and close them had always baffled me. If some thief or voyeur, lurking in the thick woods behind the house, did catch a glimpse of Abel, they'd get an eyeful.

I finally spoke up. "Someone saw me," I said.

Abel didn't respond. And reading emotion from the alien's face was a lost cause. His face was as tranquil as the odd-shaped fountain that never spouted water. Still, I hoped that this one time I could gauge his reaction. I couldn't. But I did understand he wanted more details. That was why he hadn't responded.

"I don't know how much this guy actually knows," I said, "but he saw me kidnap the last target."

"Bring him to me," Abel said. His voice emanated from a black square—the size of a ring box—which he clutched in his right hand. The voice was synthesized and flat. It didn't have a faux personality like the electronic voices in science fiction movies. Like Abel himself, the voice betrayed no emotion.

After Abel issued his order, he turned away from me and headed back down the hallway. This was the custom. He'd end our brief conversations by turning away, and that was my cue to exit.

He's going to kill the tutor, I thought. Why else would he want me to bring him here? Abel wouldn't reveal himself to the tutor unless he was planning to kill him.

I walked back through the living room to the front door, wondering whether Abel would kill the tutor himself or order me to carry out the grisly crime. When I glanced at the silent water fountain outside, I couldn't help but think that the woods beyond it would make for a secluded burial ground. One where *I'd* have to bury the tutor.

I walked out the front door, and another morbid thought hit me: I might end up in that secluded burial ground too.

EDDIE

CHAPTER TWELVE

Ben called me and told me to meet him at the Starbucks at the bottom of Coldwater. He'd taken the full week to get back to me, but I hadn't been worried. I knew he would contact me. He couldn't ignore the threat I posed to his livelihood.

My week had been busy. Jenny had had another chemo infusion, so I'd rescheduled some of my tutoring sessions to take care of her and the kids. Jake, who'd been a terrific help to both his mom and me after the first infusion, was even more of a help after the second. For me, this only reinforced the idea that he deserved to go to the school of his choice. He was a great kid—hard working and kind.

Hannah also did her share, including refraining from confrontations with her mom. She was still feisty—she wouldn't be Hannah if she wasn't—but she knew when to turn it off. Crisis had brought maturity.

The entire week, I felt close to my family. Was it the urgency of our circumstance? Was it that the value of life had been brought into sharp focus? Was it that a turning point seemed close at hand?

I felt an inner strength and an alertness that I hadn't felt in years. I was more determined than ever to earn the money my family needed to weather this storm and land securely on the other side.

And I was confident that I'd found the means to do that.

To that end, while I had waited for Ben to contact me, I had researched the grand house that he'd visited the night of the kidnapping. The house had been built in the thirties, and according to the property records, the original owner, Thomas Caraway, had never sold it. This was extremely unusual. In LA, houses turned over frequently. They hardly ever remained with one owner for a decade, much less for almost a hundred years.

I searched for information on Thomas Caraway, but I found nothing other than the dates of his birth and death. That in itself didn't raise any red flags; as a reporter, I'd researched many people of his generation, and few of them left digital footprints. Still, if you were wealthy—and Caraway must have been to have purchased that house in the thirties, during the Depression—you usually did leave a few digital footprints behind.

But I found none for Thomas Caraway.

It reminded me of my Internet search on Ben. Ben's digital footprint had been much bigger in comparison, but because Ben was of my generation, his footprint was also way too small to be "normal."

Since Caraway was dead, he obviously wasn't the current owner of the house, despite what the property records showed. But I had learned in previous homeowner searches that it was technically possible for a house to appear as if it had not changed hands, even when the original owner had died. The house could've been transferred from one generation of Caraways down to the next through a quitclaim deed. Such deeds were legal ways to transfer property, but sometimes they didn't make it into a city's digital records.

If I wanted to dig up a hard copy of a quitclaim deed, I'd have to go to the Beverly Hills City Clerk's office.

That had been next on my to-do list, but my week had been so busy with family that I hadn't had time to spend in the City Clerk's office digging through old files. And now that Ben had called, it might no longer matter anyway. It was possible that I'd be learning the answer to this mystery from the owner of the house himself, for I was fairly certain Ben had chosen the Starbucks at the bottom of Coldwater for one reason: so we could drive up to the house.

*

As I waited at Starbucks, I ran through two scenarios. One was easy to play out, more or less. If Ben arrived and told me I had the job, then I'd move forward into my new, lucrative career—though exactly what that career was, was still a mystery to me, other than the fact that I'd be wading into some kind of criminal enterprise. And there was the rub: I'd have to ignore my moral qualms about this enterprise. But how far on the other side of the law, and on the other side of morality, would this new career take me?

The second scenario was a little harder to picture. If Ben arrived and told me that I didn't have the job, then I'd have to visit the grand house myself and personally ask whoever lived there for the job. For wasn't the person in that house calling the shots?

But I wasn't too keen on heading up there alone. If there was no quitclaim deed—and the house had not passed down to Caraway's descendants—then whoever currently owned the house wanted to remain anonymous. My research had made that abundantly clear. And anyone who wanted anonymity that badly—who had had all traces of himself wiped from the Internet—might be willing to kill to *keep* that anonymity. Especially if he found out that someone had witnessed one of his crimes.

Hadn't Ben warned me not to get involved?

Through the plate glass window, I saw Ben approaching. And in that same second, I realized, with the moment of truth at hand, that my confidence—for the first time in a week—was shaky.

Ben stepped into the shop, spotted me, and headed over. He didn't look angry, but he didn't look pleased either. If I had been forced to label the expression on his face, I would've said it was confusion.

He sat down at my table and skipped the small talk. "My employer wants to meet you," he said. It came out like he was delivering bad news.

"Do I have the job?"

"I don't know. It's not my call." His jaw tightened, and he stood up. "I'll drive," he said, and headed toward the door.

I didn't like the way this was playing out. Not so much the part about visiting his employer—that was to be expected—but the way Ben was acting.

I followed him out of the Starbucks. He didn't say anything as we headed toward his car. I was beginning to fear the worst. Was I willingly marching to my own death? Was I going to be executed in cold blood?

Again I thought about Ben's warning—*You do not want to get involved.*

But I *was* involved. And therefore, I had to act. *Adapt or die.*

Ben pressed his key fob, and his car beeped. I watched him circle around to the driver's side of the car, and before he got in, I spoke up.

"I have pictures of you in your car with the woman you kidnapped," I said.

He looked over at me, more annoyed than frightened.

I went on with my ruse nonetheless. "If I don't make it back, the pictures will be delivered to the LAPD."

Ben stared at me for a second or two, studying me, as if he

doubted me. Then he said, "So you planned ahead for the worst case scenario?"

No, not really, I thought, which was why I had to resort to this pathetic bluff. And when I saw the rest of Ben's reaction to the bluff—he ignored it, got into his car, and fired up the engine—I knew I was in over my head.

I stood outside the passenger door and considered my next move. But I had only one move. The security of my family was at stake. I got in the car.

*

We drove up Coldwater in silence. There was no need for me to ask any questions; I knew they'd go unanswered. So instead, I held on to the hope that a job was waiting for me at the end of this ride. I told myself that whatever criminal activity Ben and his employer were involved in, it didn't include murder. Murder would shine a light on them. So I was safe.

Probably.

When Ben pulled up to the wrought-iron gates, I readied myself to plead my case. That I could do whatever was asked of me, and do it well. That I'd be loyal and trustworthy. That their secrets would forever be safe with me. In return, I wanted a share of those bricks of cash.

The gates opened, and Ben drove toward the house. This was where I expected him to fill me in on the man we were about to meet.

But he said nothing. He pulled up to the house. The front door was open.

Without a word, Ben got out of the car. I followed suit.

We walked into the house. No one greeted us, which made me warier than ever. In truth, it scared me. Had Ben brought me here to execute me himself? Was that why he'd been silent on the way up?

Ben walked through the living room, toward the back hallway, but I stopped. The patio doors were open. They gave way to an old fountain and a dense patch of woods. I was frightened enough to consider taking off into those woods.

When Ben noticed I was just standing there, he barked out, "Let's go."

I decided not to run. If there was a job to be had, running away from it wasn't the way to land it.

I followed Ben down the back hallway and to a door that, like the front door, had been left open in anticipation of our arrival. We stepped inside.

The room was dimly lit, and the only furniture was a large mahogany desk, which fit the grandeur of the house, and a high-backed leather chair, which faced away from us. Both sat ominously in the darkest recesses of the room. The back of a man's head was visible above the chair's backrest, and though it was too dark to know for sure, it looked like the man's head was shaved.

Ben motioned for me to step closer to the desk.

I did, and I saw that, indeed, the man was bald.

"Go ahead," Ben said to me. "Tell him what you want."

The man still hadn't turned around, so I began to wonder if he had some kind of rare disease. Was he hiding in the shadows because he didn't want anyone to see how badly the disease had disfigured him? That question led to an epiphany: the kidnappings suddenly made sense. They were the only way this disfigured man could get women.

"I want to work for you," I said.

"Why?" the man asked. His voice was synthesized, and that confirmed for me that he suffered from a terrible disorder. It had robbed him of his ability to speak, just as it had disfigured him.

"Because I need the money," I said. Suddenly honesty seemed like the best policy.

"There are plenty of other ways to earn money," he said. The synthetic voice was even-keeled. Emotionless.

"I need to earn a lot of money quickly."

"What about the consequences?"

"I know it's a risky line of work."

"I mean the consequences of coming here. The consequences of disrupting an operation you know nothing about."

He's planning to kill me, I thought. But I pleaded my case. "I can keep my mouth shut," I said. "Whether you hire me or not, I'll keep your secret."

"You had your chance to keep your mouth shut. You chose not to."

Ben smirked—an "I told you so" smirk.

"Give me a chance to work for you," I said. "You won't regret it."

"Why should I give you a chance? I don't need you."

"I guarantee you I'll go beyond the call of duty."

"You don't listen too well, do you? I said I don't need you." He suddenly swiveled around in his chair—

I braced myself for whatever horror I was about to see.

But he was still hidden in the dark. I couldn't see his face. I *did* see his gloved hand move swiftly from right to left in a cutting motion—like he was signaling someone. I held my breath, positive that he'd just signaled Ben to draw a weapon and gun me down.

But that wasn't what happened.

Instead, a cone of red light—infrared?—engulfed me. I quickly looked up to the ceiling for its source, but didn't see any. I looked down at the hardwood floor and saw nothing but a sheen of reflected red light.

What the hell was going on? Was the cone of red light a weapon? Was that how I was to die?

Panicked, I turned to run—but I hit a solid barrier. I was walled inside the cone. I didn't know if it was a weapon, but it was certainly a cage. I struck at it, but it was solid as a rock.

"I don't need two people to do one man's job," the synthetic voice said. Again, the voice was flat. Just the facts, ma'am.

So this is it, I thought. I'd be executed in a cage of red light, and there'd be no security for my family.

"No, Abel!" Ben suddenly shouted. I'd forgotten about him. But he hadn't forgotten about me—he was trying to save me.

I looked over at him and saw that he, too, was trapped in an infrared cone. But he was trying to fight his way out, frantically throwing his body this way and that. It made no difference—and I saw that his eyes were wild with terror. Then I realized why: Ben wasn't trying to save me.

He was trying to save himself.

His cone was turning a darker shade of red, a deep crimson, and it was thickening around him.

"Please, Abel!" he shouted. He was caged in what looked like a viscous, purplish-red fluid.

Then his body began to melt, conjoining with the gelatinous fluid. Tiny, thin blue lines—capillaries?—started to emerge from his liquefying body. They swam up to the top of the cone, and there, they gathered themselves into a tiny ball, the size of a marble.

A few seconds later, Ben's body completely melted away, and the cone disappeared. The only thing left of Ben was that blue marble, which still hung in the air. But what was it? *Was* it capillaries?

My heart was thumping wildly, and sweat coated my brow. My thoughts were as jumbled as my feelings. I was terrified and panicked, but I also felt relief, because whatever it was that I'd just witnessed, I was grateful that it hadn't happened to me.

"Take the blue sphere and put it in this," the synthetic voice commanded.

I turned to Abel—which was what Ben had called the disfigured man—and realized that I was no longer in the cone of light. I also noticed that there was now a white object, the size of a thimble, sitting on the mahogany desk.

I followed orders.

I stepped up to the desk, picked up the white thimble, and walked over to the blue marble, which was still suspended in the air.

As I reached for it, Abel warned, "Don't touch it with your hands."

I obeyed. I carefully scooped the marble into the thimble, and as soon as the marble was inside, a tiny lid automatically slid across the top of the thimble, sealing it.

I brought the thimble over to Abel, and as I did, I saw a new object sitting on his desk. It was gold colored, the size and shape of a credit card, but completely smooth and lustrous, with no markings.

"You now work for me," Abel said. With a gloved hand, which rose from the shadows, he slid the gold card toward me. "Keep this with you at all times."

I put the thimble down and picked up the gold card. It felt metallic, but it was as light as air. As I waited for Abel to explain what it was, my thoughts became less jumbled, at least enough to understand that I'd gotten my wish: I had the job.

And my thoughts were also clear enough to understand what would happen if I slipped up. Ben had been murdered right in front of me, and though the method of murder was bizarre, it had made one point perfectly clear: my new employer had no problem with murder.

"Time for your orientation," Abel said.

He leaned forward out of the darkness and into the dim light.

I gasped.

His face was horribly disfigured—far worse than anything I

could've imagined. It had no features, except for one. A large, almond-shaped eye. A polished black gem. The purest black I'd ever seen. No white, and no pupil.

The rest of his face was taut brown skin. No nose, no mouth, no contours. There were no wrinkles and absolutely no blemishes. It looked fake, or surreal, the effect heightened because there were no features to break up the rigid surface.

What in God's good name had happened to this man?

"Get used to it," the synthetic voice said.

That was a tall order—getting used to it was going to take time. And right now, rather than getting used to it, I was trying to make sense of it. And that led to a realization.

Abel wasn't a man at all, was he?

That would explain his peculiar appearance.

Of course, it was still possible that my first instinct had been right. That he'd been disfigured by a horrible disease.

Only—he didn't look disfigured. His skin didn't bear any signs that it had been grafted. It was perfectly smooth, without a blemish. And his single, magnificent eye—it didn't look like the result of some corrective surgery. It didn't look like a doctor had done the best he could with what he'd been given. Abel's lone eye looked perfect and all-seeing.

The man was a living Cyclops.

Except he wasn't a Cyclops.

When I took into account what else I'd witnessed tonight—the red cone that had liquefied Ben, leaving no trace of his body except for the blue marble—I had to consider the impossible.

"I'm an extraterrestrial," Abel said, as if he had been following my train of thought and wanted to help me reach this implausible conclusion. His synthetic electronic voice gave no hint of the outrageousness of his statement.

"More than that doesn't concern you," he added.

I took this in and thought this through. I was already predisposed to believe in alien life. Not in a kooky, science fiction way, but in a pragmatic, scientific way. Probability dictated that we weren't the only form of intelligent life in the universe. When you did the math, you had to conclude that in a universe so vast that its size was unfathomable, there were other forms of intelligent life. The quote from the film *Contact* put it best: "The universe is a pretty big place, so if it's just us, seems like an awful waste of space."

But I had never imagined humans would make contact with this alien life. Or that aliens were here on earth now. Or, even more far-fetched—that *I* would make contact with that alien life.

That was science fiction.

"I give you the targets," Abel said, "and you deliver them to me. When I'm done with them, you return them. Those are your duties."

I knew the targets were the women.

"I'll give you a supply of tranquilizers," he said. "You use the tranquilizers to capture the targets."

Like big game hunting, I thought. But what was Abel doing with the spoils of the hunt? What was he doing with the women?

Abel scooted his chair closer to the desk and opened a drawer. He pulled out a small tin box and what looked like a metal straw, copper-colored, about the length of a cigarette.

"Use this like a blow dart," he said, "but don't blow hard. Breathing out once is more than enough. The tranquilizer pellet travels up to twenty yards almost instantaneously. It travels through anything in its path, except for humans. Once the pellet hits a human, it immediately dissolves."

I took the tin box and the copper straw. The straw felt cold, as if it had been refrigerated, or had its own internal cooling system. I slid the straw into my pocket, then opened the tin box. There were twelve gel pellets inside. It was obvious that the pellets were to be loaded into the straw, so there was no need to confirm that with Abel—and if I did, that would probably lead him to believe that I was far too slow a learner for the job.

Somehow, I supposed because of Abel's terse manner, I knew I should ask questions only if it was absolutely necessary. I'd already gathered that this was one of the main requirements of the job.

So, though I wanted to ask him how I should pick out the targets, I decided to ask the only question that mattered. The only question worth the risk of asking it. Because the answer to that question was the reason I was here.

"What's the salary for the job?" I said. Using the term "salary" was a way for me to whitewash the illegality of the job. Wouldn't the term "bounty" have been more appropriate?

"It depends on the target," Abel said.

That left me no option but to ask a follow-up question. "How?"

His black eye stared at me, as calm as a dark, moonless night. "Some targets are more valuable than others," he said. "But the minimum payment is one hundred thousand dollars per target." The synthetic voice didn't register just how much that was.

But I did—and I was elated. My confidence surged. I stood up straighter, felt stronger. I didn't know what lay ahead, but at that moment, I was sure I'd made the right decision.

I wondered how many targets there were per year, but I didn't have to wonder too long.

"There will be one target every two weeks," Abel said.

A quick calculation left me holding my breath. He was talking about two and a half million dollars a year. *Minimum.* My financial problems were solved. *If* I could do the job. *Without* slipping up.

"You may choose to execute the assignment in any manner you wish," Abel said. "And if you execute the assignment properly, the target won't remember anything." He leaned forward and took the thimble from the desk. ""I will contact you through the gold card. The card will give you the first target."

I'd been dismissed already, which was another sign that questions were to be kept to a minimum. I wanted to ask what he meant by "execute the assignment properly." Was there a risk that a target would remember the abduction if I *didn't* execute the assignment properly?

But I didn't ask Abel anything more. Instead, I said, "Thank you." It was time to exit. I had accomplished my mission. I reached into my pocket to make sure the gold card was there. It was. And it would stay with me at all times, as he'd ordered.

I headed out of Abel's dimly lit office and down the hallway into the living room. A breeze was blowing in through the open patio doors. I took in a deep breath of fresh air—a life-affirming breath—and as I walked through the living room, I decided that on my next visit, when I delivered the target, I'd use one of my small allotment of questions. I'd ask Abel how I was supposed to keep a target from remembering she'd been abducted. For how could I know if I'd executed the assignment "properly" if I'd had no training?

I stepped outside and was suddenly confronted by Ben's car. It gave me a jolt. It brought back the harsh reality that Ben was dead. Murdered. Mason would be devastated. I had just ruined the life of a great kid. A cold chill swept through me—guilt—and I began to shake.

But I fought back against the guilt. I told myself that I'd had no idea that my determination to land this job would result in Ben's death. I couldn't have foreseen it. I thought it might result in my own death, not his.

I told myself that this was my new life—my new career—and that meant I had to accept what came with it. For better or worse. I had experienced the "better"—a lucrative job—but I had also unintentionally generated the "worse."

I had to adapt. Adapt or die. And in this case, adapting meant learning to live with guilt. Not only to live with it, but to move forward in spite of it—to thrive. Otherwise, I'd fail in my new career.

So I started right then. Rather than letting the guilt take over, I focused on my next move—my immediate move: getting back home tonight. I gathered that Abel would get rid of Ben's car; if he'd wanted me to do it, he would have ordered me to. That left walking.

It would take me an hour to walk back to the Starbucks where I'd left my own car. So I got started. As soon as I stepped up to the iron gate, it opened, and I was on my way.

A thousand questions raced through my mind as I trekked toward Mulholland. I tried to focus on only one: my role in the alien's operation. Why did he need a human employee? Wasn't he technologically advanced enough to get away with abductions without human help?

I'd seen some evidence of his superior technology: the cage of red light, which cleanly and efficiently disposed of human life; the tranquilizer pellets, which traveled through anything until they hit human targets; and the thin gold card in my pocket, through which the alien would give me my marching orders. But the most compelling evidence of his superior technology was the fact that he was here at all.

So why did he need humans?

When I hit Mulholland, I stared up at the broad night sky, at the vast reach of space from which Abel had come. But it was only when I looked down at the Valley below, with its dazzling lights strung out in long tidy rows, that an answer to that question began to take shape. My investigative reporting instincts kicked back into gear, and I realized I'd come at the question from the wrong angle.

Forget the "alien" part of Abel's operation. What mattered more was the *illegal* part—the very fact that it *was* illegal. Abel wasn't trying to run his operation with maximum efficiency as a goal. His main objective—after the abductions themselves—was the same as that of any ongoing illegal enterprise: minimize the risk of getting caught. Minimize the risk that *he'd* be exposed. He didn't want humans to suspect that aliens had anything to do with the abductions. And it was also possible—although I couldn't be sure of this—that he didn't want his own kind, his own species, to suspect either.

He was using humans to do his dirty work so he could keep his distance from the nitty-gritty vagaries of human interactions. For it was those very interactions that were the riskiest part of the operation, and no amount of superior technology or intelligence could eliminate that risk.

Abel had eliminated that risk by taking himself out of the abduction equation.

That seemed right.

I'd seen the same structure in all sorts of illegal operations, from drug rings, where the head honchos were shielded from the dirty work by their street-level employees, to corporations, where the top executives were shielded from criminal activities by their managerial-level employees, to governments, where public figures where shielded from covert operations by "unaffiliated" secret paramilitary groups.

When I made it to the Starbucks, I added another part to this analogy. Those who did the dirty work were replaceable—whether they were street dealers in a drug ring or managers in a corrupt corporation.

I was replaceable.

On the drive home, I turned that over in my mind. Before I was replaced—before I slipped up—I had to earn enough money to cover Jenny's treatments no matter how long they lasted and how expensive they got. Before Abel liquidated me, I also had to earn enough money to cover Jake and Hannah's college tuition, plus a comfortable cushion to cover them in case they wanted to go on to graduate school. And I had to earn enough money to pay off the house.

It seemed inevitable that at some point I'd slip up, just as Ben had.

I could accept that.

But I had to meet those objectives first.

CHAPTER THIRTEEN

When I walked into the house, I was ebullient, focused only on the positive. For now, my unanswered questions had been pushed to the side, along with my guilt. The gold card in my pocket was proof that I'd secured a job—a great job—and I wanted to tell Jenny. I wanted her to know that the good news she'd been expecting had been delivered.

But how would I frame that good news? That, I didn't know.

Jake was at Sam's house, along with a few of his other friends, all gathered to download some cutting-edge video game that had just been released. Hannah was at swim practice; the coach liked to schedule extra practices at night.

So it was just Jenny and me, a great opportunity to make my special announcement—and also to celebrate it.

I stepped into the kitchen. She was at the table, typing on her laptop. "Let's go out to eat," I said, ready to take on the celebratory aspect of my announcement, even though I didn't know what I was going to tell her.

"Eddie, we can't afford it," she said.

"Let's do it anyway." I didn't hide my grin.

She cocked her head, smiled, and immediately gave in. "Okay, let's live a little," she said. My grin had given away my surprise. She knew what was up.

She insisted I pick the restaurant, another sign that I'd already let the cat out of the bag. I chose The Counter, the family favorite, a place where we'd had many celebratory dinners.

The short drive over wasn't totally worry-free, but it was far more worry-free than any drive I'd taken in quite a while. I could feel a lightness on my side of the car as well as on hers. The anxiety about the cancer hadn't disappeared, but the gloom stemming from my rocky job prospects had lifted. Sure, I was feeling uneasy about coming up with a cover story for the new job, but I was no longer feeling like a loser who couldn't provide for his family.

At The Counter, we "built" our burgers, which were the restaurant's primary attraction. You created your own custom gourmet burger by ordering from a menu of a wide range of exotic toppings, from Danish Blue Cheese to Jicama.

When we finished giving the waiter our order, I added a beer, which I hadn't had in months. Jenny ordered a glass of wine, and when the waiter took off, she beamed at me. Her blue eyes sparkled with anticipation.

The grin returned to my face, but I still held back on the good news. And it wasn't because I was trying to create suspense. It was because I had to lie again, and that part wasn't sitting so well. On the other hand, the money part was sitting very well—and that was the part I needed to channel.

"Are you ready to spill the beans?" she asked. "Or do you want to wait for our drinks and make a toast?"

I reached across the table and took her hand in mine. "Let's wait for the drinks."

Her smile grew, and I supposed her anticipation grew along with it. I was also enjoying the moment, regardless of the lie I was going to have to spin, until out of nowhere—the gold card in my pocket suddenly felt heavy.

I wondered if Abel was calling me, interrupting our celebration, to give me my first target. I couldn't check the card in front of Jenny, so I told her I needed to use the restroom.

In the restroom, I pulled out the card. Nothing about it had changed. *It was me who had changed.* I was feeling self-conscious about the card. It was a reminder of the lie I was about to tell Jenny. And it was more than that. It would be with me at all times, a kind of private Scarlet Letter, reminding me that I was a sinner, and making sure I would never forget that.

When I got back to the table, the waiter was delivering our drinks. As soon as he walked away, I raised my glass, hoping I could get through the upcoming lie as fast as possible, so we could enjoy the celebratory part of the dinner.

"I got the job," I said.

"Congratulations!" Jenny raised her glass, and we clinked. "I'm really happy for you," she said. "I know it was a long haul."

"Thank you for pushing me. It was exactly what I needed."

"That's what I'm here for."

We both laughed. Then she sipped her wine, and I took a healthy gulp of my beer, savoring the taste—grainy, rich, and fresh.

"So is it the investment job?" she asked. "I've been dying to know." The lines on her brow deepened; she was wary.

Still, I went with the flow. The investment job was the top candidate for my cover story anyway. "Yep. It came through," I said. Then I tried to allay her fears. "But don't worry. The salary isn't commission. Otherwise we wouldn't be eating fifteen-dollar burgers."

"Good. Great!" The lines in her brow lessened. "And I'm sorry I was so negative about the job when you first brought it up. I just didn't want you to have the pressure of making sales."

"I understand. I should've filled you in on the details sooner. I don't know why I suddenly became superstitious about jinxing it."

"Because things haven't been going our way. That's why. But it looks like that's changing." She took a sip of her wine. "So fill me in."

"It's an investment company that trades in commodities." Why I decided to use Ben's cover story, I didn't really know. I guess I figured if it had been good enough for him, it was good enough for me.

"How did you even come across that?" Jenny asked.

"It was a total fluke. A friend of a friend brought it up," I said, and before she asked who—a question I didn't have an answer for—I plowed ahead. "It turned out that this investment firm was looking for business reporters. They wanted seasoned reporters who had experience researching and investigating businesses, and who could churn out coherent reports. Well, I didn't have the business reporting background, but I sure had the seasoned part, and the research and investigative part, and I showed them I could write a coherent report."

"Well, you sold me."

I laughed. "It was a little harder to sell them. That's why it took a while."

"It took a while, but they made the right choice. It does sound like a good fit. And it actually sounds like it's going to be intriguing."

"Luckily, I'll have the chance to find out."

"Amen to that."

Our burgers arrived a few minutes later, and we dug in. The burger tasted great, and I had to believe that the good news played a role in that.

"I'm glad we went out to dinner to celebrate," Jenny said.

"Me too. I'm even more glad I got a job."

"Oh—what's the name of the company?"

I couldn't afford to hesitate, so I immediately blurted out the first name that fit the bill. "Archer Daniels Midland," I said, remembering that in addition to being one of the largest food processing companies in the world, ADM was also one of the largest commodities traders in the world.

"Wow. Really?" she said.

"You sound surprised," I responded. Had my lie grown too big?

"I guess I imagined the job was with one of those small boutique places in Westwood or something. If I'd known the job was with a megacorporation, I don't think I would've had that negative reaction the first time you brought it up."

"Because you think a job with a huge corporation is more secure."

"Yeah—which is kind of weird." She shook her head. "I mean, look at all the layoffs Warner Brothers just had."

"It's not that weird. I think the same thing. The bigger the company, the more secure. I guess we've both been brainwashed."

She beamed again, picked up her glass, and raised it. "To bigger companies," she said.

We clinked, laughed, and went back to enjoying our burgers.

As we ate, I had second thoughts about using Archer Daniels Midland as part of my cover story. If she ever got suspicious enough to check on the job, wouldn't a more obscure company have been a better cover?

"What's the salary going to be?" she asked.

"One hundred thousand."

"That's great, Eddie." Her shoulders softened as if a great burden had been lifted from them. "And considering you're changing fields, that's more than great."

I knew she'd be pleased with the salary, and if I had added "per target" to the one hundred thousand, she would've been even more pleased. Still, there was one more thing I could add to give her peace of mind.

"And I negotiated to have the health insurance kick in with no waiting period," I said. "So if the insurance company doesn't find a way around the new you-can't-be-denied-because-of-a-prior-condition requirement, we're going to be good on that front, too."

"And Jake and Hannah are covered?"

"Yep."

Tears welled up in her eyes. "Thank you, Eddie. Thank you for making sure the kids are going to be okay. That's really all that counts."

"You don't need to thank me. It's my fault we got into this position in the first place." And it was. I was the one who had refused to adapt when the writing was on the wall.

Jenny wiped her tears away with the back of her hand.

Her tears moved me to build on my lie. I wanted her to know that we were going to be able to pay for her treatments, regardless of insurance.

"The job also pays bonuses," I said. "Big bonuses. Ones that can go a long way toward paying for treatments out of pocket if you get denied by the insurance company." That was about as close as I could come to telling her we were *definitely* going to be able to pay for her treatments, which would have been impossible for her to believe.

"Another benefit of the megacorporation," she said.

"They just keep coming."

"So how do you snag one of these bonuses?"

"By delivering."

"On the reports?"

"Yeah—if a report turns out to be especially valuable, I get a bonus."

"What makes a report especially valuable?"

"I don't know yet. But I'm going to find out."

JENNY

CHAPTER FOURTEEN

I realized that Eddie's job, or lack thereof, had weighed more on me than I'd imagined. The dinner had proved that. It had been a long time since I'd felt as normal as I had during that dinner. I actually felt happy, which played a big role in feeling normal.

When Eddie told me he'd gotten the job, and when it became clear that it was a good job, the black cloud of cancer suddenly dissipated. Not that it was replaced by blue skies, but it was replaced by partly sunny skies. And I could live with that. I could already feel the warmth of the sun shining through the clouds.

With our lives back on the upswing, we could move forward. Though there was nothing we could do about the cancer except go through the treatments and hope for the best, Eddie had done something about our financial instability. He'd sent it packing.

When we walked into the house after dinner, even the house appeared to have changed. It felt more inviting than it had in months. It felt like a place of strength, not the nexus of insurmountable problems. The truth was that money did make things easier. That was a fact of modern life.

In the kitchen, Eddie wrapped his arm around my waist, kissed me, and then said, "Why don't you go ahead and text Jake and

Hannah to see when they'll be home?"

There was no mistaking his tone. He wanted to fool around. And so did I. The warmth I'd been feeling from the partly sunny skies was turning into another kind of heat.

I kissed him back. "Are you sure?"

He grinned. "Isn't that the best way to celebrate?"

It had been a while since we were both interested in fooling around. Way too long a while.

I got my phone out and texted the kids.

Jake wasn't going to be home for another couple of hours, and Hannah had finished up with swim practice and was going out to grab a bite to eat with some of her teammates.

"Lucky us," I said to Eddie.

*

We fooled around, and it was loving and lustful and satisfying for both of us. This *was* the best way to celebrate.

Afterward, we were lying in bed, languid and tired, a good tired, when Eddie suddenly sat up, looking anxious. His eyes darted around the room.

"What's the matter, honey?" I said. "Did Hannah just come home?" I hadn't heard anything.

He took a second before answering, almost as if he was confused. "No—I just remembered something I forgot to do," he said. "For the job."

Then he got up, slipped his pants on, and exited the room.

His sudden change of mood was odd. I didn't know what to make of it.

A couple minutes later, he came back, and I thought he would volunteer what he'd forgotten to do, but he didn't.

And I didn't ask.

Maybe I should have. Maybe I should've asked a lot more questions that night.

*

In the morning, I awoke refreshed. So refreshed that I thought I overslept. Especially when I noticed Eddie was already up and around. I was usually up before him, but the clock confirmed I'd gotten up at the usual time. It was Eddie who had changed his routine.

Then I remembered that Eddie's tossing and turning had awakened me in the middle of the night. I'd gone right back to sleep, but maybe he'd just given up on getting a good night's sleep and had gotten up early.

I found him, already showered and dressed, on the couch in the den, hunched over his laptop.

"You're up early," I said.

"ADM emailed me some files to look over, so I thought I'd get started." His eyes were fixed on his computer screen.

"Do you want me to make you some breakfast?" He was in the habit of scrambling up three eggs for himself in the morning.

"No—I'm good for now."

Seeing him engrossed in his work made me feel good. "I'm really happy for you," I said. He looked fulfilled and confident.

"Thanks," he responded. Then he looked up from the laptop. "Would you mind telling Jake and Hannah the good news? I'm on a run here and I'd like to keep going."

"I'd love to be the bearer of good news," I said, but it surprised me that he didn't want to tell them himself.

"Great. I've got a lot of work to do."

A lot of work to do? I thought. Which led to the obvious question: "Have you officially started?"

"Yeah. I have."

He said it nonchalantly with just a quick glance up from his laptop.

"Why didn't you tell me?" That had come out more confrontational than I'd planned, so I was relieved when it didn't seem to faze him.

"Because I just found out. My first assignment came in last night."

Well, that cleared up the mystery of why he'd suddenly left the bedroom last night, and why he'd gotten up bright and early, and also why he didn't want to take the time to tell the kids the good news—he wanted to get a jump on the job.

But it prompted a couple of new questions: Why was he working in the den? Didn't he have an office to go to, or was he going to be working remotely?

I'd ask him later, when he took a break.

*

I made breakfast for myself, and when Jake and Hannah came into the kitchen, I told them about their father's new job.

"Good for Dad!" Hannah said, flashing an honest smile. "And the job sounds kind of cool."

Jake had a different reaction. "What exactly does Dad know about investing?" he said.

"Good job of raining on Dad's parade," Hannah responded, smirking at her brother.

"Maybe I didn't explain it well enough," I said. "It's more of a research job."

"Investment firms hire mathematicians and economists to do their research, not reporters," Jake said. He looked genuinely puzzled.

"Apparently you're wrong." Hannah was in full form.

That got Jake's goat. "So now you're the expert on financial institutions? Miss avoids-numbers-at-all-costs."

"At least I'm not a—"

"Hey." I interrupted before this mushroomed into a morning skirmish. "This is good news. Not something to fight over."

Hannah glared at her brother, ready to take him on, but Jake backed off—probably because he didn't want to upset me. If the two had been alone, he would've gladly knocked his sister down a peg. He believed that because she shied away from science and math, which were his forte, her opinions were de facto less informed.

"Well, I definitely want to hear the details from Dad," he said.

"He's working in the den if you want to ask him."

"I'll talk to him later. I have to get to school early. I'm giving a tour to incoming freshmen."

"Make sure you let them know we offer English and History classes," Hannah said.

"Hannah, please." This time I was the one doing the glaring.

"Don't worry," Jake said. "I'll let the underachievers know they have options." After tossing that grenade, he exited.

"I'm really looking forward to next year, Mom," Hannah said loudly so Jake could hear it. "When Jake is in college!"

Hannah's retort wasn't too vicious—at least not vicious enough to inspire return fire from Jake—and I was thankful for that. But it did remind me that Jake would be gone next year, and I wasn't looking forward to that. I was going to miss him terribly.

After Jake and Hannah left for school, I was tempted to go into the den to ask Eddie if he'd be working remotely. Jake's interest in the specifics of his father's new job had kindled my curiosity even more.

But I didn't want it to appear like I was interrogating Eddie, or like I wasn't supportive of his job. I *was* supportive—very. So I didn't venture back into the den.

Instead, I opened my laptop and did my own work, which consisted of two things. One, reading every scrap of information about treatment options, and two, getting the word out about my career change. In spite of my death sentence, I had decided to forge ahead, and was planning for my future in case I got a stay of execution. I had been sending out inquiries to all my productions contacts, asking them about training positions in the bookkeeping/accounting of whatever shows they were currently on.

As I was sending off another such email, an email from Lila popped into my inbox. I thought it might be a lead for a trainee position—I'd already talked to her about my plans—but it turned out to be something unexpected.

The Disney Family Channel was gearing up to shoot a TV pilot, and the production designer on the show was interviewing prop masters. Lila had recommended me for the position. After reading that email, I couldn't help but believe that things were truly on the upswing in our household. Eddie had landed a good job, and out of nowhere, I had a shot at one. It wasn't part of my master plan to switch careers, but it was still great news—*if* I could land the job.

Over the last few weeks, as I'd moving closer to finishing off this round of treatments, Lila had suggested that work would be good therapy before I started another round; that was one of the reasons I'd resumed my search for a trainee position.

But Eddie was against the whole proposition. He said that working would just weaken me more. Of course, I could understand why he'd think that, but just the thought of working had actually lifted my spirits and given me strength. And now that I'd ended the first course of treatments, the timing of this job looked pretty good. Lila's email said it was a six-week gig, so it would end well before my next round of treatments.

And the timing was good when it came to Jake and Hannah, too. Jake was set for college, enjoying the end of his senior year, so for him it was smooth sailing from here on in. And Hannah had taken her SAT and ACT, and between school, the swim team, and her extracurricular activities, she was so busy that I hardly ever saw her. She took care of herself and she didn't have time to get into trouble.

And then there was Eddie. The more I thought about him in the den, how engrossed he was in his own work already, the more I realized how demanding his new job would be. Also, ADM wouldn't have started him at that salary, considering his lack of experience, unless they were expecting a lot of him. He was going to be busy, and I'd find myself alone a lot. Wouldn't it be better to spend that time working, rather than obsessing about a disease I could do nothing about?

This *was* a good time to go back to work. The job would make me feel better about myself, maybe even close to normal. I didn't believe a positive mental attitude was a cure for cancer—that was crap—but I did believe the job would shift my focus away from an uncertain future, and that in itself was good medicine.

And who knows, maybe I could get to know someone in the accounting department. Then, if the pilot went to series, they might hire me as a bookkeeping trainee.

I emailed Lila back, thanking her for the lead, and immediately followed up with an email to Mimi Quincy, the production designer on the pilot.

Then I considered telling Eddie, but dismissed the idea. He didn't want to be interrupted, and this interruption would be a long one, maybe even one that resulted in an argument. I decided to wait until he took a break to bring it up.

But by midmorning, after sending out more resumes for trainee positions, I had decided to wait until the weekend. And by lunchtime, when Eddie still hadn't appeared from the den, I had come up with a better idea: I would wait and see if I actually got the job before bringing it up. Sure, it would be harder to explain then, but why bring it up at all if I ended up not getting the job? Why rock the boat now when Eddie had just delivered? He had come through, and it was time to enjoy that, not time to argue.

And maybe he would be so into *his* job by the time I got *my* job that he wouldn't care. That was my hope, because I suddenly realized how excited I was about the possibility of getting back to work.

EDDIE

CHAPTER FIFTEEN

I'd spent all morning profiling the target—the woman Abel wanted me to abduct. Abel had given me her name, Tracy Miles, and her address last night. The gold card had delivered the information just after Jenny and I had finished fooling around.

I'd been lying in bed, serene and dreamy, when I heard a ringing in my ears. A high-pitched hum, like tinnitus. A few seconds later, it got louder, and then, when it got louder still, I began to wonder if the sound was external, and not in my own head.

I sat up in bed and scanned the room for the source. I couldn't pinpoint it, and just as I was about to ask Jenny if she heard it— which would have been a blunder, a terrible way to start my clandestine job—she asked me what was the matter.

Right then, I understood that she wasn't hearing the ringing. So I reconsidered whether it *was* in my own head—but it was way too loud to be internal. I was confused for a couple of seconds, until my eyes fell on my pants.

That's when I made the connection: it was the gold card that was humming. *Wasn't it?* And wasn't it possible that Abel had rigged it so only I could hear it?

Of course it was possible. For Christ's sake, the guy was an alien.

I told Jenny that I'd forgotten to do something, then got out of bed and hurried over to my pants. I slipped them on and headed into the den.

When I pulled out the gold card, its smooth and lustrous surface was no longer a blank slate. It was now "embossed" with silver lettering, which spelled out a name and address, and a date and time, two days from now.

I had my work cut out for me. It was clear that I was to deliver Tracy Miles—the target—to Abel in two days. So I had to learn as much about her as I could, so I could find the least conspicuous way to abduct her.

As I processed this, the ringing in my ears stopped. Abel had given me my marching orders. A second later, the embossed silver lettering disappeared, too. The metallic gold card was a blank slate again.

I would have started to investigate Tracy right then, but that would've been too hard to explain to Jenny. So instead, I opted to go back to bed and get up bright and early.

In the morning, my first move was to sign up for a VPN, a Virtual Private Network. This was an Internet service that masked your computer's IP address, so your online searches remained hidden. As a reporter, I'd had no need to cover my tracks, but with this job, secrecy was paramount.

I knew that a VPN wasn't foolproof—if my computer was seized, my searches might still be recoverable. But I didn't have time to come up with another solution, at least, not for this first assignment. The time left to deliver the target was already ticking down. Besides, with the money I'd be earning, there was an easy solution: trash this computer when I was done with this target and buy a new one. Still, I made a note to come up with a long-term solution to cover up my identity on the Internet.

My online sleuthing into Tracy Miles yielded plenty of

information, unlike my last profiling attempt—my research into Thomas Caraway. The thought of Caraway prompted me to make another mental note: find out how Caraway was connected to Abel. Or were they one and the same person?

The search results on Tracy were just what I was used to finding as a reporter: her date of birth, her past and current employers, her home and cell phone numbers, her educational background, her credit scores. I also unearthed miscellaneous tidbits about her life by combing her social media posts and those of her friends and relatives, as well as other websites she was linked to. I knew what stores she frequented, what her political leanings were, what music she liked, et cetera.

By early afternoon, I'd gleaned as much about her as I could from the Internet. Though I didn't know anything specific about the previous target, the woman Ben had abducted, I saw at least one connection between her and my target: they were both women in their thirties. Perhaps I was jumping to conclusions based on only two examples, but I was already wondering why the alien was interested in targeting that particular demographic.

I filed that question in the back of head, in the same place where I'd stuck my remorse over Ben's death. Every time he came into my thoughts, pangs of guilt shot through me. I was complicit—no, responsible—for his death. But there was no time to dwell on it. Especially with the deadline for delivering Tracy looming over me.

My next step was to scout out her apartment building. And after that, I would scout her workplace. I also planned to follow her home from work and watch her evening routine. That would maximize my first day on the job. The tranquilizer pellets would be at my side during my vigil, just in case an opportunity to kidnap her presented itself. And I was already thinking it'd be easier to kidnap her in the Fairfax district, where she worked—because it was policed by the

LAPD, and they were spread thin—rather than in Burbank, where she lived, which had its own police force.

But if I was already worried about the police, I was going about this all wrong. I had to make sure the possibility of attracting the attention of the police was next to nothing. That was what my new job called for, above all else.

Before I headed to Tracy's workplace, I called my tutoring clients, the ones scheduled for tonight and tomorrow night, and told them I'd found a full-time job and that I'd no longer be tutoring. I'd call the rest of my clients later; they could wait until I completed this assignment.

Then I headed into the kitchen to make a late lunch. Jenny was at the table on her laptop.

"How's it going?" she said.

"Good. Just plugging away." I hoped she wouldn't ask too many questions, and then I realized that this hope was going to be a permanent one: from now on, every time I'd talk to her, I'd hope she didn't ask too many questions.

"I'm guessing you're going to be working a lot of hours," she said, sympathetically.

"That's okay. I'm ready for it." I grabbed some eggs from the fridge. "Do you want me to scramble some eggs for you too?"

"I already ate."

I pulled a skillet from under the stove.

"When is your first day at the office?" she asked.

I had prepared for that question by doing some research on ADM this morning. Luckily, it turned out that they did have offices in LA. Still, I couldn't pretend to head off to that office every day.

"The way it's set up," I said, "I don't have to go in very often." I turned the stove burner on. "I'll be working remotely, from home, so you might get sick of seeing me around the house."

"I think I can live with that."

I buttered the pan. "I hope *I* can. I'm used to having an office, even if it was just a spot in a newsroom."

"We can turn the den into your office."

"I don't want to take over the den."

"Don't worry about it. Jake and Hannah stick to their rooms most of the time. And we can move the TV into the living room. Not that any of us really watch it anymore."

"Okay. Let me think about it." I cracked three eggs into a bowl, grabbed a fork, and started scrambling. Then I laid out more of my cover story, the part that would explain my long absences from the house, at odd hours, which would start with this afternoon and evening's surveillance.

"I'm still going to be out of the house a good bit though," I said. "I have to do intensive field interviews for the reports."

She turned from her laptop. "You never told me what those reports are supposed to be about."

"I'm investigating companies that ADM wants to acquire. Basically, they assign a company to me, and I have to sum up everything I find out about it, according to this set of guidelines they gave me."

She didn't respond, and I didn't look at her. I poured my eggs into the skillet and continued to scramble them.

"That's interesting," she said, sounding contemplative, as if she wasn't totally buying it, which was evidenced by her next question. "I thought the job was all about commodities."

"It is, but my division deals with buying small companies that play different roles in commodities trading. Companies that do analytics about trading, or design software for trading, or run platforms for trading. There a lot of angles that I never knew about."

"Oh, now I'm getting a better picture." She turned back to her computer.

Good, I thought. Because that was about as far as my cover story went. I needed to bring this conversation to an end.

"I'm the guy who'll be investigating a company's management, other personnel, history, connections to other companies, et cetera," I said. "Not so much their finances. That's up to another department." I scooped the eggs from the skillet onto a plate. "After lunch, I'm going to run over to the Van Nuys courthouse and dig up some business filings for the report I'm working on."

"You're hitting the ground running, huh?" she said.

"Yeah, I'm running toward those bonuses."

She laughed, and that was my cue to make a clean getaway.

In the den, I ate my scrambled eggs while I scrolled through the police blotter websites. I was checking to see if Ben's disappearance had been reported. First, I went through the blotters available to the public, but they didn't have anything listed. Then I checked the private blotters, which I knew how to access from my years at the *Times.* They didn't have anything either.

I was tempted to act on one of my mental notes from earlier—to research the connection between Caraway and Abel—but I decided to hold off on that. There'd be plenty of time after I completed the assignment. Besides, I already suspected that they were one and the same person. That would explain why the house appeared not to have changed hands for over a century. And it would also explain why Tom Caraway, aka Abel, had barely left a trace in the historical record.

I brought my empty plate back into the kitchen, ready to venture out and scout Tracy Miles, my first target. Jenny was no longer in the kitchen, and I couldn't help but feel relief. Ask me no questions, and I'll tell you no lies.

*

I headed to Tracy's home turf in Burbank, which wasn't too far from my home turf, Valley Village. I wondered if Abel had picked Tracy as my first target for that very reason: she was a good "starter" assignment.

Tracy's two-story apartment building sat at the corner of Pass Avenue and Heffron Drive. It was designed in a Southwestern style, painted pastel pink, and it looked fairly new. That, along with its ornate balconies and manicured grounds, told me the place was too nice to be a rental property. It was probably condos. But would it make a difference to my plan whether the target was a renter or an owner?

I had no idea, but I was sure that as I became better at my job—if I survived long enough to become better at my job—I'd get to know if it made a difference.

I drove around the block a couple of times to get a closer look at the building. It had a gated underground parking garage and a large central courtyard. Each individual condo had an entrance along that central courtyard.

That layout told me that breaking into Tracy's unit wasn't in the cards. Each unit had a view of the goings-on in the courtyard, so a neighbor could easily spot me. Not that breaking and entering was the best course of action anyway—I doubted I could pull it off.

I pulled into a strip mall that was conveniently located across Pass Avenue, and parked in a space from which I could watch Tracy's building. Then I grabbed a coffee from the Starbucks in the mall and got back in my car. As I sipped the coffee and stared at Tracy's building, I pretended to be absorbed in a cell phone conversation, like any other mall patron.

By the time I'd finished my coffee, I'd had an insight. An insight that inspired the inkling of a plan. I'd realized that observing Ben—the man I didn't want to think about—had been my only training for the job. And Ben had abducted his targets in public. He must have concluded that this was an acceptable method—maybe even the best method—for completing an assignment.

Of course, I couldn't be sure that this was his standard operating procedure. There was the possibility that what I'd witnessed was specific to that one target, but it was also possible that after much trial and error, Ben had concluded that abducting targets right under everyone's nose was the best approach.

Regardless of whether I was right or wrong, this line of reasoning informed my plan.

I realized that Tracy probably headed over to this strip mall on foot whenever she needed to pick up something she could find in one of the mall's stores. Contrary to popular belief, anytime Angelenos had the opportunity to avoid driving, they took advantage of it. And there was a lot Tracy could take advantage of in this mall: a Vons grocery store, a bank, a dry cleaner, three casual restaurants, an upscale restaurant, a nail salon, a flower shop, a frozen yogurt shop, and of course—what strip mall would be complete without it?—a Starbucks.

I looked over the layout of the mall and formed a plan similar to what I envisioned Ben's plan would have been. But my plan had two major differences. First, there would be no fake doctor bit—I wasn't prepared to pull that off. And second, for what I had in mind, I'd need to get very close to Tracy, without her noticing me, *before* tranquilizing her. There'd be no hanging back and tranquilizing her from the safety of my car, like Ben had done that night when I followed him.

I scanned Pass Avenue, identifying the path Tracy would likely take to walk from her building to the mall. Then I studied the mall's layout again, imagining the path she would take from north to south as she made her way past each store. Of course, I couldn't possibly know what her ultimate destination would be. She could duck into any store at any time. That was the wild card.

Still, shaky though it was, I had a plan.

I decided I could move on to Tracy's place of employment. I took Cahuenga out of the Valley and into Hollywood. As I headed down La Brea into the Fairfax District, I again weighed the risk of getting away with the abduction in Burbank versus LA proper. Even though I'd originally thought LA would be better, my Burbank plan was growing on me—probably because of the time crunch.

I turned west on Wilshire Boulevard, and seven blocks later I pulled into a metered parking space just down the street from Tracy's office building. It offered a view of the building's underground parking garage. From my online investigation, I knew what kind of car Tracy drove, so my intention was to follow her home from work. Maybe she'd stop off somewhere that would present me with the opportunity to abduct her with minimum risk.

I watched professional men and women walking along the broad sidewalks of Wilshire, heading in and out of office buildings. Lawyers, managers, analysts, all chatting and going about their normal business, just as I had when I'd been a reporter. But my business had changed. I was now in the lone wolf business. A true lone wolf—for how many other people carried out alien abductions?

Suddenly that lone wolf cliché led me to a decision. I needed to take my own counsel.

I would kidnap Tracy in the Valley, and that was that.

I'd do it either tonight or tomorrow night.

And everything I would do from this moment on, until I delivered her to Abel, would be taking me closer to that end.

Which meant that sitting here watching Tracy's workplace, waiting to follow her home, was a waste of time. And I couldn't afford to waste time. I didn't have to wonder what would happen if

I missed my deadline. There was no doubt I'd lose the job. And "lose the job" was a euphemism for being liquefied.

I pulled out of my parking space and headed back to the Valley. The only decision left for today was whether to go home for a few hours before heading back to Burbank, or head over there now.

JENNY

CHAPTER SIXTEEN

Shortly after Eddie had left for the courthouse, I'd received an email back from Mimi Quincy, the production designer. She said that she was more than happy to interview me. Not only that, she was delighted that someone with my experience was applying for the position.

Not as delighted as I am, I thought.

Mimi asked if I could meet her at Disney at four this afternoon. I wrote back yes, and then looked up Mimi's credits so I'd be prepared for the interview.

Mimi had worked her way up the food chain fairly quickly—from set dresser to prop master to art director to production designer. And she'd gone from small productions to large ones fairly quickly too. Just by looking at the progression of her career and the quality of shows she'd worked on, I knew this could be a great gig. *If* I landed it. And judging from Mimi's email, I might just land it this afternoon.

I leaned back in my chair and took a moment to enjoy the feeling of getting back on the horse. The cancer was still part of my life, but soon it wasn't going to be *all* of my life.

Of course, I knew that Eddie would still be an obstacle. The key thing was not to get too angry with him and to let him say his piece. I didn't want to get into a major argument with him, one that would interfere with his new job. My pilot gig would be temporary, while his job was critical to the long-term stability of our family, especially if—God forbid—I only had a couple of years to live. I wanted to make sure he got off to a good start in his new career.

And in the end, I knew his opposition to the job wasn't going to stop me from taking it. He'd know that, too. I would do what was best for me, and in the end, that would also be what was best for both of us.

I spent an hour reading about the pilot so I'd know as much about it as possible for the interview. There was no script floating around online, but I was able to learn a lot about the show from articles in the trades. When I finished with that, I moved on to getting dressed for the interview. With any Hollywood job interview, you had to look as young as possible, regardless of your age. So I changed into a good pair of jeans and a nice blouse, and took my time putting on my makeup. My problem wasn't looking younger than my age—that I could pull off. My problem was looking full of vim and vigor. I was still pale and a bit gaunt from my treatments, and no one wants to hire an employee who looks ill.

When I was done with my makeup, I slipped on stylish low heels and looked myself over in the full-length mirror. I had cleaned up nicely, and again I took a minute to enjoy the feeling of getting back on the horse.

Then I printed out my resume. I knew Mimi had probably already looked up my credits and called some of my old employers— no one in the film industry wasted time interviewing candidates for a job unless they'd already vetted them—but I'd be ready with my résumé anyway. I also grabbed my computer, which held my portfolio. After twenty years in the business, I had an extensive portfolio of photos of the dozens of sets I'd worked on.

Hannah and Jake walked into the house as I was slipping everything into my bag. Though their voices were subdued, I picked up that they were arguing. I was used to them arguing, so that didn't faze me, but what did faze me was that Hannah was home early. Except for a rare day off here and there, she always had swim practice after school. And as far as I knew, today wasn't one of those rare days.

When I walked out to the living room, Hannah was there, heading to the kitchen. She looked me up and down, and said, "You headed out on a date?"

I grinned. I *had* cleaned up nicely. "Yep," I said. "One of those cute oncologists wants to cheer me up."

Hannah didn't return my grin, and for a second I wondered if she thought my joke was meant to cover up the truth, like I'd been caught red-handed, so I added, "I'm kidding. I'm going to visit a friend on the Disney lot."

"Good for you," she said. "You need to get out more."

"No argument from me on that front. Now if only you could convince your dad of that."

"Why does he need to be convinced?"

I don't know why I answered, but I did. "He thinks the more I rest, the faster I'll get better."

"That makes sense."

I should've guessed she'd take his side of the argument, so I didn't defend myself.

Jake walked into the living room and shot a glance at her. "So did you tell Mom?"

"What is *wrong* with you?" Hannah snapped. "I wanted to wait until Dad got home."

"Tell me what?" I asked, already concerned. Hannah was the unpredictable child.

"I don't want to talk about it right now," she said.

"Is it something important?" I already knew the answer—Hannah's defensiveness told me that it was.

She glared at Jake for a second or two before conceding the point. "I guess it is. But I want to talk to you and Dad together."

"You can talk to me. I promise I won't get mad." That was a promise I might not be able to keep, depending on what she said.

"I think it's better if I wait."

"Just tell her," Jake said. "It's not like Dad's gonna change Mom's mind."

Hannah looked at me as if she was actually considering taking her brother's advice.

"Go ahead, honey," I said. "What is it?"

"You have to keep an open mind."

"I will."

"You're not going to like this. But it's my life."

"I understand."

Hannah looked away. "I quit the swim team."

"*What?*" I couldn't help myself. This was a far cry from anything I'd been expecting. Hannah's entire extracurricular life was wrapped around the swim team—the practices, the weight training, the swim meets, the tournaments. And I liked knowing that it kept her too busy and too tired to get into any trouble.

"See—you're already mad." Hannah shook her head.

"I'm not." I was furious.

"Yes, you are," Hannah insisted.

"It doesn't matter—just tell me why you quit."

"I got a job."

I took a deep breath. Hannah wasn't like Jake at all, and this was a big reminder of that. Jake would have discussed quitting the team with me. And he would have discussed taking a job.

"What's the job?" I asked.

"I'm going to work part time at Gregory Brothers." Gregory Brothers was an art supply store on Ventura Boulevard.

"Can't you work there *and* stay on the swim team?"

"I can't. Gregory Brothers wants me to work fifteen to twenty hours a week."

"Tell them you can only work five." But I knew that even five hours would be tough. With swim team, plus homework, plus studying for the SAT, ACT, and the APs, Hannah's plate was full.

"They're not looking for someone who can only work five hours a week," she said.

"But you love swimming."

"If you listened to what I've been saying all year, you'd know that isn't true. It used to be fun, but now it's a grind."

Actually, I did know. But Eddie and I had both hoped that she'd get through this period and learn to like it again.

"Don't you want to see it all the way through?" I said. "Do it for all four years?"

"You mean 'don't quit'? Is that what you think? That I'm a quitter?"

"Of course not—it's just that it's been such a big part of your life."

"Well, that part of my life is over."

"What about colleges—what will they think?"

"Are you kidding me? You're telling me that not only do you think I'm a quitter—but so will colleges?"

"No—not at all—I'm just saying that—"

"Jake—doesn't it sound to you like that's what she's saying?" Hannah said, interrupting me and swinging around to her brother.

"Leave me out of this," he said, then turned to leave.

"Jake!" she said. "You wanted me to tell her. I did. So now you

175

need to tell her what you told me. Please."

Jake stopped and looked back at me. He hesitated, then said, "She isn't doing anything wrong." Even though he and his sister argued all the time, the kid did know when to put aside petty differences.

He looked at me for another beat, calm and collected, sure that he was in the right, and then he walked out of the living room.

"Listen, honey," I said to Hannah, "I don't think you're a quitter, or that colleges will think that. It's just that—you might have to explain why you left the team on your college applications."

"I don't think so. I'm not a superstar swimmer. I'm not getting into college on a swimming scholarship. And I do have an explanation! A good one. I got a job. Don't you think colleges will like that?"

I did—but I still didn't want her to quit the team.

"We need to talk more about this before you decide," I said. "We should talk to Mr. Teller, too." Mr. Teller was her high school counselor.

"Mom—you're not listening! It's a done deal! I already quit the team! I took the job!"

Right then, as if on cue, the front door swung open and Eddie walked in. So now, in addition to dealing with Hannah, I'd have to face him. I had hoped to get out of the house without him seeing me all dolled up, because he'd definitely ask where I was headed.

"What's going on?" Eddie said.

"I quit the swim team and got a job," Hannah answered. "*That's* what's going on."

Eddie glanced at me, then back at Hannah. "Wow," he said. His tone reflected genuine surprise rather than anger.

"Believe it or not," Hannah said, "I made a decision about my own life *on my own*."

I looked over at Eddie. "I think we should all talk about this before any final decision is made."

"Mom doesn't seem to understand that I already made the decision," Hannah said.

That made me so angry that I was afraid of what I might say next. So I didn't say anything, hoping that Eddie would take up the mantle.

But I noticed that his cheeks weren't reddening and his eyes weren't fiery. He didn't look angry in the least. Was it because he was engrossed in his new job? Or did he truly believe it was just fine and dandy for their daughter to have made this huge decision without consulting them?

"What's the job?" Eddie asked.

"A sales clerk at Gregory Brothers." Hannah sounded pleased with herself.

"Can you tell me why you didn't want to talk to us first?" Unlike me, Eddie didn't sound confrontational.

"Because I didn't want to fight about it day in and day out while I was waiting to see if I actually got the job."

Just then, in spite of my anger, it dawned on me: what Hannah had done was exactly what I was planning to do. I was planning on not telling Eddie about my potential prop master job until I actually got the job.

Eddie didn't respond to Hannah's explanation right away, as if he was weighing what his options were. When in came to Hannah's high school years, this was certainly her most rebellious act.

Finally, Eddie spoke up. "I guess you can always go back to the team if the job doesn't work out," he said.

I was dumbfounded. "That's your solution?"

Hannah had managed to divide and conquer, so she jumped on her opportunity for a quick exit.

"I don't think I'll ever go back to the swim team, Dad," she said.

Now her tone was no longer confrontational. And why should it be? She'd gotten her way. "And I promise you the job will work out," she added. "Because it really is what I want to do."

She started to head toward her bedroom.

"We're not done talking about this," I said.

"*I'm* done," she said, before stepping into the hallway.

I spun toward Eddie. "So you're letting her get away with this?"

"She already got away with it."

"You're not furious at her?" I asked.

"You can't say we didn't see this coming. She's been telling us for months that she wasn't into the swim team."

"That doesn't make it okay."

"I know. But maybe she's changing."

"Changing? This is her to a T—pulling this stunt behind our backs."

"What if she had talked to us about it first?"

"I would've put my foot down. And you would've done the same."

"You're right. But maybe she needed this change. And if we had stopped her, she would've been miserable."

"So you're saying you're fine with this?"

"It's not so much that I'm fine with it. It's more that I'm fine with her making the decision on her own." He was doing his best to appease me. "And since she already did, there's nothing we can do about it anyway."

"We can tell her that if she doesn't go back to the team, I won't do her laundry, cook her meals, or drive her anywhere."

Eddie stared at me for a long beat, and I suddenly felt petty. But I didn't give an inch.

After a few more seconds, Eddie said, "I'm fine with punishing her, if that's what you want to do."

"I think we should."

"Okay," he said. "Then why don't we cool off and talk about it again tomorrow?" But by "we," I knew he meant me—that I should cool off before we talked about it again.

"All right," I said.

But I didn't agree to drop it because I was done talking about this. I agreed because it was time to head over to Disney for my interview. And with that thought, it hit me once again that I was acting like Hannah, hiding my possible job from Eddie. That made my anger toward Hannah dissolve a little.

"By the way," Eddie said, "tonight my tutoring is going to go late."

"Aren't you done with tutoring?" I asked.

"I am. But I didn't want to leave some of the kids in the lurch. So I'm doing a couple more sessions with them while they're locking down new tutors."

"That's nice of you."

"What can I say? I'm a nice guy."

"I guess you are. That's probably why you didn't get mad at Hannah."

"You were mad enough for both of us."

I smiled. "You're right."

He looked me up and down. "Do you have a hot date or something?"

"Yeah—with Lila. I'm going over to Disney to grab a cup of coffee with her."

"Great. Let me know what's new at the Mouse House." He kissed me on the cheek. "I'm going to do some more work."

As he headed to the den, I wondered if we'd have another argument when I came back from the Mouse House. Not about Hannah's new job, but about mine.

EDDIE

CHAPTER SEVENTEEN

I'd been in the den just a few minutes—checking out police blotter sites again to see if Ben's disappearance had been reported yet—when Jake entered. I didn't expect him. I expected Hannah would be the child who'd next want to talk to me. I thought she'd want to verify that I had her back when it came to Jenny's next onslaught over the decision to quit the swim team.

I also didn't expect Jake's request. "Tell me about your job, Dad," he said.

"There isn't that much to tell," I said. I loved that my son wanted to talk to me—what dad wouldn't?—but this was the one topic I wanted to avoid. Still, if I wanted to avoid a cross-examination, I had to give him something. So I added, "It's with Archer Daniels Midland, a large ag—"

"I know what ADM is," he said. "It's a gigantic agricultural company that rapes the earth to provide us all with food."

I chuckled. Maybe this wasn't going to be so bad after all. "Yeah, but on the other hand," I said, "they feed hundreds of millions at a relatively low cost."

"You mean poison hundreds of millions."

"That's debatable—and for a guy interested in economics and

business, you don't sound like a big fan of capitalism."

"ADM isn't capitalism. It's a megacorporation unfairly crushing the competition. ADM isn't what Adam Smith was talking about when he wrote his capitalist manifesto."

This was turning out to be an enjoyable little debate and not the cross-examination I'd feared.

"So you're for the little guy," I said. "The little corporation."

"If you actually read *The Wealth of Nations*, you'd know that's what capitalism is all about. Competition on a level playing field. Not one megacorporation crushing the competition."

"So how do you stop the megacorporation?"

"That's what government is for."

"Good luck with that. You've got a big chunk of the country trained to think that government is bad. They have no idea that Adam Smith meant for government to intercede."

"That's because of those megacorporations—the ones your generation let get out of hand. They've brainwashed people into hating the government."

"Can't argue with that." I basically agreed with his assessment of capitalism, that it had gone off the rails, and I was proud that he could articulate his point of view.

"Good," he said. "Now that we've got that squared away, exactly what are you doing for your new corporate overlord?" The good times had ended, and the cross-examination was back on.

"I'm doing research for their commodities trading division," I said.

"ADM also *trades* commodities? If that's not a conflict of interest, I don't know what is. They grow the stuff *and* get to bet on it?"

"It's a hedge," I said. "A way to protect themselves and stabilize prices."

"I know what a hedge is. But the truth is that it's a hedge when farmers do it. When ADM does it, it's cheating. They have inside information, so it's a big money-making scam."

"Well… then… I guess I'm part of that scam." That almost got a grin out of him.

"And what role will you be playing in that scam?" he said.

I gave him the same cover story that I'd given Jenny, that I'd be researching small companies that play different roles in commodities trading, companies that ADM was interested in buying.

"You mean you're going to crush the competition," he said.

"We like to think of it as acquisitions."

That not only got him to grin, it got him to laugh. And I thought I might be out of the woods. But he came up with another question.

"Are you working with economists and mathematicians?" he asked.

"I don't know," I said, and regretted it immediately. If I had understood what he was getting at, I would've said "yes" instead of the weak "I don't know," which betrayed a lack of understanding about acquisitions.

"You'd think they'd have someone who can crunch the numbers to do the quantitative analysis of the companies," he said.

They probably would—wouldn't they? "I focus on the management," I said, trying to regroup. "But I'm sure they have financial analysts who pore through the numbers."

Jake raised his eyebrows skeptically. But I couldn't tell if he was skeptical about my answer or about the job itself. And I didn't have a chance to find out because his phone buzzed.

He pulled it out of his pocket, glanced at it, and then said, "I gotta go."

He made a quick exit—and just like that, the cross-examination was over.

But I was left with the task of fleshing out my cover story, just in case Jake asked for more details later on. And since I had some time left before I needed to head to Burbank, I started in on that task, looking up commodity trading firms.

But my thoughts soon went from my own son to Mason, Ben Kingsley's son.

I'd ruined his life.

Mason was more than likely in some sort of psychological limbo. He was probably in denial about his dad's disappearance, because only a day had passed. But soon his denial would grow into anguish, and then—in a few days, or in a week, or maybe in a month—his anguish would grow into unbearable heartbreak. He'd have to accept that something awful had happened to his dad. He'd have to accept that he'd never see his dad again. He'd be devastated.

I wanted to help the kid. But there wasn't anything I could do.

No—that isn't true.

I could help him financially, as I was doing with my own family. Certainly Ben had made some investments that would help Mason and his mom. But I was sure that Ben had also kept lot of his earnings in cash—in that safe behind the tapestry. Otherwise he would've risked being audited.

I made a decision. I'd anonymously tell Mason or his mom about that safe—for I was sure that neither of them knew about it. And if there wasn't enough cash in that safe for Mason to live his life without financial worry, I'd anonymously deliver more cash from my own earnings. This wouldn't cushion the emotional blow of losing a father, but it would cushion the financial blow.

With that commitment assuaging my guilt, I turned my attention back to the target: Tracy Miles. But not to profile her. I'd done enough of that. It was time to focus on the abduction. I played out what I'd witnessed when Ben had abducted his target, combing through the footage in my mind as if it were the Zapruder film, looking to pick up any tricks of the trade.

And I did pick one up. One that I should've used when I'd scouted Tracy's apartment building this morning.

I needed to remove the license plates from my car—just as Ben had done with his car—before heading back to Burbank.

Why the hell hadn't I done that this morning?

Because I was still in training—on-the-job training, the kind of training that was dangerous.

Well, thank God I remembered to take off the license plates now. Otherwise abducting Tracy in front of bystanders would be even riskier than it already was. I was far more likely to get caught because someone jotted down my license plate number than because someone saw me commit the crime. I was well aware of the unreliability of eyewitness accounts. Six years ago, I'd written a feature story about it. Even in cases where witnesses were actively paying attention to the events unfolding in front of them, their descriptions of the people participating in those events were, for the most part, wrong.

Jenny had gone to meet Lila, so I didn't have to worry about her seeing me strip the license plates from my car. But Jake or Hannah might spot me, and if they did, they'd surely ask what I was up to. And pulling the car into the garage to do the deed wasn't an option. The garage was packed with junk.

I added another mental note to my growing list: clean out the damn garage. Not only would it provide a discreet place to remove and reattach my license plates, it would also give me privacy if I needed to load up the car with supplies for the job.

For today though, I'd have to remove my license plates somewhere else. I considered a few secluded side streets, the ones that dead-ended at the 101, but decided to go with the underground parking lot at Marshall's. That lot was rarely full, and it had some dark niches.

*

Before I headed out, I changed into the least conspicuous outfit I could put together—a button-down blue shirt, and a pair of jeans that weren't too faded or too new.

But when I stepped up to front door, ready to head out on my first assignment, an odd feeling came over me. Not odd as in weird, but odd as in foreign.

I felt full—emotionally full.

Sure, I felt nervous and anxious, but those feelings were overwhelmed by soaring exhilaration. The exhilaration of embarking on a unique adventure, a lucrative adventure.

But this feeling of fullness—completeness—was so powerful that I knew it was more than exhilaration. It was also the overwhelming love I felt for Jenny, and Jake, and Hannah.

I was going to secure their futures.

And this love for them inspired me to make one stop before I walked out of the house.

I knocked on Hannah's door. She didn't answer.

I knew her well enough to know she wasn't going to answer unless I was persistent. She was in there, angry at her mom—her cheeks flushed with fury—texting to her friends about what jerks her parents were.

I knocked again, louder. "Hannah, can I talk to you for a minute?"

Still no answer.

Another knock and another plea: "Hannah, I know you're mad, but let me talk to you for a sec," I said.

Still no word from the other side of the barrier.

I reached for the doorknob, expecting her door to be locked, but it wasn't. Probably an oversight on her part. After an argument, she always locked her door.

I opened the door and found her clutching her iPhone, sitting on her bed, her back against the wall, her knees close to her chest. She shot me a look of loathing—her eyes were narrowed and her eyebrows stitched. "What do you want?" she said.

"I just wanted to talk for a minute."

"I know you're trying to play good cop. But I'm not changing my mind."

"I'm not trying to play good cop."

"So you're a bad cop too. Like Mom."

"No—I'm—"

"It doesn't matter. I quit the swim team, and I'm not going back."

"I'm fine with that."

"No you're not. You're just saying that so you can ease me into a dialogue and try to talk me out of quitting."

I couldn't help but smile. She was feisty.

"Why are you laughing at me?" she snapped.

"I'm not laughing. I just wanted to tell you that I understand. Swimming has run its course, right? You want to move on with your life."

She cocked her head as if she was gauging my honesty. "Yeah... I guess."

"That's fine. We don't have to do everything forever. We all change."

"But you don't think I'm changing. You think I'm quitting."

"You're about as far from a quitter as I can imagine." I looked at the paintings on her wall. Paintings she'd done herself. Stunning landscapes of Yosemite, inspired by a family vacation we'd taken there. One of the paintings had won a national art award for high school students.

"Remember that painting class you took in fifth grade?" I said.

"You cried every time you came home from it. You said the other kids' paintings looked like paintings, but your paintings looked like—"

"Shit," Hannah said.

"Yeah—and I think I got mad at you for using that word."

She reluctantly broke into a smile. "You did."

"You were so miserable that I wanted you to stop taking the class. But you wouldn't give up. And when it was all said and done, your final painting was the only one chosen for that district contest." I sat down on the bed next to her. "That's how you are with everything. You stick with it until you're good at it. You don't quit. Even when—for some crazy reason—you decide to take German instead of Spanish."

"Yeah—well *that* I should have quit. It's still hell."

We both laughed.

"I'm proud of you, honey." And I was. "Leaving the team must've been hard. I understand that. And I'm proud of you for going out and getting the job with Gregory Brothers. You made the decision that working there was more important than swimming."

She studied me for a few seconds. "So you're really okay with it?"

"Yes. Really."

She leaned forward and hugged me. "Thanks."

"But now we have to ease your mom into this. Okay?"

She nodded.

"You don't need to flaunt it. I'm backing you up on this. And I promise you she'll eventually come around."

"Okay."

I got up to go, but before exiting, I turned back to her. "I love you, sweetheart."

"I love you, too," she said. Her rage was gone, and her smile was bright and beautiful.

CHAPTER EIGHTEEN

I pulled into the underground parking structure at Marshall's and parked in a quiet area far from the escalator. There were just three other cars parked nearby.

I quickly went to work removing my license plates. As I did, I wondered if I should have rented a car for this assignment. Had Ben ever done that? Or was a rental car easier to trace than your own car? I supposed I could use a fake driver's license and pay cash for the rental. Still, my mug would be right there on the security camera footage from the rental car place. I concluded that the reason Ben had used his own car was that it was the safest bet.

But that train of thought led to the recognition of another precaution I needed to take. When I got to the strip mall on Pass Avenue, I would need to locate the security cameras. I should have done that this morning. Another oversight; another part of my on-the-job training.

I had a lot to learn, and no time to practice. I'd either sink or swim. And in my new line of work, sinking had serious repercussions. Why had Abel designed the job this way? Why not give me instructions based on lessons learned from abducting past targets?

After the license plates were off and tucked in the trunk, I came up with an answer to those questions. Maybe the alien *hadn't* designed the job this way. After all, I'd forced my way into the job. Maybe it was just me who hadn't been given any instructions. Maybe Abel *did* give new recruits training. The recruits *he* chose.

Wasn't it possible that when Abel saw me—a nobody who'd stumbled onto his operation—trying to pull a fast one on him, he thought, *Okay, let him sink or swim?*

*

I parked in the strip mall on Pass Avenue, across from Tracy's building. The first thing I did was check out the strip mall from my car, looking for security cameras. But that wasn't good enough; I had to walk the mall too. Of course, that act alone put me in the crosshairs of some of those cameras. But that couldn't be helped. It was critical that I knew where the cameras were, so the abduction itself wouldn't be caught on tape.

When I got the lay of the land down—the parts of the mall not covered by security cameras—I went back to my car. Rush hour was starting, which meant more traffic along Pass Avenue. That was a good thing. It made me less conspicuous than I'd been on my first vigil here. And there was more activity in the strip mall itself—a constant flow of cars pulling in and out, as commuters, on their way home, stopped to pick something up. That went a long way in helping me blend into the scenery.

In the midst of all this activity, I kept an eye on the garage entrance to Tracy's building. Sure, there was always the possibility that she had plans after work, and therefore wouldn't be arriving home for a while, but there was nothing I could do about that. Eventually she'd return home.

Over the course of the next three hours, I saw plenty of Acuras, which was the model of car Tracy drove. I'd found that tidbit when profiling her online. Then, near the end of that third hour, I spotted the one Acura I was interested in.

Tracy pulled up to her building and waited for the gate to the underground garage to open.

Now came the next vigil, the one where I waited for Tracy to leave her place. Already, this vigil felt different. My heart was thumping in my chest because I understood that as soon as Tracy left her apartment, I'd have to be prepared to abduct her. After all, I only had tonight and tomorrow night before the deadline expired.

Tracy drove into the garage, and I was suddenly filled with doubt. What if she didn't leave her apartment tonight or tomorrow night? Would I have to abduct her from work? Or from her apartment, which I already knew would be next to impossible?

I told myself not to worry about that yet—I'd cross that bridge tomorrow. Right now, I had to keep my eyes glued to the entrance of Tracy's building.

About thirty minutes later, when my heartbeat had finally slowed, the front door of the apartment building swung open, and to my great surprise—and relief—Tracy walked out. Immediately I knew where she headed, because in addition to her purse, she was carrying a canvas bag. In California, you paid extra for paper bags, so if you were on top of it, you brought your own bags when you went shopping for groceries. That made me fairly certain Tracy was headed to Vons, the grocery store right here in the strip mall.

Luck was on my side tonight, and I was thankful for it. But I'd need more luck to pull off the kidnapping.

As I watched Tracy walking down Pass Avenue toward the traffic light, my heart began to thump hard once again. But this time my body was shaking too, almost vibrating.

I tried to slow my breathing in the hope of fooling my body into thinking that this whole abduction thing was no big deal. But the magnitude of what I was about to do was hitting me hard and my body just wouldn't comply.

So with my heart racing wildly and my body quivering, I focused on executing my plan—and thank God I did, because it dawned on me that I had never decided if I should abduct the target before or after she completed her errand.

I had to decide now.

I watched the target step up to the intersection at the south end of the block, where she'd cross over to the mall. There she waited for the crosswalk light. She looked calm and collected, and that made me more nervous—sweat was forming on my brow. I wiped it off with my shirtsleeve and made my decision.

I'd abduct her before she did her errand.

I opened the glove compartment and pulled out the copper straw and the tin of tranquilizer pellets. Then I opened the tin, took a pellet out, and put it in the straw. It wedged in perfectly.

Tracy crossed the street. She appeared relaxed and innocent, and her girl-next-door good looks accentuated that innocence. I suddenly felt bad for her—but I pushed that anguish away, stuffing it into the same place where I'd locked up my guilt over Ben's death.

I concentrated on my plan: I'd walk behind the target, very close to her, as if I were with her. As soon as it looked like we might actually be a couple, I'd tranquilize her, then catch her as she began to pass out—catching her from behind so she wouldn't be able to identify me.

I'd play the role of concerned boyfriend—*Are you okay, honey? Tracy, did you miss your injection?* I'd play it so that bystanders would understand that Tracy was a diabetic. I'd use her name a few times, and terms of endearment, so there'd be no doubt we were a couple.

If a bystander was particularly concerned, I'd let them know that this had happened before, that I was capable of handling it, and that we were headed to the hospital.

Tracy was now walking along the wide sidewalk that fronted the strip mall. I quickly scanned ahead of her, refreshing my memory as to what areas weren't covered by the security cameras. Then I put my car in gear and headed across the parking lot, closer to the storefronts. Sweat now covered my palms, and I hoped I wouldn't become one big vibrating, sweaty mess by the time I moved in on the target.

I drove to the parking aisle perpendicular to the nail salon. I had decided to make my move in front of the salon—there were no security cameras there—so I wanted to park in a space close by. The farther I had to carry the target in my arms, the more attention I'd draw to myself.

Unfortunately, there were no open parking spaces along this aisle.

So I started up the next parking aisle, knowing that Tracy was closing in on Vons, which was next door to the nail salon. I had to hurry; I needed to park, scoot back through the parking lot on foot until I was behind her, then catch up to her from behind before she got to the nail salon.

I found an open space, pulled in, and got out of my car. I didn't lock the doors because I didn't want to trigger the "beep beep" sound of my car doors unlocking during my return trip. That would bring unwanted attention to my girlfriend and me when I whisked her away.

As I scooted through the parking lot, circling back around behind Tracy, a kink in my plan hit me, and hit me hard. Why hadn't I thought of this kink before?

On-the-job training—that's why.

The kink was the possibility that someone who knew me would see me abducting the target. They'd know I wasn't Tracy's boyfriend. It was true that I wasn't in my own neighborhood, but I wasn't that far from it either.

And then another kink hit me. What if one of the bystanders to the abduction knew Tracy? They would know she didn't have a boyfriend—*that* was why Ben had impersonated a doctor, rather than someone who knew the target.

And if that wasn't enough, a third kink hit me. Even if I managed to pull off the abduction outside the view of security cameras, there would still be footage of me right before the abduction.

Too late now.

Too late to consider any of these kinks.

In the end, the only way to get away with this—the only way to earn those bricks of cash—was to make my shaky plan work. I had to execute my plan "properly," as Abel had put it.

I made it to the storefronts, then headed toward Tracy. She was closing in on the nail salon, so I had to pick up my pace.

I avoided making eye contact with the people walking toward me. Though I knew eyewitness accounts were faulty, I still didn't want to invite attention. But because I was hurrying to catch up to Tracy, I was also passing people moving in the same direction I was. These people could prove to be trouble later on down the line. They might realize that I hadn't really been with Tracy in the first place, but had been trying to catch her from behind.

When I made it to within five yards of Tracy, everything around me suddenly looked sharp and clear, as if a kind of hyper-alertness had kicked in. If my heart was still beating wildly, or if my palms were still sweaty, I didn't know it. My focus was no longer on myself, but on my target and on my surroundings.

There were no red flags, and the nail salon was coming up quickly. I wanted to be right behind my target, off to one side, for at least a couple seconds before she got there. Long enough to pull off the boyfriend act for bystanders, but not long enough for Tracy to sense that there was someone suspicious by her side.

As I ran my thumb along the tranquilizer tube, which I clutched tightly in my hand, I sped up. Conversely, the scene around me slowed down, as if my hyperawareness had become more acute. As I bore down on Tracy—I was one yard behind her, on her right—the four people headed in my direction appeared to be walking in slow motion, which was exactly what I needed. Their deliberate, measured movements gave me enough time to glance from one to the other, looking for a window—the window where I could bring the straw to my lips without being spotted.

I glanced at each: an elderly woman wearing a straw hat, a young man with tortoise-shell glasses, a young woman with heavy eyeliner staring down at her phone, and a man in a business suit, also staring down at his phone.

The coast was clear.

I stepped closer to Tracy, and after a second on her heels, I whipped the straw up to my lips, aimed it at her shoulder, and blew.

She stumbled and swayed.

I swooped in as she was falling.

But I screwed up.

And I knew it as soon as I caught her in my arms. Because I immediately felt that she wasn't yet a bag of bones crumpling to the ground. She was still fighting the wooziness—and though that fight lasted but a second, during that second, she turned her head slightly and looked me in the eye.

There was no doubt she'd seen my face.

Then her eyes fluttered and closed, and she went limp, collapsing completely into my arms.

I held her tightly, but instead of going into my act—calling her by her name, advertising that she was a diabetic, and setting myself up as her boyfriend—I was berating myself. Why hadn't I waited just a fraction of a second longer to catch her? What if she remembered seeing my face? Abel had said she wouldn't remember anything—*if* I executed the assignment "properly."

Had I?

It seemed not.

"Is she okay?" someone asked.

"She's a diabetic," I answered, getting on with my spiel before it was too late.

"Do you need any help?" the same voice asked.

I looked up to see who was so concerned. It was the young man with the tortoise-shell glasses.

"I think I can manage," I said. "This has happened before. Her blood sugar just dropped all of a sudden." I placed one of my arms under Tracy's legs, then lifted her up.

"Do you want me to call 911?" the man in the business suit chimed in.

"I'm going to take her to the emergency room." I began to walk away with Tracy in my arms.

"Do you want me to drive you?" That question came from the young woman with the heavy eyeliner. She was standing among the other bystanders, whose number had now grown to eight or nine.

"Thanks, but our car is right here," I said, and stepped off the sidewalk onto the blacktop. I wanted to leave parting words to strengthen my poor performance, so I added, "She'll be fine."

That was stupid. I should've picked a line that played into her diabetes. That would have been more convincing.

Someone behind me shouted, "Wait!"

I didn't wait.

"Wait!" the voice said again, this time more insistent *and* closer. The owner of the voice was following me.

I instinctually picked up my pace. Sweat pitted under my arms and across my brow. I felt like a criminal on the run. I *was* a criminal on the run.

And when the owner of the voice caught up to me—it turned out to be the woman with the heavy eyeliner—I was no longer hyperaware. Instead, I was nothing but a shaky, sweaty, panicky mess.

I turned to the woman, not sure what I was going to say—and thinking that I should just give up and cut my losses—when she suddenly thrust a purse at me.

"You forgot her purse," she said.

My mouth hung agape for a full second before I responded, "Oh, thank you. You're a lifesaver."

I reached out with the arm that was under Tracy's legs, and the woman placed the purse in my hand.

"Are you sure you don't need any help?" she said.

"I'm okay. The hospital is just three minutes away. We've been there before. They know us."

"Good luck," she said.

"Thanks."

Without looking back, I hurried to my car, opened the passenger door, dropped the purse inside, then buckled Tracy in. After closing the door, I was tempted to glance back to see if the woman with the heavy eyeliner was still waiting in the wings, wanting to help, but I forced myself not to.

Instead, I ran over to the driver's side of the car, got in, and pulled out. As I turned onto Pass Avenue, I again thought about the poor job I'd done.

But after a few minutes on the road, I felt a surge of energy, a surge of exhilaration, and I saw the flip side: I was driving away with the target.

I had completed my first alien abduction.

CHAPTER NINETEEN

It was bizarre driving through the familiar Valley streets with an unconscious woman in my passenger seat. No—"bizarre" was putting it too mildly. Using the word "bizarre" made it more palatable. It was downright creepy, and I didn't like it. With Tracy out cold, drugged, just a foot away from me, I felt like a low-life criminal. And I was, wasn't I?

There was nothing redeeming about kidnapping an innocent stranger, even if it was an alien abduction. Just because an alien was the ringleader didn't make it some kind of highbrow mission.

As I made my way down Ventura toward Coldwater, I kept glancing around, in all directions and into the rearview mirror, on the lookout for police cruisers. And when I stopped at traffic lights, I surreptitiously checked out the other drivers around me, gauging whether they were peeking into my car at Tracy. Some did peek in, but I could tell by their blasé reactions that if anything registered at all, it was that a woman was sleeping in the passenger seat. I now understood why Ben could drive around in public with an unconscious woman riding shotgun next to him. Other drivers weren't bothered in the least by what they saw.

But I was.

When I glanced over at Tracy and saw her face, which was turned toward me, I saw an innocent victim, one that I'd preyed upon. As if I were a psychopath. She was serene, and her breathing was calm and shallow. I had complete power over this sleeping beauty. But I didn't want that power—at all.

Now that the adrenaline rush of the abduction had mellowed a bit, the magnitude of the crime itself was looming larger in my thoughts. Before it could paralyze me, I dealt with it: I escorted the magnitude of my crime to the back of my mind, to the place where I'd locked up my guilt over Ben's death and the anguish I'd felt when I first saw Sleeping Beauty crossing Pass Avenue. That place in the back of my mind—which I now thought of as a prison cell—was fast becoming crowded.

Then another worry hit me: I was driving through Studio City, my home base, and that meant I was increasing the odds of a neighbor spotting me. A neighbor who'd wonder why I was driving around with a young woman sleeping in my passenger seat.

What if Jenny saw me?

I should have taken Barham to the 101 and taken the 101 straight to Coldwater.

Again—too late now.

Next time, I'd map out my drive back to Abel's.

And next time, I wouldn't jump in so soon to catch the target before she tumbled to the ground.

And I wouldn't use the boyfriend cover story—a cover story that wouldn't have stood up if one of the bystanders had known Tracy.

I'd made a lot of stupid choices, and I was tempted to continue to list them, berating myself along the way. But instead I forced myself to accept that this was on-the-job training, and the best I could do was apply the lessons learned tonight to the next abduction.

But it wouldn't be that easy, would it?

The next assignment might have requirements that were totally different from this one. Only after I'd done a number of assignments would I start to learn how to better execute them. Of course, that assumed that there'd be more assignments. After my weak performance tonight, that wasn't guaranteed.

As I drove up Coldwater, closing in on Abel's house, my thoughts shifted from abducting targets to returning them. I knew it took Abel fifteen minutes to do whatever it was he did to the targets—that was how long Ben had been at the house with his target—so in less than thirty minutes I'd be heading back down Coldwater. With Tracy. To return her.

Return her to where?

I didn't get to see where Ben had returned his target. Had he released her back on Tujunga, where he'd abducted her? Was the "return" part of the assignment similar to releasing an animal back into the wild? Like I'd seen on the Discovery Channel, where animals were tranquilized, captured, and tagged?

I glanced over at Sleeping Beauty. To Abel, Tracy was an animal—all humans were. But what did he do with these animals during those fifteen minutes?

I turned onto Mulholland and continued to play out my nature analogy: What did *we* do with our animals after we captured them and before we returned them to the wild? We studied them, or experimented on them, to learn more about them. Or to learn more about us.

My gut told me that Abel wasn't capturing targets to learn more about them, or to learn more about his own alien species. He was capturing them for some other purpose. Why was my gut telling me this? Because of my earlier insight: that Abel was operating as if he was running a criminal enterprise.

I wound down the secluded Beverly Hills hillside and turned onto the dead-end street of grand houses. Again, I noticed how the houses showed off Hollywood's golden age even under the pale moonlight. Then, for the first time, I wondered if anyone in those houses suspected that one of their neighbors was an extraterrestrial. I doubted it. It was too absurd to even consider. Abel's neighbors probably thought that the home at the end of the lane was owned by a wealthy eccentric who treasured his privacy.

I pulled up to the wrought-iron gate, and it slid open as if Abel had been expecting me. I drove up the driveway, and as I approached the house, the garage door started to open. I didn't need to be told that I was supposed to pull into the garage.

Once inside, I stayed in my car until the garage door closed—I didn't need to be told that either. I thought I might find Ben's BMW in the garage, but the four-car garage was empty. My guess was that Abel had liquefied the car just as he'd liquefied Ben.

The interior door to the house was open. It was an invitation to enter—with the target.

I got out of the car, walked around to the passenger side, and unbuckled Tracy. I picked her up and cradled her in my arms, but when I saw her tranquil, innocent face up close again—Sleeping Beauty—I had to quickly look away. I didn't want the magnitude of my crime to escape from its prison cell in the back of mind.

I carried Sleeping Beauty through the open door, which led to the same hallway I'd walked down last night from the other end—the layman's end, as compared to the employees' end, which was now my territory. For a second, I wished I had remained a layman, that I'd never followed Ben up into the hills. But if I hadn't followed him, I wouldn't be able to give Jenny and Jake and Hannah everything they deserved.

All the doors along the hallway were shut, except one. But tonight the open door wasn't the door to Abel's office. It was a door leading into another room—a room where I was sure I was to deliver the illegal bounty.

I carried Tracy inside and found Abel waiting for me. He was standing next to the only stick of furniture in the room: a loveseat. *If that's not ironic*, I thought, *I don't know what is.* Because whatever was going to happen here, I was certain it didn't have anything to do with love.

I placed Tracy on the loveseat. She drooped sideways onto the armrest, so I adjusted her—my feeble attempt to make her comfortable, pathetic amends for committing a terrible crime against her.

Abel stepped forward as if to say, *I can take over from here.*

I didn't look him up and down, though I desperately wanted to. He was no longer cloaked in the veil of darkness behind his desk. Still, without gawking at him, I took in the basics:

His body was small, maybe four and half feet tall, brown, leathery, and with no distinguishing marks. He was basically humanoid: two legs, two arms, and two hands, one of which was clutching a small black square.

Taking in his entire body didn't change the fact that his all-seeing eye was his dominant feature. He was still the alien Cyclops. And if human eyes were the windows to the soul, the alien's eye was a window whose blind was drawn. The large gleaming oval was a tranquil black sea, its surface completely opaque.

"Wait in the living room," Abel said. "It'll be ten minutes." The alien's electronic voice came from the black square he clutched in his spindly fingers.

As I headed toward the door, I took a closer look at the room. I hoped to gather more information about what Abel was planning to do. But the room gave me no hints. Except for the loveseat, there was absolutely nothing else here.

In the living room, I sat down on the couch. The patio door was open again, and I couldn't help but wonder why. Did the alien like the fresh breeze? Tonight the breeze was light, and I wished it was stronger, much stronger—strong enough to cleanse me of my crime.

Without much to look at inside, I stared at the fountain outside. The base of the fountain had no water in it, as if it hadn't been working for a while. And the gray stone sculpture that rose from the base was so old and worn that, in the moonlight, it looked almost metallic. I couldn't figure out what it was supposed to be. It wasn't a Greek god or goddess, or a lion or bear, or intertwined lovers. It was shaped like an egg or a pinecone, and I wondered whether in the thirties, when this house was built, it was chic to have a fountain that was more abstract.

A sudden gust of wind blew through the woods and into the house, and with it my attention was brought back to the crime— specifically, to the part of the crime I still had to execute: releasing my target back into the wild. Where would I take her? Wouldn't it have to be a place she'd recognize instantly when she came to? But even if that was the case, wouldn't she follow up on why she'd suddenly passed out?

Regardless, I needed to come up with a plan, one where she wouldn't see my face for the second time.

I starting going over the possibilities, but by the time Abel walked into the living room, I hadn't yet decided on a course of action.

"You can return the target now," he said.

I stood up, at his beck and call. "How much time do I have before the tranquilizer wears off?"

Abel handed me a tin box, exactly like the one that held the tranquilizer pellets.

"Place one of these capsules in her mouth," he said. "She'll come to one minute later."

I pocketed the box.

"How did it go when you picked her up?" he asked. His question caught me by surprise. I had expected him to dismiss me.

"Good," I said.

"No problems?"

"No, not really."

"Not really? Does that mean yes, there were problems, or no, there weren't any? I can help with problems."

If Abel had had a regular voice, instead of the monotone synthetic simulation, I might've been able to tell from his tone whether he was genuinely willing to help or not. But as it stood, it was likely that by "help," Abel meant that he'd liquefy me to make the problem go away.

"It went well," I said.

"Good, because I gave you an easy target to start out with."

"Easy?" That worried me.

"I weigh the benefits against the risks for each target. If a target is more valuable, then it's worth more risk. Isn't that how you operate?"

"Yes." But that was a lie. I wasn't a risk taker.

And this must have been easy to pick up on, because Abel asked me point-blank, "Are you a risk taker?"

"I am now." I smiled, and wondered if Abel had gotten the humor. There was just no way to tell.

"What makes one target more valuable than another?" I asked, taking advantage of Abel's sudden interest in conversation.

"To answer that, I'd have to explain more than I want to right now." The synthetic voice was actually sounding friendly. But I was probably imagining that.

"They're commodities, aren't they?" I said. That epiphany had come to me in that moment.

"Yes. They're crops we've grown."

"Crops? How?"

"To use one of your expressions: it's a long story. And it's time for you to return the target."

I didn't press him further. The alien had already given me more information than I ever expected to get on this one visit. Maybe he was friendlier than I'd originally thought—or maybe he was lonely.

Before I exited the living room, I did want to ask him another question. A practical question. A question about returning targets, because I hadn't come up with a plan of my own. *Was there a procedure to follow?*

But I didn't ask. It was clear from his lack of instructions about abducting targets that he wasn't going to give me instructions about returning them either. The nitty-gritty part of the operation fell on the employee, not the employer. But so what? That was no different than any other modern American business, was it?

As I headed back through the living room and down the hallway to pick up Tracy, I remembered my earlier line of reasoning: Abel wasn't giving me any guidance because I'd forced my way into the job. *Sink or swim.* And with that in mind, I entered the "loveseat room," scooped up Tracy, and told myself I had to learn to swim.

When I turned back to the doorway, Abel was standing there.

"Return her to a place she's familiar with," he said, "and when she regains consciousness, she'll believe that's where she passed out. The human mind is easy to fool unless it's faced with major unanswered questions."

Again, I took advantage of Abel's willingness to share. I came up with a roundabout way of asking him my most pressing question.

"Will she remember anything that happened before she passed out?" I asked. I had to know if there was any chance of Tracy remembering that she'd seen my face.

"No," he said. "Which is why she won't remember where she lost consciousness. If the assignment is executed properly, the targets only remember that they passed out. Not the circumstances surrounding it. They may go to a physician to find out why they passed out. But that's where it ends."

That sounded good, except for that pesky adjective "properly" again.

Abel moved aside, indicating it was time for me to get on with the job.

I complied, and headed out of the room, down the hallway, and into the garage. Every step of the way, I was wondering whether I'd executed the assignment "properly"—properly enough to ensure that Tracy wouldn't remember the last face she'd seen before passing out.

I opened the passenger door to my car, and when I bent down to put Tracy into her seat, I saw the bricks of cash: six of them on the driver's seat. Though I didn't know how much they added up to, I saw that they were stacks of hundred-dollar bills, and I knew that there were at least a hundred thousand dollars' worth of those bills.

Nice, I thought. *Very nice.*

I buckled Tracy's seatbelt, then reached over and grabbed the money.

I walked around to the back of the car, and as I put the cash in the trunk, a new question came to me: Where did Abel get the cash?

I was sure that the alien never left his lair, so my bet was that this was an area where his superior technology did all the heavy lifting. He probably siphoned money from bank accounts digitally, converted that money to cash, then had it delivered. Of course, I didn't care how the alien ran this part of his operation, as long as the bricks of cash kept showing up on my driver's seat.

Back on Coldwater, heading down into the Valley, I considered Abel's instructions: return the target to a place she's familiar with. The problem was that I wasn't familiar with the places she was familiar with. I would have been if I'd had more time to trail her. But I needed to work with what I had.

I came up with her gym. I remembered from profiling her that it was in Burbank, on Alameda, about a mile from her place. Alameda was mostly a street of office buildings, so it would be empty for the night. There might be a dimly lit parking structure near her gym where I could leave her.

When I hit Ventura, I didn't turn right onto the boulevard, into the heart of my home turf. Instead, I continued north on Coldwater toward the 101. I'd take the 101 back to Burbank without driving through the streets of Studio City or Valley Village.

On the 101, I realized I couldn't leave the target near her gym. Because of her car. She wouldn't remember where she passed out, but she'd surely realize something was wrong when she regained consciousness in a place she hadn't driven to. As soon as she saw that her car wasn't at the gym, she'd know something was up.

The human mind is easy to fool, Abel had said, *unless it's faced with major unanswered questions.* Leaving Tracy at the gym would give rise to a major unanswered question: How the hell did I get here without my car? And in LA, that question would always demand an answer.

So I had to return her to a location near her apartment. My first thought was to return her to the strip mall—but I didn't see how that could work. I didn't see how I could get away with dropping off a comatose woman at a mall. If someone spotted me, they'd follow up on it. And this time the security cameras wouldn't be recording a boyfriend helping out his diabetic girlfriend. They'd be recording a criminal dumping off his victim.

As I approached the Pass Avenue exit, I thought this through a little more. I considered leaving Tracy right outside her apartment building. Not on Pass Avenue, where there was a lot of traffic, but on the side street, south of her building. Except that, even on a side street, there was a chance a motorist or a pedestrian might spot me dumping her off. I'd have to time it perfectly.

Then another flaw in that plan reared its ugly head: even if I could time it perfectly—making sure the coast was clear on the street—a tenant in Tracy's apartment building, or in one of the other nearby apartment buildings, might peer out their window and spot me.

What I needed was a truly secluded place to dump her. Unlike the abduction itself, which could be pulled off in plain view, the release back into the wild couldn't be.

I approached Tracy's neighborhood without a fixed plan, but when her apartment came into view, I had a flash. I'd rummage through her purse, fish out her keys, wait until the dead of night— when all the tenants in her building were sleeping—and use those keys to enter her building and then her condo.

I'd leave her on her own couch, and no one would be the wiser.

But that crazy flash didn't even last two seconds. It was a desperate idea, diametrically opposed to what I'd concluded at the very start of this assignment. In no way was I ready to break into anyone's apartment.

I looked over at the strip mall, and realized it was my only real option. It was pretty clear that driving aimlessly around Tracy's neighborhood, with her passed out in my car, was stupid. I'd have to leave her in the strip mall, then get on my way. I promised myself that from here on in, I'd always have a plan about returning the targets *before* I delivered them to Abel—if I still had the job after this debacle.

I pulled into the mall parking lot, ready to execute a simple maneuver. My plan was to pull into an open parking space between two cars, far from the security cameras and storefronts. Then I'd get out of my car and casually walk over to the passenger side, checking to make sure no one was close by. If all looked good, I'd open the door, kneel down, out of sight, and pull Tracy out and onto the asphalt. I'd put the capsule in her mouth—the capsule that would revive her—get back into my car, and hightail it out of there.

She'd regain consciousness a minute later, close to home. I imagined she'd wonder what she was doing in the parking lot, but it would be familiar enough, wouldn't it? If Abel's capsule really did its job as advertised, this plan wouldn't leave Tracy with a major unanswered question. After all, I was releasing the target back into the wild less than fifty yards from where I'd captured her. Her only question would be why she had passed out, which Abel had said was normal.

I found an open parking space between a Lexus and an SUV, and I pulled in. *Not bad,* I thought. I was fairly far from the stores, and the SUV acted as a shield. It stood between me and the patrons who were walking along the storefronts.

But then I realized the downside. Though the SUV was a great shield for my dirty work, it kept me from seeing if the coast was clear. Still, no space would be perfect, and the more I cruised around the parking lot with this unconscious woman at my side, the more I risked one of Tracy's neighbors spotting her. To the uninitiated, she was just Sleeping Beauty, but to someone who knew her, she was an unconscious captive in a stranger's car. I'd already gotten away with abducting her on her home court; there was no reason to push my luck.

I got out of my car, then took a couple of seconds to check out the mall. As long as I was standing up, I could see over the SUV. No one was approaching, but the parking aisle I'd chosen gave way to the Starbucks—not the best choice. There was always a lot of foot traffic going in and out of Starbucks. Still, right now, all looked good, so I got on with the job.

I hurried over to the passenger side of my car, then checked the

Starbucks again. Two hipsters stepped out of the store with large coffees. *It figures,* I thought. Hipsters would be the main demo loading up on coffee at this time of night. Hopefully they weren't headed in my direction, but I didn't wait to find out.

I knelt down out of sight, opened the passenger door, and unbuckled Tracy. Then I pulled her into my arms and laid her down on the asphalt. I started to shut the door when—thank God—I saw her purse on the floor.

I grabbed it and placed it beside her.

When I closed the door, my stomach suddenly tightened with fear. She'd been carrying a canvas bag when I'd abducted her. *Shit!* That had been left in the dust. The young woman with the heavy eyeliner, who had trailed me with Tracy's purse, had left behind the canvas bag.

I'd left behind the canvas bag.

Again, it was too late to do anything about it. Way too late.

I pulled the tin box from my pocket, opened it, and grabbed one of the capsules from inside.

I placed it in Tracy's mouth.

Now I had one minute to get the hell out of there.

I stood up, and my eyes immediately fell on the hipsters. They were walking down the row of cars toward me—and I was already calculating the distance between us. Was there enough time to pull out before they got too close? I thought there was. But the worst-case scenario was that I'd pull out just as the hipsters got to my parking space. If that happened, they'd be able to connect my car to the woman lying on the blacktop.

I hurried back around to the driver's side of my car, slid in, started the engine, and began to back out. I didn't dare turn the wheel until I was clear of the entire parking space. Running over the target would be a fitting end to my first mission—a bumbling effort that at best could be called a learning experience.

212

When I cleared the parked space, I turned the wheel and checked over my shoulder for the hipsters—another mistake. They were ten yards away, chatting with each other and not paying attention to me—until I looked at them.

One of them glanced at me and made eye contact.

I looked away, turned the wheel, and drove off. It was appropriate that this assignment had ended the way it had started. Tracy got a look at me during the abduction, and this hipster got a look at me during the return.

Note to self: avoid amateurish bookends.

As I pulled out of the parking lot onto Pass Avenue, I wondered if the hipsters had spotted Tracy's body. She wouldn't yet have regained consciousness as they walked by her, but they would have passed within fifteen feet of her.

I'd never know if they had spotted her or not.

And I hoped I never would.

Because if I did find out, that meant the hipsters had connected me to the body lying unconscious on the blacktop.

I didn't take the 101 home. I didn't need to. It was now safe for me to drive through my home turf. There was no longer any reason to fear neighbors or acquaintances glancing into my car and spotting Sleeping Beauty.

On Moorpark, which was a good distance from the scene of the crime, I went back to the word Abel had used when referring to the targets: "crops." The targets were crops. What did that mean? That humans were nothing but crops to Abel and his species? Crops that grew wild on planet Earth? Was Abel here to *harvest* these crops?

I pictured the entire human race as a wheat field. A wheat field that was ambulatory and far more intelligent than your usual wheat field. These crops could think and feel and create a lasting culture. But still, in the end, they were only a wheat field waiting to be harvested.

But why return the wheat to the field? Why not kill the crop and process it as you would any other crop? That's what we humans did with our crops.

This question had an obvious answer.

You could harvest agricultural crops, kill them, and process them, well within the confines of the law—our laws. But not so if the crops were human. Killing human crops would bring the authorities into the picture. So Abel needed to harvest the crops *and* return them to keep his operation on the down low.

But the crop analogy didn't help when it came to answering the million-dollar question: Why did Abel want the crops at all? What was he taking from the crops? Because he must have been taking something, since the harvest wasn't really the abduction, was it? The harvest was what he was taking from the humans during those fifteen minutes on the loveseat.

Maybe Abel would give me the answer if I was patient. Of course, this was contingent upon Abel giving me another assignment. I supposed he'd first want to see how this one played out. He'd want to see if there was any negative fallout. And I'd be checking for that too—scouring the news and checking police blotters to see if Tracy Miles reported her mysterious abduction.

But the most pressing item on my agenda now was where to stash those bricks of cash. I couldn't deposit them all at once into our bank accounts, even if I spread it around. That amount of money would definitely raise red flags with both Jenny and the banks. I needed to find a safe place to hide the money.

This was a high-class problem if ever there was one—and it rekindled the exhilaration I'd felt at the start of this assignment. That elation came soaring back, and with it came a surge of confidence. I'd started my new job, and for better or worse, I had one assignment under my belt.

JENNY

CHAPTER TWENTY

I couldn't wait much longer. I had to tell Eddie about the new job. I'd already waited far too long. So long that I now found myself sitting next to him in the passenger seat, on the way to meet my oncologist, with this lie of omission still hanging between us. We were on the verge of finding out the results of my first round of chemo treatments, and there was this chasm between us—of my own making. I wanted to be of one mind with my husband. Whether the test results were good or bad, I wanted to look Eddie in the eye and discuss what to do next without this dividing us.

It had already been two weeks since Mimi Quincy had offered me the job—which I'd accepted on the spot. So every time I'd had a conversation with Eddie since then, I'd been lying to him. For how could any conversation be truthful when I was withholding such critical information?

Sure, I had hidden things from him in the past, but they'd all been minor things with no serious repercussions. Like when Jake had gotten a C on that Calculus test in tenth grade. He hadn't studied because he'd spent the weekend prior to the test at a friend's house. He'd asked me not to tell his dad about the grade and promised he'd get an A in the course, which he did.

But hiding a job from Eddie was different. This was a big deal. Especially because I was only one week away from starting. I buttressed myself and turned to Eddie, ready to spill the beans. But when I saw him, absorbed in his own thoughts, staring ahead at the road, my will weakened. It weakened because I had the feeling Eddie already had enough problems of his own.

Since he'd started his new job, he'd been more reticent than usual. I suspected this was because he was under tremendous pressure to deliver, and the learning curve was steep. But I also had this uneasy feeling that his position with ADM wasn't secure—that it was provisional. That though he was paid well, ADM expected him to prove himself before they'd commit to a long-term contract. I even wondered if he'd lied to me—that the job was commission-based and not salaried.

"I think it's going to be good news," Eddie said.

"I hope so." The doctor hadn't given us any hints about the test results.

"You've been feeling pretty good, and that must mean something."

"Maybe... but cancer is sneaky." I'd been feeling good because of the job.

"Boy, you really don't want to get your hopes up, do you?"

"It seems easier to prepare for the worst."

He looked over at me and gave me a warm smile. "We'll be okay no matter what the results are."

He was trying to make me feel better, and I appreciated it, but I didn't have a response. My mind was still on the chasm between us. The longer I waited to tell him about the pilot gig, the bigger our argument would be.

After about a minute of silence, he turned to me again and said, "Oh, I wanted to tell you: ADM is going to reimburse us directly for our medical expenses. They couldn't get around the waiting period for the insurance, so to make good on our agreement, they're paying out of pocket until the waiting period is over."

"Great. That's good." But that worried me. Was the real problem that the job didn't include insurance until he proved himself? *Was the job provisional?* But it felt wrong to be asking questions about his job when I was still being secretive about my own. If I wanted him to be honest about his job, I needed to be honest about mine.

It was possible that I was just using that line of reasoning as an excuse to do what I had to do: tell him the truth so we could be of one mind when talking to the oncologist. But regardless of what the catalyst really was, I forged ahead.

"Eddie, I have something to tell you that you might not like," I said.

He glanced at me, curious. "Sounds kind of ominous."

"Not at all. It's just that… I made a decision about something, and it's a decision you're not going to agree with."

"Okay…"

I could see that he was already getting annoyed. It was time to stop beating around the bush.

"I took a job on a pilot," I said, evenly and calmly.

He reacted immediately: his jaw tightened and his lips pursed. But he didn't say anything.

"You're mad," I said. "And you have every right to be. I should've talked to you about it first."

"I don't want you taking the job," he said. His voice was forceful, but not raised. Not yet anyhow.

"I know. But *I* want the job."

"We don't need the money. And you don't need the physical strain."

"It's a big-budget show," I said, trying not to sound defensive.

"So I'm going to have lots of help."

"I still don't want you to do it." His voice was louder now—and more insistent.

"I need to do it."

"You don't need the physical strain." He pulled into the parking structure next to the medical offices.

"Eddie, I'm not dead. I'm very much alive, and I can work."

"I didn't say you're dead. But we talked about this: you wouldn't work while Hannah and Jake wrap up high school. We agreed to that."

"I know, but things have changed. Drastically. I don't want to sit around the house and think about cancer. Working is the best therapy."

"You don't know that."

"I know that I don't want to sit around the house and wait for test results and count the days between treatments. I know that for sure."

"What about Hannah?" he said. He pulled into a parking space, cut the engine, and turned to me. "She needs you around now. She's making some big decisions on her own and she might need some guidance."

"But you support those decisions."

"I support her new job—that's true."

"Well, I want you to support *my* new job." I got out of the car.

He followed suit, and we headed through the parking structure toward the stairwell.

Because he'd turned silent, I spoke up. "I'm not changing my mind," I said.

"Let's talk about it after we see the doctor." His was response was curt, and that left me cold.

In the waiting room, the receptionist asked for my full payment up front because I was uninsured. And the bill was hefty—eight thousand dollars—because it included a few of the tests I'd just taken.

As I was fishing around in my purse for my wallet, trying to decide what credit card to use, Eddie stepped up to the counter and pulled out his checkbook.

"Can we pay with a check?" he asked the receptionist.

"Yes," she said.

Then Eddie wrote out a check for the full amount. I noticed that it wasn't a check from one of our two checking accounts, but before I could ask him about it, he volunteered an answer.

"I opened a new checking account so that we can keep our medical expenses separate," he said. "That way it's easier for ADM to reimburse us."

"Oh," I said. This was a surprise. A good one.

We sat down to wait for the doctor.

Eddie pulled out his phone and buried himself in the online edition of the *New York Times*. I picked up the nearest magazine—an *Entertainment Weekly*, which I hated—and flipped through it.

Neither of us said a word. When I glanced at Eddie, I saw that his face was taut and his eyes narrowed. He was angry.

Luckily, the doctor didn't make us wait long, and as the nurse led us back to his office, Eddie and I made eye contact for the first time since our argument in the parking lot. The look between us said it all. No words were needed. It was clear that the battle over my job had been overwhelmed by the gravity of what was to unfold in the next few minutes: Would the news be good or bad?

We sat down in front of the doctor's desk.

"The doctor will be with you in a couple of minutes," the nurse said. Then she exited.

We sat in silence. But this time the silence was deafening. And it seemed to be full of dread. Which was probably why I decided to resume our argument. Arguing was better than dread.

"Eddie," I said, "the job is only for six weeks. And it fits right in between treatments."

"We can talk about it later."

"I know. I just wanted to tell you. It's only six weeks."

"I got it."

I didn't say anything more. He was angrier than I'd thought. Maybe the doctor's appearance would lessen the tension between us.

Dr. Rainer was an upbeat guy. When I'd been told I could pick any oncologist as my lead doctor—which was the only silver lining of not having health insurance—I settled on Dr. Rainer almost immediately. He was calm and had a positive attitude that wasn't phony. He didn't sugarcoat my diagnosis, and he didn't pretend that a miracle was around the corner. But when it came to treatments, he was optimistic. He believed in what he prescribed. He told me that every treatment he prescribed, for me and for any of his patients, was the best option out there today.

And I believed him. It was hard not to. He'd had cancer himself. And when he'd chosen his own treatments, he'd thoroughly researched them all. He told me that he'd promised himself that he'd always do the same when it came to the treatments for his patients.

He walked into the office and greeted me with a direct question, as usual. "How are you feeling, Jenny?" he asked.

"Good," I said. "Especially the last couple of weeks."

"Great! I'm glad to hear it." He sat down at his desk, but he didn't open a file and glance at some report, as if he needed a reminder of what was going on with his patients.

"I know you want to get right down to business," he said.

"That would be nice." I looked over at Eddie, and then back to the doctor.

"Well, you'll be happy then," he said.

"Really?" I was shocked. So shocked that I finally admitted to myself that I really had been expecting the worst.

I reached out, put my hand on Eddie's arm, and glanced at him. He was already smiling, his anger long gone.

"The results were good," Dr. Rainer said. "The tumor shrank. Not much, but considering that at this stage we're only hoping to keep it in check, it's a great outcome."

"Wow," I said. "I can't believe it." I was as thankful as I'd ever been.

"I'm adding my own 'wow,'" Eddie said. "And I know this is probably too much to hope for, but does this mean that the long-term prognosis is better now?"

"Great question," Dr. Rainer said. "But that's a tough call at this point. It's way too early to say. But for now, it's pretty much the best outcome you could hope for."

"Thank you, doctor," I said.

Rainer laughed. "I didn't do anything."

"You picked the right treatment," I said.

"In this case, it wasn't rocket science. The choices were limited."

I leaned back in my chair and let the good news sink in deeper. Had I been feeling better over the last couple of weeks because I actually *was* better? Maybe it wasn't the anticipation of the pilot gig.

Eddie put his hand over mine. That felt nice. He was enjoying the moment with me.

"Does this change the course of the treatments from here on in?" I asked.

"No." Rainer seemed confident in his answer. "I think we should continue with the next phase as planned."

"So we're still going to wait eight weeks to start again?"

"Yes."

"You don't think it might be worth getting more aggressive now?"

223

IRVING BELATECHE

I kind of wanted to go in for the kill, while the tumor was on the run. For that, I'd forgo taking the pilot job.

"I think we should stick to the plan for now," Dr. Rainer said. "If it ain't broke, don't fix it. And we have to consider the big picture. If we jump into the next treatment too soon, we won't be giving your immune system enough time to recover. And that's part of the calculation."

"That makes sense," I said.

Dr. Rainer smiled. "Just enjoy the next eight weeks."

*

On the way back to the car, I felt even better than I had over the last two weeks. But I understood that I wasn't home free. It was crystal clear that Rainer hadn't changed my prognosis. Regardless of the good news, I still had only two years to live—actually less now, since it had been months since my original diagnosis.

When Eddie and I made it back to the parking structure, he turned to me and said, "This was great news. I'm sorry we argued."

"Me too." But we hadn't settled the argument, had we?

"Why don't you text the kids and let them know?" he said.

"I don't want to get their hopes up."

"Why not?" He grinned.

He was right. Better to get their hopes up and let them enjoy the good times, rather than having them live in a constant state of fear that the worst was just around the corner.

As soon as we got in the car, I pulled out my phone and texted Jake. And while I was composing my text to Hannah, Jake texted me back. His text was pure joy: "Congratulations" followed by five exclamation points, two smiley faces, and a hands clapping icon. *He's a great kid,* I thought.

I sent the text off to Hannah. "Okay. I'm done getting their hopes up," I said.

224

Eddie laughed.

Then neither of us said anything as we started on our way home.

The seconds turned into minutes, and I realized that the tension between us was growing again.

He addressed it first. "You want to talk about the pilot," he said.

"Yeah—I do. But I don't want to fight again."

"Then let's not."

"I don't see how that's possible."

"It's possible like this: I'm okay with you taking the job."

"What?" The turnaround shocked me almost as much as Dr. Rainer's good news had.

"I'm sorry I made a big deal about it," he said.

"Why'd you change your mind?"

"It's like you said. Everything's changed. And it's continuing to change. And I have to get used to it."

So that was that. I was going to be working on the Disney pilot.

*

When we got home, we got another piece of good news. At least, I thought it was good news. Eddie got a call from Larry about a job possibility—a job as a journalist. But his reaction was strange. He didn't ask Larry any questions about it, as if he wasn't planning to follow up on the lead. And he didn't seem too excited about the prospect of getting back into the journalism game either.

So when he got off the phone, I said, "I guess you're liking the new job."

"Yeah. I am. So far," he said. "But I'm still learning the ropes."

"So you wouldn't consider going back to journalism?"

"I don't know. I guess the money is better at ADM, and I kind of like that."

"Nothing beats the money when you're working for the man," I said.

"Yep," he said, as if that was the bottom line. Which—
considering he just wrote a check for more than eight thousand
dollars—it was.

He then set himself down in the den and buried himself in his
computer. This was part of his routine with ADM. He'd spend a
good chunk of time on his computer, doing research, then he'd spend
a few days out of the house conducting interviews. And whether or
not the job was provisional, he'd decided to go all in. He'd bought a
more expensive and more powerful computer a couple of weeks
ago—a MacBook Air—which didn't surprise me because he was
spending so much time on the computer.

What did surprise me was that he didn't give his old computer to
Jake. Not that Jake needed another laptop; he had a fairly new laptop
himself. But Jake wanted it so he could experiment with it—get into
the operating system, play with the code, et cetera. I didn't
understand the details, except that "modifications" was the operative
word.

Eddie told him that he needed to keep the old computer, just in
case he later found out that some information didn't get transferred
over to the new MacBook Air. And even though Jake volunteered to
make sure everything was transferred, Eddie didn't budge.

Then I noticed that the old computer had disappeared. Or at
least, it wasn't anywhere to be found in the house. And when I asked
Eddie what he'd done with it, he said he'd sold it on Craigslist.

"I thought you wanted to keep it," I said.

"Jake was right. All the information was transferred."

"Then why didn't you give it to Jake?"

"Every penny counts," he said. "I got a few hundred bucks for it."

I couldn't argue with that—I was the reason we needed every
penny. But I still thought it was strange that he didn't give the
computer to Jake.

*

When evening fell, Eddie was still entrenched in the den. I made dinner, and he took a break to eat with Jake and me. Hannah didn't get off work at Gregory Brothers until eight.

It would have been nice for all of us to have dinner together, basking in the good news as a family, but I was happy that at least Jake could join us. I had gotten his hopes up, and Eddie had been right about that. It hadn't been a bad thing to do. And it put me in an even better frame of mind than I already was.

In the midst of a lively conversation—where Eddie, Jake, and I were debating the merits of China's state-controlled capitalism—I guiltily admitted to myself that this dinner was more fun without Hannah here. If she'd been at the table, there would have been a constant threat of a flare-up. She resented my lack of support over her decision to quit the swim team. And truth be told, I still wasn't totally on board with her decision.

After dinner, Eddie went back to work in the den, and I went through the production design notes that Mimi had sent me. I'd already made a list of the props I'd definitely need, and I was now working on a list of props that would add to Mimi's vision for the show, but which weren't necessary. What I called the "sprinkles on the cake."

At eight-thirty, I heard Hannah walk through the front door. I had asked her to text me when she got off work and was ready for a ride home, but she hadn't. And walking home alone at night was already becoming a habit. I didn't like it, and neither did Eddie, regardless of Hannah's argument that we lived in a good neighborhood. Eddie had bought her a small can of mace, which she reluctantly agreed to keep in her purse, but that didn't ease our worry.

Still, I knew I'd have to get over it, unless I wanted to fight about it on regular basis.

When Hannah walked into the kitchen, I offered to warm up some dinner for her.

"Great," she said. "I have to study for a French quiz, and I'd like to get started."

"Okay. Come back in ten minutes, and it'll be ready."

"Thanks. And I'm really happy about your test results, Mom." She followed that up with one of her beautiful, beaming smiles—genuinely happy—and it melted my heart.

"Thank you, sweetheart," I said. I felt terribly guilty for thinking our dinner was more fun without her at the table. I was a terrible mother.

Hannah turned to go when I remembered that I hadn't told her the other bit of news.

"Oh—that reminds me," I said. "There's another update. I'm going to be working on a pilot starting next week."

She turned back to me. "You're kidding. I thought no work until you get rid of me and Jake."

"I thought so, too. But I wanted to take this job."

"Hmm, sounds familiar," she said, grinning.

I could've said, *But I didn't quit the swim team,* upping the stakes, but I was the adult, so I kept my mouth shut.

"Are you sure you should do it?" she said.

"You don't think I should?"

"I don't mean because you have to wait until Jake and I are out of your hair, but because you're sick. Maybe it's not the best idea."

Like father, like daughter, I thought, but I said, "It'll be okay. It's six weeks and the timing is perfect. It's between treatments." Then I got up to get her dinner ready.

"I don't know…" she said, hesitating, like she was thinking it through. "Aren't you supposed to use the break between treatments to take it easy? To recover?"

"Thank you, doctor," I said, and regretted it immediately. It was harsh—the kind of thing Jake would have said to her.

"It's just my opinion," she said. "But we know what you think about my opinion. Not much!"

"I'm sorry, honey—it's just that—"

"Save your apology. I get it. You can do what you want, and you don't give a crap about what anyone else thinks. But if I do what *I* want, all hell breaks loose!"

She marched out of the kitchen.

I knew better than to follow her out and try to repair the damage. If I did, all hell *would* break loose. That's just the way it went between us. So I let it go and prepared a dinner plate for her. I'd bring it to her room, where I was sure she'd accept it with a terse "thank you." I'd respond with a friendly "you're welcome," and we'd pretend that all was well between us.

That was fine. Because today had turned out to be a great day. My cancer was on the run—sort of—and I was no longer hiding anything from Eddie. There were no longer any lies between us. The chasm was gone.

EDDIE

CHAPTER TWENTY-ONE

I had packed some clothes and was waiting for the morning rush hour to die down before heading to San Diego, home of my next target. Jenny was running errands, still catching up on the various things she'd fallen behind on during the pilot gig—which had turned out well for both of us.

She'd been tired but cheerful during the entire stretch, and that cheer had lasted. It had now been over month since the gig had ended, and she was still riding high. It had worked out well for me, too. During the gig, Jenny had almost always been on the set or out gathering more props, so I'd had the house to myself for hours on end and didn't have to hide my nefarious activities from her. Maybe that was the reason there'd been no more major screw-ups since that first abduction.

I had now abducted six more targets, and with each abduction, I felt like I'd gotten better at the job. I'd started using Ben's MO, instead of the boyfriend-carries-his-diabetic-girlfriend-to-the-car routine. I felt more comfortable with my original ruse, but it had one major flaw: there was always the chance that a bystander to the abduction might know the target and thus know I was not the target's boyfriend. Ben's doctor routine didn't have that flaw, but I still wanted to come up with an MO that better fit my temperament.

By my fifth abduction, I was able to pull off the doctor ruse fairly smoothly. Smoothly enough that the highlight of the job wasn't some little mistake I'd made, it was the conversation I'd had with Abel after I delivered the target. Up to that point on the job, Abel had been tight-lipped. The alien had said so little that I no longer thought he was lonely. But that night, Abel wanted to talk.

He walked into the living room after finishing with the target, but instead of telling me tersely that it was time to return her, he said, "I'm going to give you an assignment outside of Los Angeles. It won't be your next target, but the one after that."

"Should I prepare anything special?" I asked.

"No."

So I wondered why he had told me in advance, if I didn't have to make any extra preparations. But when he didn't turn to exit, I thought maybe he just wanted to talk. So I tested out my theory by asking another question.

"Abel. Will you tell me what you actually do with the targets?" I asked. I figured if he wanted to talk, I might as well make it worth it.

"Is it important that you know?"

"I'm curious. Especially because you used the term 'crops.'"

"You know what they say. Curiosity killed the cat."

"That's what *we* say."

"That's my point. There's a reason you say it.'"

I couldn't argue with that, and though he wasn't answering my question, he also wasn't exiting the room. For me, that confirmed that he wanted to continue the conversation.

So I followed up with a less intrusive question, one I thought I already knew the answer to, but which would lay the groundwork for what I really wanted to ask. "Abel," I said, "why do you need human agents to carry out the abductions?"

"Your predecessor figured that one out pretty quickly."

"Too many wildcards outside these walls," I said. "Anything can go wrong at any time, and it's not worth taking that chance."

"That's right."

With that confirmed, I thought I could move on to the topic I really wanted to explore. I had come to believe that the alien's primary concern—what kept him from interacting with humans any more than he needed to—was not that humans might discover him, but that his *own kind* might discover him. He feared them, and that was the chief motivation behind his hands-off approach. And the longer I worked for the alien, the more I was convinced that this was his real concern. After all, it seemed that Abel had enough technological tricks up his sleeve to evade human detection fairly easily. He could point any investigation in another direction by creating phony, digital footprints—fake evidence.

But just before I was about to ask about this, I decided not to. I don't know why. Maybe it was my instinct suddenly telling me that I had to keep some cards to myself. But whatever it was that led to that decision, I'd later be thankful for it. Because, as it turned out, there would a far better time to bring this up.

And then, as if Abel knew that I had zeroed in on his real fear, he said, "Time to return the target." And he turned away and headed out of the living room, bringing the conversation to an end.

*

I put my overnight bag in the car, which I now kept in the garage, then went back into the house. I went online and checked the 5 for traffic, scanning all the way down to San Diego to see if the rush hour had abated. It hadn't.

So I turned on the TV and began to flip through the channels until I landed on the KTLA morning show; it was running a report about Ben's disappearance. The report was just a rehashing of old facts. It had been months since Ben had vanished, so his disappearance had dropped off of everyone's radar screen—except mine. And Ben's wife's and Mason's. That was for sure.

Diane, Ben's wife, had reported him missing in the wee hours of the morning after Abel had murdered him. But I didn't see the report appear in any of the police blotters until forty-eight hours later. When it hit the blotters, the local news ran with it, and ran with it hard. It made for a good mystery on two levels. First, Ben had vanished without a trace. And second, reporters had found the same thing I'd found when looking into Ben's past—that the last ten years of the man's life had been spent in relative anonymity.

And soon, information about the case itself started to trickle out—information that added to the mystery and made it more intriguing. I first saw these "facts" on the police blotters. Detectives had dug up evidence that Ben had met with a Russian businessman in Malaysia, that he'd flown to Moscow twice, and that he'd also traveled to New York and Dallas for unspecified and secretive meetings. There was also evidence that linked Ben to a mysterious hedge fund, incorporated offshore.

I was sure that all of these "facts," these digital footprints, were misinformation. Misinformation planted by Abel. As a matter of fact, it was the way this case had unfolded that had led me to conclude that Abel had the means to redirect any investigation.

When reporters got hold of some of these facts, they spun a story, connecting Ben's work with this mysterious hedge fund to his sudden disappearance. Their theories ranged from Ben taking the fall for a big investment gone horribly wrong to Ben double-crossing a Russian investor.

But eventually the story faded, and that faded version was what I was watching now on KTLA. The story was part of a continuing series on KTLA's late morning show, a series where a reporter revisited old, unsolved police cases. But the series never revealed any new information about those cases. Still, I somehow thought that maybe there'd be something new. Not that I wanted there to be. For why would I want KTLA, or the police, any closer to solving the case?

Guilt. That was why.

The clip ended, and it left me thinking about Mason and the promise I'd made to myself months ago—to make sure the kid and his mom knew about the money in the safe. To make up for my sin. Mason was smart and had a great future ahead of him—if he was surviving this tragic setback. The tragic setback that I'd caused.

I considered offering to tutor him again. Wouldn't that lead to a natural way to let Mason and his mom know about the safe?

*

The drive down to San Diego went by fast. I had timed it perfectly.

I pulled into Del Mar, a small coastal enclave a few miles north of San Diego proper, and home to Wendy Bester, my next target. She lived in the heart of a wealthy hillside neighborhood that overlooked Del Mar's quaint town center and the Pacific Ocean. But she didn't live in one of the expensive houses on that hillside; she lived in a small guesthouse behind one of those houses.

I drove up to Lunela Drive, her street. From the Google satellite image, I knew that the guesthouse was located at the back of the property, far from the main house, and that a small cluster of trees and bushes shielded it from the main house. I was sure this was for privacy purposes—to separate landlord from tenant—and I would use it to my advantage.

I would kidnap the target right outside her home.

The main hurdle would be getting to the back of the property without being seen. A long driveway went from the street, past the main house, to the guesthouse in the back. But to determine if I could use the driveway without being spotted by Rose David—the elderly woman who lived in the main house—I first had to take a closer look at the property.

So I parked a couple of blocks ways, then walked back to Lunela Drive, acting as if I was a tourist taking in Del Mar's hillside views of the Pacific Ocean, taking pictures of the sweeping vistas with my cell phone. It was a ruse I liked far better, and felt far more comfortable with, than playing doctor.

When I got to Rose David's property, I slowed down to study it. I decided that the best way to make it to the back of the property without being seen was to go along the south side of the house, the side without the driveway, because it had fewer first-floor windows. So if I stuck very close to the house and ducked under those windows, no one in the house would see me. And I didn't have to worry about neighbors, because Leyland cypress trees stood in tall, neat rows, like guards on perpetual duty, creating what amounted to a wall around the property.

But to get to the south side of the house, I would first need to make it across the front lawn without being seen. I would be totally exposed for that stretch, which was roughly twenty-five yards. Again, neighbors weren't a problem; I would be shielded to the north and south by those cypress trees, and the house across the street was much farther down the hillside, as were all the houses on the opposite side of Lunela Drive.

The only risk of being spotted during those twenty-five yards came from Rose David herself. There was a large bay window at the front of the house through which she could survey the front lawn. Because of her age—she was eighty—I doubted she'd be lurking near that window, or any other windows, but it was still a possibility.

I had also checked to see if she had family that might be nearby and could potentially be visiting during the abduction. But it turned out that her only child, a son, lived and worked in San Francisco, and I'd checked to confirm that he wasn't visiting.

After looking over the property, I decided that I would risk the trip across the lawn. I was confident that I could pull it off because I was going to have an accomplice: the cover of night.

Then I turned my attention to where to park my car during the abduction. I was uneasy about parking it in front of the house. It would sit there during the operation, and it might raise a red flag, especially because there were no other cars on the street. Rose's neighbors parked their cars in their driveways.

I supposed that if one of Rose's neighbors drove by and saw my car parked on the street, they'd think Rose had a visitor, which I was fine with. But if Rose herself spotted my car, she'd wonder what it was doing parked in front of her house.

However, I needed my car stationed at the edge of Rose's lawn because I'd be returning from the guesthouse with Wendy Bester in my arms.

So far, I didn't have a solution to this problem.

There was also the matter of video surveillance cameras. Though I'd done a thorough Internet search to confirm that no home security firm listed Rose David as a client, that wasn't ironclad proof that she didn't have cameras set up. I perused the property, but didn't see any.

I then walked back to my car and drove down the serpentine hillside streets to the town center. Here, unlike the deserted streets above, there were plenty of locals and tourists. They were shopping, taking in the sights, and eating in the many restaurants.

I found a parking spot, pulled in, and opened my new MacBook Air. Not only had I decided to use a VPN when researching targets on the Internet, I'd also decided to buy a new computer every few weeks and dump the old one. Of course, I was buying the exact same model so that Jenny, Jake, and Hannah wouldn't notice how fast I was going through computers.

I connected to the Internet using a Mobi hotspot, one that I'd paid for in cash, then checked out the satellite maps of the hillside again. Now that I'd walked the neighborhood, I wanted to see if I'd missed a place where I could park my car so it wouldn't raise a red flag. I came up empty.

I closed my laptop, then got out of my car and looked for a place to grab some lunch. I ended up at a small café called the Sun and Moon, where I ordered a coffee and sandwich. While I ate, I ran through my plan again, but I didn't have any breakthroughs about where to park the car.

After lunch, I had a few hours to kill before the target would return home from work. I strolled along the streets until I came to a small, beautiful park that faced the ocean. There, I found an empty bench and made myself at home.

I stared out at the blue Pacific. The ocean was calm and the sun glinted off the water. After about ten minutes or so, that same calmness settled over me, too. I was feeling relaxed. More so than I'd felt for a long, long time. My family was doing well and the job was going fine.

And the money was piling up.

I breathed in the salty air, and my gaze slowly followed the blue-green ocean out to the horizon. I was enjoying the scenery, far different from the Valley's long ribbons of light, and thinking about the target. Wendy Bester managed a small art gallery in La Jolla, which was a ritzy beachfront town a dozen miles south of Del Mar. On weekdays, the art gallery closed at seven, so she'd be pulling up to her guesthouse at around seven-thirty—

Right then, I had a breakthrough. I solved the problem of where to park my car. Just like that, the solution was crystal clear.

I'd use *her* car.

I'd find a long-term parking lot where I would park my own car, then I'd walk up to Lunela Drive, and under the cover of night I'd stealthily make my way to the guesthouse and wait in the shadows for Wendy to return from the art gallery. She'd drive up the driveway, to the back of the property, get out of her car, and I'd tranquilize her as she stepped up to the guesthouse. Then I'd carry her back to her own car and whisk her away. And if Rose noticed Wendy's car pulling into the driveway and then pulling out shortly afterward, so what? It might seem a bit weird, but certainly not call-the-police weird.

After transferring Wendy to my car—I wouldn't want to get pulled over in hers—I'd leave her car in the parking lot while I drove to LA. To pull this off, I needed to find a parking lot without an attendant, so I wouldn't have to conceal Sleeping Beauty as I drove onto the lot and out in different cars.

Were there other problems I needed to work out with this scenario? I decided that there probably were, but I wasn't picking up on them for now.

I went back to my car and opened my laptop to search for a parking lot. But before I even began, I realized I couldn't park in a lot in Del Mar. I didn't want to risk someone recognizing Wendy's car. I'd have to park farther away, then take a cab back to Del Mar before walking up to Lunela.

After googling parking lots, I found one near a cluster of large hotels just north of San Diego, off the 5. It was about thirty minutes away.

I drove over there to see if it fit the bill.

The lot turned out to be a five-story parking structure, and as advertised, it was automated; there was no attendant. It required a ticket for entry and exit, and you paid the parking fee at a credit card kiosk before exiting.

I pulled into the structure and drove up to the fourth level, where there were fewer than a dozen cars parked. I checked for video surveillance cameras. There weren't any. Then I staked out a parking space that couldn't be seen from the stairwell or from the outer perimeter of the parking structure.

I parked, walked over to one of the nearby hotels, five blocks away, and took a cab back to the Del Mar town center. I had a few more hours to go before my next move, and I spent them checking out the little shops. When day turned into evening, I walked back to the oceanfront and took in the gorgeous sunset. They sky went from a blazing reddish orange, to purple, to a deep, rich blue.

In the luminous twilight, I headed up to Lunela. I wanted to be lying in wait before Wendy got back from work.

But the time I hit Lunela, night had fallen. Again, the street was deserted. No cars and no people. I walked casually toward Rose David's house.

When I got to the front of Rose David's property, I saw that first-floor lights were on, as were a couple of second-floor lights. But I didn't see anyone on the other side of the bay window.

I stepped onto the lawn and scooted toward the south side of the house, checking the second-floor windows as I went. And then my plan suddenly went awry—

Rose David was staring out the bay window.

Panic surged through me, and I froze.

But then—and the only possible explanation for this was that I was actually changing—I adapted. I did my job. I came up with a new plan on the spot.

I'd hide in plain sight.

I smiled at Rose David, though I wasn't sure she could see my face from this distance, and I headed to the front door and rang the doorbell.

It took Rose more than a minute to get to the door, and when she opened it, I was presented with a slightly built woman, her white hair done neatly up in a bun. She wore a wide smile, and the wrinkles on her face made her look every bit her age. But she had aged gracefully—those wrinkles were smiling too, as if she always saw the bright side of life.

"Hello," she said. "What can I do for you?"

"I'm looking to rent a place in Del Mar, and one of your neighbors mentioned that you rented out your guesthouse."

"That's right. But I'm sorry. I've already got a tenant."

"Oh. That's too bad." I laughed. "I mean too bad for me."

She laughed with me. "I wish I could suggest another rental property in the hills, but there aren't many. Most of the rentals are down by the beach."

"Yeah. I know. I checked a lot of them out, but I like the seclusion up here."

"So do we," she said, and chuckled. She was charming.

"Is there any chance that your tenant might be moving out in the next few months?" I asked.

"I don't think so. She's pretty stable."

"Okay…" I said, and shook my head, feigning disappointment. "I'm sorry I bothered you."

"No bother. I hope you find a place."

"Thank you." I turned to leave, and as I slowly walked away, I listened for the door to close behind me.

As soon as I heard it click shut, I sprinted over to the driveway and ran down it toward the guesthouse. I knew I could get to the guesthouse before Rose had gotten anywhere near a window, judging by how long it had taken her to get to the front door.

Less than a minute later, I was standing next to the guesthouse. And just like the satellite images had revealed, it was isolated from the main house.

But not as isolated as I'd thought.

The north side, where the driveway ended, was completely shielded from the main house. But the front of the guesthouse, which faced the main house, wasn't. On the satellite image, it had looked like the cluster of trees and bushes between the houses was thicker.

This meant it was time to refine my plan once again. I couldn't tranquilize Wendy in front of the guesthouse without taking a chance on Rose spotting the whole nasty affair. I had to tranquilize Wendy as soon as she got out of her car.

So the next step was to find a spot where I could station myself. And, like a big game hunter waiting for his prey, it had to be a spot where Wendy wouldn't see me as she pulled in. But it also had to be a spot that was close enough to her to allow me to fire the tranquilizer pellet without missing her.

There weren't any trees, hedges, or shrubs along the driveway behind which I could hide. I considered hiding behind the back corner of the guesthouse, but then what? When Wendy stepped out of her car and I stepped out from behind the house, she'd spot me.

I had roughly fifteen minutes to come up with a better plan. I scanned the terrain a few times before I reluctantly accepted that I couldn't tranquilize Wendy as soon as she got out of her car. Under the circumstances, the best plan was to hide in the cluster of trees and bushes in front of the guesthouse. From there, not only would I be able to track Wendy as she made her way from her car to her front door, but after she passed by me, I'd also be able to surreptitiously creep out from my hiding spot, without being seen, until I was right behind her.

The downside was that I risked being spotted by Rose. But I had no choice.

So I decided to head to the cluster of trees by going around the back of the guesthouse; there was no reason to risk Rose spotting me before the abduction had even begun.

That decision changed everything.

As I was walking along the back of the guesthouse, I saw that a window was cracked open. I didn't hesitate; this was my chance to tranquilize Wendy in the privacy of her own home. There was no possibility of Rose witnessing it.

I pushed the window open, climbed into Wendy's house, and found myself in her bedroom. I didn't spend any time there. I headed into the living room, which gave way to the front door. After a quick look around, I knew what to do.

I positioned myself to the side of the front door.

When Wendy entered, she'd open the door toward me, so I'd be hidden. Then she'd step inside, reach back to close the door behind her, and I'd fire the tranquilizer. It would take effect before the door even closed. I just had to make sure to stay out of her field of vision for a second and a half.

I pulled the copper straw and tin of pellets from my pocket, and I stuck a pellet in the straw.

Then I began the vigil. It was a short one. Eight minutes later— eight minutes of wondering why the hell I'd changed my MO now that I had it down, and telling myself it was because I was learning to adapt and that I was more comfortable with this scenario—I heard Wendy's car rolling up the driveway.

Though I felt anxious, I had long since stopped feeling panicky when it came to the actual abduction. I'd learned to let my exhilaration, which was now building, take over, rather than my fear. I guess when it came right down to it, practice had given me more confidence, and instead of succumbing to worry and panic, I rode the buzz of the hunt.

The sound of the car's engine died, and a few seconds later, a car door slammed. I gripped the copper tube tightly, and I took a couple of slow, calming breaths.

Twenty seconds later, a key turned in the lock. Then I saw the doorknob twist—and the door swung open toward me.

I brought the copper straw to my lips, and when I caught sight of Wendy moving past the door—before she reached back to close it—I blew through the straw.

Instantly she lost her balance and stumbled. She tried to catch herself, but the tranquilizer was too powerful.

I waited—for exactly a second and a half.

When she lost consciousness and her body fell toward the floor, I glided forward and caught her. Then I pushed the door closed with my foot, pulled her more securely into my arms, and carried her to the couch. I laid her down and took a few seconds to let the buzz of the hunt wear off.

The next step was to get her into her car and drive off the property. But I suddenly realized I had the opportunity to improve my plan a hundredfold. I wouldn't head out right away. I'd wait fifteen minutes, so Rose wouldn't wonder why her tenant had arrived home and then left seconds later. Instead, it would look like Wendy had come home, taken a few minutes to change, and then headed back out.

I turned on the lights, as Wendy would have done when she arrived home after dark; Rose would expect to see the lights on back here. Then I went through Wendy's purse, fished out her car keys, and sat down. I didn't look at Wendy. I no longer liked to look at the targets. Keeping my eyes averted from them was a form of denial, but it was necessary. It was one of the reasons my confidence was high.

Instead of staring at the target, I looked over her place. She had good taste, which didn't surprise me since she worked in an art gallery. The furniture was graceful and warm, and so were the paintings on the walls. I turned my attention to them to pass the time.

They were original oils of one of the magnificent hillsides of Del Mar. Each painting featured the hillside at a different time of day, from dawn to dusk. You could see how the change in light transformed the hillside. In the dawn's muted light, everything was just shadows and shapes, full of potential. In the midmorning's bright light, the hillside was sharp, the colors almost too brilliant to distinguish from one another. In the afternoon's light, the hill had turned into a swatch of bursting color, with dozens of hues of orange, green, pink, and purple.

After about fifteen minutes had passed, during which I studied those paintings, I decided it was time to go. I got up, shut off the lights, and walked over to the couch. I scooped Wendy up and headed to the door. There, I stopped and braced myself for the next step: I had to get to the driveway, which was hidden from Rose's view, as fast as possible.

I took in a deep breath, let it out, and opened the door—

Rose was standing on the doorstep, holding a plate covered with aluminum foil.

Her eyes immediately fell on Wendy, cradled in my arms.

Then she looked up at me. She wasn't smiling.

"What's going on?" she said.

"I don't know," I said. "She passed out and I'm taking her to the hospital." *Lame.*

"But why you are back here?" she asked.

It was clear that she wasn't buying my lie, but I went on with it anyway. "I came back here to talk to her directly about renting the place. To see she if she was planning to move out soon."

"But I don't under—" she said, then stopped herself, probably concluding that she *did* understand.

"I'm calling the police," she blurted out, and turned to go.

I let Wendy's legs drop to the ground, and with my free hand I reached into my pocket and pulled out the copper straw and tin of pellets. But to do what I needed to do, I had to have both hands free.

So I laid Wendy down on the floor and took off after Rose.

As I did, I loaded a pellet into the straw. Rose was shuffling across the back yard, trying her damnedest to move quickly, but her age worked against her. I caught up to her in the blink of an eye and shot the tranquilizer pellet into her back.

The plate she was carrying fell to the ground, and its contents— chicken breast and broccoli—spilled out.

A second later, Rose was falling into my arms, unconscious.

I carried her into the guesthouse, stepping over Wendy's body in the doorway, and placed her on the couch. I wondered if the tranquilizer would affect her in the same way it affected the targets, who were all much younger women.

Would Rose rest peacefully?

Or more to the point: Would the tranquilizer kill her because of her age?

I could see she was breathing, so the answer was no. At least, for now.

Now what? Time to adapt—again.

I could revive Rose, but I didn't like the idea of doing so and then leaving her to her own devices while I trekked up to LA and back with Wendy. What if the revival capsules worked differently on victims that weren't the intended targets? What if the capsules didn't wipe out Rose's memory? What if she came to and remembered she'd witnessed the abduction?

She'd go to the police.

I decided it would be far better to revive Rose after returning from LA with Wendy. That way, when Rose came to, Wendy wouldn't be missing. So even if Rose did remember what happened, Wendy wouldn't—and I knew this for sure from the other abductions. Wendy wouldn't be able to confirm Rose's story, except for the part about fainting. And if Rose went to the police, they'd quickly lose interest in the case: the victim was fine and recalled nothing, and there was no evidence of a crime.

Also, if I was lucky, the police might suspect Rose had imagined the whole thing due to her advanced age.

With my decision made, I moved forward as fast I could.

First, I dealt with a minor detail that for some reason worried me. I went back outside and scooped the chicken and broccoli back onto the plate, using the aluminum foil. Then I buried it all, including the plate, in one of the trash bags in Rose's trashcan.

With that done, I got on with the rest of my night.

On the way to the parking structure, with the latest incarnation of Sleeping Beauty riding shotgun, I admitted to myself that there was another reason to wait until after returning from LA to revive Rose—a reason that had influenced my decision even though I hadn't wanted to think about it. By waiting to revive Rose, I'd given myself the opportunity to ask Abel how I could fix the problem. Of course, this meant admitting to the alien that I'd screwed up. Only then could I ask him for help.

I'd never told him about my first screw-up—the night the target had seen my face just before she'd lost consciousness. I supposed I could've told him about it anytime during the string of successful abductions that had followed. Certainly by then I'd gained a little of the alien's trust. If I had told him—and survived the consequences—I would have known a little more about how he might react to tonight's blunder.

But this blunder was much bigger. And that was one of the very reasons I *had* to tell Abel about it. Before I did something that made it worse.

I made it to the parking structure, parked Wendy's car next to my own, and transferred her over.

Ten minutes later, I was on the 5, headed back to LA.

On the trip, I braced myself for my confession. I knew I had no choice but to let Abel know I'd tranquilized an innocent bystander. If I couldn't find the courage to confess my screw-up to Abel, then I would confess out of fear. The fear that I'd executed this assignment about as far away from "properly" as possible.

*

I sat in Abel's living room, waiting for the alien to harvest whatever it was he was harvesting. I stared at the fireplace and girded myself for my confession. My eyes fell on the poker, tong, and shovel set, and I suddenly flashed onto a horrible image: Abel uncharacteristically getting upset at my stupidity, and lashing out at me by grabbing the fire poker and bashing me to death with it. Wouldn't that be a far better death than Abel liquefying me in the red cone of light?

Abel walked into the living room. "You can return the target now," he said, and immediately turned to leave.

I wished he had said something more, indicating he wanted to chat, like he'd done on the night of the fifth abduction. That would have made it easier to confess. But he didn't.

So I stood up. "I had a slight problem with the target," I blurted out. Then I clarified my statement. "Actually, not with her, but with her landlord."

Abel turned back to me. His large black eye was emotionless, a sea of tranquility. There was just no way to read his reaction.

I went on. "As I was carrying the target out of her house, I ran into her landlord." I stopped myself and waited for a reaction. There was none.

"So I used the tranquilizer on her," I said.

Surely my unauthorized use of the tranquilizer would elicit a reaction. Or at least a question.

But Abel said nothing.

Cold silence filled the room.

I wrapped up my confession. "The landlord is safe and sound, and I'm sure no one will find her before I return." Of course, I had no way of knowing if that was true. One of the many worries that had come up during my drive back to LA was that Rose had a live-in housekeeper. What if that housekeeper had come out to the guesthouse to find out why Rose hadn't returned?

Abel still hadn't said a word, and I didn't want to continue with my tale of woe. So instead, I went with a question.

"Do you want more details?" I asked.

"No." Abel's synthesized voice gave no hint of anger.

I waited for him to say more. To ask a question or two. But what came next wasn't a question. It was a decree.

"You have to dispose of the landlord," he said.

CHAPTER TWENTY-TWO

I drove back to San Diego with Wendy by my side.

And murder on my mind.

I didn't want to kill Rose, but I also didn't want to disobey Abel. I wanted to follow orders, but murder was a tough order to follow. I didn't think I was capable of it. Of course, it wasn't so long ago that I didn't think I was capable of kidnapping innocent women.

Still, murder was different. Very different.

You have to dispose of the landlord, Abel had said. Without malice or ill will. Just the facts, ma'am.

And what made this whole mess even worse was finding out how lucrative this assignment was. Wendy must have been a valuable target, a top crop, because Abel had left two hundred fifty thousand dollars in my car—the most I'd ever received for an assignment. So now, instead of wrapping up what could've been a lucrative *and* easy assignment, I was stuck in the middle of a nightmare.

I pulled into the parking structure, drove up to the fourth level, and switched from my car to Wendy's car. Less than twenty minutes later, I was approaching Del Mar and caught sight of the Pacific—dark and endless, with glints of gold moonlight streaking its surface. When I had stared out over the Pacific this afternoon, from that beautiful park in Del Mar, I had felt all was well.

Now, everything had changed.

Would my life go back to the way it had been this afternoon, or would it take a turn for the worse?

I couldn't go through with the murder. That I knew. But I also knew that disobeying Abel carried a huge risk. I was almost a hundred percent sure it would result in my own death.

As I drove up to Lunela Drive, I concluded that my best option was to revive Rose and then somehow ensure that she wouldn't implicate me in the crime. And I had a plan to try and make that happen. If I could pull it off, then it would be a case of all's well that ends well. And if Abel saw that, wouldn't he agree that no further action was needed? As in, there was no reason to dispose of me.

Whether I actually believed that or not, I felt I had no other choice.

I pulled into the driveway and drove to the guesthouse in the back. I carried Wendy inside, where my eyes immediately fell on Rose. She was still on the couch just as I'd left her. *Good.*

I put Wendy down on the floor near the front door, so when the time came for her to regain consciousness, she'd be in the same place where she'd fainted.

Then I approached Rose. She looked ashen, her face completely drained of color, and her cheeks sunken. But the most alarming change in her appearance was her wrinkles. They were no longer smiling, but were frozen into expressionless ridges.

It was clear that she wasn't weathering the tranquilizer as well as the other targets had. Her age was probably the cause.

I bent down to scoop her up—my plan included reviving her in her own home—when the obvious finally registered.

I stood back up and looked at her again. This time I focused on her chest and stomach, looking for the gentle movement of shallow breathing.

I didn't see it, and my stomach tightened.

Rose was dead.

Wasn't she?

I leaned down, bringing my face close to hers, and then I turned my head so my ear was right over her nose and mouth.

I listened for shallow breathing.

I didn't hear it.

My face suddenly felt hot, and my stomach tightened further. But I didn't segue into panicking. *Not yet,* I told myself. Not at all, if I could help it.

First, I had to be certain Rose had passed away. I couldn't just assume she was dead. I knew how to check a person's pulse from a first aid course I'd taken years ago. I placed my index and middle fingers on the inside of Rose's wrist, just below her thumb—and waited.

Rose had no pulse.

But in desperation—my body was trembling now, as it had on the night of my first abduction—I placed my index and middle fingers on the side of Rose's neck, just under her jaw. I remembered that this was another way to check a person's pulse. Maybe Rose's pulse would be easier to detect here.

It wasn't.

And after thirty seconds or so, I had to accept that Rose was dead.

I turned from her to look back at Wendy—Sleeping Beauty on the floor—and the correct term for what had happened to Rose entered my thoughts.

Rose had been murdered.

By me.

I'd murdered her with the tranquilizer pellet. I'd been right: the tranquilizer had affected her far differently than it had affected the intended targets.

Then Abel's words came back to me again. *You have to dispose of the landlord.*

For the first time, I understood what he'd really meant. He hadn't meant for me to commit murder. I had *already* committed murder, and Abel knew it. He'd literally meant for me to dispose of the body.

Why? I thought. *Why can't I just put the landlord back in her house?* Eventually someone—maybe Wendy—would discover her body and conclude that Rose had died of natural causes.

But if that was true, Abel wouldn't have issued his edict. There was a reason he didn't want Rose's body found. Maybe the alien drug was detectable if the host died, and an autopsy could reveal it.

Whatever the reason was, it didn't really matter. My job was not to question why, my job was but to do or die.

My stomach was tighter than a drum, but I was no longer trembling. At least I hadn't committed murder. This was an accident: I had panicked when Rose appeared on Wendy's doorstep, and by panicking, I'd accidentally killed her.

Whether I truly believed that or not, I needed to stop rationalizing and take action. I needed to make this all go away. Without thinking it through, my gut told me that I had to dispose of Rose's body before I revived Wendy. But I immediately dismissed the idea of transporting Rose to another location. That would entail too much risk.

Was it possible to hide her in the main house? Of course it was, but that hardly qualified as disposing of her. Her body would rot, and eventually the smell would be detectable.

Unless I could bury her in the basement.

I headed to the main house to see if that was even a possibility. Still worried about the possibility of a live-in housekeeper, I first scoped out the house through the windows.

There was no sign of a housekeeper.

Still, I entered the house as quietly as possible and crept up to the second floor to check; at this time of night, a housekeeper might be fast asleep in her bedroom.

She wasn't. The house was empty.

I headed to the basement.

Unfortunately, the basement floor was a concrete slab. I couldn't bury Rose here unless I broke through the concrete. And even if I could do that, then what? I couldn't mix and pour a concrete slab to repair the damage.

Another idea came to me, and this idea was proof of just how out of my depth I was. I wondered if I could dissolve Rose's body like I'd seen Jesse do in *Breaking Bad*. That's right—I was desperate enough to consider lifting ideas from the plots of TV shows. But in that episode, Jesse, the character tasked with dissolving the body, had badly botched the job because the acid used to dissolve the body had required using all sorts of safety gear, which he didn't have. So not only would I have to track down the acid, I'd have to track down the required safety gear.

Why couldn't Abel have offered to liquefy Rose?

I dismissed the *Breaking Bad* plan.

Instead, I decided to go with the most old-fashioned way to get rid of a body: I'd bury it in the ground, right here on the property. The property was big, and shielded from the neighbors, and there were many secluded spots. I had no idea how long it took to dig a grave, but I decided that if I wasn't finished by morning, I'd take Rose's body's into the main house, revive Wendy, wait until Wendy left the property, and then finish the job.

My plan required a shovel. Since I was already in the basement, I searched it first, but found nothing. I checked the garage next, entering through an interior door. Inside, along with an old Mercedes, in mint condition, I found a full complement of gardening tools—including a shovel.

I grabbed it, went back to the guesthouse, and used the shovel to measure Rose.

Then, under the light of a waxing moon, I scouted the back yard, looking for a good spot to dig the grave.

The best place turned out to be north of the guesthouse and driveway, close to the Leyland cypress trees that bordered the yard. Not only was this spot well hidden from neighbors, it also couldn't be seen from the guesthouse or from the main house. In addition, it was separated from the rest of the property by a flowerbed that hadn't been tended for a while. Plants and weeds grew wild there, obscuring the patch of land immediately behind it. The patch of land that would soon be Rose's gravesite.

Using the shovel as my measuring tool once more, I laid out the dimensions of the grave. Then I stripped away small patches of the lawn, creating my own sod, which I'd place over the top of the finished grave.

Finally, I started digging. I was determined to bury Rose deep, so deep that I'd never think about her again. But I knew this was wishful thinking. I'd think about Rose every day for the rest of my life.

The topsoil was soft, so at first I was making good time. But the deeper I dug, the harder the soil. I kept at it, undeterred, settling into a steady pace. I didn't let my thoughts drift. I didn't want to be distracted from the task at hand.

But it was fortunate that one thought managed to rise to my attention. I knew that at some point, Rose's son, or a friend of Rose's, or maybe even Wendy herself, would report that Rose had disappeared. And then the cops would search Rose's house, which meant I had another task to do before leaving Del Mar behind. A task I'd never had to do during my previous assignments.

I needed to wipe my fingerprints off of everything I'd touched in the main house.

I kept digging. When dawn approached, I upped my pace.

By the time full-fledged morning arrived—which meant the time to revive Wendy was almost at hand—I had transformed the patch of land hidden behind the flowerbed into a grave. A grave deep enough to bury Rose.

But it wasn't deep enough for me. It wasn't deep enough to hide the crime from myself. And even though there was probably no way I could bury her deep enough for that, I decided I had to try.

If I had buried Rose right then, everything that followed could have been avoided.

But I didn't bury Rose then. I wanted to dig a deeper grave.

So I walked around the flowerbed, and then to the guesthouse. Inside, I scooped up Rose, carried her past Wendy, still unconscious on the floor, and took her across the back yard and into the main house. I laid Rose out on the couch in her living room. I still hadn't looked at her face. I couldn't.

I headed back to the guesthouse, stepped inside, and checked my phone for the time. I'd wait ten minutes before reviving Wendy. That would give her just enough time to get ready for work, but no extra time to dilly-dally. Of course, she might decide not to go to work, but instead go to her doctor to check on her fainting spell. Regardless, as soon as she left, I'd get back to work on digging a deeper grave.

While the minutes passed, I stared at Wendy's stomach and chest to confirm that she was breathing normally. I half-expected her to die, though that fear was unfounded. I saw the signs of shallow, calm breathing, the kind of breathing I was very familiar with. I'd seen it with all the other targets.

Finally, I took the tin box from my pocket, opened it, and pulled out a recovery capsule. I knelt down next to Wendy and put the capsule in her mouth.

Less than a minute later, I was back in Rose's house, waiting for

Wendy to make the next move. As I anxiously awaited the sound of Wendy's car starting up, I couldn't help but glance at Rose a few times.

This is her wake, I thought. There were no relatives at this wake, no loved ones. The only guest was a murderer. *The only guest is the man who killed you,* I thought.

But Rose had lived a long life, and, judging from her smile, a good life. And it wasn't like she had wanted for anything. Just one look at her house told you that.

Sure, I was rationalizing—again—but so what? It was true. Rose had *not* been cut down in the prime of her life.

It was ten minutes into this uneasy wake when I felt like I had to check on what was going on out back. I didn't want to risk peering out the kitchen window, even if I was partially obscured by the cluster of trees out back, so I headed upstairs to the second floor and found a bedroom with a window that looked down on the guesthouse. The view was still partially obscured, but I was sure Wendy couldn't spot me.

I waited there, hoping to see some activity.

There wasn't any.

Maybe she'd called in to work and told them she'd be late. Or maybe she was calling her doctor, trying to get an appointment.

I headed back downstairs, accepting the fact that Rose's wake would go on longer than I'd expected; it might be a while before Wendy headed out.

But just as I stepped into the living room, I heard a sound—

A sound that made my heart leap from my chest into my throat.

Someone was knocking at the back door.

No, not someone.

Wendy was knocking at the back door. I was sure of it.

But why?

Did she think she'd fainted because of something her landlord was responsible for? Like a gas leak? Or was it part of Wendy's routine to check on Rose every morning? Maybe that was part of her duty as a tenant. Maybe she got a discount on the rent because of it.

There were a million possible reasons for her to come by this morning. But whatever the reason, I should've foreseen that she might. I'd been given an obvious clue that this was a possibility: Rose had brought that meal over to Wendy last night. That meant the two probably had a close relationship. Close enough for Wendy to pay Rose a visit.

Wendy knocked again, this time a little louder. When she stopped, I realized I'd made another horrible mistake: I'd left the back door unlocked. What an idiotic move. What if Wendy decided to come right in and check up on Rose?

As I waited for more knocking, I weighed whether to grab Rose's body and race down into the basement or into the garage. I had to hide the body in case Wendy barged in and started searching for Rose.

But I didn't move.

I was no longer making decisions quickly. The exertion of digging the grave had slowed me down.

My mind went blank for a few seconds.

Then, like a loud clap of thunder roaring through the house, the phone rang. The ringing kicked my mind back into gear; I had a hunch as to who was on the other end of that phone call. I stood there frozen, waiting for the hunch to be confirmed.

An old-style answering machine picked up after the fifth ring, and Rose's voice sprang forth from it—coming from the kitchen. Her message was cheery; I could hear the smile in her voice.

After the beep, a younger voice took over. "Rose, this is Wendy," it said. "I just knocked at the back door and didn't get any response.

I thought if I called you, you might hear the phone."

Wendy paused, but not long enough for the machine to hang up. "Are you there, Rose?" she said, then waited again.

The seconds passed. I knew Wendy was standing just outside the kitchen door, waiting.

The answering machine abruptly clicked off. Wendy had hung up.

I heard another click—a doorknob turning.

Like a shot, I took off toward the couch, scooped Rose up, and raced to the garage. The basement was no longer an option; I couldn't get to it without crossing Wendy's path.

I moved quickly, but I tried to keep my footsteps soft and measured. I gently opened the door to the garage, then closed it behind me. I scurried around to the back of the mint-condition Mercedes, like a cockroach on the run from sudden light, then placed Rose's body on the floor and crouched down next to her.

After about a minute or so, I heard Wendy's voice calling Rose's name. Wendy was moving down the hallway on the other side of the door. Her voice got louder as she got closer. If she peeked into the garage, she wouldn't see Rose or me; she'd just see the front of the Mercedes. But if she ventured into the garage, I was a sitting duck.

I heard Wendy call Rose's name again. She was closer; I crouched down lower. If Wendy was going to open the door, it would happen any second now.

But it didn't happen.

A minute passed, then another minute. Still nothing.

I stayed in the garage, hovering over Rose's body, but not looking at it, waiting for a sign that the house was clear. I supposed Wendy continued to search the house, but I couldn't know for sure, because once she receded from the hallway, I could no longer hear her voice.

Finally, after ten minutes, I heard Wendy's car backing down the driveway, right past the garage.

I was safe. Though "safe" was a wild exaggeration. I was probably safe from this immediate threat, but I was in danger from every other angle.

As I carried Rose back into the house, I wondered if Wendy had already followed up on Rose's disappearance. Had she called the police, or Rose's son, or one of Rose's friends? There was no way to know.

But I did know this: I wasn't going to make the grave any deeper. It was deep enough. I needed to bury Rose right now, clear the house of my fingerprints, and get the hell away from here. And if I had any hope of surviving this nightmare and keeping my job—as well as my life—I had to do it all quickly and efficiently.

I carried Rose out to the gravesite and placed her in it. I wasn't religious, but I still said a prayer. It was more of an apology to her, and to God, and to whoever would listen to my flimsy excuse: that this was a horrible accident.

Then I shoveled dirt over her and packed it down. I completed the funeral—the worst funeral ever—by laying the sod out over the grave. It turned out to be good camouflage.

But I was left with extra soil. Not a lot. Rose was small. Using the shovel, I hauled the extra soil from the gravesite to the cypress trees and scattered it between them. It only took a few trips, and the trees were good cover. They were so tightly packed together that the extra soil disappeared into the shadows under the bushy leaves at their base.

I washed the shovel using a spigot at the back of the guesthouse. I made sure not to get my shoes wet or muddied. Then I wiped the shovel dry by running it back and forth on the grass.

After returning the shovel to the garage, I moved on to the fingerprints. Using a dishtowel, I wiped down the doorknobs I'd touched, and the shovel. I was pretty sure I hadn't touched anything else. I also checked to see if there were any visible shoe prints on the hardwood floors or area rugs. There weren't any.

Taking the dishtowel with me, I exited the main house for good. Then I wiped my prints off of the guesthouse's front doorknob, but because Wendy had locked the door, I couldn't get inside to wipe them off of the inside doorknob.

I went around back to see if the bedroom window was still cracked open. It was.

But I'd done enough, hadn't I? It seemed stupid to risk breaking into Wendy's place again. What if she returned while I was inside? What if I climbed in, and while inside, I accidentally left more evidence that would incriminate me?

All told, I was on the verge of making a clean getaway—or the cleanest one now possible considering how badly I'd botched this assignment. It was time to cruise.

I wiped my prints off the window, stuffed the dishtowel into my pocket, and made my way to the front of the property. I clung close to the south side of the main house, and stopped at the front edge to check out Lunela Drive. It was barren as usual. No cars and no people. But there was no way to scout out what was going on farther down the street on either side. The property's privacy was now working against me.

If I wanted to scope out the street, I had no choice but to move down to the front of the property.

So that's what I did.

The street was deserted on either side, and that validated my choice to leave while the going was good.

I morphed into a tourist and strolled down Lunela Drive, with my cell phone at the ready, awed by the views of the Pacific. From Lunela, I made my way down through the wealthy enclave to the town center. There, I called for a cab—I thought using Uber would leave too much of digital trail—and took it to the parking structure.

It was a great relief when I stepped up to my car. I was comforted by its familiarity, and I couldn't wait to slide in and drive away.

On the way back to LA, I decided I wouldn't give Abel a blow-by-blow description of how I'd implemented his decree. After all, I had done as I'd been told. I had disposed of Rose's body. It hadn't gone perfectly, but it might have gone well enough to get away with it. That would depend on what happened after the police got involved. For there was no doubt that they would. At some point, if that point hadn't already come, Wendy would realize that Rose had disappeared, and she'd call the police.

And then my fate would largely depend on when Rose's body was discovered. There were many cases where it took decades for the police, or for anyone, to discover that a victim's body was buried right on their own property. I hoped this would be one of those cases. After all, there was no evidence to indicate that Rose had even been murdered.

And if the police discovered the body sooner, as in months from now, there still shouldn't be enough forensic evidence to link me to the murder. At least, I didn't think there was.

ABEL

CHAPTER TWENTY-THREE

I checked the numbers again, even though I knew they were right. The equipment was in excellent shape; I had nothing better to do than to keep it well maintained. And the numbers confirmed that the latest target had yielded the most potent batch of Kalera yet. It was ninety-one percent pure, which was basically as good as it got. Prior to this batch, the most potent one I'd harvested had been seventy-three percent pure. And that had been a long time ago. Thirty cycles ago.

I took one of the tablets—made from the potent Kalera—and headed up to the second floor of the house. I had a decision to make, but I wanted to think about it a little longer.

As I climbed the stairs, I wondered if this batch was a fluke, or if there were other humans that might yield similar batches. I hadn't heard of crops on other planets ever yielding anything close to this.

But that didn't mean it hadn't happened. Earth was so distant from any significant part of the universe that it was hard to get any news here at all. And because I didn't want to compromise my location, I didn't troll the galaxy in search of news.

I walked into the master bedroom—a huge, empty room with large windows looking out on the wooded hillside. I hadn't yet made my decision, but I was getting closer.

I spotted an owl nestled in a nearby birch tree. I'd watched that birch tree grow into the king of the hillside over the last hundred years. But it was the owl that captured my attention for the moment. The owl was another fine example of just how varied life was on this planet. On Tracea, millions and millions of cycles hadn't produced such a wide variety of life. The bulk of the evolutionary momentum had gone into developing my own species, so there was nothing on my planet as spectacular as owls—or as magnificent as the mountain lions, deer, and coyotes that roamed this hillside.

Surely my species had had no idea that life on Earth would flower into so many forms. If they had, they wouldn't have seeded Earth with Kalera. But one billion cycles ago, Earth looked no different than millions of other planets that were desolate, yet had the two ingredients necessary to grow and harvest Kalera: the right climate, and a simple life form to act as a host.

On Earth, that life form was cyanobacteria. Or at least that's what I'd come to believe. I wasn't a biologist or a chemist, but I'd had plenty of time to study Earth. Still, I couldn't be certain that my species had chosen cyanobacteria, because so much had changed on Earth since then. In fact, so much had changed that I was lucky to have discovered Kalera had been planted here at all.

As humans were fond of saying—and I liked many of their idioms: I'd "hit the jackpot." Starting my life again, on this distant planet, had been tough, but finding Kalera here had been my big break. And it wasn't my only big break. The other was a lucky quirk of biological fate: life on this planet had evolved in such a way as to allow the Kalera seeds to pass from one life form to another. So as the seeds had matured into plants, they had also clung to their evolving hosts.

I took my eyes off of the owl and looked at the Kalera tablet in my hand. I was leaning toward taking it—this batch of Kalera was certainly worth taking—but I still wasn't totally convinced this was the best decision.

I rarely took the drug. I'd taken it only three times since I'd arrived on Earth, and those three times had been during my first ten cycles on the planet. I'd felt lonely and miserable, homesick in the worst of ways—because I knew I could never return home. I had convinced myself that it was okay to take the drug because my biological and mental makeup made it unlikely that I'd become addicted. And it did help a little with my loneliness. But then I stopped taking it, because the truth was, anyone could get addicted to Kalera, regardless of what their biological and mental makeup predicted. As confirmation of this, all I had to do was look at how many members of my species, and of other species, were addicted.

But this tablet of Kalera was worth taking in spite of that. And wasn't that why I'd sent Eddie to San Diego? It wasn't just that I wanted to harvest what I suspected might be a valuable batch of Kalera. I had to admit to myself that once I'd discovered this target, I'd instantly had the urge to try the Kalera that would result from the harvest—*if* it turned out to be as potent as I suspected.

Which it had.

I'd been feeling terribly homesick over the last cycle. Far more homesick than I'd ever felt. I physically ached for companionship, and for the familiarity of Tracea.

Kalera would ease my longing. I knew the sense of peace it would provide was a false one, but I didn't care. I welcomed it. And I could hardly wait for it.

I welcomed the other effects of the drug, too. Especially one particular effect, which might prove to be an even greater benefit than the sense of peace. Kalera would propel my mind into hyper-drive. And given the potency of this batch, it would be a hyper-drive more powerful than any I'd ever experienced—one so powerful that I'd be capable of generating a plan to end my stay on Earth.

For the last few cycles, I'd been desperately trying to come up with such a plan. I thought that by planning, perhaps I could fight the misery that had taken root deep within me. The misery I couldn't shake. And it had worked, partially anyway. Thinking about how I could get back to Tracea gave me hope. The hope that my time as a fugitive would soon be coming to an end.

But I hadn't been able to come up with a plan. And that was because I couldn't come up with a solution to the most vexing part of the problem: finding a way to secretly reintegrate myself back into life on Tracea—the only place I loved.

To do that, I would need to create a new identity. An identity that would completely shield me from the Council, the governing body on Tracea—and from all my fellow Traceans. An identity with no link to my former self. An identity that was impenetrable.

No Tracean could ever suspect who I really was.

I turned the Kalera tablet over in my hand. I was expecting a lot from this tablet. But I knew it could deliver—or had the potential to deliver. Sure, Kalera always delivered on the false sense of peace— that was why it was the most popular drug in the universe. But it didn't always deliver on the hyper-drive in a way that made any difference. For that you needed potency.

I thought I held that potency in my hand.

I lifted the tablet to my eye, ready to absorb it. But just before I let it touch the surface of my eye—just before it would instantly dissolve and there'd be no turning back—doubt came over me.

This wasn't the time for taking the drug.

It was better to wait until the situation with the human was settled. The current situation, anyway. With a man like Eddie, there was bound to be another, eventually. Eddie was a desperate man, and desperate men did desperate things. Things that had dangerous repercussions. Other species were no different; I was an example of that. It was my own desperation that had led to me being a fugitive.

I had always screened my human employees before offering them the job. And even though Eddie had volunteered, I had screened him, too. But the man had turned out to be far more of a wild card than I'd thought. He concealed details about his abductions to a degree that I hadn't seen with my prior employees.

I chalked this up to the fact that even though I *had* screened him, all my other employees had started at much younger ages and hadn't been desperate. For them, the job had quickly turned into careers— lucrative careers. Careers they didn't want to jeopardize. I had hoped Eddie would also see the job as a career. But instead, he saw it as a quick fix for his troubles.

I blamed myself for that. If I hadn't disposed of Ben in front of him, then he might not have started the job thinking that his days were already numbered. But I'd made that decision on the spot. My misery had led to poor judgment. My homesickness had gotten the better of my reason.

I should have disposed of Ben the way I always did when it was time to replace an employee: send him on an assignment that was designed to kill him. Of course, there was no guarantee that if I'd followed my usual protocol—and then had also disposed of Eddie— that a fresh screening process would've led to an employee any better than Eddie.

As proof, all I had to do was look back to Richard Deaks, the man who'd worked for me in the nineteen fifties. By all measures, he'd been an ideal candidate. The man was resourceful and reliable and innovative. He'd taken to the job like a duck to water. That was another of my favorite idioms. I often wished that this idiom applied to me, as in: I had taken to the life of a fugitive like a duck to water.

But that wasn't the case. The appropriate human idiom for my situation here on Earth was: I was a square peg in a round hole. Which was why I wanted to take the Kalera. I was desperate to go home. But though I was still holding the tablet within a few inches of my eye, I wasn't making the next move. Instead, my thoughts were on Deaks.

The man took to the job better than any other employee I'd ever hired; he delivered each target without complications. And he always gave me a full report on each assignment. Also, he didn't ask many questions, which I appreciated.

But around the five-year mark, even though he'd never asked questions, he started searching for answers on his own. He began to spy on me and the house. He thought my operation was part of a much larger conspiracy. He had come to believe that I was part of an advanced scout team, and that I'd been sent here to examine humans before my alien brethren launched a full-fledged invasion.

Deaks had been influenced by the media of the time. Films, books, and news stories had latched on to the idea that aliens were just itching to invade Earth—and that the invasion was imminent. The idea was ridiculous. Earth didn't have the kind of resources that other species wanted or needed. This planet's only valuable resource was Kalera, and that resource could be had on many other planets. We, the Traceans, had seeded it all across the universe.

The ridiculous idea that Earth was worth invading was purely an American invention. The US had an inflated view of itself back then. It had become the dominant global power as a result of that dreadful war, and that power had led to hubris. The same hubris that had sparked Deaks's delusion. He wanted to be an American hero. And the considerable money that he was earning as my employee wasn't enough to overcome his delusion.

The media convinced him that the invasion was just around the corner, and he believed that if he could stop it, he'd save mankind and be hailed as a hero for all eternity. He'd be the superman who'd stopped a deadly alien enemy from wiping out the human race.

His delusion of grandeur inspired him to cart a telescope into the woods so he could watch the house. It also inspired him to take pictures with a telephoto lens. Within a year, he was taking his mission even more seriously. Every time he delivered a target, he'd bring a small recording device into the house, hidden under his shirt. He kept hoping I'd say something to prove I was part of the alien scout team. And while I was harvesting the Kalera from the target, he'd search the house looking for evidence that would prove the invasion was imminent.

I put up with Deaks's shenanigans—that was how great an employee the man was—until he did the unthinkable. Up to that point, I had thought there was still a chance I could keep him on. He wasn't outing me because he wanted to first find solid evidence of the invasion. So I took advantage of that extra time he'd bought himself by volunteering information about what I was actually doing—hinting that I was a lone farmer, harvesting crops—hoping he would conclude for himself that there was no planned invasion and drop his investigation.

It didn't work.

Deaks's final insubordination came in February 1956. The idea of the alien invasion had been growing on him for a year, the same year during which he'd spied on the house and searched it up and down. Then, that month, *Invasion of the Body Snatchers*, a film about an alien invasion, was released.

Deaks went to see it on opening weekend.

And then he did something with the next target that none of my employees had ever done.

The night started out normally. Deaks brought the target to the house—this was a couple of days after he'd seen the movie—and waited for me to harvest the Kalera.

After I harvested it and put Deaks's pay in his car, I walked into the living room and said, "You can return the target."

Instead of getting right to it, which he almost always did, Deaks extended the conversation. "Hollywood has some crazy ideas about you guys," he said.

"For instance?" I said, pleased that I didn't have to be the one extending the conversation, which I'd tried to do a few times when dropping hints that I was a lone farmer.

"I just saw a movie," he said, "where aliens invade Earth by comin' in as plant spores." He stared at me as if he was looking for confirmation.

"Seems farfetched," I said.

"They got it backwards, don't they?" He let out a derisive laugh, as if he couldn't believe how foolish Hollywood was. "*We're* the plants."

"It's possible that there are species that travel as spores," I said, though I knew it wasn't possible. But I was pleased to discover that he'd picked up on the tidbits of information I'd been dispensing over the last year. This was the first indication that he understood what I was doing on the planet.

"Aliens as plants is dumb," he said. "Aliens ain't that primitive. Just look at you."

"I'll take that as a compliment," I said.

"I'm just not buyin' this spore thing." He shook his head.

I decided to use *Invasion of the Body Snatchers* to make a point. "Why did the aliens in that movie invade Earth?"

Deaks didn't respond. I could tell his brain was working overtime to come up with an answer. Finally, he realized why he couldn't come up with one.

"It didn't say," he said.

I hoped to steer him in the right direction, so I continued. "It seems like an awful lot of trouble to mount an invasion of a planet, if there's no point."

"Resources," he blurted out.

"So the spores came for resources?"

"Nah—that was just a stupid movie. In a real invasion, aliens would be comin' for our resources."

"What makes you think aliens would need Earth's resources?"

"You're here, ain't ya? You must need somethin'." This was delivered with a smile, an *I got ya* smile.

And he had gotten me. My only comeback was to lay it out a little more explicitly.

"There's a difference between need and want," I said, and I let that sink in for a couple of seconds.

His eyes narrowed as if he was thinking this through.

I continued. "My species doesn't need what I harvest here. But some of them want it."

Again, I let him think about that for a few seconds before I went on.

"Humans need water," I said. "But they don't need tomatoes. They might invade another planet if they ever ran out of water, but they wouldn't invade another planet if they ran out of tomatoes."

"Okay... so?"

"So some people still may *want* tomatoes, and if it's worth it economically, a few people might go to another planet to get tomatoes. But the human race isn't going to mount an invasion to make sure they have a steady supply of tomatoes."

He studied me, then said, "Okay... I can see that."

But as it turned out, he couldn't.

When he left with the target, I believed I'd gotten through to him—not completely, but partially. Enough to begin to counter the ridiculous idea that one extraterrestrial, stuck in the hills of Beverly, with minimal assets, was the lead scout for an alien invasion.

But I hadn't gotten through to him at all, and I found that out by listening to police transmissions. Through those transmissions, which gave a good recap of the story Deaks had told, I learned that my best employee had become my worst.

Deaks didn't return the target to Culver City, where she lived. Instead, he took her to Cedars Sinai Hospital and revived her there. He told the doctors that an alien had abducted her, and he convinced them to examine her. He was able to pull that off because the target did corroborate part of Deaks's story. She confirmed that she'd fainted unexpectedly, though that was all she could confirm, because the revival capsule had done its job.

So it was Deaks who insisted the police come to the hospital. And when they arrived, he told them his tall tale. He didn't want to incriminate himself, so he didn't mention his five-year stint as a kidnapper, and the income he'd earned from it. Instead, he told the police that he'd witnessed this strange-looking creature shoot a tranquilizer dart at this woman—the woman he'd brought to the hospital.

He was driving down Venice Boulevard in Culver City, minding his own business, when he turned a corner and saw a woman step out of her car, then suddenly pass out. Out of nowhere, an alien creature grabbed the woman, loaded her back into her car, and got in himself. Deaks said he followed the car up Motor Avenue, through Beverly Hills, and up Dixie Canyon Road, all the way to a fancy house. He gave the police the address of that fancy house—my address.

Though the police transmissions were detailed, they left out one element. Whether it was on purpose or not, I didn't know. But I did know that this element—the only real evidence that Deaks had—was probably the reason the police were willing to consider Deaks's outlandish claim at all.

I had no doubt that Deaks had shown the police the copper straw, the tranquilizer pellets, and the revival capsules. And I thought it likely that the doctors at Cedars had confirmed that the pellets and capsules were unfamiliar. But the doctors were professionals. They would withhold judgment until a proper chemical analysis of the pellets and capsules was complete.

Too bad for Deaks. Because that forensic evidence would disintegrate, if it hadn't already. For as soon as someone other than Deaks reached into either of those tin boxes, whether with gloved hands or tweezers, the pellets and capsules would disintegrate, and the elements from which they were made would disperse into the atmosphere, never to be recovered. Same with the copper straw. As soon as someone other than Deaks touched it, it would disintegrate.

And that was that.

Back then, I didn't have to worry about the gold card because I didn't use it to contact employees. There was no need to. Using a landline had been fine. Back then, I could hide my landline communications quite well, which brought to mind another idiom: it had been child's play. Everything was easier in those days.

In the fifties, those freewheeling police transmissions were all I'd needed to fix the damage Deaks had wrought. They provided a step-by-step guide to what I needed to do to throw the police off my trail. I used phony dispatches and phone calls, and a few other tricks—facilitated by using the limited equipment I'd managed to smuggle off of Tracea during my escape. Changing the facts that made up Deaks's tall tale was easy.

One of those new facts gave me a sense of satisfaction—and a good laugh. By the time the address Deaks had given to the police made it to the detective assigned to the case, I had changed it. It was no longer my address, it was Pete Wilson's address. Pete was a gaffer on a film in production on the Paramount lot.

The film was about an alien invasion. And lo and behold, when the detective paid a visit to Pete's house, a little bungalow on Gower, Pete identified Deaks as someone who dropped by the film set often. "Deaks was obsessed with the film" was the way Pete put it.

Pete was more than happy to lie to the detective because I'd sent him a special delivery: one hundred thousand dollars, which was close to a decade's worth of his salary. And to earn it, all he had to do was stick to the story I'd sent him, which was that Deaks believed an alien invasion was imminent, and that the poor schmuck was a nutcase.

Damage control hadn't been too tough back then. Now it was much harder, which was another reason I wanted off this planet. I could still manipulate human technology just well enough to cover my tracks, but as human technology had improved, my limited equipment was less able to do the job.

Still, being discovered by humans wasn't my biggest fear. My biggest fear was that the Traceans would find me. If my own species found me, I'd have to go on the run again—*if* I was lucky enough to escape again. Otherwise, they'd dispose of me faster than I had disposed of Ben Kingsley.

With every passing cycle, it was getting harder to monitor and manipulate all the information that might give the Traceans a clue that I was here on Earth—which was another reason I had to come up with a plan to get back home now. I knew my cover here would eventually be blown.

That thought forced my hand.

I moved the capsule toward my eye, and this time I didn't stop. When it made contact with my eye, it dissolved.

As I waited for the drug to take effect, I stared out the window at the sprawling birch tree. I hoped the Kalera would deliver on the hyper-drive, and that the hyper-drive would be powerful enough to generate a plan.

A few minutes later the Kalera took hold.

There's no place like home, I thought.

EDDIE

CHAPTER TWENTY-FOUR

I'd been home from San Diego for a couple days, and during those days I'd thought about driving up to Abel's house to let him know how I'd disposed of Rose. But thinking about it was as far as I'd gone. That was because I hadn't read anything about Rose's disappearance on the San Diego police blotters. I knew the story would eventually make it to the blotters, and then into the news, but the fact that it hadn't yet gave me hope. Why? Because the longer it took to investigate the crime, the higher the likelihood that whatever evidence I'd accidentally left behind would fade.

Still, I was getting antsy. I desperately wanted to know what Abel was up to. Was he waiting it out? Was he waiting to see if I'd executed the assignment "properly"?

I also wanted Abel to give me the next target. That would get my mind off of Rose. It would also mean that I was still employed by the alien—that he wasn't planning to liquefy me.

On the morning of my third day back from San Diego, Larry called. He was following up on that job he'd told me about a while ago. He wanted to know if the prospect of a return to journalism had grown on me. After the nightmare in Del Mar, I had to admit to myself that segueing back into journalism sounded appealing. Not that that mattered. Regardless of the appeal, I knew there was no going back. There was no way to quit the job with Abel. It was lifetime employment.

In the end, the only reason I agreed to head over to Larry's to talk about the job was to put a temporary stop to obsessing over Rose. And as it turned out, the visit to Larry's didn't deliver on that.

By the time I left his place, I would be in an absolute panic over Rose.

*

Larry led me into his office, which had sprouted a second desk. And sitting at that desk, in front of two computer monitors—which brought the total for the office up to five—was a sharp-looking kid in his mid-twenties.

"Eddie," Larry said, "meet Josh. A proud graduate of the USC Annenberg School of Journalism—with a joint degree in Computer Science."

"A degree of the future," I said.

Larry smiled. "A degree of the present."

"I'm just happy it was a degree that led to a job," Josh said.

Larry leaned over the kid's shoulder and stared at the two computer monitors for a couple of seconds. Then he said, "Go back even further and see if you can confirm the pattern for another decade."

"Sure," Josh said, and started typing.

Larry then walked over to his own desk and checked his own computer monitors. I was sure he was checking for news updates. If his news site was one of the first with a story, he'd get more clicks, and that meant more advertising dollars.

After a minute of perusing his monitors, Larry grabbed an iPad from his desk—so he'd stay connected and wouldn't miss anything—

and turned to me. "Let's go talk on the patio," he said.

Outside, we both sat down and Larry plopped the iPad on the table between us. "So, how do you feel about being an editor in chief?"

"You're kidding." He hadn't told me what the job was over the phone, and this wasn't what I'd expected.

"Nope," he said.

"What paper needs an editor in chief?"

"It's a website."

"That explains it." I shook my head.

"Don't scoff," he said. "It's a great job, and you'd be a great fit."

Even though I knew another career change wasn't in the cards for me, it seemed rude not to hear him out. Especially because he thought that's why I had come over.

"Okay, you've piqued my curiosity," I said.

"Great. So here's the scoop: a bunch of news sites, similar to mine, want to band together to produce more in-depth pieces. We'd all run the pieces—like running a syndicated column."

"Can't you pick up syndicated columns now?"

"We can—but the idea is that we want to create our own content with our sensibilities."

"You mean you want to bypass the middleman," I said.

He laughed. "That's part of it."

"So where do I fit in?" I asked.

"You'd be the editor for the syndicate."

I didn't respond. Larry was coming through for me. And I knew the job was legitimate. He wasn't the type of friend who'd present me with a half-baked idea. This was a real editor in chief job, in the landscape of new media.

He waited for my response, raising his eyebrows, as if to say, *So, what do you think?*

"It sounds intriguing," I said, "but I have to tell you, I'm kind of liking my new job."

"Maybe I can sweeten the deal if you tell me more about the competition."

When he'd originally asked me about the job, I had told him what I'd told Jenny—that I was researching potential acquisition targets for ADM. And I wasn't inclined to add anything more now. So I told him what I'd told Jenny when she'd asked for more details.

"I can't really get into specifics because I'm not supposed to talk about ADM's acquisition targets," I said. And then I came up with a great additional line on the fly. "And I'm guessing that talking to a reporter about those targets would be the worst kind of violation."

He grinned. "So now I'm the enemy?"

I smiled. "Yep. Sorry."

"How about the money? Is the pay good?"

I thought I could cop to that without giving too much away. "Yep. It's actually kind of nice to see how the other half lives."

"The money's that good?"

I decided to play it down. "Let's just say it's good enough."

He leaned back in his chair, cocked his head, and narrowed his eyes.

I recognized that look. Hell, I'd spent more than a decade in the same newsroom with the guy. He was curious, bordering on suspicious.

"How'd you land the job?" he said. "You never told me."

"It was a fluke. Someone told me about the opening, and somehow I was able to finagle ADM's HR to give me an interview. They weren't so sure about me, but I convinced them to let me interview with the actual department I'd be working for. Once I got that interview, I went for broke."

"You mean you begged them?"

"Not quite. But close. I was desperate. But I also knew I could do the job."

Larry wasn't quite buying my story; his eyes were still bright with suspicion. He leaned forward and I braced myself for another question—but his iPad suddenly got his attention. His eyes scanned the screen, and he quickly stood up, ready to jump into action.

"Can you excuse me for a minute?" he said. "I want to get something up on the website."

"Sure—what's up?"

"I can't get into specifics about my work," he said with a straight face, and then grinned. "I'm kidding. Walk me back to the office and I'll fill you in."

He didn't walk back to his office—he hurried, with me at his heels.

"It's a crime story," he said, "with a human interest element. And with those stories, if you're in the first wave, you get great traffic. Especially with Josh on board now."

"How does he figure into it?"

"I'll write a two-paragraph story and an irresistible headline. Then he'll take over and do the SEO. Before, I had to do both, so it took me twice as long to get something up on the site."

We stepped into his office, and as Larry rushed toward his chair, he barked out instructions. "Josh, bring up the *San Diego Union-Tribune*. Pat's blog has a crime story we're going to run with."

Hearing "San Diego'" immediately put me on high alert. But before I could check to see whether it was a false alarm—and less than three seconds after Larry had told Josh to bring up the story—Josh said, "I got it," and both of them began to bang away at their keyboards.

From where I stood, I could see Larry's monitors. On one, his story was unfurling as he typed madly. On another, the *San Diego*

Union-Tribune banner topped the screen—but I couldn't make out the headline underneath the banner.

I also noticed that as Larry pounded out the copy for his story, it was also unfurling simultaneously on one of Josh's monitors. And Josh was already changing the copy—optimizing the story for search engines.

But I couldn't see the actual text of story.

So to find out if there was reason for alarm, I moved a little closer to Larry's desk and focused in on the original story in the *San Diego Union-Tribune*. The headline left no doubt that my nightmare was just about to get bigger—

"Woman Found Buried In Yard," it said.

Amid Larry and Josh's intense race to get the story out, I was invisible. So I moved even closer to Larry's desk and began to read the *Union-Tribune* story. My heart was pounding, and my breathing was halting. I was already in a panic. Why hadn't I seen the crime on the San Diego police blotter earlier? Were the police already closing in on me?

My first question was answered in the story. In the age of Internet journalism, the speed at which news traveled was almost instantaneous. It turned out that the police had discovered the body less than an hour ago, so the crime report must have hit the police blotter while I was on my way over here. And the reporter for the *Union-Tribune* had undoubtedly put the news up on his blog immediately, without going through the paper's editorial staff.

But I could see why the reporter wanted to get it up there fast. It was an intriguing mystery—and that's how he'd painted it—and it would draw eyeballs to his blog and to the paper. The story had all the right phrases: "shallow backyard grave," "kindly widow," "wealthy neighborhood," "possible homicide," and "many unanswered questions."

I hoped those questions would remain unanswered.

I looked over to check on Larry's story and saw his headline: "Trouble in Paradise: Del Mar Woman Found Buried In Her Own Yard."

Then I read his version of the story. It added a dash of gruesomeness—"no report yet on how long the body had been buried"—and a dash of character: "Rose David was a long-time resident of Del Mar" and "a well-known member of Del Mar's preservation society." That information hadn't been in the *Union-Tribune* story, so where had it come from?

I found the answer on Larry's third computer monitor. That monitor showed the results of a search on Rose, which must have been initiated by Josh—the reason for his furious typing at the start of this sprint. Josh and Larry were already a well-oiled machine.

"What do you think?" Larry said, his first words since the sprint had begun.

I thought he was talking to me, but Josh answered him immediately. "I'm ready to go," he said.

"Okay," Larry responded. "Let's give it the once-over."

Then they both stopped typing and read the story.

A minute later, Larry said, "I'm good."

"Me too," Josh concurred, then followed this up with, "Posted."

I felt the frantic energy in the room dissipate. Josh was back to typing, but at a normal pace. I looked back at Larry's monitors, and this time one of them featured his news site. The headline for the new story was on it, accompanied by a small photo underneath—a view of the Del Mar hillside I knew so well.

Larry stood up, his face flush from the burst of adrenaline. "Sorry for the interruption," he said.

"No problem," I said.

"You ready to let me sell you on the editor job?"

I glanced at Larry's website again. "Trouble in Paradise" screamed out at me.

"I think I want to stick with ADM. At least for now," I answered.

"Okay—then let's just catch up," Larry said.

"I've gotta take off. Maybe we can grab lunch this weekend."

"Sounds good. And I might hold you to it."

Was he still suspicious about my job? It didn't really matter. It was time to hit the road.

Two minutes later, after Larry had asked me again if I'd consider the editor job, I was on my way home. But the closer I got to home, the more I wanted to drive past it, then on to Coldwater and up to Abel's.

By now Abel knew that the business of disposing of Rose's body had gone badly. *It's all over the Internet,* I thought, and that's when it dawned on me: Abel probably hadn't been waiting to find out if I had botched implementing his order. He'd probably *known* that I had. That explained why he hadn't contacted me with the next assignment.

He'd already decided to dispose of me.

JENNY

CHAPTER TWENTY-FIVE

Working on the pilot already seemed like a distant memory, even though it hadn't really been that long. And I missed it, even though the job had been hectic, the workload heavy, and I'd been on call 24/7. Mimi had turned out to be a perfectionist, more so than any other production designer I'd worked for, so our entire department had been kept busy.

After the gig had ended, it had felt good to have a break, but now I was yearning to get back into action. I'd recovered, and I had time before my next round of treatments. I was restless to work again, and it was that restlessness that allowed my suspicions about Eddie to rise to the surface. If I had been working, I might've been able to keep from acting on my suspicions. But as it stood, I was fixated on the idea that Eddie's job was commission-based.

The day had started out well. It was a Sunday, so Hannah had an eight-hour shift at Gregory Brothers. She'd gotten up early and joined me for breakfast. We'd been getting along better, and the reason for that was ironic. Her job—the very thing I'd been against—had made her more responsible. It had driven her to manage her time more effectively, more so than being on the swim team had. When she had schoolwork to do, she focused on it, with no interruptions for social media or chats with friends. And she didn't waste time arguing with Jake or me.

"I'm really proud of how you're handling the job," I told her at breakfast.

"Thanks," she said.

I went on to let her know how wrong I'd been, ending with: "Do you want to tell me 'I told you so'? You've earned it."

"Nah. I'd rather use the goodwill for something more useful."

I laughed. "Uh-oh."

"Don't worry," she said. "I'm talking about material goods. Not permission to do something outlandish."

"Whew." I mock-wiped my brow.

She looked over at the clock. "I'd better head out," she said.

Then she picked up her dishes, carried them over to the sink, and rinsed them. In the past, she wouldn't have voluntarily done that. I would've had to ask her to.

"Do you want a ride?" I said.

"I'm fine." She headed to the door. "I'll see you this evening."

I cleared the rest of the dishes, then headed to the bedroom to see if Eddie was still in bed. If he was already up, I hoped he might want to go with me to the farmer's market. I thought it might be relaxing for him. When he'd come home from San Diego a few days ago, he'd been tired and anxious, more anxious than he'd been in weeks. And when I had asked him how the assignment had gone, he'd said it had gone well, but not as well as it could have.

I got the impression he was sugarcoating it, as in it hadn't gone well at all. And that impression was reinforced by the poor way he'd slept. He was usually a sound sleeper—except when under extreme pressure. He had tossed and turned after that first massive pay cut at the *Times*, and again after he'd found out about my cancer diagnosis. And ever since San Diego, he'd been doing it yet again.

As I walked down the hallway, I heard the shower going, and what I should have done was continue forward, pop my head into the bathroom, and ask my husband if he wanted to go to the farmer's market to relax a little. But instead I stopped when I spotted his laptop on the coffee table in the den. He never left it out in the open anymore. When he wasn't using it—and he'd been on it pretty much non-stop since returning from San Diego—he'd taken to putting it in his desk drawer. The desk he never used because he preferred to work on the couch.

It was seeing the laptop out there in plain sight that made me wonder what had been disappointing about his trip to San Diego. What if his job was based on straight commission and he'd lost out on the commission for the San Diego assignment? That would explain his anxiety—he was behind the eight ball when it came to his next paycheck.

So I marched into the den and opened the laptop, thinking I might find out something that would reveal whether Eddie worked for straight commission. But the screen didn't show a desktop packed with files; the screen was black except for a prompt asking for a password.

Eddie had never before used a password to log on to his computer. I guess it made sense that he might do so now, because he'd told me that his job required secrecy. Still, it bothered me.

I quickly moved to the doorway and listened to see if the shower was still running. It was. I hurried back to the laptop, feeling like an underhanded snoop, but I couldn't help myself. My instincts told me something was up.

I tried a few different passwords—the ones we used for our various other accounts. Citibank, Netflix, Amazon, et cetera.

None of them worked.

I tried other passwords based on significant dates in Eddie's life, then significant places.

Finally, after checking the shower again and hearing that it was no longer running, I gave up and closed the computer, ready to scoot out of the den before Eddie caught me. But right then, I noticed something odd. Something about Eddie's computer—something about seeing it closed—but I couldn't quite put my finger on exactly what was odd about it.

In the kitchen, I poured myself a second cup of coffee. I never drank a second cup of coffee unless I had a lot of work to do, but right now I felt I needed it. And as I sipped it, I decided that if Eddie was hiding something, it would be better to press him for answers, rather than to snoop.

I reached over to my computer bag and pulled out my laptop, thinking I would get my mind off my suspicions by answering a few emails. But right before I opened my laptop, I suddenly realized what had seemed odd about Eddie's computer. The extra cup of coffee must have given me a jolt of alertness, enough to understand what I'd seen.

Something about the laptop was different.

Weeks ago, I'd felt weak—weaker than normal. So, worried that I had an infection, I'd asked Eddie to take me to Cedars. I knew it was possible that I still had a compromised immune system, even though months had passed since the chemo treatments—and thus if I waited too long to take action, an infection could quickly turn into a crippling setback.

At the hospital, the doctor ordered up a dose of antibiotics as a precaution until the blood culture came back. The antibiotic IV drip took an hour to administer, and Eddie stayed with me during that hour in the treatment room. He had his MacBook Air with him, the one he'd bought because he'd needed a more powerful computer for ADM.

While we waited for the drip to finish, he worked on his laptop, but I was sure that what he was really doing was the same thing I was doing: hoping this didn't turn out to be an infection and a setback. I could tell he was apprehensive, anxious to get the results from the culture, because he was avoiding eye contact with me.

He was facing me, hunched over his computer, which meant I did a lot of staring at the computer's lid.

I noticed a scratch on it.

And that scratch was now gone.

The computer in the den—the one I'd just tried to break into—bore no sign of that scratch. Which meant Eddie had gotten another new computer, another MacBook Air. But that seemed ludicrous. Unless, of course, the first MacBook Air had died. But that didn't make sense either. If that was the case, he would've said something to me; he would've complained quite a few times that his computer had died even though it was practically brand new.

I gulped down the rest of my coffee.

There was a second explanation: Eddie had two MacBook Airs. *But why?*

Before I could come up with an answer, Eddie stepped into the kitchen.

"Good morning," he said.

"How was your sleep?" I asked.

"Good." He poured himself a cup of coffee.

"Honey, I know I already asked you this, but how did it go in San Diego—really?" I wanted to bring up the computer, but couldn't figure out how.

"Honestly, I didn't get as much information about the company as I wanted. So I'm having a hard time evaluating them."

"What happened in San Diego that stopped you from getting the information you need?"

"I guess you could chalk it up to bad luck. One of the executives who agreed to an interview got buried in something and canceled on me."

"Can't you just reschedule?"

"It's too late. ADM wants the report tomorrow. Everything is time-sensitive when it comes to acquisitions. I'm going to have to get the information I need from other sources. But the problem is that the only way to get the good stuff is straight from the horse's mouth."

"I hope you can cobble together a report," I said.

"I will," he responded. Then, with coffee in hand, he headed toward the kitchen door. "I just hope it's good enough."

"Do you want me to warm up a blueberry muffin for you?" I asked.

"Sure—thanks," he answered as he exited.

The blueberry muffin would give me another chance to bring up the computer. I pulled one out from the fridge and placed it in the oven. As I waited for the muffin to warm, I wondered if Eddie's tossing and turning was due to his failed trip to San Diego and nothing else. Maybe it had nothing to do with whether or not he was going to get a commission check.

I put the muffin on a plate and headed to the den, ready to ask him about the computer, rather than delve into the bigger issue of his paychecks. Eddie was on the couch, hunched over his laptop, which he promptly closed as I approached him.

I handed him the plate, and he gave me a gracious smile. "Thank you," he said.

"You're welcome." I glanced down at his laptop, trying to do so casually. "Hey, is that a new computer?" I asked.

He didn't answer immediately, but his gracious smile disappeared. He looked at me for a beat, like he'd been caught off-guard—and that was all I needed to see to know I'd ensnared him. But exactly what I'd ensnared him in, I had no idea.

"Yeah," he said, sitting up a little straighter, like he was regrouping. "I dropped the other one and damaged the hard drive, so I had to replace it."

Innocent enough explanation, except that he hadn't said anything about it earlier. When you drop your new computer and break it, you talk about that, berating yourself for your carelessness. But he hadn't mentioned it at all. Why?

Because—and I had no doubt about this—he had just made up that explanation on the spot.

"Why didn't they just replace the hard drive?"

He averted his eyes and again hesitated before answering. Then he said, "I was worried there was more damage, so I went with a new computer."

"Apple Care covered it?"

"Yeah. They're not supposed to if you cause the damage yourself, but I got lucky and had a nice store manager." He glanced at the computer. "How could you tell this baby was new?"

"Your other computer had a scratch on the lid."

"Oh," he said, and then reached for the muffin. He took a bite, and his smile returned.

"I'll let you get back to work," I said.

In the kitchen, I sat down and tried to figure out why he'd lied about his computer. If he had two computers, why didn't he just tell me? And if he really had replaced the first MacBook Air, why not tell me the reason why? His lie had been so obvious. And I couldn't help but remember that when he'd upgraded computers when starting his new job, he hadn't wanted to give his old computer to Jake.

I concluded that the only way to find out what he was hiding was to get a look at what was actually on his computer. So basically I was back to snooping. I guess that was because I didn't know what I was looking for anymore—just that something was up.

After googling methods for breaking into a password-protected MacBook Air, it became clear to me that the fastest way for me to do this was to enlist Jake's help. He'd be able to cut to the chase, which I couldn't do from the various methods I'd found. But I had to find a way to pull Jake into this without letting him know that I was suspicious about his dad.

Jake rolled into the kitchen about an hour later, grabbed a bowl of cereal, and sat down at the table. I didn't want to lie to him, but I justified it to myself by blaming Eddie. It was *his* lie that begat *my* lie.

"I've been meaning to ask you something," I said to him. "I need your advice."

"Go for it." He chowed down on his cereal.

"It's about computers."

"My forte."

"Lila wants to log on to one of her old computers and she can't remember the password. Is there a way for her to log on without the password?"

Jake looked up from his cereal and smirked. "I know what you're up to, Mom."

I blushed, feeling ashamed—but ready to double down on my lie to keep him away from the truth.

But before I could say anything, he continued. "Lila wants to break into her daughter's computer."

"You're right," I said, relieved. "I'm sorry I lied."

"I'm not big on invasion of privacy," he responded.

"I'm not either," I said, "but in this case it's a good thing. Lila thinks her daughter is getting bullied and that she's hiding it from her."

Jake took a few bites of his cereal before replying. "Why can't she just talk to her daughter about it?"

"She's tried. But her daughter says it's nothing—that Lila is blowing it all out of proportion."

Jake took a deep breath.

"She just wants to help her daughter," I said. "If it turns out she needs help."

"This isn't fair, Mom."

"What's not fair?"

"You're putting me in a moral dilemma. If I don't help you break into this girl's computer and something happens to her, then it's kinda my fault for not helping. But if I do help you, I'm doing something illegal and unethical."

I should've known Jake would take this very seriously—he always thought things through. I should've stuck to my original story of Lila breaking into her own computer. But there was no turning back.

"I didn't mean to put you in this position," I said, "but I'd appreciate the help."

Jake took his cereal bowl over to the sink and rinsed it out. Then he stood there for a few seconds as if he was considering my request.

"Okay," he said. "It's pretty simple. There are a couple of ways to do it."

He then went on to explain how, and I asked him to write it all down, so I could relay it to Lila. He did, but he left me with a caveat before heading back to his room.

"I hope Lila isn't doing this just to snoop," he said.

I didn't respond. I'd already lied enough to him.

After he exited the kitchen, I went back onto my computer, but all I was really doing was biding my time until I could break into Eddie's computer.

That opportunity came less than two hours later.

EDDIE

CHAPTER TWENTY-SIX

I wished I had come up with a better explanation for why I'd purchased another new computer. But there were only two options: either the first computer had been damaged beyond repair, or it had been stolen. Maybe I should've gone with stolen, but when Jenny asked her question, not only was my mind on the investigation into Rose's murder, but I was blindsided. I had never expected Jenny to say anything about my computer.

The whole incident did make me wonder if it would be better to just rely on VPN's to cover my tracks, rather than buying new computers. For if I ever did become the focus of an investigation, wouldn't it come out that I'd been buying new computers way too often? I didn't know if paying cash was enough to cover my tracks. I needed to think this through more thoroughly and come up with a definite solution. And I vowed to do that—if Abel didn't end my employment, and my life, first.

And to find out if that was on the horizon, I had been searching every corner of the Internet for new information on the investigation in San Diego. Since my chat with Larry, I'd been tracking stories about Rose David, the kind, elderly woman found buried in her own yard, in an idyllic neighborhood overlooking the Pacific.

The investigation had gained a lot of traction in the press in a short amount of time, but what I didn't know was whether that traction extended to the police as well. The press, especially the Internet press, was running wild with the story. But without being down there and investigating the old-fashioned way—as a reporter on the scene, hassling the police detectives in person—I didn't know if the evidence popping up in the news was leaks from the police, or evidence dug up by reporters. And the police blotters weren't much help on that front because the story was unfolding so quickly.

The one thing that worried me the most wasn't even a piece of evidence—at least, not any of the evidence I knew about so far. What worried me most was simply the fact that Rose's body had been discovered so soon after the crime. With her body fresh and not yet rotting in the ground, and with her clothes not yet decaying, I feared that I'd left damning evidence intact. Forensic analysis might discover fibers from my clothes, or worse, skin detritus, from which came DNA. All of this could have been avoided if I'd taken the right precautions, and not blithely—or was it out of panic?—counted on the body being discovered in the distant future.

But even if the police collected forensic evidence from Rose's body and clothes, they'd still need evidence that would point them in my direction—for forensic evidence would only help if they had a suspect to tie it to.

Right then, a new story on Rose David posted. It was on the *Union-Tribune* blog.

I paled as I read it.

It was reported that Wendy Bester, Rose David's tenant, had told the police that she'd passed out the night before Rose disappeared. I could have lived with that part, since I knew for sure that Wendy remembered nothing else from that night and that even if she underwent the most thorough physical examination, it would reveal nothing. In those two ways, she was like any other target.

But what I had paled at was the story's conclusion: that there was a connection between Wendy's fainting spell and Rose's murder. Of course, I didn't know if that was the reporter's conclusion or the police's conclusion. But it didn't really matter, did it? It was now out there.

I had to talk to Abel; I had to ask him for help. My cover-up was falling apart. And when I asked for help, I also had to beg for leniency. I had to beg for a second chance. For it was possible, or even likely, that Abel had already made up his mind to get rid of me.

I took a deep breath and told myself to think everything through again, slowly and without panicking.

After five minutes of doing so, during which I pushed my fear away, I concluded that Abel was just as motivated to keep the police as far away from the truth as I was. Maybe he needed me to go back down to San Diego and help clean up this mess. Because if the police linked Rose to me, whether I was dead or alive, they'd be one step closer to Abel, too.

That line of reasoning led me to consider a new possibility. Was there a way to use my link to Abel to protect myself from *him*, too? Could I blackmail Abel just as I'd blackmailed Ben? I could tell the alien that if anything happened to me, evidence of his existence would be delivered to the *LA Times*.

But I knew that blackmailing him wasn't going to be as easy as it had been with Ben. And would the *LA Times* even run the story? Bob, the editor in chief, would need evidence. It wouldn't matter that I'd been on the paper's staff for two decades, or that I was his friend. But I *had* evidence, didn't I?

The tranquilizer pellets, the recovery capsules, and the copper straw.

I could deliver these items to Bob—a "blackmail package" to be opened should something happen to me. And if my blackmail plan worked, Abel would have to replace the tools of my trade with a new set.

Still, I strongly suspected I couldn't count on just these items. Certainly Abel wouldn't let me walk around with evidence proving an alien presence right here on Earth. Either they were made from compounds found on Earth, or they were designed like those tapes in the old *Mission Impossible* TV series and would self-destruct if they fell into the wrong hands.

I also had the gold card through which the alien contacted me— and, as I'd come to believe months ago, through which he tracked me. But I couldn't make the gold card part of the blackmail package. It would give away the location of the package while I kept it hidden and carried out my threat. And also, because Abel would know that the card wasn't with me anymore, he'd be tipped off about my planned betrayal.

No, I needed more evidence. Hard evidence. And that meant I had to go to Abel's. Which was a good move regardless. I could ask for help in covering up the Del Mar fiasco, and at the same time I could look to gather evidence with which to blackmail him. Evidence that left no doubt that an alien lived in the hills of Beverly.

I hesitated before starting my next Internet search. I had always assumed that Abel monitored my searches, regardless of the VPN— the VPN may have kept humans off my digital trail, but not Abel. And I didn't want him to be privy to this next search.

I sat there frozen until I convinced myself, rightly or wrongly, that it was okay if Abel saw what I was up to: he'd think I was worried about the trail of evidence I'd left behind now that Rose's body had been discovered. So I dug in and researched how forensic investigators gathered genetic material for DNA testing. But what I was really looking for was how *I* could gather genetic material for DNA testing.

I figured the only evidence that would be truly convincing to anyone was DNA evidence. If I could get a sample of the alien's skin, surely it would reveal some anomaly, something so strange—maybe even completely unknown genetic material—that although it might not prove my outlandish claim, it would raise enough red flags to get reporters, law enforcement, and other interested parties to investigate further.

The Internet yielded only one strong possibility when it came to collecting DNA samples from Abel's house—a procedure called "Touch DNA." Just like its name implied, the procedure relied on gathering skin cells left behind after a person touched something. The other ways to collect DNA samples—through blood, hair, fingernails, et cetera—were out of the question.

I made mental notes on how to collect a proper sample, then I shut off my laptop, stuck it in the desk drawer, and went into the kitchen. Jenny was on her laptop.

"Guess what?" I said. "I caught a break."

She looked up. "How?"

"I lined up an interview with a former employee of that San Diego company. The guy now lives in Thousand Oaks. So I'm going to drive up there."

"You think he's willing to give you the information you need for your report?"

"I don't know for sure, but when I talked to him on the phone, he seemed open to it." I turned to go, leaving another lie in my wake.

At CVS, I bought cotton swabs and tiny plastic bags.

Then, on the way to Abel's, I considered both the worst-case scenario and the best case. The worst case was that I never left Abel's house. That the alien liquefied me as he had Ben. But if it looked like that scenario was playing out, I'd issue my blackmail threat right then and there—even though it was premature, since I had no blackmail package ready to be delivered.

The best-case scenario was that Abel would ask me to go back down to San Diego and clean up the mess. That would give me time to make my blackmail threat real.

As I drove down the small winding roads that led to Abel's grand home, I went through the exact words I'd use to issue my blackmail threat, in case it came to that. While I was rehearsing, it hit me: I could leave the blackmail package with Larry instead of with the *LA Times*. I could take advantage of the very media I hated; he'd run with the story even if the evidence was flimsy.

Talk about clickbait.

And he could protect himself by running the story with his own commentary doubting the veracity of my story. He'd merely be laying out the flimsy evidence for the reader to decide for him or herself.

So the decision was made. If I made it out of Abel's alive, I'd prepare a blackmail package for Larry. Then maybe, in addition, one for the *LA Times*.

When I pulled up to the gate in front of Abel's house, it opened. He was expecting me because he was tracking me through the gold card. As I drove toward the house, the garage door opened, as it always did.

I pulled into the garage and waited until the door closed behind me before I got out of the car. Another ritual I was used to. The door to the house was open, inviting me in.

I walked inside, and my eyes immediately fell on the door leading to the harvesting room—the room with the loveseat. But the door was closed, because I didn't have a target. The door to Abel's office was closed as well.

So I walked down the hallway and into the living room.

A few seconds later, Abel came down the staircase from the second floor. This was the first time I'd seen him enter the living room from upstairs.

I immediately noticed the alien's gait was different. He was moving slowly, as if he wasn't really paying attention to his surroundings. And as he got closer, I noticed something else different about him: his large black eye had an extra gleam to it. It was as if its surface was glassier, more reflective, shinier.

Was the alien betraying some kind of emotion for the first time? If so, I would've expected to see anger, and this didn't look like anger. But I was anthropomorphizing him. Maybe for his species, anger looked exactly like this.

I reminded myself that I needed to focus on the surfaces the alien touched, if any, and not on trying to read his emotional state. The only way to get a Touch DNA sample was to make sure I swabbed the exact spot that Abel touched.

Abel stopped about four feet away from me. That was also a change. He usually stopped much farther away. But what didn't change was his electronic voice.

"I expected you to contact me sooner," he said.

"I should've. I made a mistake." My eyes flicked to the device in Abel's hand, the one from which the electronic voice emanated. There was no doubt the device was covered with skin samples.

"You were supposed to dispose of her body," he said. "Didn't you understand what that meant?"

"I did. But I thought it was too risky to drive around with a dead body in my car. I should've buried her much deeper."

"You should have made sure there was no body to be found."

I remembered that this had crossed my mind. The *Breaking Bad* solution.

"I did a poor job," I said. "Is there something I can do to fix it?"

"No."

"Is there something you can do?"

"What would you have me do?"

Was Abel asking me for advice? That didn't make any sense. I stared into the alien's eye, trying to figure out if he was actually being snarky. But all I saw was that glassy surface, gleaming with its newfound sheen.

"My guess," I said, "is that you've already done everything you can to keep yourself isolated from the crime."

Rather than acknowledge whether or not he had, he asked, "Is there anything else I need to know about what went on in Del Mar?"

"Just that I did my best to cover my tracks." That wasn't a lie. The problem was that, although I'd become better at my job—abducting targets and returning them—I was far from a pro when it came to covering up a crime scene.

Abel didn't respond.

Again, I got the same impression I'd had when he came down the stairs: that he wasn't paying attention to his surroundings. Was his mind on something else? Had he already moved on to a new employee? Should I issue my blackmail threat now?

"Are you going to give me my next assignment?" I said, hoping his answer would give me some indication of what he was thinking.

"Yes. But it won't be the usual assignment."

"What do you want me to do?" I asked. I couldn't help but think he was going to send me on a suicide mission.

"I'll contact you."

I didn't know whether I should follow up with another question. As it stood, it looked like issuing my blackmail threat would be premature. The alien wasn't making a move to liquefy me, which gave me time to put teeth into my blackmail threat; I could gather more evidence.

He turned and started back toward the staircase. He hadn't

touched anything in the room, but I wondered if I should still swab a surface. Of course, I'd be relying on luck—for only luck would steer me to swabbing a spot that Abel had touched.

I looked at the open patio door—had he touched the handle? The door had always stood open; for all I knew it had been open for years. I looked at the fireplace tools—had he touched the poker? The fireplace looked like it had never been used, so he'd probably never touched the poker.

But then I realized, I couldn't swab anything in this room because I couldn't just hang back while Abel headed up the staircase. He'd see with his all-knowing eye that I was hanging back. I'd have to swab a surface in another part of the house.

So I moved toward the hallway, as if I was planning to leave, and I slipped my hand into my pocket. I wrapped my fingers around a tiny plastic baggie, one of three, into which I'd put a cotton swab.

I glanced at Abel just before I stepped into the hallway. He was progressing up the staircase slowly, as if his mind was a million miles away.

In the hallway, I headed toward the garage. As I passed the door to Abel's office, I saw a swabbable surface staring me in the face: the doorknob. Abel *had* to have touched it.

But then I had a better idea. I didn't know when Abel had last touched this doorknob, but there was another doorknob that he had touched probably less than thirty minutes ago: the knob on the door leading into the garage.

That door had been open for me when I'd pulled into garage—as it always was when I arrived—and there was no doubt that Abel had opened it himself, since there was no one else to do it.

I pulled the plastic baggie from my pocket and glanced over to my shoulder to make sure Abel hadn't changed course. He hadn't.

When I reached the door, I'd already pulled the cotton swab out of the baggie. But before I swabbed the doorknob, I checked the hallway behind me again, nervous that Abel would appear and catch me red-handed.

The coast was clear, so it was now or never.

I leaned down and swabbed the doorknob. Then I carefully placed the swab in the baggie.

I stepped into the garage, leaving the door open behind me as I always did. But as I moved toward my car, I had a moment of doubt. Should I close the door behind me? I never had before, but that's because I'd always had a target in my arms. Would leaving the door open now give away my betrayal?

I told myself I was overthinking it. I climbed into my car and put the baggie with the sample in it in the glove compartment.

A minute later, when I drove through the gate and off the property, I felt a sense of relief. I'd gotten out alive.

But could I stay alive?

ABEL

CHAPTER TWENTY-SEVEN

The human feared for his life—and rightly so. If it wasn't for the Kalera, I would have disposed of him during his impromptu visit. He'd never know that the Kalera had saved his life.

And it had done so much more. This batch had turned out to be even more powerful than I'd thought. The clarity and speed and complexity of my thoughts were unparalleled. As soon as the drug had permeated my system, my mind shifted into a hyper-intelligent state. I was able to instantly dissect numerous plans to integrate myself back into life on Tracea.

One plan passed all the checks.

I had been working on that plan for a few days, non-stop, under the influence of the Kalera, when Eddie dropped by. I should've expected the visit because, even as I'd been working on my plan, I'd been paying attention to the unfolding investigation into Rose David's death. The human had done a terrible job of covering up his tracks, and unfortunately, I wasn't in a position to do as much as I would've liked myself. If this had happened decades ago, I could've easily pointed the investigation in another direction. If this had happened during the Richard Deaks years, I could've made the problem go away days ago.

But as it stood now, I wasn't able to manipulate the investigation enough to throw the police completely off-track. There was still the possibility that the investigation could eventually lead to me.

I had hoped my heightened intellect, thanks to the Kalera, would enable me to come up with some new way to manipulate the case. But regardless of what angle I took, it was clear there wasn't much I could do. So instead of helping me come up with a solution, the Kalera only reinforced what I'd already concluded: that over the last few cycles, it had become much harder for me to manipulate information without leaving a trail.

The Kalera did deliver on another front though. During Eddie's visit, I'd picked up cues that indicated he'd become the new Richard Deaks. The human wanted to expose me. But this time, it wasn't because he wanted to go down in the annals of history as a hero. Eddie was motivated by pure selfishness. He wanted to protect himself and his job. He reflected the values of his generation, just as Deaks had reflected the values of his.

But though the values that humans held dear changed from generation to generation, it had become clear that their behavioral characteristics didn't. For example, in all my cycles here, I'd seen that the species was consistently empathetic. I believed that their capacity for empathy was far greater than that of any other species. At least of the ones I knew about. I often wondered whether their capacity for empathy was what made up for the species' lack of intellect—or at least, whether it would eventually do so. By empathizing with each other, might they as a species make great strides? There was power in unity. I'd seen that across the universe.

My thoughts suddenly slowed down; the Kalera's effect was waning. It was time to focus on putting the final touches on my plan. The plan had to be perfect if I was going to have any chance of reintegrating myself into life on Tracea. But the more my thoughts slowed, the harder it was to focus.

I was tempted to take another Kalera capsule right then. Sure, it was a terrible idea. The second time wouldn't be as powerful as the first—and the second time was the road to addiction.

I postponed that decision, and instead ran another simulation of my plan on my workstation. I also continued to monitor the Rose David investigation. I was plugged into the internal police communications in San Diego as well as the private networks of the news outlets. And the number of news outlets covering the story had grown exponentially.

If Eddie had known the truth about how far the police investigation had progressed, he would no doubt have threatened to expose me during his visit, rather than wait. Although the human knew the situation wasn't good, he didn't know that one of Rose David's neighbors had reported seeing something unusual on the day before Rose David went missing. The neighbor told the police that he'd seen a tourist strolling along Lunela Drive taking in the view of the Pacific. That wasn't unusual for the neighborhood, but what was unusual was that he'd seen the tourist a second time, on the same day, taking the same stroll.

And there was something else the human didn't know: the police were looking through security camera footage from businesses in Del Mar to see if anyone who'd walked by or stopped in on that day fit the description of the tourist that the neighbor had given.

I felt my mind slowing even more, but now I was fine with it. I'd finished running the simulation of my plan, and it looked good. More than good; it looked excellent. But unfortunately, the plan still called for one element I couldn't get by myself. I'd tried to work it out so this element wouldn't be necessary, but I hadn't been able to. This was the reason I hadn't disposed of the human during the visit; this was the reason the Kalera had saved him. I needed him for one more job. I needed him to get this element. That was why I'd let him walk out alive.

Next time the human wouldn't be so lucky.

JENNY

CHAPTER TWENTY-EIGHT

Jake's method of breaking into Eddie's computer had worked like a charm. *An evil charm used by a snoopy wife,* I thought, because I'd felt guilty every step of the way. Still, my suspicion had overpowered my guilt.

When I checked Eddie's computer files, I didn't see any evidence he was doing research on companies that ADM was looking to acquire. I couldn't find a single Word document or Excel spreadsheet about an acquisition target. I couldn't find one PDF download from a company website. And I couldn't find any summary of an interview with a company executive.

There wasn't a single file on his computer indicating that he'd been conducting research on even one company, much less a bunch of companies. And what surprised me even more than that—*shocked* was the right word—was something else I couldn't find: any file, document, or email that had anything to do with Archer Daniels Midland. That set off alarms. If he was working for ADM, surely there would have been some sign of that.

There wasn't.

There also wasn't anything on his computer to indicate that he was working for any other organization. In short, there was no indication that he had a job at all.

So how was he paying for our expenses? How was he paying for our medical bills?

After checking a few more files, I looked at his search history and saw that he'd deleted it.

I was tempted to ask Jake if there was a way to retrieve someone's search history, but I thought I'd already lied to him enough. Besides, I'd confirmed my suspicions. Eddie was definitely hiding something.

As I checked a couple more files, ready to end my snooping, I realized something else. Eddie didn't have many files on this laptop. It was as if he'd transferred very little from his other MacBook Air onto this one. And what about the files from the original computer? The one he'd owned for years, the one he hadn't wanted to pass on to Jake—where were those files? He'd had thousands of files related to his work at the *LA Times* on that computer. Had he purged them all?

That didn't seem right. He'd want access to those files—they contained resources, research, and contacts he'd spent years collecting. So where were they?

Had he kept his old computer? The one he claimed to sell on Craigslist?

I put this question aside for now and circled back to the matter of his job. If Eddie wasn't working for ADM, what had he been doing for the last few months? And what was he doing when he left the house for hours on end? Where the hell did he go?

I suddenly felt queasy and chilled. Not because of chemo—the effects were long gone—but because my string of questions had led me to a question I didn't want to think about: Was Eddie having an affair?

That was ridiculous. He was lying about a job that he didn't have, and he had found a source of money that I didn't know about. None of that suggested anything to do with an affair.

Still, I couldn't push the thoughts of infidelity away; I was already trying to string together evidence to prove it. But the evidence was all circumstantial: primarily his odd schedule, which included a lot of interviews with executives at night. He had explained these away by telling me that they had to be low profile, so no one would get wind of ADM's acquisition plans.

I wondered if his trip to San Diego hadn't been a business trip, but an illicit jaunt with his mistress. And that upsetting thought suddenly led to another piece of circumstantial evidence—a very personal one. Since my cancer diagnosis, though most things in our relationship had remained the same, a few hadn't. We'd always had a great sex life, but the cancer had changed that. Specifically, the chemo aspect of the cancer. I didn't feel like having sex as much as I had before the treatments, and my desire to have sex was only just now returning.

A bit late, I thought.

Surely, my lack of desire had affected Eddie. When we'd talked about it, he'd been understanding. But what kind of husband *wouldn't* be understanding? Or at least say he was?

I decided that when Eddie returned from Thousand Oaks—or from wherever he really was—I would confront him. Not about infidelity—I understood that on that front, I was jumping to conclusions—but about his job. I'd demand to know the truth about ADM. Then from there, I'd decide if I'd also accuse him of being unfaithful. That would depend on what he said about ADM, on whether or not he really had a job.

*

Eddie came back shortly after noon, but I had to wait a little longer before confronting him. I didn't want Jake in the house when Eddie and I talked. But as soon as Jake left for Sam's, I marched into the den—where Eddie had been holed up on his laptop since returning—and got right into it.

"Eddie, we need to talk," I said.

He closed his computer. "Is something up with Hannah?"

"No. Something's up with you."

"What are you talking about?"

"I think you're lying about your job."

He swallowed, and his eyes widened.

"No. Not really," he said.

"'Not really'? What does 'not really' mean? Are you lying or not?"

"It's just that there are some things about my job that I can't talk about."

"Then let's start with the things you can talk about."

"I've told you all those things."

He was sticking to his lie, and the anger I'd been repressing since I'd walked into the room was starting to assert itself.

"I don't believe you," I said firmly.

"What don't you believe?"

"Any of it. All of it."

"I'm sorry," he said, and for a second I thought he was about to come clean. But instead he said, "I'm sorry you don't believe me."

"What is *wrong* with you?" I couldn't keep my anger in check any longer. "Why can't you tell me what's going on? I'm your wife, for Christ's sake!"

His face contorted as if he was in pain. But he didn't say anything. He stared at me as if he was hoping my anger would subside.

I didn't say anything either for about thirty seconds or so. Finally, when the silence was unbearable, I said, "Tell me the truth about your job. Right now."

He took a deep breath. "I'm working for a private investigation firm."

"What?" I was totally taken by surprise.

"I couldn't bring myself to tell you."

"Why not?"

"Because it's a nasty business. Most of my work is investigating cheating husbands."

I almost blurt-laughed over the irony. I suspected him of infidelity, not of exposing infidelity.

"I tail cheating husbands," he continued, "and/or their suspected mistresses. If it looks like the two are having an affair, then I try to build an airtight case."

"Seriously?" This was so different from what I'd expected that it was hard to swallow. It was a far cry from the fictitious job at ADM.

"Yeah, seriously," he said. "It's not as low-down as it sounds though. Most of the time, the investigation is part of a legitimate lawsuit—a messy divorce. But I also work on other types of cases."

"Like what?" I was now trying to fit this admission into what I knew about his behavior.

"Like sometimes a family with too much money on their hands hires us to find out whether the guy who's dating their daughter is a gold-digger. You'd be surprised how many families do that."

I'd recently heard a case like that on the news.

"Or a guy wants to know if the woman he's planning to propose to has been cheating on him." Eddie shook his head and let out a little chuckle. "And believe it or not, I had one case where a husband who was cheating on his wife was investigating his mistress to make sure *she* wasn't cheating on *him*."

Eddie looked less pained, like he was relieved to get this off his chest.

"So why do you spend so much time on your computer?" I asked.

"Because these days, you can get a lot of digital evidence that helps prove a case. Especially with some of the software tools the PI firm has." He let out a breath, then glanced at his computer. "And now I can also tell you the real reason I have a new computer: the PI firm doesn't want anything traced back to them or me. So every couple of months, they give me a computer that's outfitted with protective software, then dump the old one as a precaution."

"That's crazy."

"Yeah. I think so, too. But it's because of the law firms who hire them. They want everything hush-hush. Especially if our investigation is tied to a pending lawsuit. They're the ones who don't want anything traced back to them."

"Why did you tell me you were working with ADM?" I asked. "Why the whole acquisition story?"

"Since both involved investigating, I thought it was a good cover. I was stupid."

"I agree with that," I said, and then realized he had another reason for wanting to hide the job from me. It wasn't just because it was shady.

"It's dangerous, isn't it?" I asked.

"Yeah," he said, without hesitation.

I didn't have to ask the next question: Why did you take the job if it was dangerous? The answer was obvious: money. The job paid my medical bills. But I did have another question.

"Eddie—why did they offer *you* the job?"

He let out another chuckle. "Honey, they didn't offer me the job. I begged them for it. A reporter I knew from the *Seattle Times* had become a private investigator and was doing well. So I asked around and found a couple of openings. But when I applied, they told me they were only interested in former cops. So I begged them for a shot—selling my *LA Times* experience and that Seattle reporter's success. When they still said no, I asked them to give me one case, freelance. I'd do it for free. They did, and the rest is history." He smiled. "But I'm sorry I didn't tell you right off the bat."

"I'm glad you told me now," I said, and I was. The bottom line was that he'd taken a job in a shady business and, therefore, had been acting shady.

Eddie got up and we both instinctually hugged. I felt good, and I was positive he did, too. I would be worried about his safety from here on in, but I'd have to live with that. Still, it was better than living with a lie.

We embraced, enjoying a moment of closeness, until a ringing phone interrupted us.

I walked over to the desk, picked up the phone, and said, "Hello." It turned out to be one of Eddie's former tutoring students. I covered the mouthpiece and turned to Eddie. "It's Mason Kingsley," I said. "He wants to talk to you."

"Wow," Eddie said. "Those tutoring days seem like ancient history."

As he walked over to take the phone, I noticed that the pained look had returned to his face.

EDDIE

CHAPTER TWENTY-NINE

"Things are going okay," Mason said on the phone, after I'd asked him how he was holding up. "At least, better than they were," he added tentatively. "But I let my studies slide."

"That's understandable," I said. Of course it was. You didn't just move on from losing your dad and blindly get on with your life.

"But I think I'm ready to regroup," Mason said. "And I need some help. I mean with my studies. I want to catch up."

I knew what was coming next—and I wished it wasn't. But it came anyway.

"Will you tutor me again?" Mason asked. "I know you can bring me up to speed better than any other tutor."

I wanted to say the timing was all wrong, but man, did I owe this kid big time. I'd ruined his life. So after a second of hesitation, I did the right thing. "Of course," I said. "I don't tutor anymore, but I'll be more than happy to get you back on track."

"Thank you, Mr. Hart. I really appreciate it."

How could I refuse the kid? He was reaching out for help, reaching out to the very man who was responsible for leaving him fatherless and for sending his life into a tailspin. This was a chance to make amends for my terrible sin.

But I wasn't fooling myself; I knew no amends would bring Mason's father back. But I'd do what I could, including, if necessary, anonymously getting the boy and his mother cash, in case they hadn't found the safe or gotten access to wherever else Ben kept his ill-gotten gains.

When I got off the phone, I explained to Jenny that tragedy had struck Mason's family, and that the kid had fallen way behind in his studies; I was going to try and help him catch up.

So that afternoon, rather than sitting around waiting for more bad news to dribble out from Rose David's murder investigation, or waiting for Abel to contact me with this new mystery assignment— which might be a suicide assignment—I headed over to Mason's house. But not before I'd loaded a hundred thousand dollars in cash into the trunk of my car. I kept the bulk of my earnings in a couple of boxes in the garage, among dozens of boxes of memorabilia that we hadn't looked at in two decades. I'd planned to move the money to a more secure location, but still hadn't gotten around to it.

I had no idea how I'd actually give the money to Mason anonymously. But if I saw that he and his mom were in dire straits, I'd figure out a way.

When I pulled out of the garage, I questioned what I was doing. Shouldn't I use this time to get the sample in the glove compartment tested? Shouldn't I start implementing my blackmail plan? Why was I assuaging my guilt instead?

Because my guilt was growing stronger, taking over, when I needed to push it back. I was ashamed of the new lie I'd thrown at Jenny; it had added to my guilt. But I knew the ADM story wasn't cutting it. It never had, had it?

As I drove up Beverly Glen, nostalgia swept over me. I hadn't driven this route since I'd stopped tutoring, and it now felt like those tutoring days were carefree compared to my new life, where I was trying to stay one step ahead of a murder charge. That was how drastically my perspective had changed, for the reality was that those tutoring days hadn't been carefree. I'd been desperate to find a job and desperate for money, which was how I'd ended up zeroing in on Mason's father in the first place.

No, those days weren't carefree. The unvarnished truth was that I'd been transported into a brutish, ugly reality—a menacing reality—when compared to my days as a tutor.

I turned onto Tiffany Circle and drove down the familiar street of McMansions. If I was going to be of any help to Mason, I had to change my frame of mind and channel the confidence I'd gained through my job. The confidence I'd been high on before my blunder in Del Mar.

That confidence was the best part of my new life. I'd adapted. I'd reinvented myself. I'd come a hell of a long way. *And* I'd earned a hell of a lot of money.

I pulled up to Mason's house and parked.

As soon as I stepped up to the front door, the door swung open, and Mason greeted me. "Thanks for coming, Mr. Hart," he said, and invited me inside.

He led me toward the den and didn't try to make small talk.

"I'm sorry you fell behind in your studies," I said, breaking the uncomfortable silence. "But you're a great student. You'll catch up in no time."

"I hope so." He didn't sound very sure of himself.

"We'll get you there."

We stepped into the den, and I noticed the desk had nothing on it. He'd always had his computer and whatever school textbooks and papers we'd need ready to go.

"Do you want to get your stuff and show me where you are with everything?" I asked.

"I can talk you through it first," he said. But he didn't sit down, and he didn't bring a second chair over to the desk.

"Sounds good," I said.

"I haven't been able to concentrate for a while," he said. "Even on the subjects I'm good at."

"That's perfectly natural."

"You mean because of my dad." He wasn't going to be obtuse, and that was probably a healthy thing.

"Yeah," I said. "No one can get right back to business after a family tragedy, Mason."

"But it's been months and months, Mr. Hart."

I wasn't a grief counselor, but I wanted to say the right things, so I spoke from my heart. "Learning to live with a change in your life as big as this takes time. Especially when it's something so sad and unexpected. I know you're hard on yourself, but this isn't something to be hard on yourself about."

"Yes, it is," he said, a bit harsher than I'd expected.

"I know it seems that way. Because we're helpless. We can't do anything to change what happened. That's why it's tough."

"But there *is* something I can do."

I was confused, and I waited for him to elaborate. But he just stared at me with a hard look on his face.

"I guess I'm not following you," I said.

"There's an answer to what happened to my dad," he responded.

I wanted to change the subject as fast as possible, but I knew that was a terrible idea. So instead I asked, "Is that what's bothering you?"

"Yeah—the police don't have an answer. Just theories. But there's an answer out there, and I want to find it."

"And that's why you can't concentrate on your schoolwork," I said.

"Yeah."

"I'm sorry."

"*Everyone* is sorry."

"And that's no help, right?" I said. "Not when you want answers. I get it."

"If you get it, then I want you to give me some answers."

"I don't think I'm qualified to help out there, Mason," I said.

"I think you are."

"How do you think I can help?" I asked, worried that this conversation had quickly headed into territory I didn't want to explore.

"The police have all these theories," he said, "but not one of them has any real evidence behind it—and they never found my dad's body, or his car, or anything."

Instinctively, I almost said "I'm sorry" again, but I caught myself. "I'm sure they turned over every rock," I said.

"Maybe. But I haven't." He took a beat to stare me directly in the eyes. "I want to ask you about the argument you had with my dad."

"What argument?" I asked, then instantly regretted it. Mason was smart. If the kid overheard the argument, I wouldn't be able to deny it and keep my credibility.

"The last night you were here," he said. "You two had an argument at the front door."

I furrowed my brow and cocked my head, like I was thinking back to that night. But I was frantically racing to come up with a way to handle this.

"It wasn't an argument," I said.

"I don't care what you call it." There was anger in his voice. "Just tell me what you were talking about."

"We were talking about tutoring," I said. "I let him know that I was going to be moving on to a new job."

"So why was that a big deal?"

"It wasn't a big deal."

"I could tell when my dad was mad. And at the end of whatever you guys were talking about, he was mad. Why would he get mad over you moving on?"

"I don't think he was mad. Maybe a little insulted. He offered to double my rate and I said no. Then he offered to triple it and I still said no."

"Is that what you told the police?" Mason said.

That threw me for a loop. "The police? What do you mean?"

"I told the police about your argument. Didn't they question you about it?"

It was too late to backpedal. "No," I said, sure that Abel had intervened to keep the police from pursuing this lead.

"I wonder how many other clues they didn't follow up on," Mason said.

"I'm sure they followed up on everything that mattered."

"How would they know if something mattered unless they followed up on it?"

Again, the kid was right. So I moved on to something tangential. "I know there's nothing I can do to make things better," I said. "Losing your dad is terrible. And you want answers. But I'm old enough to tell you that sometimes there aren't answers—"

"In *this* case, there is an answer." And he was determined to find it.

It was time to extricate myself from this conversation and go home. "I don't know how to help you find that answer, Mason," I said.

"I'm going to find out what you and my dad were arguing about."

"We weren't arguing."

"I don't believe you."

"Okay. But I don't know what else to tell you."

"How about telling me the truth?" He stared at me, as if challenging me to confess.

"I told you the truth," I said.

"Then you can leave," he responded.

I stood there for a few seconds, weighing whether there was a way to stop him from pursuing this. If there was, I didn't yet know what it could be.

So I walked out of the den and let myself out of the house.

CHAPTER THIRTY

I had put out the fire with Jenny, but not with Mason. On the drive back home, I wondered how worried I should be. The good news was that, unlike Jenny, the kid didn't have access to me. Unless he decided to investigate me in person, his main source of information would be the Internet, and I didn't think that would lead to anything. Abel would have made sure of that.

But I wasn't off the hook. What if the kid went back to the police and insisted they question me or investigate me? That possibility terrified me. Would Abel once again throw the police off my trail? Or was there a way he could give me up without implicating himself? Of course, there was a way. I was sure Abel was capable of that.

I should have talked to Mason's mom. She might have dropped hints as to how far the kid was willing to go to connect me to his dad's disappearance. But I didn't have to talk to Mason's mom, did I? I already knew how far the kid was willing to go. After all, he'd called me out of the blue and he'd confronted me in person.

Mason was going to leave no stone unturned. And there was no denying that his strategy was working. He had already picked out the right suspect.

My stomach churned, and I suddenly felt queasy—sick.

What if Mason got too close to the truth? Abel would kill the boy. And that led to the most awful of revelations.

What if that was my mystery assignment?

What if Abel wanted *me* to kill the boy?

I understood that this awful revelation might be nothing but paranoia. But with Jenny's sudden demand to know the truth, and Mason's accusations, and Rose David's murder being investigated by the police—not to mention the press, including Larry, who was tracking it closely—I guess it made sense that I was seeing threats everywhere I looked. I felt like the walls were closing in. The queasiness in my stomach had seeped into my legs, which had turned rubbery. If I hadn't been behind the wheel, I would've had to sit down.

The confidence I'd had before my meeting with Mason was gone. And the only way to get it back was to assert some control. Sitting back and letting the walls close in, without taking action, was asking for disaster. It was time to get back to basics. I needed to take care of my family.

And to do that, I had to accomplish two things. First, I had to get Abel to run interference for me, and keep anyone and everyone off my trail. And second, I had to get the alien to keep me on as an employee. Blackmail was the only way to accomplish these two things, so I had to get on with it immediately.

Abel had to believe that his lowly employee had the evidence to out him as an alien.

I quickly thought through my catalogue of evidence again, racking my brain for anything more to add to the pellets, copper straw, capsules, and swab. I came up with a few other items—like the strange chain of title to Abel's house—but they were all circumstantial evidence.

In the end, my blackmail threat really came down to the DNA

evidence—if I actually had any DNA evidence. And that left me with a choice: I could put the cotton swab into my blackmail package for the *LA Times* and for Larry, along with instructions to have it tested, or I could test it first before adding it to the package.

It was a no-brainer, wasn't it? Abel wouldn't respond to an empty threat about a swab that may or may not have his genetic material— and may or may not even exist, for all he knew. But if I could show Abel the test results, then my blackmail threat would have teeth. He'd see that I had incontrovertible evidence that would reveal to the world that there was an alien among us. Of course, this assumed that I'd actually collected genetic material from that doorknob. And the only way to find that out was to have the cotton swab tested.

I turned off of Ventura and onto Vantage, then pulled into the parking lot behind the CVS. I took out my cell phone, but weighed whether to use it. I wanted to search for a lab that could test the sample. I never used my cell phone to search for anything that had to do with my assignments—if the police ever connected me to a target, I didn't want my phone records to confirm the connection— but I figured this search didn't have anything to do with an assignment. Besides, at this point, I had a much bigger worry—the police connecting me to a murder.

But what about Abel? Just as I'd always assumed he monitored my computer searches, I also assumed he monitored my cell phone. Once again, I'd have to hope the alien would think I was worried about the police using a DNA sample to connect me to the crime in San Diego. I knew this was probably wishful thinking, but I was motivated by a sense of urgency. I had to implement this blackmail plan as fast as possible. The walls were closing in.

I searched for the nearest lab under the guise of searching how long it would take to test a sample, thinking this ruse might throw Abel off the trail. It turned out that there were quite a number of

DNA testing labs in LA. Many of them had specialties, like testing for paternity, or for ethnicity, or for genetic mutations.

I decided on a lab in Northridge. It ran a large variety of DNA tests for a large variety of clients, from hospitals to law enforcement agencies to biotech firms, which meant it was more likely to have the capability to analyze a sample with strange characteristics. I also liked that it offered an express service. The service still wasn't fast enough, but I hoped that if I offered to double their fee—and I was willing to pay far more than double—I'd get the fastest service available.

Before I headed up to Northridge, I walked into the Bookstar next to CVS. I headed to an empty aisle, then slipped the gold card into a book on the bottom shelf. If Abel used the card to track me, he wouldn't see that I'd driven to a DNA testing lab. I'd pick up the device on the way back. I also shut off my cell phone, in case the alien also used it to track me.

Thirty minutes later, I arrived at the lab, during a shift change. Technicians were streaming out of the lab and others were heading inside. I parked in front of the building, in one of the spots marked "dropoff," then headed into the lobby, where I stepped up to a receiving window.

From behind the window, a large woman in her forties, wearing big round glasses, looked up from logging a package into her computer terminal.

"Dropping off?" she said.

"Yeah," I answered.

"From where?" She reached for a form.

"What do you mean 'from where'?"

"Doctor group, hospital, or clinic?"

"None of those."

She put the form back. "If you're a cop, you can't check a sample in through the receiving window."

"I'm not a cop."

She raised her eyebrows skeptically. "So where you from then?"

"It's a personal sample."

"We can't take it," she said, shaking her head. "You gotta go through a doctor, hospital, or clinic."

"I don't have time for that."

"That's the way it works, and there's nothing I can do about it."

I thought about bribing her, but before I went through with it, I realized that she was the wrong person to bribe. Even if I had been able to bribe her to fake whatever information she needed on that form, I'd still need a technician to perform the test immediately. So my next move was to find that technician.

"Okay. I understand," I said, and headed back outside.

I got in my car, pulled out of the "dropoff" spot, and drove deeper into the large parking lot, until I was surrounded by employees on the shift change. I parked right in the thick of it and eyed the workers. Some were headed to their cars, while others were milling about, chatting.

I evaluated them, one by one. As a reporter, I was fairly good at picking up a few details about a person just through observation. I was looking for someone who'd jump at the chance to earn a large chunk of change, and it also had to be someone who had the authority to cut through the red tape and get the test done now, or who could do the test themselves.

After about five minutes of quickly sizing up two dozen candidates, I decided the best candidate was a woman who looked to be in her late thirties, and who appeared self-assured as she spoke to a colleague. Her age and her demeanor led me to believe she was probably a technician, or possibly a manager, which might mean she was higher up on the food chain in the lab.

And there were other things about her that helped with my decision. The woman's hair was pulled back in a ponytail, not styled in any way, and she was wearing flats—practical shoes—and plain tan slacks. She also looked fatigued, and as she chatted with her coworker, I could see she was continuously inching away from the conversation, as if she wanted to get home as soon as she could. Her generic outfit, her desire to get home, and her fatigue told me she was almost undoubtedly a woman juggling work and motherhood.

I got out of my car and made a beeline toward her. As I approached her, she finally broke away from her coworker and stepped up to a late nineties Ford Explorer—old but dependable; I'd had one. And when she opened her car door, I saw not one but two kids' car seats in the back.

I'd hit the jackpot. I was confident I'd picked the right person.

"Miss," I said, as I closed the distance between us.

She didn't react. She was focused on getting home to her kids.

"Miss," I repeated, louder, as she closed the door.

She must have heard me, because just before the door shut, she turned toward me.

I gave her a quick wave and hurried to her car.

She rolled down the window.

"Miss, I'm sorry to bother you," I said, "but I was wondering if I can ask you for a favor."

"I'm kind of in a rush." She started the Explorer.

"I understand, but please give me just a few seconds." I smiled.

She gave me a quick once-over. "Sure. What's up?"

"Would you be willing to test a DNA sample for me? I'll pa—"

"Receiving is in the front lobby. Just drop it off there, and they'll take care of it."

"I know, but I need it done right away."

"They can take care of that, too. There's an express service."

"I understand, but they said it would take a week, and I can't wait a week."

She took a deep breath; I was trying her patience. "I'm sorry," she said. "That's the best we can do."

"I'll pay you five thousand dollars if you can do it right away."

That got her attention. She leaned back in her seat and stared at me.

I went on. "This is a really private matter. I don't want to go through 'official' channels."

She cocked her head, frowned, and glanced at my hands. I knew she was checking for a wedding ring—which, indeed, I was wearing—thinking that I was a philandering husband worried about paternity. From my Internet search, it was clear that determining paternity made up a big percentage of DNA testing.

"Listen," she said. "I don't know what you're up to, but I'm not going to risk my job. Okay?"

"Hear me out. I can pay y—"

"I did hear you out." She put the Explorer in gear.

For a second, I thought I'd picked the wrong person. But then I remembered the most basic lesson I'd learned since getting fired from the *Times*: a parent will do anything to guarantee the financial security of his or her family. I was the prime example. And wasn't that the primary reason why I'd picked this woman? Because I'd suspected she was a parent.

"Wait. Please. What's your salary?" I said.

"What?"

"What's your salary? How much do you earn a year?"

She shook her head, looked at her rearview mirror, and began to pull out.

"I'll double your salary. In cash."

She looked back at me and stopped her car; I knew the tide had turned.

"You can have it now. All up front," I said.

Her brow furrowed with curiosity. "But I earn thirty-two thousand a year."

"Twice that is sixty-four," I said.

She gave me another once-over. "You're saying you'll give me sixty-four thousand dollars? Now?"

"Can you run the test now?"

"Yeah."

"Great," I said. "Stand by."

I headed over to my car, opened the trunk, and surreptitiously counted out sixty-four thousand dollars from the hundred thousand I'd packed for Mason.

When I got back to the Explorer, the woman was standing outside it. She told me to hold on to the cash until this part of the parking lot was clear of employees. As we waited, I told her I wasn't looking for a paternity test, but for something more comprehensive. *And* I told her she had to keep everything about the test confidential. She agreed, then went on to explain that there were different kinds of DNA tests, and that some took a lot longer than others.

I wished I had done more research on what kind of test I needed, but luckily, the cash I'd promised this woman had turned her into a fount of knowledge. I asked her if there was a specific test that could determine if the DNA sample was "abnormal," a term I used because I couldn't use "extraterrestrial."

She translated "abnormal" to mean testing for specific genetic "markers." Genetic markers referred to certain genes, some of which were used to identify people. After she explained a little more about genetic markers, it became clear that this test would definitely reveal whether there was something highly "abnormal" about the sample or not.

I gave her the cash, and she told me to come back in six hours.

*

After retrieving the gold card from the Bookstar, I headed home, prepared to answer more of Jenny's questions about the PI job. But when I walked into the house, she was talking to Hannah.

I overheard them in the kitchen, and it sounded like they were in the middle of a serious conversation. My first thought was that Hannah was insisting on doing something crazy during the upcoming summer break. Last summer she'd wanted to go backpacking through Kenya—not with a tour group, but by herself. It had been a non-starter, but she thought she could bully us into it and had thrown more than half a dozen temper tantrums before accepting that it was never going to happen.

I headed to the kitchen with the intent of bailing Jenny out in case she felt cornered. But when I entered the room, both of them went quiet.

"What's wrong?" I said.

"Nothing. Everything's fine," Hannah answered. But I could see in her face that everything wasn't fine. She looked frightened.

I looked over at Jenny, hoping she'd spilled the beans.

Jenny turned to Hannah. "It's okay, honey. I understand that it has nothing to do with the job. I really do. You can tell your dad."

Hannah stared at me for a beat, then looked away.

"I'm not going to get mad," I said.

"You might," Hannah responded.

Jenny moved closer to Hannah and gently touched her arm. "If I didn't get mad, you know he won't. He's the pushover when it comes to you." She smiled sympathetically.

Though this didn't elicit a matching smile from Hannah, she did look me in the eye. "I'm not overworked," she said. "I just want to make sure you know that."

"I know that," I said.

"I'm not doing too much."

"I don't think you are, honey."

"Maybe I didn't eat enough. That's all."

I didn't understand what she was getting at, so I looked over at Jenny.

"She fainted on the way to work," Jenny said.

My body went numb. A second later, that numbness was replaced with fear and panic, which I fought to hide from Hannah and Jenny. Had Abel targeted my precious daughter? I wanted to reach out and hug her, envelop her, and protect her. But she'd think I was overreacting.

And I was, wasn't I?

It's not Abel, I told myself. *It can't be.* This was nothing more than a weird coincidence. The targets were always women in their late twenties or early thirties. Hannah—my innocent daughter—didn't fit the bill.

I finally managed to croak out a response. "Are you okay, sweetheart?"

"I'm fine," Hannah said, defensively. She'd heard the fear in my voice—I hadn't been able to mask it. "I just wanted Mom to know," she continued, "in case Mrs. Waller said anything."

"Why would Mrs. Waller say anything?" I asked.

"Because Mrs. Waller found her," Jenny said. "She passed out in her yard."

"So what happened exactly?" I said.

"I was walking home from work, and out of the blue I felt faint." Hannah's tone was muted, which was unlike her. "I must have been near Mrs. Waller's, because next thing I knew she was standing over me, asking me if I was okay. I guess I wandered into her yard before I actually passed out."

My heart was pounding now. This was Abel's MO—*my* MO—and I wanted to kill him. My precious daughter had been drugged, hauled like an animal to Abel's, stripped of something—I still didn't know of what, but now more than ever I wished to God I did—and then released back into the wild.

But who'd abducted her? Did Abel have another employee—one who targeted teens?

"How long were you passed out?" I said, hoping I was doing a better job of masking not only my fear, but also my rage.

"I don't know... an hour and a half, I think."

This was exactly how long it would take for someone to drive her from our neighborhood to Abel's and back, including the time Abel would have to spend harvesting.

And there was another detail that made me think Abel was behind this: the Wallers' yard. If you were going to drop a target back into our neighborhood, which for Hannah was familiar territory, then the Wallers' yard was the best choice. It had a hedge obscuring it from the street, and it had a gate that opened onto an alleyway that ran behind the houses on that side of the block. Whoever had returned Hannah had undoubtedly checked to see if the alleyway was clear, then pulled in right alongside that gate and dumped her body in the yard.

"Did you wake up near the gate?" I asked before I could censor myself.

"Yeah—why?" Hannah looked at me curiously.

I shrugged and tried to come up with a reason for my strange question. "I thought you might have taken the alleyway as a shortcut."

"Maybe... To tell you the truth, I don't remember much before I fainted."

"I think we should go to urgent care," Jenny said, "to make sure you're okay."

"I'm fine, Mom."

"Better safe than sorry," I said, even though I knew a doctor wouldn't find anything wrong with her—if this had been Abel's handiwork. But what if it wasn't?

"I really feel fine," Hannah said.

"Can you at least let your father take you to urgent care in the morning?" Jenny said. "Or to the doctor if he can get an appointment? I'd do it myself, but I have my own doctor's appointment first thing in the morning."

"Nothing's wrong," Hannah insisted.

"I know, honey," I said. "But please do it, for our sake, so we don't have to be worried sick about you."

Hannah took a couple of beats to look from me to her mom, then relented. "Okay. But it's nothing."

I hoped it was nothing—nothing to do with Abel. But if that was the case, did that mean Hannah had fainted from some other cause? That idea frightened me as well.

The gold card in my pocket suddenly vibrated. Abel was calling me with the new assignment. Was it a suicide mission?

CHAPTER THIRTY-ONE

My new assignment had to be completed by ten p.m. tonight, which meant I'd have to hit the road right away to give myself time to pull it off. But before I left, I checked the murder investigation. Unfortunately, I discovered more bad news. Larry's website had an update based on an anonymous source: the police were looking through the security camera footage of businesses in Del Mar. The update hadn't said who the police were looking for, but the implication was that they had a suspect.

I badly wanted to scour the Internet looking for more details, but I didn't have time. First of all, I wanted to prepare the blackmail package before taking off for the assignment, and second of all, I wanted to check out the alien's strange request. He didn't have a target for me this time; instead, he wanted me to steal something called "cerium"—and I wanted to know what that was.

I looked it up and found that it was a rare earth mineral, and that it had a number of uses. It was used as a catalyst to refine petroleum and as an alloy to make special metals. It was also used to make common everyday items like flint and carbon arc lights. But I wondered if Abel needed the mineral to harvest his human crops. Maybe it was a catalyst for the extraction process, and he'd run out of it. Or did he need it for a piece of equipment that allowed him to survive on Earth?

After searching for a few minutes, I realized I wasn't going to be able to determine what Abel wanted it for. But it didn't appear that he was sending me on a suicide mission.

So I moved on to preparing the blackmail package. It consisted of the pellets, the copper straw, and the recovery capsules. Of course, the missing piece—the most important piece—was the sample. If, indeed, it turned out to be a valid sample.

When I had the package together and safely in the trunk of my car, I told Jenny that I had to drive down to LAX. "I have to verify that someone's mistress is flying in from Las Vegas," I said.

She didn't question me about it, but I suspected that was because she was more worried about Hannah than about my job. As was I.

"Please remember to call Dr. Eisner first thing in the morning," she said, "and see if you can get an appointment for Hannah. Tell his office what happened."

"Don't worry. I'll take care of it," I said.

And I would, if I was still alive in the morning.

I got in my car and headed to Carson, which was where Abel wanted me to go, a city in the South Bay. My plan was to head to Northridge for the sample and test results afterward.

As soon as I got on the 405 and started the trek south, my thoughts went back to my assignment. I was to break into the storeroom of a high-tech manufacturing company located in Carson's large industrial corridor, steal the cerium, and take it to Abel. For my abductions, he always gave me at least two days, and usually double that. But for this one, he wanted it right away, which struck me as odd. Why not allow me more time?

But the biggest difference with this assignment, and the biggest surprise, was that Abel was actually helping me. He had prepared everything in advance, rolling out the red carpet for me. The company's exterior gate, which led to the building that housed the storeroom, would be open at seven-forty, ready for my arrival. And the storeroom itself would be accessible for a twenty-minute window, unguarded by security guards and alarms. Abel had also arranged for the company's security cameras to malfunction during the theft.

In essence, I was little more than a delivery boy, picking up the cerium and delivering it to the alien. But that was fine by me.

The only downside was that, with nothing to prepare for, I had time to think about Hannah. I was tortured by the possibility that I was responsible for her abduction and for whatever had followed at Abel's house. I'd taken on my new line of work—kidnapping women—to *help* my family; but now my family had become victim to it.

Unless this had been a coincidence. But I'd never know, would I?

I desperately wanted to know what effect the harvesting had on its victims. If Hannah had been a victim, had she suffered irreparable harm? The alien had never told me if there was lasting damage to the targets. And of course I'd never pressed him to find out. I supposed I hadn't really wanted to know. I liked thinking that after I released the targets back into the wild, not only would they never know what had happened to them, but they'd also be just as healthy as if I'd never abducted them at all.

I felt less sanguine about that when it was my own daughter.

By the time I made it to Carson, I'd decided that when I delivered the cerium to Abel, I'd ask him if there was lasting damage to the targets. I'd try to get an answer before I blackmailed him.

I'd also try to get another question answered: Did Abel have other employees? I felt the answer was self-evident. If Hannah had been abducted—and I was talking myself into believing that she almost certainly had—then Abel did indeed have other employees.

Which made me even more disposable than I'd thought.

*

I picked up the cerium without a hitch, then headed back north up the 405 to Northridge. The 405 slowed near LAX, but after that it was smooth sailing, so it wasn't long before I was driving through the Sepulveda Pass, down into the Valley. When the 405 hit Ventura Boulevard, I exited, as if I was planning to head back to my place or to Abel's.

But I wasn't.

I pulled into the parking structure at the Galleria, which was just off the freeway, and drove to the top floor. It was empty. I parked and walked toward the elevator. To the left of it was one of those concrete trash receptacles that stood an inch or so off the ground.

I pulled the gold card from my pocket and slid it underneath the receptacle, so that it was completely hidden from view. Then, after once again shutting off my cell phone, I got back on the 405 and headed to Northridge.

When I neared the Northridge exit, I went through what I'd tell Larry if the DNA test revealed something that might prove my outlandish claim. I decided I'd tell him what I'd told Jenny: that I'd lied about the ADM job, and that I was working for a PI firm. Then I'd go on to say that I was now working on a dangerous case, and that if anything happened to me, he should follow up on the contents of the package that I was leaving with him. He should investigate the contents himself and also have the *LA Times* investigate.

But if my blackmail plan worked? What if Abel didn't dispose of me, but instead kept me on as an employee? Wouldn't Larry open the blackmail package anyway? And I couldn't take it back, because from here on in, my relationship with Abel would change, even if he kept me on. The threat of blackmail would become my only protection. So I needed to come up with a way to ensure that Larry would *only* open the blackmail package if something went wrong.

I exited the 405, and ten minutes later, I was pulling into the lab's parking lot.

The woman was there waiting for me, lit by the blue-green vapor lights high overhead. She was leaning against her Ford Explorer, staring at her cell phone. She appeared calm, which made me think the sample had turned out to be a dud. There hadn't been any DNA on that cotton swab because the alien had never touched that doorknob.

I parked, got out of my car, and walked toward her. As soon as she noticed me, she headed toward me. She wasn't holding anything in her hands but her phone. No sample, no report. I was disappointed—and I could feel sweat beading on my forehead. How was I going to protect myself now?

When the woman was a couple of cars away from me, she said, "Let's meet at the Petco over on Nordoff."

"Why?" I asked, surprised by her request.

"Because I'm not an idiot," she said. "Take De Soto to Nordoff, turn left, and you'll see the Petco on the right." She turned and headed back to the Explorer.

I wanted to ask her what was going on, but it was clear she wasn't going to answer any questions here. So I headed back to my car, wondering why she'd said, "I'm not an idiot." Had she felt I'd duped her in some way? That didn't compute. How would I have duped her?

On the way to the Petco, I started to believe that I'd gotten her into some kind of trouble. Maybe she'd been caught running the test and she didn't want to be seen with me. That was a logical reason for wanting a clandestine meeting.

I pulled into the Petco parking lot, picked out her SUV, and parked alongside it. She didn't get out of her car, so I got out of mine and walked over to hers. Her driver's side window was already rolled down.

"What's up?" I said. "Why the cloak and dagger stuff?"

"Because I shouldn't have been running a sample like that." She no longer appeared calm. Her eyes were wide and wild.

"Why? What did you find?" I asked.

She pulled a sheet of paper from her pocket, unfolded it, and handed it to me. It was the lab report.

"Why'd you bring that sample to me?" she said. "I'm just a lab technician. Why didn't you bring it to Cal Tech or JPL or—"

"I'll explain," I interrupted, "but please, first tell me what you found."

"It's all in there," she said, nodding toward the report.

"What does it say?" I asked.

She took a breath, looked at me for a second, then said, "That sample had extra base pairs."

"What do you mean, extra base pairs?" I felt my confidence returning.

"I'm not gonna give you a full biology lesson in front of a Petco in the Valley," she said, "but DNA is made up of certain nucleotides—compounds—four, to be exact. And they're repeated over and over again. But they can only pair up in certain ways. Sometimes there are mutations—mistakes—but that's it." Her eyes narrowed. "But there can't be *other* base pairs. That's impossible."

"Are you saying there are other base pairs in that sample?" I'd hit the jackpot. My blackmail scheme suddenly had teeth.

"Yeah—I'm glad you're following along. But I can't tell you what those base pairs are. We're not equipped for that." She took in a breath and stared at me for a few beats. She looked frightened. Finally, she asked, "What's that a sample of?"

"To tell you the truth, I don't know."

"Give me a break. You got it from somewhere and you were frantic to have it tested." Her fear was turning into anger. "That's why you paid me the big bucks. You have to tell me what you're up to because you got me in over my head. Someone's going to be asking me a lot of questions."

"This was supposed to be confidential."

"That was the plan, but this isn't something I can sweep under the rug."

"That was part of the deal."

"Yeah, well, I was counting on that too. It wasn't hard for me to shuffle some paperwork around and make your sample look like a legit job. But I didn't know that I'd have to worry about the results."

"Why does that make a difference?"

"The results of every test automatically get fed into a giant database. That's how the lab makes extra money."

"That sounds illegal."

"It's not. It's part of the terms that everyone agrees to when they sign their release for a test. It's in the small print that no one reads. But it's no big deal—all the results are submitted anonymously into this database. And the database is just for universities to tap into. It gives them access to a lot of DNA tests that they can use for statistical analysis."

I realized I'd screwed up. "So the results have already been forwarded to this databank?"

"You're catching on."

"But it's anonymous, right?"

"It is until something like this pops up." She shook her head. "Someone's gonna see those weird base pairs, and they're going to want to know where that sample came from. Then they're going to track it down to the lab that submitted it. And when they find the lab, they're going to track down the paperwork. And then they're going to track it down to me."

And Abel's gonna track it down to me, I thought. If the murder investigation wasn't enough for him to dispose of me, this surely was.

"Tell them I threatened you," I said. Then I nodded to the kids' car seats in the back. "Tell them I threatened your kids. But please don't identify me. Tell them you never saw my face."

"I don't know if that's going to work, but it's better than telling them you bribed me. For that I'd get fired. And I need this job." She let out a deep breath. "But you have to tell me where you got the sample. That way I'll know if saying you threatened me will be enough to end this. How much are they going to want to dig into this? What's this all about?"

"I can't tell you that."

"The money you gave me means it's a big deal. They're going to want to dig deeper into this, aren't they?"

"How long will it be before they contact you about the sample?"

"I have no idea."

"Please tell them I threatened you and you never saw my face."

"If I want to keep my job, I have no choice." She stared at me and didn't say anything for a few seconds. Then she said, "But they're going to want to know how I got the sample, and what happened to it, and if I gave you the report."

"Tell them you picked it up here. In this parking lot." I looked toward the Petco, where I spotted a familiar sight: a concrete trash receptacle.

"You picked it up under that trashcan." I nodded at it. "And you dropped the report off there, too."

She looked over her shoulder and took in the trashcan. "They're gonna ask me how you got in touch with me."

That was a tougher question to answer. And she knew it, because she began to rule out some of the options. "I can't say you called me because they wouldn't find a record of the phone call, and I can't say you emailed me, texted me, or sent me a handwritten note because there's no record of those either."

"If these are university researchers who are going to track you down, you sure make them sound relentless."

"I think I already mentioned that I'm not an idiot. I don't know what that sample is, but I know it's going to go beyond university researchers."

I wasn't going to argue with her—because she was right. So what *could* she say about how I'd first contacted her?

"You know what?" I said, realizing the answer was simple. "Forget about the trashcan. Tell them I came to you in person. Just like what actually happened. But give them a description of someone else."

She let out a nervous laugh. "That's not bad."

"Just leave out the bribe and add the threat," I said.

"Oh—I got that part." She started her car and put it in reverse.

"Wait." There was a big piece of information I needed to know. "What happened to the actual sample? I was hoping to get it back."

"Not gonna happen. Once we test a sample, both the part we test and whatever is left over immediately gets discarded as biohazard waste."

I didn't like that answer. It meant that if I wanted to make the blackmail package stronger, I'd have to add another sample along with the lab report. "There's no way to retrieve it?"

"Nope," she said, and added, "I hope this works out. For both of us." Then she pulled out.

I walked back to my car, lab report in hand, and climbed in. I was feeling good about the blackmail—the sample had come through, big time. But I didn't like the sample sitting there in the databank like a ticking bomb. And I wished I'd gotten some of the sample back. Still, a bit of luck had come my way. And if this woman could hold her own when and if anyone asked her questions—then everything might work out just fine.

So I got on with my night.

I swung by the Galleria and picked up the gold card, then made a copy of the lab report at CVS. Afterward—before delivering the cerium to Abel—I headed to Larry's house, thinking through exactly what I'd say once I got there.

I already knew I'd use the PI story to explain why I suspected I might be in danger, but I still hadn't come up with a way to make sure Larry wouldn't open the blackmail package prematurely. It would be a monumental failure on my part if my blackmail threat actually worked—saving my life and my job—but Larry went ahead and followed up on the contents of that package anyway. And, of course, I had no doubt he would follow up once he saw what was in there. It was the story of the century, if not of all time: aliens are here.

I weighed whether there was some way to use the *LA Times* to keep Larry from opening the package prematurely. But when I pulled up to his house, I still hadn't come up with an angle to keep him in check. Nonetheless I moved forward, because I had no choice but to get the package into Larry's hands before threatening Abel with blackmail.

I jotted down Abel's address on the lab report, then added a note next to it saying this was where you'd find the alien with the extra base pairs. Then I stuck the report in a manila envelope, which already contained the other evidence. I sealed the package with tape, which I'd brought with me. And finally, I folded the copy I'd made of the lab report and tucked it neatly into my pocket.

With that done, I walked up to Larry's front door and rang the doorbell.

Larry opened the door a few seconds later. "Eddie—what a coincidence," he said. "I was just going to call you."

"Really? What's up?"

"I want to show you something." He led me through the house with a sense of urgency.

"Another breaking story?" I asked.

"No, it's the same one that was breaking when you were here a few days ago. The one about that old woman they found buried in her yard in Del Mar."

"Oh…" A new wave of panic swept over me. Those beads of sweat appeared on my forehead again, and I wiped them off. This sounded like bad news. News that implicated me in the case. Why else would Larry have been about to call me?

"What's in the envelope?" he asked.

"Something that I'd like you to help me out with," I said.

He glanced back at me—and in that moment, I had an awful thought: he was thinking that whatever was in the envelope had to do with Rose David's murder.

"Okay," he said, then we both stepped into his office. "I want you to look at something first." He headed to his desk, sat down, and clicked away until a video window appeared on one of his three monitors.

"The police are looking at security cam footage from businesses in Del Mar," he said. "Footage from around the time they think the woman was murdered."

"So they have a suspect?" I asked, as if I hadn't been following every last detail about the case.

"Yeah." He pointed to the monitor with the video window, then rolled the video—it was security cam footage. "Take a look at this," he said.

I moved closer to the monitor and stared at the grainy black and white footage. I recognized the café, the Sun and Moon—and I knew what to pay attention to—but I played dumb. "What am I looking for?" I said.

"You'll see."

The security camera didn't take in the entire café. It was pointed down at the front counter and register. Ten seconds passed, then an employee walked into frame and up to the register. I knew what was going to unfold next, and I tried to keep from sweating.

I watched myself walk into frame. The camera was looking down on me, from a severe perspective, and you could only see about a third of my face, if that much. And just like the rest of the footage, my face was grainy—thank God.

"Is that you?" Larry said, turning to me.

"Of course not." I chuckled.

"It sure looks like you."

"Is that why you wanted to call me?"

"Yeah."

I watched myself pay for my food, take the table number card from the cashier, and walk out of frame to wait for my sandwich.

"Is that what the police are focused on?" I asked.

"It's one of the things they're focused on," he answered, then queued the footage back to the start. "It sure looks like you, Eddie. Enough that it was my first thought—even though I knew it was a crazy thought." He cocked his head. "You're telling me it's not you."

"And you're telling me you actually think I killed that old woman."

He pursed his lips, sighed, then turned back to the monitor and rolled the footage again. We both watched as I walked into frame, paid for my food, and walked out of frame.

"I think that's you," he said. "But it doesn't mean you had anything to do with that woman's murder."

If there was ever a moment of truth when it came to my Del Mar blunder—at least up to this point—this was it. I had to decide, on the spot, how to move forward, and a lot was riding on how I dealt with this, including the blackmail package that I clutched by my side.

"I'm in trouble, Larry," I said. "I didn't kill that old woman, but I know who did." I swung the blackmail package forward. "It's a long story, and it's all in here."

Larry reached out for the package, but I didn't hand it to him.

"First I have to explain a couple of things," I said.

"I'm all ears."

"I don't work for ADM. I just tell people that because I don't like to talk about my job—and I shouldn't talk about it." I went on to tell him the same PI story I'd told Jenny. The same story I'd planned to tell him before I handed over the blackmail package. But that story would now be embellished to include the reason why I was in that security cam footage.

When I finished with the preliminaries—the warm-up for the main act, the explanation of exactly how I was involved in Rose David's murder—I paused to gauge Larry's reaction.

"Wow," Larry said. "So you liked this PI work enough to reject my offer of the editor in chief job?"

"Let's just say I lied about a lot, but I didn't lie about the money. I like the money." I let out a deep breath, as if I was about to unload a burden, then patted the manila envelope. "It's an inheritance case."

"You're talking about the murder."

"Yeah. It's a fight over Rose David's money, plain and simple."

"From what I'm reading, both on the record and off," he said, "the police are about as far away from that angle as possible."

"That's because there's no legal case yet. The fight over the money hasn't even started. The son—Blaine David—hired my PI firm to see if he could build a case against Rose David's tenant."

"Wendy Bester?"

"Yeah."

"Why? How is she involved?"

"Blaine thinks Bester was duping his mom, Rose, into writing her into the will."

"And was she?"

"I didn't get far enough into the case to find out if the duping part was true, but Rose *was* planning to change the will. She was going to split her estate between Bester and the son."

"And how does homicide fit into all this?"

"I don't know, except that *I* fit into it: I walked into a trap. I broke into the house to set up a bug, for eavesdropping. We wanted to get Bester and Rose on tape talking. We thought it was a good way to start. We might have been able to prove that Bester was manipulating Rose."

"Breaking and entering, huh?"

"I told you, it's a dirty job. A lot of surveillance. Anyway, I checked out the property, and scoped out Rose and Wendy's routines. Then I broke into the house to set up the bug." I shook my head, feigning disgust with myself. "When I broke in, I found Rose's body."

"You were framed."

"Not exactly—but the will won't ever get changed now. Blaine inherits everything."

"What does 'not exactly' mean? You *don't* think you were framed?"

"I did at first, but it didn't make sense. Why me? Then I got it: I wasn't supposed to find the body. I interrupted something already in progress. Whoever buried the body killed Rose David."

"You didn't bury her?"

"Of course not. I got the hell away from there. But it was too late. Every piece of evidence points to me. I was doing surveillance on the house. I was doing surveillance on Rose. I was doing surveillance on Bester." I nodded toward his computer monitor. "And I was in Del

Mar at the time of the murder."

"How the hell did you go from working for the *LA Times* to getting mixed up in this?"

"Stupidity."

"Well, you gotta go to the police and explain."

"That's where the shit really hits the fan," I said. "My entire job is based on the fact that it doesn't exist. The PI firm won't back me up. It's part of the job. We're freelancers, doing the dirty work that doesn't get traced back to them or the law firms who hired them."

"Yeah, well, this is a murder case. You have to come clean."

"I know. But I can't. Not yet anyway." I handed Larry the manila envelope. "But if I get connected to the case, or if I become a suspect, or if... if something worse happens, then I want you to open this. I want you to open it with Bob. I want both you and the *LA Times* to follow up on what you find in there."

Larry took the envelope and turned it over in his hands.

"But please don't open it unless something happens to me," I added.

Larry didn't respond. He looked contemplative. Like any good reporter, he was probably wondering if there was more to the story, and that's what I played into next.

"I know this sounds insane—way out of my league—but there's more," I said. "There's more about Rose David and her inheritance. More than what I told you. More about why Blaine would hire us, then do this under our noses. It's all in there." I motioned to the envelope again. "But please don't open it unless something happens. If nothing happens, then it's better if you don't know anything more about the case."

"You mean that I'll be in danger, too? Or that you're embarrassed by what's in here."

"Both. Just promise me you won't open it. Promise me that if all this blows over and the police never connect me to the case, you won't open it."

Larry pursed his lips and shook his head. He looked overwhelmed, as if he would much rather have dealt with this as an Internet story as opposed to a flesh and bone story, living and breathing in his office. He turned it over again in his hands, took another contemplative beat, then said, "I won't open it."

"Thanks," I said, about the only honest thing I'd said to my friend that night. And I followed it up with a little more honesty. "Listen, I have to hit the road. There are a couple of other things I need to do if I have any chance of cleaning up this mess."

ABEL

CHAPTER THIRTY-TWO

I was once again sitting behind my desk in the shadows, hiding my identity in preparation for a visitor. Except this time, the visitor wasn't going to be a potential employee.

I was waiting for Henry Rohm, the president of the Beverly Hills Historical Foundation, and for the foundation's attorney. I'd already had a long talk with Henry on the phone, during which I'd painted a vivid picture of myself: a wealthy and eccentric recluse, and an invalid with an unnatural sensitivity to light. I'd also thrown in a few other quirks to complete the picture.

Henry Rohm had hung up the phone thinking I was a hypochondriac, an old world eccentric in the mold of Howard Hughes. My odd behavior, manner, and sensitivities also laid the groundwork for the unusual circumstances surrounding the meeting. Due to my sensitivity to light, I only took meetings at night. Due to my odd behavior, I never greeted anyone at the door; my guests always let themselves into my home. And due to my odd manner, my meetings were always of the urgent variety.

As I put on my gloves in preparation for the human ritual of the handshake, I realized just how tired I felt. The Kalera had left me physically worn out, as if my body had been running a marathon at top speed. But I needed to push through my fatigue and wrap up my business here on Earth. I wanted to properly dispose of my home—and of Eddie.

Since coming down from the Kalera, I'd been covering up all evidence of my stay here on Earth. Not that I'd left much of it. I'd kept a low profile and cleaned up after myself every step of the way. Still, I'd left enough of a trail, especially over the last cycle, that it might pose a threat in the future if I didn't clean it up now. If the authorities on Tracea ever became suspicious about my new identity, I wanted to make sure they couldn't find a clue to my former identity here on Earth.

I was also careful not to create any new evidence of my presence. Thus, I was no longer monitoring, manipulating, or interfering with any data or communications, including those dealing with the San Diego murder investigation.

Unfortunately, there was still some evidence of my presence from the planet's "paper" era that I couldn't remove. Records in the filing cabinets of Los Angeles's government agencies—the original deed to the house, property records, tax records, et cetera. But no one from Tracea would ever get to those filing cabinets unless they found something in the digital records first—and those were now clean.

When I heard the front door open, I scooted farther back into the shadows. A minute later, a silver-haired man, dressed in khaki pants and a polo shirt, appeared in the doorway. "Mr. Caraway?" he said.

"Please come in," I responded.

"I'm Henry Rohm," the silver-haired man said, jovially, as he entered the office. Another man, dressed in a suit, and carrying a thick, expandable folder, followed him in. Rohm motioned to his colleague. "This is the foundation's attorney, Sam Greenberg."

"Thank you both for coming," I said, and then reached out from the shadows with a gloved hand. "As I mentioned, please forgive my voice—an electronic monstrosity—but my rapid decline has also taken part of my larynx."

Henry shook my hand. "I'm sorry about your health problems."

"No need to be sorry." I waved off his concern. "I've lived a good, long life."

Sam, the attorney, shifted the thick folder from his right hand to his left, shook my hand, and then both men sat down.

"I apologize for the short notice, but I just couldn't put this off any longer," I said. "I wanted to do it while I was still of sound mind. Were you able to prepare all the legal documents?"

"They're all here," Sam said. He opened the folder. "I'll go through each one with you."

"There's no need for that. I trust it's all in order. After all, we're talking about a ten-million-dollar asset, and I don't doubt for a minute that you've made absolutely sure the house and property transfer properly."

"It's a great piece of property," Henry said. He smiled graciously.

"That's why I want the historical foundation to open it up to the public as soon as possible."

"No worries there, Mr. Caraway," Sam said. He pulled out a document from the folder and placed it on my desk. "As you requested, your home will be designated a museum, just as we did with the Delray property on Canon."

"And don't worry," Henry chimed in. "Just as you asked, we'll differentiate this site from the Canon site by focusing on LA's history rather than just Beverly Hills."

"I don't want people to have to leave Beverly Hills to learn about the rest of LA's history," I said.

"You have my word that this house will be transformed into a showcase for LA's rich history." Henry's obsequiousness was nauseating. "The displays will be top of the line. And I already spoke with Mayor Grayson about the parking issue. She assured me that the zoning will be changed to allow for a parking lot on the north part of the property."

"Good. I want to make sure the museum gets plenty of visitors," I said. And I did, because that was the whole point: I wanted the property overrun by humans so that any trace of extraterrestrial life would be stamped out. It was a simple plan, and while under the influence of Kalera, I'd determined it was also the best plan. It was a universal law that when one species took over the habitat of another, after enough time had passed, traces of the original species all but completely disappeared from that habitat.

"You're leaving behind a great legacy, Mr. Caraway," Henry said. "The city of Beverly Hills will be forever grateful."

"Please," I responded. "It's really my father you should be thanking, Tom Caraway, Senior. He was the one who fell in love with Beverly Hills and had the foresight to build the first house up in these parts. He was a man of great vision."

"Indeed he was," Henry said, though it was impossible for him to know anything about the man since there was no record of him except for his birth and death.

For the next fifteen minutes, I signed contracts that transferred the property over to the foundation. I didn't say much, except for a few comments that implied I was planning to leave the country to live out my few remaining months in some secluded mansion in southern Europe.

For their part, Henry Rohm and Sam Greenberg didn't say much either. But as they watched my gloved hand sign the contracts, I saw flashes of worry cross their faces—worry about the rushed transaction. I wished I could've told them that there was nothing to worry about. No one was going to contest this gracious gift, because there were no other interested parties. If it weren't for the legal requirements of transferring property rights, I wouldn't have even bothered with the paperwork. I would've just told Henry that the foundation could have my place.

After Henry and Sam left, signed contracts in hand, I went on to prepare for Eddie's arrival. Or more specifically, to prepare for the cerium's arrival. I prepared a mixture of compounds that would convert the cerium into a form my body could easily absorb. Under the influence of the Kalera, I'd discovered that cerium was the key to changing my identity. At least when it came to making use of the limited resources available here on Earth.

Tracea identified—and tracked, if need be—their citizens by their electromagnetic fields. Each Tracean had a unique electromagnetic pattern. But cerium could change this pattern permanently, and that's what I was planning to do. I would do it tonight, before I left Earth.

And when I arrived on Tracea, I would immediately do two other things. First, I'd insert the records of my new identity into the Tracean information network; my heightened intelligence under the influence of the Kalera had shown me the way to hack into that system and seamlessly insert the records. And second, I'd change my physical appearance. This would be easy—it was a common procedure on Tracea.

With the mixture prepared, and with Eddie on his way, I decided to check over the transport again. I ran a systems check for the fifth time. The transport was in fine shape; it had only been used once. Still, I was worried that its curvature drive might fail me. I hadn't been able to get the sturdiest nor the best-designed transport when I'd left, because I hadn't planned on such a quick exit.

The systems check showed that all was perfect, just as it had the first four times I'd run it. But now that I was almost ready to go, I wished I had run a systems check while I'd been under the influence of Kalera. I would've been able to actually interpret the numbers that the check spewed out, rather than just accept that they were all in the "good" range. After all, just as I wasn't a scientist, I wasn't an engineer. And as it stood now, without Kalera bathing my brain, I was like any layman, relying on a systems check to give me the go-ahead.

And hadn't I heard—in my former life—that this curvature drive functioned better the more it was used? Well, I had only used it once, which was why I was worried, regardless of the systems check. If the drive didn't power up to its full capacity, and stay at that capacity during the entire length of my trip, I'd never make it home. I'd end up somewhere between here and there, and die in the transport.

No, I thought. *I won't let that happen.* And right then, I decided I had to be absolutely sure that the curvature drive would function perfectly.

So I took the Kalera again.

As I waited for the drug to take over, I thought about the one thing I was leaving behind on this planet. A treasure that would yield me great wealth once I was back on Tracea. I had come up with the idea, and executed it, while on Kalera. Just as my species had planted Kalera here millions of years ago, I planted my own crop—a more powerful kind of Kalera, based on the Kalera I'd harvested from Wendy Bester. This new crop would grow with each new generation of women, passed on from one generation to the next, until it matured into a drug more powerful than any Kalera in the universe.

Or so I hoped.

If my hope was realized, I'd come back here and harvest the new drug. But I wouldn't come back in exile. I'd come back in triumph. For this new drug wouldn't be illegal. At least, not yet. I had modified the seeds I'd planted so it wouldn't be recognizable as Kalera. Eventually the Traceans, or other species, would probably make this new drug illegal—but that would come long after I'd made my fortune off of it.

I had hired one new employee to help me execute my plan. He'd brought me back seven targets, and I'd planted the seeds in them. I had already disposed of that employee and cleaned up any connection between him and me.

These seven targets had the perfect biology to incubate the seeds and to pass them on. My hyper-intelligence had told me that planting the seeds in these seven women gave me nearly a one hundred percent chance that, cycles from now, there'd be an abundant harvest.

And I felt pride in one of the targets I'd chosen: Eddie's daughter. Not only was she a perfect match, but there was a nice symmetry to this choice—

My thoughts suddenly sped up and turned razor sharp.

The Kalera had kicked in.

I immediately started another systems check on the transport, focusing all my attention on the curvature drive. But minutes later, I heard the high-pitched hum that indicated Eddie had pulled up to the gate. I wanted to focus solely on the task before me, but I also knew that the cerium had arrived, which meant it was time to add the mineral to the mixture I'd prepared—and also time to dispose of the human.

It was hard to shift gears. The curvature drive had captured my attention, and my heightened mental state had already given me the ability to make millions of inferences from the numbers the systems check was generating. *This* was the reason I'd taken the Kalera. It wasn't for the mundane tasks of absorbing the cerium and disposing of the human.

But I had no choice. So I forced myself to go back to my office, where I checked to make sure it was Eddie at the gate. It was, and I let him in. But I didn't wait for him in the office, even though I would dispose of him here.

The Kalera made me impatient. So impatient that even though it would be only a couple of minutes before the human made his way through the gate, into the garage, and then to my office, I went back to the transport. I figured the extra minutes I'd get to spend on the drive would be worth it. I'd come back to the office in two minutes to collect the cerium and dispose of the human.

EDDIE

CHAPTER THIRTY-THREE

I parked the car in the garage and got out with the cerium in hand. The mineral was in a small metal box, labeled only with a serial code, exactly as I'd found it in the storage locker.

I opened the door to the interior of the house and entered. As I closed the door behind me, I couldn't help but glance at the doorknob, the one that had been a boon to my blackmail plan.

As I walked down the hall, I saw that, as on my last visit, both the door to the harvesting room and the door to Abel's office were closed. So I continued forward into the living room.

There I waited, buoyed by the knowledge that my blackmail plan had teeth, and soured by the knowledge that the San Diego police were closing in on me. But I knew that if Abel took my blackmail threat seriously, he'd make sure I wasn't implicated in Rose David's murder.

Abel walked into the room, and again I noticed that he was moving slowly—and this time his gait seemed even slower than during my previous visit. And when he got closer, I saw that his eye was glassy again.

He stopped a few feet from me, but he didn't say anything. It appeared as if his mind was elsewhere—as if he was looking right through me instead of at me.

So I spoke first. "I have the cerium," I said, and when he didn't respond, I added, "The job went well."

It took him a full second, maybe even two, before he finally spoke. "Okay," he said, and raised his arm.

I stepped forward and handed him the cerium.

He took it, but he seemed to be moving in slow motion. Either he was sick, which might explain that extra gloss on the surface of his eye, or his mind was completely focused on something else. *Was there another crisis brewing?* Maybe my blackmail plan could be put on hold.

"Follow me," he said, and he turned and started to walk toward the hallway. His pace was unhurried, like he was a million miles away, not at all interested in his current surroundings.

I followed, weighing whether to ask him where we were headed. Usually, after our transactions it was time for me to bid a hasty exit. And if he was planning to pay me for the cerium, wouldn't he have left the money in my car seat as he always did?

Just then I realized that there were two other potential spots from which I could have gathered DNA samples: my car's door handle, which the alien must've touched when he put the money in my car, and the money itself. The fact that I hadn't thought about this earlier made me doubt my blackmail plan as it now stood. What other obvious things had I overlooked?

And as soon as that question came to mind, I realized what else I'd overlooked. Something far more critical to my plan: I couldn't show him the lab report. It had the lab's address on it. And with that address, he didn't need me alive. He'd kill me, then wipe out evidence that the sample had ever existed at all.

The alien walked by the door to the harvesting room, which meant we were headed to his office. The only other time I'd been in the alien's office, he'd disposed of Ben. I immediately considered making a run for my car; the door to the garage was right there at the end of the hallway, and I could easily scoot by the slow-moving alien. But I reminded myself that Abel would eventually catch me—which was why I'd come up with the blackmail plan. But how could I make my blackmail plan work without showing him the lab report?

And there was another thing that kept me from running: the alien's demeanor. He showed a complete lack of interest in his surroundings and in me. It just didn't feel like he was concerned with getting rid of me right now.

We both entered his office and walked toward his desk. He moved behind it and sat down, while I stood in front of it. He placed the cerium on his desk, then stared at me as if he was trying to get his bearings—almost as if he was trying to remember why he'd asked me to follow him in here in the first place.

I was staring at his eye—the glassy sheen was bright even in the dim light—but I should have been watching his hands. Too late. His right hand moved swiftly from right to left—that same cutting motion I recognized from my first encounter with him.

Instantly the red cone of light enclosed me, and my heart began to pound. Fear had taken hold of me. I was imprisoned, and there was no way out. I pictured Ben's body liquefying, conjoining with the thick red light, until it completely disappeared.

But my body wasn't melting. At least, not yet. Though the alien had tuned in to me long enough to literally lower the boom, he either had tuned out again or was simply moving too slowly to start the liquefying process.

With my heart in my throat, I croaked out my threat. "If you kill me, everyone will learn that you're here. Now. On Earth."

When he didn't respond right away, I didn't say anything more. I gathered that he had to tune back in first.

After a couple of long beats, he said, "Your threat is hollow—"

I interrupted him for fear that now that he'd tuned back in, he'd kill me before I could explain. "If anything happens to me," I said, "I have proof that you're here, and it's ready to go wide."

Again, he didn't respond right away, and I couldn't be sure, but he appeared to be drifting off again. My threat wasn't strong enough.

"I took a sample," I said. "And it's ready to go."

"You're bluffing." That was the quickest response he'd given me.

I wasn't bluffing. But if I couldn't show him the report, what proof could I give him? I knew that whatever I did, I needed to do it *right now*. It was do-or-die time.

It came to me like sudden manna from heaven. I *did* have proof. It had been handed to me on a silver platter in that Petco parking lot in the heart of the Valley. The lab technician had told me all I needed to know about the report.

"Extra base pairs," I said. "You have extra base pairs."

ABEL

CHAPTER THIRTY-FOUR

That got my attention. The human was now my only focus. It was possible that he'd just taken a random guess, but under the influence of Kalera, I was able to rule that out in less than a fraction of a second. My mind ran through the odds that he'd just happened to guess correctly, and the conclusion was clear.

The human wasn't bluffing.

Besides, in my current state—with all my focus on the human—I could *see* that he wasn't bluffing. Just as I could see that the human was terrified, gripped with the fear that he was seconds away from dying, I could also see that he was telling the truth. It was written in his eyes and on his face.

The human had gotten a genetic sample and had gotten it tested.

I would still dispose of him, of course. But before I did, I needed more information. And the human was in no position to deny me that information.

"Who knows about the sample?" I asked.

EDDIE

CHAPTER THIRTY-FIVE

Everyone knows about the sample, I thought. *Because I screwed up royally and let it out into the world.* But then, with my heart pounding, I suddenly understood that my screw-up was also my salvation. My screw-up was better than my original plan. Because at this very moment there was a real and immediate threat already out there in the world—and not just a report in a manila envelope.

"Right now, it's sitting in a databank," I said. "It hasn't been flagged or tracked. But it will be. The clock is ticking."

"Where is this databank?" he asked.

"I'll tell you once you let me go." The ticking clock was my get out of jail free card, because with every passing minute, there was the chance that someone would flag the sample.

"I let you walk out of here safe and sound," he said, "and you tell me where the sample is."

"Deal." I tried to sound confident. "And I also keep working for you."

The red cone of light disappeared, and I knew that I was free to go. But I also knew that this was the end game. After I told him where the sample was, I was no longer going to be working for him. There was no deal. He'd still kill me—unless I killed him first. And I had no doubt that he knew this too.

But right now, I had the upper hand. He didn't want any hint of his existence getting out there, and time was of the essence.

"There's also the problem in San Diego," I said, playing along with the mutual lie that we had some kind of deal.

"I'll fix it," he said.

I knew he couldn't. If he could have, he would have done so already.

So with that exchange, we'd both finished telling our lies. And when he didn't say any more, I knew to expect to hear from him shortly through the gold card. He'd let me know how to get him the information about the lab and databank.

I headed out. It was every man—and every alien—for himself.

ABEL

CHAPTER THIRTY-SIX

I watched the human leave my office, and resisted the urge to head back to the curvature drive. With my thoughts driven by the Kalera, I'd been able to go through my options in a few seconds. I could have held the human captive until he told me where the sample was, or I could have just disposed of him on the spot. I didn't need him to help me find the databank or the sample there—with the Kalera's help, I was confident I could track those things down on my own. But I was sure the human had another sample stashed somewhere else, along with some way to reveal it. So I needed to track down that extra sample too.

And the easiest way to find that other sample was to let the human go—he'd think he had outsmarted me—and then see if he led me straight to it.

Still, as the human had said, the clock was ticking, and I wouldn't just wait around for him to slip up. I had to immediately set to work eliminating the sample at the databank, as that was my most pressing concern. If the sample was flagged before I got to it, I'd be exposed. Even if it took a while for the scientists who examined it to understand exactly what they were studying, the Traceans would immediately know that one of their own was on Earth. And worse, the sample would tell them exactly which Tracean it was, which would lead to my capture.

So now I had to venture back out into the digital world, which I didn't want to do since I had already cleaned up my trail, but I had no choice. I'd find the databank, find the sample, and then wipe out all evidence that it had ever existed. Then I'd move on to finding Eddie's other sample. Maybe he would lead me to it, which would save me some time. But if not, I had other ways to track it down.

Unfortunately, I now had to use my time under the influence of the Kalera to do these things, instead of using it on the curvature drive. Which meant I might have to take Kalera a third time to focus on the curvature drive.

But with this, too, I had no choice.

And then, once I checked these items off my list, I'd have one final job: to dispose of Eddie. I knew I'd never get Eddie to come back to the house, so I'd have to hire a human to handle that for me.

I now wished that I hadn't disposed of the employee who'd planted the seven seeds. I could've used him to do the job.

EDDIE

CHAPTER THIRTY-SEVEN

As I wound up toward Mulholland, farther away from the shadow of death, I kept expecting the gold card in my pocket to hum to life, but it didn't. It remained dead in my pocket. And by the time I was on Coldwater, I began to believe that Abel had gone back to whatever he'd been so involved in when I'd arrived. He'd ask me about the databank when he finished with that.

For a few seconds, I even considered the fanciful possibility that he hadn't contacted me yet because this *wasn't* the end game. I actually considered a storybook ending to this crisis: that after I told the alien where the sample was, we'd continue with business as usual. The Rose David murder would somehow fade in the rearview mirror, and I'd continue to deliver targets in return for bricks of cash.

But this was wishful thinking, and I knew it. Abel would have murdered me on the spot if it hadn't been for my blackmail threat. And now that I was no longer under the threat of immediate execution, I also understood he might have murdered me anyway if not for the fact that he was worried he might miss something. Something that I hadn't confessed to—and with me dead, there was the chance he wouldn't be able to find it. I had evened the playing field. For now.

But how was I going to kill Abel before he killed me?

Just as the clock was ticking on when some professor, or researcher, or grad student, discovered that abnormal test result in the databank, so was the clock ticking on how much time I had to kill the alien. I supposed I could buy myself more time by lying to him about the sample's location. But would that really buy me more time? When he found out that I'd lied, he might not ask me again. He could easily conclude that once a liar, always a liar, and get rid of me.

I was now on Ventura, closing in on Valley Village and my house. If Jake and Hannah were going to be saved from suffering through the tragedy of losing their dad, I had to act. I had to implement my next move before the clock stopped ticking and Abel was back in the driver's seat.

By the time I pulled into my driveway, I had made a fateful decision. I'd tell Abel the truth about the location of the sample.

Then I'd head to his house to kill him.

I realized that if I told him the truth, rather than lying, he wouldn't contact me again. He'd immediately start the job of covering up all traces that the sample had ever existed, *and* he'd put into motion his plan to murder me. During this, I'd be on my way to his house. But if I lied, I couldn't be sure what he'd do next, so that option was off the table.

I walked into my house and found it eerily silent. The silence felt ominous, but I told myself this was only because it was late and everyone was already in bed. On the kitchen counter, I found a note from Jenny. *Don't forget to call Dr. Eisner and make an appointment. Let's make sure Hannah is fine.*

That hit me like a punch to the gut—Abel had messed with my daughter, and I regretted not confronting him about it. But what good would that have done? If the alien was responsible for Hannah's fainting spell, it was my fault. I was the one who had forced myself into the alien's life. The guilt welled up inside me again; I was culpable in turning my daughter into a crop.

I went into the den and pulled the gold card from my pocket. Why hadn't Abel contacted me yet? Was it really because he was busy with something else? Wasn't there another possibly? A horrible one? What if Abel hadn't contacted me because he'd already found the sample and no longer needed me?

I'm just standing here waiting to be executed, I thought. And if that was true, then I needed to drive back up to the alien's house and kill him before he killed me. Which led to a conundrum. If I drove up to his house, I had to leave the gold card behind. Otherwise he'd know I was on my way up there, unannounced, and under the circumstances, he'd know exactly *why* I was headed up there.

But if I left the gold card behind, and he tried to contact me with instructions on how to get him the databank's location, I wouldn't be here to get the message and act on it. He'd know I was up to something.

There was no time to carefully weigh my options.

I decided to leave the gold card here and head to Abel's.

I knew I could get onto his property from the back, through the woods, and that I could get into the house through that open patio door. I also knew that the house didn't appear to have an alarm. Of course, it was quite possible that it had some kind of "alien" alarm, but that was a risk I was going to have to take.

I needed a weapon, and the most logical weapon was a gun. But I didn't own one, and there was no time to get one. But another option quickly came to me. While working for Abel, I had become good at coming up with ad hoc solutions to unexpected problems. Say what you will about the San Diego assignment, but the truth was that every step of the way I'd come up with a solution to an unexpected problem.

I headed to Hannah's bedroom and found that there wasn't any light spilling out from under her door. She was in bed and hopefully fast asleep.

I cracked open the door, and when there was no reaction, I knew she was asleep. So I opened the door farther, enough to let light from the hallway illuminate parts of her room. I scanned her room until I spotted what I was looking for—her purse.

I crept into her room, opened her purse, and pulled out her mace. I'd use it to disable the alien. I'd blind his all-knowing and all-seeing eye.

Of course, there was the chance that his eye wouldn't respond to the mace in the same way human eyes did, but I believed it would. I'd stared at that eye many times, and I had the unshakable conviction that it was a terribly fragile piece of biology. Far more fragile than our own eyes. It was the alien's way of interacting with the outside world, of understanding it, and of analyzing it. I had no doubt that his eye went beyond the capabilities of all our five senses put together. The rest of his body looked impermeable, but not his eye.

Still, the mace would only stun him; it wouldn't kill him. That would come next. While the alien was dazed, I'd go for the fire poker to finish the job.

Back in the den, I shut off my cell phone and stuck it in the desk drawer. Then I pulled the gold card from my pocket and tucked it under a couch cushion—under the exact spot where I was usually stationed while in the house. If Abel checked on my location using the gold card, he'd find me in my normal spot.

Then I headed back out to my car and pulled out of the garage. But before driving away, I stared at my house. Would I get to see Jake and Hannah grow up? A wave of sadness coursed through my body. If Jenny didn't recover from the cancer, would Jake and

Hannah be left without either of us?

Before the enormity of my failings as a father and husband could crush me, I drove away.

ABEL

CHAPTER THIRTY-EIGHT

Tracking down the sample hadn't taken much time. It turned out there were only a few national databanks that gathered information on DNA samples.

I found the test result in a databank in Seattle and wiped clean all evidence of its existence. Then I traced the sample back to a lab in Northridge and wiped out any evidence that the lab had ever had it or tested it. Of course, the Northridge lab still had the physical sample, but with that I had a choice about how to proceed. I could hire an employee to dispose of it and the technician who'd tested it—the same employee I'd hire to dispose of Eddie. Or I could do nothing. After a sample was tested, the lab's procedure was to trash it. I had learned that all the lab's samples went undifferentiated into biohazard waste containers, which meant it would be nearly impossible to isolate and resurrect one sample. In addition, the trash would be picked up in two days and carted away to a dump, where it would be mixed in with thousands of pounds of other biohazard waste. This wouldn't take care of the technician, but without the sample, the technician would be just another nutjob claiming aliens were here on Earth.

After wiping clean the test results, I hunted through Eddie's list of friends, relatives, neighbors, and former employers at warp speed, fueled by Kalera, looking for someone he'd entrust with blackmail evidence—for as I said, I was sure he had a backup plan. I also searched through all his movements, Internet searches, and cell phone calls, as well as those of his friends and family.

In the end, although there were a few candidates he might have trusted with the evidence, one stood out: a former employee of the *LA Times* who currently owned a rather popular news website. The clincher was that Eddie had visited this man just prior to heading over here. I could tell, because though he'd been careful to dump the gold card before he'd gone to Northridge, he'd picked it up again before going to his former colleague's house.

I called Eddie's colleague and told him that if he didn't immediately burn whatever Eddie had given him, he'd lose his website and his entire business.

The man's voice quavered at the threat, but he stood firm for a couple of minutes, asking questions, and getting no answers. He didn't cave in until I told him to check his website and his bank accounts.

His website—his business and livelihood—was gone, as was any trace of it, and his bank balances were all at zero.

I monitored the man's frantic Internet searches. He checked servers, backup servers, and all his failsafe systems to find out what had happened to his business. He also checked his bank accounts, confirming that every one of them had a zero balance.

When he came back on the phone, his voice cracked with distress and anguish.

I told him he'd never get his business back up or see his money again until he complied with my request.

He didn't need any more convincing.

I set up a direct video stream from his smartphone and watched him burn the evidence.

When that was done, and with his voice still cracking, he asked me about Eddie. He wanted to know if I'd killed his friend. The man was compassionate. Again, this was the species' empathy coming through loud and clear. Maybe this characteristic really would be enough to overcome the species' weaknesses. And if I got a chance to come back to this planet to harvest the new drug, I'd get a chance to find out.

But I didn't answer the man. The curvature drive was waiting.

Ten minutes later, I had completed another systems check and had determined that the drive would function perfectly.

There were only three more things I needed to do before I left. The first one I did quickly. Thanks to the Kalera, whose effects unfortunately were rapidly beginning to wear off, I'd finally come up with a way to spin the Rose David investigation in a completely different direction. Once that was done, I went on to the second task.

I covered up the new digital trails that I'd left in my wake over the last couple of hours. I'd have to do this one more time, after I accomplished my third task, which was to dispose of the human. This was going to be more complicated than I'd wanted.

But I wondered: Was it really so complicated? Or was it the waning effect of the Kalera, and the commensurate loss of intelligence, that led me to *believe* it was too complicated? I didn't know.

And I also suddenly found myself doubting that I'd taken care of every loose end.

So I took a third Kalera tablet.

I wasn't addicted.

But I had to be sure all was in order before I left for Tracea.

Which reminded me. I packed the rest of this batch of Kalera, in case I ran into trouble during the trip and needed heightened intelligence to solve it.

Then I waited for the Kalera to kick in before reviewing my plan for disposing of the human.

EDDIE

CHAPTER THIRTY-NINE

When I got up to Mulholland, I was still feeling a deep, heart-wrenching sadness about leaving my kids without a father. My body felt cold and empty, and my limbs were numb. Except for the sadness coursing through me, I felt as though I was already dead. This did nothing to help with my confidence. My plan was already amateurish enough; without the confidence that I could pull it off, it seemed doomed to failure.

But I had to move forward.

It was kill or be killed.

I made my way down the hillside along winding, narrow roads until I arrived at my destination: a street that had direct access to a forested area above Abel's neighborhood. The patch of land abutted the back of Abel's property down below. I had discovered this way to access the property way back when I was researching the house's history—in the innocent days before I blackmailed Ben into giving me a shot at the "investment" job.

I parked, then hiked down through the woods. Fifteen minutes later, I caught sight of Abel's house. As I moved closer, I wondered if the alien was still engrossed in whatever he'd been doing when I'd interrupted him.

The pale moonlight lit my way to the edge of the woods, which gave way to Abel's back yard and the odd stone fountain. The patio doors were open. As usual.

I looked over the house and didn't see anything to stop me from going forward. A few lights were on, as they always were when I arrived. Still, I hesitated before moving forward. I clutched the mace in one hand, as if it was truly a life-saving weapon. I wished that it was.

After taking a deep breath and trying to convince myself that I had a shot at surviving—and maybe I did, if Abel was still distracted by whatever he'd been fixated on—I ran through the yard, past the fountain. Up close, the fountain looked like it had been buffed and spruced up since I'd last stared at it. But strangely enough, it looked more metallic, not less.

I hurried across the patio and into the living room, where my eyes fell on the hallway that led to Abel's office and the harvesting room. If it hadn't been for the one time I'd seen Abel enter and exit the living room using the staircase, I would've immediately headed down the hallway, looking to ambush Abel in either his office or the harvesting room. But now I had to consider the possibility that he was upstairs.

I didn't consider it for more than a couple of seconds though. I decided to go with the hallway because I'd last seen the alien in his office. I grabbed the poker from the fireplace and crept toward the hallway.

Just before I got there, I heard a high-pitched hum. I whipped around, looking for the source, and as I did, the hum became unbearably loud.

Was it a burglar alarm? Was I trapped?

The hum suddenly grew impossibly loud and was now reverberating through my body. The penetrating vibrations made my insides feel like they were turning into jello.

I panicked—I was being liquefied.

But there was no red cone, and I wasn't encased in red light.

And when I looked down at my body, I saw that I was fine. *Intact.* My insides were vibrating from the deafening hum, but I was otherwise okay. The only pain I felt was coming from the sheer strength of the sound pushing at my body and through it.

I glanced down the hallway. Nothing had changed.

I looked out the patio door—and my breath caught in my throat.

The metallic fountain was now glowing—a deeply luminescent blue. The hum was emanating from it, and as the hum got louder, the blue glowed even more deeply.

A second later, the fountain was gone.

And so was Abel—I had never been more sure of anything in my life. And, as if to confirm this revelation, I was suddenly filled to the brim with sweet and utter relief. I let out a deep breath, and took in another.

The alien was gone, and I was still alive.

The odd fountain had been Abel's interstellar transport—and he had just used it to get the hell out of Dodge. But why? Why had he left? Could he have felt threatened by the DNA sample? Had word of its discovery already leaked out?

I didn't believe that for a second. The blackmail was a way of protecting myself, but it was never a winning strategy. The best it could ever do was buy me time. As I stared at the empty space where the fountain had stood, I had no doubt that the alien had *chosen* to leave. He hadn't been forced.

I was one lucky man. I'd survived my employment in the alien abduction business.

ABEL

CHAPTER FORTY

As soon as the Kalera took over, I realized I didn't need to dispose of the human at all. I could head home—because once I was gone, he wasn't going to reveal my existence. Why would he if I was no longer a threat to him? How would it benefit him? It wouldn't. His reaction to my departure would be relief and joy. Relief that he was no longer working a job for which he was unsuited. And joy that I hadn't disposed of him. He'd be as happy to start his new life as I was to start mine.

The curvature drive was working nicely. I relaxed and glanced over at my stash of Kalera tablets. I wondered how long they would last me.

EDDIE

CHAPTER FORTY-ONE

When I walked into my house, I was met with silence again. But the silence no longer felt ominous. It felt inviting. My family was safe and secure, sleeping in peace, and I was home.

As in home free.

I stood there, letting the feeling of liberation wash over me. I felt as if I'd been released from prison. I didn't feel on guard, like the other shoe was about to drop. I felt calm, my body no longer shot through with adrenaline, which had kept every inch of me jumpy and apprehensive.

I was no longer chained to a vile job.

But although I felt physically secure, I *didn't* feel that same sense of liberation in my heart and soul—and I wondered if I ever would. I had committed terrible sins. And though I told myself I'd committed them out of desperation, they were sins nonetheless. I'd have to push them away and learn to enjoy the outer peace I now felt. I would rededicate myself to my family and focus on them, rather than on a road I wished I'd never taken.

I headed to the bedroom, and when I entered, I saw Jenny sleeping. She was far braver than I was. She'd made it through the first rounds of chemotherapy with no complaints, and she'd worked the demanding production job even though she was far from healed. She'd never been desperate about her situation, and she hadn't made any stupid decisions. *And* she'd put up with my lies, even when it was clear that I'd been up to no good.

As I changed out of my clothes and into my pajamas, I wondered when I should tell her about my return to the ranks of the unemployed. She'd be happy to know that I was no longer living a lie. Of course, I'd have to explain why money wasn't a problem when I had no job. And money wouldn't be a problem for quite a while. I supposed it was possible that I'd land a new job with a high enough salary that it wouldn't seem like we had more money than we should.

No, that wasn't possible.

No job would give me the kind of salary that would explain how I could pay our medical bills and Jake and Hannah's college expenses in full every semester. But this was a high-class problem to have. It was a blessing that I'd be able to pay for these things. Couldn't I take the good that had come out of the job? I'd helped my family, and though it hadn't been pretty, it had worked. And another good thing had come out of it, too: I had finally learned to adapt.

I slid into bed, careful not to disturb Jenny, and wondered if I'd have to hide the real source of our money forever. I would, wouldn't I? For who in their right mind would ever believe that aliens were abducting humans?

*

When I woke up, Jenny was already out of bed. I checked the clock. It was eight, which meant the kids were at school and she'd probably already left for her doctor's appointment.

In the kitchen, as soon as I saw the note to call Dr. Eisner, nausea welled up in my stomach. Abel was gone, but it was still possible that his handiwork wasn't. My guilt over Hannah was another thing I'd have to store in the back of my mind. For what else could I do except hope that whatever Abel had harvested from her wouldn't leave her damaged for life?

I called Dr. Eisner and made an appointment. Of course, I knew the doctor wouldn't find anything. That was how the harvesting worked. But I wondered if I should say something to Eisner. Tell him to do a more thorough examination. I didn't have a reason to ask for that—I couldn't tell him I suspected that Hannah had been abducted by aliens—but I could lie. Once again, I could lie.

I could pull Eisner aside and tell him I'd observed some things about Hannah's behavior that worried me. But what could those things be, and what if Eisner asked Hannah about them? She'd tell him I was lying. And in the end, would a more thorough examination—a blood panel, an EKG, an MRI—reveal anything?

I was sure it wouldn't. Abel had never worried about a target going to a doctor.

But just because an examination wouldn't reveal any evidence of the harvest, it didn't mean the harvest didn't do any damage. This damage might manifest itself later in Hannah's life—years later. And I'd have to live my life with this time bomb waiting to go off.

More importantly, Hannah would have to live with it.

After making the appointment, I went into the den to check on the gold card, the one piece of evidence I hadn't given to Larry. I reached under the couch cushion, but it wasn't there. I panicked, then realized I must've shoved it farther back.

I lifted the cushion. The gold card was gone—and my panic was back. Had Jenny found the device? But if she did, what difference did that make? The alien was gone. Sure, I'd have to lie as to what the gold card was, but that would be the end of it. There wouldn't be the need for an ongoing cover story.

My panic subsided, and when it did, I noticed that there *was* something under the cushion. A small fleck of gold dust no bigger than a dime. Had Abel remotely disposed of the device? Of course he had.

I reached for the gold dust, then stopped myself, thinking I should preserve it, for this was the only trace of the gold card left. *Just in case,* I thought. *But just in case of what?*

There was no reason to preserve it.

I reached for the gold dust, and as soon as I touched it, it dissipated and disappeared.

So, Abel had gotten rid of this evidence completely. And right then I wondered if he'd gotten rid of the other evidence, too.

I went over to the desk drawer, fished out my cell phone, and turned it on. I had five messages from Larry. I didn't listen to them, but called him straight away, understanding that something was up, and that it was urgent.

Larry picked up on the first ring. "Why didn't you call me?" he said. "I thought you were dead."

"Why? What happened?"

"Someone with a hell of a lot of power called and threatened me. They must be connected to the Rose David investigation—I don't know—but they're fucking serious as hell, Eddie."

My heart started to race and my entire body tensed, back on high alert. Had Abel left me a parting gift? Was I going to be arrested for the murder of Rose David?

"Tell me exactly what's going on," I said.

"Someone called and told me to burn the evidence. They wiped out my entire business and took my bank accounts down to zero. I don't how they did it, but they did."

"*Who* called?"

"How the hell should I know? He disguised his voice. It was electronic."

"I'm sorry about your business—it's my fault. I should've never dragged—"

"No, no—it's back, Eddie. The business, the bank account. It's all back. As soon as I burned the evidence, it was all restored. That's what I mean by this guy has power. If I didn't know any better, I'd say he was NSA. I mean, one minute everything disappears, and five minutes later it's all back."

I didn't say anything for a few seconds. I wasn't sure how to spin this. And at the same time I realized something: I had no doubt that Abel had also taken care of the DNA evidence in the databank.

Larry spoke up again. "Whatever you're mixed up in goes high up the food chain, doesn't it?"

"Yeah—that's why I think I might be a goner. That's why I gave you the package."

"Well, you're not a goner when it comes to getting framed for Rose David's murder."

"What?"

"The case took a big turn," he said. "Though after that phone call, I'm not surprised. After what that guy pulled, he obviously has the capability and access to steer the investigation in any direction he wants."

"Are you saying they're not closing in on me anymore?"

"They're focusing on some guy with prior convictions. He was a suspect in some burglaries in Del Mar last year."

For the second time in as many days, a great sense of relief overcame me. Abel had figured out a way to fix the Rose David blunder after all. And though I'd never know what had changed to make that possible, I suspected that fixing this blunder was one of the things he'd been preoccupied with during our last two meetings. Not because he wanted to protect me, but because he wanted to protect himself.

Of course, I also now understood that he'd been preoccupied with his impending departure. It had consumed him to the point where he couldn't even pretend to be focused on me. He'd been focused on fixing the biggest problem in his life. The one that I'd suspected was haunting him when I first started to work for him: his loneliness. The lonely alien had decided he couldn't take it anymore.

He wanted to go home.

*

Over the next six months, I settled into my new life. I was the editor in chief of the "Dig Deeper" feature that ran on Larry's website and on thirty other sites. The job came with insurance, so I didn't have to lie to Jenny about where the money for our medical expenses was coming from. Better than that, Jenny was in remission. Or what was more accurately called partial remission, which meant the treatments were reducing the tumor.

After Dr. Rainer officially delivered the good news, we celebrated at The Counter. Jake and Hannah only argued once. With Jake leaving for college soon, we all understood that this was one of the last times we'd all be at a celebratory dinner together. We all wanted to enjoy it, so enjoy it we did.

Still, we knew we weren't out of the woods. Dr. Rainer had told us: this was good news, but the future could still hold bad news. We understood that, and it made the dinner that much more precious.

A week later, Jenny got another offer to work on a pilot, and she took it. Again, the timing worked out perfectly. One round of treatments was in the rearview mirror, and the next was a few months off.

Summer turned into fall, Jake went off to college, and Hannah settled into her senior year. By then, I was well into my new job, which, as it turned out, I liked. I wrote in-depth stories for Larry's news site and the other sites that were part of his loose syndicate, and I also commissioned and edited stories from seasoned journalists who, like me, had lost their jobs with traditional news outlets. And the aggregate views for these stories, across the syndication of websites, turned out to be good.

One morning, while I was in the den, getting ready to edit a piece I had commissioned, I clicked on Larry's website to see if another of my syndicated stories was still being featured. It was, but what caught my eye was a new story. It wasn't the exaggerated headline, "Beverly Hills to Selfishly Keep LA Tourists to Itself," that jumped out at me—I was used to Larry's headlines. It was the accompanying photo.

A photo of Abel's house.

I clicked on the story and found out that the house was being converted into a small museum featuring the history of Los Angeles. According to the article, the former owner, a reclusive and wealthy Beverly Hills native, had donated the property to the Beverly Hills Historical Foundation with one major stipulation: the museum had to open within a year.

And that requirement was going to be met. The museum would open early next year—and I planned to pay a visit. I wasn't interested in learning more about the history of LA, but I was interested in learning more about this wealthy donor. Maybe there'd be a plaque in the museum telling the public more about him. I wondered what story Abel had left behind. I knew that whatever it was, it didn't include a digital trail—I had checked.

When Christmas came around, Jake flew back from Northwestern. The university had turned out to be a perfect fit for him. He loved it, and we were glad to have some time to hear all about it. Jenny was in tears when we met him at the airport. She'd missed him greatly. I had, too, but I wasn't worried about him like I was about Hannah. Hannah appeared to be in good health, but doubt lingered with me always.

When I took her to see Dr. Eisner, I had insisted on talking to the doctor myself after the examination. Hannah had protested, but I didn't budge. So she stood there, annoyed, while I spoke to the doctor.

"She appears to be in good health," Eisner told me right off the bat.

Hannah shot me a smug look.

"Do you have any idea why she might have fainted?" I asked. Though I knew it would probably be futile, I wanted to get him to run some tests. I wanted to know what Abel had done to my daughter.

"At this point," he said, "I can't give you a definitive cause. But I can say that there's no reason to worry. When we see something like this, the vast majority of the time it really is no big deal."

"I know, but I'm really worried about it," I said.

"Don't be. A fainting spell doesn't by itself mean anything. It's the result of a sudden decrease in blood flow. It can come from a sudden drop in blood pressure, or from low blood sugar. If she didn't eat enough that day, that would explain it."

"That's what it was, Dad," Hannah chimed in, irritated by my concern. "I already told you that."

"And I did rule out other common causes," Eisner said. "Fear, hyperventilation—and I didn't see any signs of dehydration." He began to fill out a form on his clipboard. "But we are going to draw some blood and do bloodwork."

Great. That was a start. But I wanted him to run other tests. "Will bloodwork catch most of what could have caused it?" I asked.

"Yes."

"What about an MRI or genetic testing?"

Eisner looked up from his form, but before he could say anything,

Hannah spoke up. "Dad—what's wrong with you?" she said.

"I just want to make sure you're fine."

Eisner signed the form, then said, "Let's do the bloodwork and follow up from there."

Of course, a few days later, the bloodwork came back normal, so there was nothing to follow up on. But whenever Hannah was around, I watched her like a hawk, trying to determine whether anything had changed about her. I realized that this was one of my penances for what I'd done to those other women—the targets I'd abducted. After returning those women, I had divorced myself from whatever the future held for them. I had divorced myself from whatever Abel had done to them.

With Hannah, I could never divorce myself from that. So even during our joyous Christmas dinner, with Jake home from college, and with all of us thankful for the blessings in our lives, that was still on my mind. And it would always be on my mind.

THE END

Made in the USA
Middletown, DE
02 October 2018